DIVIDING
EDEN

DIVIDING
EDEN

JOELLE CHARBONNEAU

An Imprint of HarperCollinsPublishers

HarperTeen is an imprint of HarperCollins Publishers.

Dividing Eden

ISBN 978-0-06-245385-3

Typography by Jenna Stempel
18 19 20 21 22 PC/LSCH 10 9 8 7 6 5 4 3 2 1
❖
First paperback edition, 2018

For my son, Max, who makes my heart smile.
You certainly are not the doom.

1

Freedom was a myth.

Carys's brother Andreus didn't think so. He said a person could feel free even when walls surrounded him.

Carys loved her twin, but he was wrong. Freedom was a mirage. It taunted and promised a great deal as it hung just out of reach.

Back when they were young, her brother loved pointing out the women carrying trays of bread through one of the city's squares— or the commoners' children chasing each other, laughter echoing through the narrow alleys. They were all surrounded by walls, and yet they were happy. The walls kept them safe. The walls made them feel strong and secure. That, he argued, was freedom.

As they sat on the battlements he would sketch designs for a new windmill while she watched the guards practice, picking up tips on how to help Andreus improve his skill in combat.

Those who lived in the town below the Palace of Winds didn't understand that danger came in many guises. Not only in the form of darkness, or winter, or the Xhelozi that hunted during the cold months. Those were dangers that could be seen. Anticipated. Defeated. The massive gray stones erected at the perimeter of the town kept those dangers at bay. The white stones that bordered the castle grounds high above on the plateau doubly secured the powerful and those under their protection. But the walls were a double-edged sword. Even as they pushed back outside dangers, they kept in the things that made Carys wish for some other kind of life. One that didn't require she hide everything she was.

Carys placed her hand on the trunk of the Tree of Virtues and bowed her head, pretending to ask it for some blessing or other, as girls did when they wanted a husband or a baby or a pretty ribbon for their hair.

Foolish girls. They thought the tree, like the walls, was a sign of safety and blessing. How anything planted in the middle of town to commemorate the slaughter of an entire royal family symbolized anything positive was beyond Carys. Of course, in Eden, it was only Carys's family who need worry about that fate. Perspective was everything.

Duty to simpering femininity done, Carys turned toward the royal guards. "Let's go."

She kept her eyes on their backs as she walked, not looking left or right. Not meeting the eyes of those who fell into bows or curtsies as they noticed her.

The streets beneath her feet were soon to be paved white to match the castle walls. It had been her father's order. He said the white would show the city dwellers were as virtuous as those who lived above. He insisted the work would begin once the war was over. Carys supposed the Council of Elders would figure out how to keep the horses from mucking up the white of those stones. A fitting job for people as virtuous as animal droppings.

She caught sight of her destination and hurried her steps toward the tailor's shop on the far western square. "Stay outside," she ordered the guards as she walked to the door.

"How long will you be, Your Highness?" the freckle-faced guard asked.

Carys turned and stared at him for a long moment. She watched as his face turned red, making his freckles almost pop off his skin. Carys had that effect on people. It would amuse her, if their discomfort weren't so clear.

When the hand at her guard's side began to tremble she answered, "I shall be exactly the amount of time I require and not a second longer. And if you question me again, I shall see to it that your commanding officer teaches you the value of holding your tongue."

"Of course, Your Highness." The guard swallowed hard and looked down at the ground. "I apologize for any offense, Highness."

The apology was a start. If she were her mother, it would also be his end. But she wasn't her mother. She could only hope he'd remember this moment. If he learned from embarrassment, he might have a chance to survive behind the white walls. If not, he had only himself to blame.

Gathering her skirts, Carys stepped out of the last rays of sunlight, into the tailor's shop, and shut the door. As soon as the latch clicked, Carys heard a familiar voice. "Welcome, Princess Carys. We've been expecting you."

Carys smiled. She felt herself relax in the warmth of the greeting and of the fire crackling in the hearth on the opposite side of the stone room. A large mass of tawny fur was curled into a ball close to the fire. The fur ball opened its eyes, blinked twice, and then went back to sleep. No bows or curtsying from felines. They had no enemies to avenge, power to amass, or familial interests to protect, so they had little need to curry favor. How did cats get so lucky?

She nodded to the reed-thin man, who, straightened to his full height, barely reached the tip of her nose. The lines etched into his face were deeper than they had been the last time she saw him. Life had gotten harder in Garden City with the war. "Goodman Marcus," she said with fondness. "Thank you for accommodating my request so quickly."

They both turned at the sound of footsteps pounding the stairs. Carys barely had time to brace herself before Larkin threw her arms around her and hugged her tight.

"Daughter." Goodman Marcus's voice was sharp. "You forget yourself. The two of you are no longer children."

"Pity, since we both were so adorable when we were small. Weren't we, Your Highness?" Larkin stepped back, tossed her mass of long, frizzy dark curls, and laughed the way Carys so often wished she could.

"Royalty always strives for dignity," Carys replied with mock sincerity, "which means we are far too controlled to ever be called adorable."

"I'm certain you looked very dignified the day you fell into that pile of horse manure, Your Highness," Larkin said with a deep curtsy.

Carys laughed. How could she not? "I wouldn't have fallen if you hadn't pushed me."

"I didn't push *you*," Larkin said. "I was giving Prince Andreus a well-deserved shove. You, Princess, simply obstructed my path."

Goodman Marcus's eye twitched at his daughter's antics. Carys remembered that look well from the days when he would bring Larkin to the palace to help with the court's dress fittings. She was too enthusiastic and filled with energy to carefully pin hems and display bolts of silk. Typically, Larkin ended up feeling her father's hand before being put in a corner to wait until his work was complete. A corner was where Andreus found and rescued her.

At first, Carys didn't talk to the sniffling girl with the tear-streaked cheeks. Even at five, Carys had been told time and again that she was to avoid strangers, to protect her brother from anyone who might get close enough to learn what must be hidden. Even then she understood her duty—to quiet the whispers in the Hall of Virtues and stymie those who would do anything to remove her family from power.

But Andreus never paid attention to the rules, and he could never ignore a child in distress. Not now. Not then, either. And he refused to leave the dimpled, dark-haired girl weeping in a crook of the castle. No amount of arguing made Andreus relent in his quest to free Larkin from her punishment. That was the beginning of the friendship. It was the first time Carys trusted anyone besides her twin. It was also the last.

For the next several months, the Queen frowned whenever she spotted Larkin giggling in the castle halls, but their mother never said anything pointed about the dangers of outsiders when Andreus was around. She saved that for the moments she and Carys were alone. She assured Carys that Larkin would be used against them. Maybe even hurt by others who wished to do the King and his family harm. Carys was ordered to let the friendship die. By the time winter came, Andreus had found a new friend to rescue and had forgotten about Larkin. Carys swore to do the same.

She lied. It was a minor fabrication compared to all the others, but it had always felt like a victory to her. And even small victories were significant in the middle of a lifelong war.

"Larkin," Carys said smoothly, "perhaps we should focus on my order instead of worrying your father over events long past."

"Of course, Highness," Larkin sang out with a hastily bobbed curtsy. "This way."

Larkin bounced up the stone steps leading to the second floor. As Carys followed, Goodman Marcus cleared his throat and said, "I apologize for my daughter, Your Highness."

Carys stopped at the top of the stone steps. She looked back down at Larkin's father as he twisted a length of hemp between his hands. A man who loved his daughter. A man who lived life with a virtue none in the castle could ever understand. "You have nothing to apologize for, Goodman."

Carys walked through the doorway at the top of the stairs. Larkin closed the door, turned, and perched her hands upon her hips with a frown. "Now that we have Father convinced we are still giggling children with nary a true thought in our heads, tell me what's wrong. You're troubled."

"Don't you know it is not acceptable to tell a lady she looks out of sorts?"

"You have never been a traditional lady."

And wasn't that the heart of her problem? "My mother would have you locked in the tower for saying that."

"Compliments come in many forms, Highness. Especially outside the white castle walls. Ladies are boring. Every move in every situation already prescribed. Gods, they're barely even people." Larkin walked over to a large wardrobe and opened the doors to reveal several gowns. "I sewed through the last several nights to complete the special accommodations you asked for. Try them on."

Larkin selected the most important dress first.

Ignoring the questions in Larkin's eyes, Carys allowed her friend to pull the corset tight, as if willing curves out of thin air. But as much as Larkin tried, Carys was never going to be soft and curvy. Her edges were hard, inside and out. Still, the dress fit like a glove. Her mother would appreciate that.

Carys cared more about what she'd asked Larkin to add to the dress. The compartments were hidden in the seams, impossible to spot even for one who knew they existed. Larkin was both cunning and skilled.

Carys slid her hands into the pockets and smiled.

"Extra deep, lined with leather, each with a built-in sheath, just as requested." Larkin paused, staring at Carys for several long seconds. Carys knew her friend was waiting for her to explain. But Carys said nothing and Larkin understood her well enough to simply nod before walking to the table near the window. When she turned she was holding an iron stiletto. "For my lady's inspection."

"Where did you get that?" Carys hissed, looking toward the door.

"Never fear, Your Highness." Larkin smiled again. "It belongs to Father. He hasn't used it in years, and I doubt he even knows where he last saw it. I did, however, and felt a royal request was a proper enough reason to borrow it. I'll return it to its very dusty chest after you leave."

The handle was less intricate and the blade inferior to the ones Carys had asked her twin to commission two years ago. No princess could commission the castle blacksmith to make weapons. Not unless she wanted the rest of the court and the Council to find out and start asking questions. Questions were the last thing Carys or her brother needed.

Carys felt inside the pocket for the sheath opening, then practiced sliding the blade into the concealed carrier and drawing it again. The first three draws caught on the fabric. The fourth came free without incident. With an hour of practice she would be able to draw and brandish the weapon with both speed and ease. Knowing that made the knot of anxiety wedged deep in her stomach ease a bit. It had been growing there for weeks as if trying to warn her of—something. When she'd mentioned her unease to Andreus, he'd told her she was just jumping at shadows, that she shouldn't look for problems where there were none.

Perhaps she *was* being paranoid, but she liked having her blades near. With so little she could control, it was good to have command over this and to know that no one, not even her brother, was aware of the secret. To survive in the castle, a girl needed all the secrets she could get.

Out of the corner of her eye, Carys spotted Larkin poking a stick into the small fireplace. Once the end was ablaze, she began lighting candles throughout the room to chase away the lengthening shadows.

"Is there a reason you're not using the overhead lights?" Carys asked. Every business in the town was allotted a share of the power harnessed by the windmills atop the castle towers. Seven massive windmills to represent the seven virtues of the kingdom and the power that those who lived by those virtues wielded.

Power. It came in many forms. Running the lights. Operating the water. Raising people above their stations. Ordering people to their deaths. In Eden, he who controlled the wind had the power.

"Candlelight is not as harsh as the overhead glow." Larkin glanced at the window, then finished lighting the last candle before placing the burning stick into the fire. "Shall we move on to the next garment, Your Highness?"

"Larkin, what do I not know?" Carys asked as her friend busied herself at the wardrobe. Larkin always changed the subject when she was hiding something. When she looked away the trouble was even greater, and right now Larkin was keeping Carys at her back. "Larkin, tell me. Is there something wrong with the lights?"

Her friend turned with a sigh. "People are saying the wind has not blown as strong as it should in recent weeks, Highness, and that's why there isn't as much power. The shortage has caused some . . . tension."

Tension was never a good word when it referred to the King's subjects. When there was tension, trouble followed.

Carys moved to the window and looked up at the palace windmills. The massive structures loomed above the white walls and cut through the backdrop of a darkening sky. The sound of their churning was the accompaniment to life in Garden City. Carys could hear their pulsing hum now, but could the blades be moving less speedily than in the past? Andreus would be able to tell. He'd made studying the windmills and the power they created his life's work. The orb—the light that sat high atop the tallest tower of the palace—used his design. The light was supposed to welcome all who wished to add their talents to strengthen the kingdom and promised safety in its glow, because the things that hid in the darkness could never triumph when there was a light powered by virtue pushing them back.

Her twin had helped build the newest light, but even he had

known that the brightest orb would never banish the darkness completely—no matter how big it got or how hard the windmills turned.

Andreus would know if there were a problem with power production. Without her brother's knowledge, all Carys could say was that the hallways and great rooms in the palace were still illuminated just as brightly by the wind-powered light. Not that it mattered. Lack of power in the palace would cause little inconvenience; down here in the city, it would lead to much larger problems.

"Where is the tension greatest?" The gown rustled as Carys turned her back to the window.

"A few of the millers have expressed some upset, but Father has given them some of our wind power allotment. That has helped quiet the loudest of the complaints." Larkin helped Carys out of the formal gown and into the next dress. "But there are still whispers, and those whispers are getting louder with every day."

"What do the whispers say, Larkin?"

Larkin bit her lip and sighed. "The whispers say the cold is coming. The days are getting shorter and the Xhelozi will be waking to hunt if they haven't come out of slumber already. People are making offerings at the old shrine to keep the winds blowing—especially now that we have so few guardsmen to keep the walls safe if there is an attack."

"I thought most people avoided the shrine." The first of Eden's seers had ordered it constructed to give citizens a place to appeal directly to the Gods in times of struggle—and they had, until five years ago. A cyclone had appeared above the castle, and though the seer drove the wind tunnel back into the mountains, he warned that the deadly winds had been an answer to a careless request made at the sacred site. After that, the common people stayed away. Only the most troubled were driven to visit the grove on the edge of the city.

"They did, Highness." Larkin sighed. "But that was before, when the old seer was alive and there was enough wind power in the city. The new seer is lovely, but they wonder how someone who looks as if she can be blown over by the wind can possibly have the power to control it. Those who visit the shrine say they are trying to send her strength."

"And those who aren't visiting the shrine? What are they saying?"

"They say your family and the Council have put us all in danger by installing Lady Imogen as Eden's seer. They are wondering if your family truly wishes to keep Eden safe."

Carys stiffened. "Do they speak of the Bastians?"

"Not where I can hear them," Larkin assured her. "A new seer is bound to make people nervous, especially as the first cold season approaches, but those I have talked to trust Prince Micah to keep the kingdom safe. They know he would not be planning to wed Lady Imogen if he wasn't convinced of her skills. Once they are wed and the warm months return, things will settle down."

Carys forced a smile. "I'm sure you're right. I value your thoughts on this."

Larkin looked at Carys. "But if you don't mind me asking, Highness, what are *your* thoughts of our seer? All anyone in town knows for sure is that she is young and lovely."

In the shifting shadows cast by the candlelight, Carys stepped into the next garment. Careful not to meet Larkin's gaze, Carys pictured the dark-eyed oracle who moved through the castle as quiet as a ghost but seemed to be everywhere and see everything.

"She's . . . smart," Carys offered. It was no lie. On the rare occasion Imogen spoke of matters other than the wind and the stars, her future sister showed vast knowledge of the kingdom's history and the inner workings of the castle.

"And she's dedicated," Carys added. In the six months since the seer had been summoned from the Guild to court, Imogen had spent several hours of each day on the battlements, either in meditation with the stars or in consultation with the Masters in charge of the windmills.

"My father and the Council believe Lady Imogen has great power."

"I didn't ask what *they* thought, Highness." Larkin pulled the laces of the white-and-rust dress tight. "I asked about *you*."

Carys shrugged and turned again to the looking glass. Her long pale hair glowed almost silver in the shifting light. "I have not spent enough time alone with Imogen to know her well." Or to trust her.

"Has Andreus spent much time with her?"

Carys looked hard at her friend. "Why do you ask about Andreus? Have there been whispers in the city about the two of them?"

Her brother's study of the windmills was almost as well known to the people of the kingdom as his *other* hobby.

Larkin took a step back. "I meant no offense, Highness. There has been no gossip about Lord Andreus and Lady Imogen. Only about how quickly she charmed Prince Micah."

Carys let out a breath in relief. Her twin wasn't known to have many boundaries when it came to attractive women, and many of the women he encountered seemed to have even fewer than he did. While she did her best to stand by her brother, there were some things she couldn't protect him from: first and foremost, himself.

Larkin looked as if she wanted to say something more, but then she shook her head and asked instead about the details of the upcoming wedding. Carys was happy to switch the conversation to talk of the ceremonies and balls and tournaments that would be held in the royal couple's honor in the glow of Eden's orb. With the cold coming and the expense of the war looming, the Council of Elders had suggested the festivities stay within the castle walls. Her father had agreed with the Council, but Micah refused to accept their decision since everyone in the kingdom would hear of the lack of typical amusements. They would speculate about the depth of the Council's support for the Crown Prince and his betrothed, or whether the descendants of the exiled House of Bastian might be the Elders' true choice for the throne.

Carys understood her elder brother's concerns. Rumors alone could be enough to spur another contest for the crown, especially with a war depleting their guards. So she'd bided her time until she found her brother alone in his rooms, then laid out her plans for expanding the celebrations.

"You must tell Father you've been approached by people who are certain the lack of festivities means that we are losing the war. Have some of your friends say they've heard from their fathers that a smaller than normal wedding celebration is the signal to the highest lords to flee the city."

"You want people to think we're losing the war?"

"No." People thought that anyway. "I want Father to believe his lukewarm support for your wedding confirms for our people that Eden is losing the war. He and the Council will be forced to make the celebration the grandest seen in centuries to prove their confidence in victory. And once the people witness the generosity you show at your wedding tournament, they will look forward to your reign. You will make them feel safe in their homes and gain their loyalty all in one sweep."

It only took a day for Carys to hear the rumors about what the dearth of pomp and circumstance meant for the realm, and a day more for the proclamation of a celebratory tournament, street fair, and ball to be held in honor of the nuptials. The construction of the tournament challenges had begun almost immediately on the contest field a league from Garden City's walls. They were supposed to be done by the time Micah and Father returned from their review of the battlefields to the south.

The sun had set by the time the last dress had been fitted. Carys walked to the window and studied the sky as Larkin tucked the garments away. "The days are so much shorter now that autumn is coming to a close."

"The planters all believe there will be more snow than usual this year. If so, people will be doubly grateful for the memory of the wedding festivities. They will have stories to tell on days too bitter and dangerous to venture outside." Larkin closed the wardrobe doors and turned. "I only wish I could be here to see it all."

"The wedding is in five weeks," Carys said. "Surely you and your father will be in town. Will it not be too late in the season for you to go out on commission trips by then?" Goodman Marcus's skills were often sought by lords and ladies throughout the strongholds of Eden, and Larkin, now equally skilled, accompanied him. Carys envied their closeness and their freedom to do as they wished without always having to be on their guard. But Goodman Marcus was careful to stay close to Garden City in the winter months. He was wise to do so. The Xhelozi, growing in number every year, were fierce, and winter was their hunting season.

Larkin smiled. "It *is* late in the season to travel for work, but not too late to travel to my new home."

Everything inside Carys went still.

"New . . . home?"

Larkin looked down at her hands. "I didn't know how to tell you. I met someone. His name is Zylan—a furrier whose family lives in Acetia in the shadow of the Citadel. And, well . . . " She looked up with a shy smile. "I'm betrothed."

"Betrothed. You are moving away?" Other than Andreus, Larkin was her only true friend. And now she was going to Acetia—the district of Eden farthest from the palace's orb—in order to get married and live a life of her own. A life with responsibilities she chose instead of ones pressed upon her through schemes or circumstances of birth. A life no longer filled with those thirsting for power.

"Is this what you wish to do?" Everything inside her churned. The candles and hearth fire flickered. "If your father is insisting you marry, I could intercede on your behalf. Explain that you are still young and wish to wait."

"I'm four months older than you, Highness. Zylan is a good man. He said he knew the moment we met that we would wed. He cares for me."

"Of course he does." Carys blinked back the sting of tears. Crying was a weakness she couldn't afford. Not even for a friend. "You are one of the best people I have ever met. He would not be worth marrying if he didn't see that. When do you plan to wed?"

"On Winter Solstice. I will live with Zylan's sister's family until then. Father believes we should travel as soon as possible since the days are getting shorter. He says it will be good for Zylan and me to have several weeks to get to know each other better before the ceremony. I think he's hoping I'll change my mind so he doesn't have to cook for himself."

"But you won't." Once Larkin's mind was made up, she rarely changed it. And once her steadfast heart was given, it never was taken back. She'd proven that time and again over the years.

Larkin placed a hand on Carys's arm. "I know when you meet him you will understand why I have to go. You will love him, too."

Perhaps. But Carys would also hate him for taking her friend.

She never wished anything so much as that she, too, could go to Acetia, at least to attend Larkin's marriage. But it could never be. People would talk if Carys left the city. They'd realize how important Larkin was to her. Carys's wedding gift to Larkin would have to be the gift of letting her go without the threat of the darkness following her. Maybe then Larkin could be free for the both of them.

"I shall hope for strong winds to guide your steps, but I will miss you dearly." Carys wrapped her arms around her friend, wishing she could be happy. Instead, there was emptiness.

"If only you *could* be with me," Larkin suggested with a laugh that didn't cover her tears. "Think of the trouble we could cause."

For a minute, Carys let herself think of it—of finally being able to be herself and use her skills without anyone passing judgment. What would it be like to finally do something *she* wanted to do without using schemes or deceit? Who would she be then?

More than anything she wanted to find out. Instead, she said, "I do not think the world is ready for the problems the two of us would create."

Larkin gave her a wistful smile. "Well, maybe someday. You never know how the winds will blow, Your Highness."

"Maybe," she said, even though she did know.

Her lofty, much-admired life was right here in Garden City. As long as Andreus needed her to guard his secrets and keep them all from harm, *someday* would never be.

2

"Almost done," Andreus announced as he shifted his weight.

He could feel the chief of the Masters of Light breathing behind him. While he wasn't opposed to having someone's hot breath on his neck, he'd much rather the person be encased by the scent of perfume and be wearing skirts instead of reeking of grease and sweat.

Soon, he told himself as he tightened his grip on the iron pliers in his ice-cold hand. He should have thought to wear gloves, but the sun had been warm earlier despite the chill of the wind. Now the wind had started to blow much stronger and Andreus was ready to find somewhere comfortable to get warm.

"The updates will be ready to test in one more turn," he announced.

Yes. That did it. Still he gave the pliers one more try to make sure the bolt was tightened before dropping the tool to the ground and rising.

Brushing his hands on his pants, he turned and nodded to Master Triden, who had moved closer to the base of the windmill, next to the control levers. "Ready when you are, Master."

Andreus leaned against the white battlements and pretended not to hold his breath as Master Triden threw the switch closing the electrical circuit Andreus had just upgraded. If he'd done everything right, the beacons on the wall should be shining already against the darkening night sky. If he hadn't . . . his father would never let him hear the end of it.

You're a prince, not some common laborer. Act like it.

You should be more like your brother.

If you were less of a distraction, the Masters of Light wouldn't be having such problems with the power on the walls.

"It works!" an apprentice half-hanging over the battlements yelled. "The lights are all shining—even brighter than before!"

The other apprentices cheered as Andreus pushed away from the white wall and walked over to where three Masters were huddled over the control panel.

"How does it look?" he asked.

Master Triden turned and grinned, showing off his broken front tooth. "The gauges show less power loss from this line. We are going to have the boys watching all of the power measurements through-out the next week. If this design continues to prove superior—as I expect it will, Prince Andreus—we will begin the process of replac-ing them all. With any luck, this winter there will be no outages and the kingdom will have you to thank. The King will be pleased."

Andreus scoffed. The King was rarely pleased with a son who spent more time studying windmills than brandishing a sword. "I think we'll all be pleased if Garden City gets through the winter without an attack."

"The Council, our seer, and the King will all hear about your success in my next report, as will everyone else in the city. Your work to keep Garden City and the rest of Eden safe makes you no less a hero than Prince Micah fighting on the battlefields."

Of course it did. Andreus should be with Micah and his father, winning glory on the battlefield. If death were the only thing to fear, he *would* be there—without question. It was revealing his secret that was far more threatening.

Master Triden bowed, then turned to shout orders at the apprentices. The gusting wind made Andreus pull his cloak tighter around himself as he turned and headed toward the closest tower staircase. The wind was blowing steady and strong. The temperature was dropping. Now that he'd been successful, he wanted to get to his next appointment, which was not only out of the cold but would, if the lady could be taken at her word, make him very, very warm.

Still, as cold as it was, Andreus stopped before he reached the tower door and walked to the wall to look at the city far below. The glow of the beacons was faint at this time of day, but soon they'd create a bright outline of the sprawling city. It was this light that kept the tens of thousands of people below safe from the soon-to-be hunting Xhelozi.

Not bad for a day's work.

Smiling, Andreus walked out of the fading light and jogged down the staircase, trying to decide if he should wash before meeting the lovely Lady Mirabella or if she would find the streaks of grease on his hands appealing. He sniffed at his tunic and veered down the hall toward the royal family's private section of the castle. There was nothing sexy about smelling like a rusted pot. A quick wash, fresh clothes, and—

"Prince Andreus," a familiar silken voice called at his back.

"Excuse me, Your Highness, but the Queen sent me to look for you."

Andreus sighed, then turned and gave his mother's favored lady-in-waiting his most charming smile. "Lady Therese, I hope my mother isn't the only reason you're looking for me. Because the Queen is certainly not the reason I'm happy to see you."

The dress Lady Therese wore today showed off rounded hips, and the low neckline gave him a peek at her other assets. Since she'd come to court two months ago, the young widow had managed to dodge his interest, even turning down his offer of an up close and personal look at the orb of Eden. It was, at first, vexing. But he had to admit, her refusal made for an interesting change of pace. Having a crown meant that, more often than not, he didn't have to chase his quarry.

"I am here at the Queen's bidding, Your Highness. Your mother needs to speak with you." Lady Therese curtsied and lowered her gaze.

"Did my mother tell you what she needed to speak about?"

Lady Therese shook her head. "She only said that it is urgent."

The Queen thought discussing his breakfast menu was urgent. Heaven forbid he skip a meal and get lightheaded.

"Tell my mother you searched everywhere and couldn't find me inside the castle."

Lady Therese's blue eyes widened. "You wish me to *lie*?"

Yes. Women liked him better when he didn't tell the truth. "Would I ask you to betray your own conscience for me?" He gave her a mocking bow. A spark of amusement lit her features and he smiled in return. "If you turn your back and I suddenly disappear, you'd be able to return to my mother and tell her the absolute truth."

His words pulled a low chuckle from Therese. "You don't believe she'll see through the ruse?"

"Of course she will. She will also assume that I used the charm she taught me in order to misdirect you. Believe me, the Queen will not punish you for what is essentially her fault."

"You're incorrigible, Your Highness."

Andreus closed the distance between them and lowered his voice so she had to lean in to hear his words. "And you are bewitching when you smile."

Closer now. So close the fabric of her sleeve was brushing against his vest. "We both have dealt with my mother's urgent matters long enough to know that whatever problem she has can wait. And since you are supposed to be scouring the castle for me, my mother will not expect you to report back anytime soon. We could . . . pass some time together." Suddenly, the smell of rust and grease didn't seem all that unpleasant.

"And risk upsetting the Queen?"

Andreus smiled and ran a finger down Therese's hand. "What my mother doesn't know cannot upset her." Cliché, but clichés existed for a reason. He lifted Therese's hand to kiss it and was surprised when she pulled her fingers away.

"I'm afraid I have other plans, Highness. But rest assured, I will first let the Queen know you have received her message. She'll be expecting you."

With that Therese turned and disappeared down the hall, leaving Andreus to sigh at the sway of her hips and his miscalculation. Most of the girls in the castle were happy to do his bidding. Clearly, Therese was different. He admired her even as he cursed her for ensuring that now he'd have to go deal with his mother.

He turned the corner and in the distance spotted Chief Elder

Cestrum. The white-haired advisor put his iron claw on Elder Ulrich's arm as they talked in front of the entrance to the Council's chamber. Quickly, Andreus turned, put up the hood of his cloak, and veered down the hall to the left. He was more than willing to take the long route in order to avoid the Chief Elder.

While Andreus was grateful to Elder Cestrum for convincing his father to allow Andreus to work with the Masters of Light, Andreus wasn't stupid. Nothing the Council did was out of the goodness of their hearts.

Maybe if things were different he would be like the others in court, brokering favor and pitting people against one another to gain power. But his secret needed to stay just that. So he'd tried to let people know how little his father cared about the youngest royal son—and they'd believed him. It was the only explanation they understood for why a prince was always working among commoners with their rusty tools.

Carys *did* play the game—mainly for him—so she could distract people from looking too closely or asking questions he couldn't answer. Ever since the Council had helped him with his request to work with the Masters, she'd been worried that the Chief Elder might start asking for favors. Andreus was hoping Carys was wrong. Being caught between his father and the Council sounded more than a little uncomfortable.

Determined not to run into anyone else he didn't want to speak with, Andreus ducked into one of the back hallways used only by servants. Footmen and maids bowed and curtsied as he hurried through the torchlit areas of the castle where power was no longer provided. His father believed that during a time of war there was no benefit in using the wind resources to illuminate areas most lords and ladies never would think to tread.

"Prince Andreus."

Andreus cringed. Then smiled when he recognized the small boy coming down the hall, carrying a vase of winter jasmine. "Max! How are you feeling?"

"I'm well, Your Highness." The boy skipped and almost dropped the vase. When he righted himself, he gave Andreus a gap-toothed grin. "The remedy Madame Jillian made me fixed my breathing. It tastes bad, but she says I gotta keep taking it."

"Listen to Madame Jillian," Andreus counseled.

The woman was waspish, but when it came to healing she knew what she was doing and she never failed to come running when Andreus had her summoned. She was also discreet, which was equally valuable.

"Oh, I will, Prince Andreus. I need to grow up strong if I'm going to be a Master of Light like you." Before Andreus could correct him about his status as Master, Max was off again. "Did the test you was doing go all right, then? I wanted to come up and see for m'self, but Lady Yasmie had me running lots of chores. It wasn't till she asked me to fetch these flowers that I got to look out a window at the city. The lights are on. Bright as the sun! That means it worked, right?"

The boy gulped air and Andreus laughed. "Yes. It worked. If it keeps working, the Masters of Light will change the entire system. With any luck, this winter there will be no part of the city wall that stays dark when it's night."

Max sighed and kicked his newly made boot against the ground. "I wish I coulda seen it today, Prince Andreus."

"How about I take you up to the battlements so you can see it for yourself?"

"Really? That would be—" His face fell as he looked down at the vase in his hands. "I gotta get these flowers to Lady Yasmie now or my backside'll get tarred."

"Let me know when Lady Yasmie and her friends give you a moment to yourself." Andreus snapped off a stem of tiny yellow flowers and said, "And tell her that Prince Andreus said the flowers pale in beauty in comparison to her."

Max frowned. "Do girls really like when you say that kind of silly stuff?"

He thought of the way he and Lady Yasmie had spent the day in her rooms a few weeks ago. "Yes, Max. They really do. Now hurry off and keep the sass to a minimum. I don't want you to get thrown out of the castle just after I got you in."

"Don't worry, Your Highness." And with a half bow, the kid bolted down the hall, almost barreling into two very young servants as they rounded the corner. Whatever Max said to them had one of the girls blushing. Andreus laughed. A quick study, then. Good. Max would need his wits if he was going to make a go of it in the castle. The boy glanced back toward Andreus, gave him a jaunty salute, and hurried off.

Hard to believe Max had been lying in the dirt, barely breathing, just a few short weeks ago. Andreus had spotted him when he was riding back from inspecting the wiring on the city's outer walls. The child was almost blue under all the grime by the time Madame Jillian got her hands on him.

Despite her care, and his obvious cure, his family didn't want him back. They believed devils were possessing him every time he struggled for air. If they could believe such a thing, Andreus had thundered, then they didn't deserve him. Breathing condition or no,

Max would serve in the castle as a page. When he was old enough he could act as Andreus's squire. He would make sure the child had a place—just like his mother and sister made sure Andreus retained his, despite his own secret. It was the just thing to do.

By the time Andreus had climbed the narrow servants' staircase to the third floor and reached the double doors of his parents' solar, he was out of breath. He leaned against the wall for several minutes and waited for the tightness in his chest to dissipate. When it did, he wiped the sweat from his forehead and made sure his cloak was arranged to hide the worst of the grease stains marring his white shirt. Then he knocked. Less than ten seconds later, Oben, his mother's longtime chamberlain, opened the dark wooden doors and Andreus stepped into the room that he and Carys had spent much of their childhood avoiding.

The rug on the floor had been replaced at least a dozen times since those years, his mother always searching for the perfect style. This one was yellow. Blue velvet-covered chairs he didn't remember being here on his last visit as well as several lounges were scattered throughout the room. When his father was out of the castle, as he was today, the seats were almost always filled with women knitting or doing needlework. Mother liked to monitor the gossip circulating through the palace and use the best bits as she saw fit. Now, however, the only people in the room were his mother, Oben, and two of the Queen's attendants pouring tea.

"You summoned me, Mother?" Andreus said as his mother turned.

Her dark brown hair was the same color as his, but her eyes were the deepest of browns—very different from his hazel ones. Right now her dark eyes shimmered with anger. Perfect since she was wearing a dress of red. Still, his mother's voice was controlled as she spoke. "The word *summoned* implies that I had to compel you as your queen to visit. One might assume you would not have come had it simply been your mother who asked for your company."

"I misspoke. Summoned was the wrong word." He changed tactics. "Forgive me, Mother. Of course I enjoy your company."

"Do you?" She looked at him as she crossed to the table and took a seat. "I can't help but notice that you have only visited with me three times since your father and brother went to observe the guard fighting the war."

"I've been busy, Mother." Andreus slipped into the seat across from the Queen and presented her the stem of flowers. "Besides, Micah told me you were going to be spending time with Imogen. Something to do with wedding plans and picking out dresses. Activities not aligned with my enthusiasms."

"Lady Imogen has no need of my help, and if I have my way she won't be around long enough to become the next Queen." His mother sniffed the flower before placing it on the table. She then picked up her tea and downed the entire cup in one gulp. She gave a contented sigh and signaled her maid for a refill. "Would you like some, dear?"

"No." He put his hand over the cup. He'd learned from his sister's troubles that it was best to be cautious of his mother's brew. One was never certain what it might contain.

His mother looked down at his hand and stared long and hard. The silence was deafening with condemnation. When he looked down he realized why.

The grease. It not only streaked up the back of the hand, but was dug under his fingernails.

Quickly, he gave his mother his best boyish smile. "My apologies for my appearance, Mother. I was heading to clean up before I got your message. I figured it was best not to keep you waiting just because of a little dirt."

It was a lot of dirt, but at the moment he failed to think quantity mattered.

"Your father is right. You shouldn't be working as a commoner. It makes you look like one. People look to their kings and queens for inspiration, especially in times of war. No one is inspired by soil."

Clearly, his mother hadn't met Max.

"I'm sure you didn't call me here to discuss the dirt under my fingernails. You were talking about Imogen. Did the two of you have a falling out?"

His mother took another long drink of tea as she studied him over her cup. Finally, she sat the delicate cup down on its saucer and signaled the maids to leave. As soon as they closed the door, she leaned forward and said, "I've asked Imogen several times to look into the future and tell me what she sees. Do you know what she says?"

"No." Now that Imogen had made a point of asking him to keep his distance, he knew very little what was in her mind or her heart.

"She says there will be darkness. When the darkness fades, two paths will appear in front of our kingdom and there is no telling which one will be chosen."

"Sounds like the same kind of mystical nonsense Seer Kheldin used to say. You were always happy with his fortune-telling."

"Fortune-tellers guess at the future," his mother snapped as she pushed back her chair and began to pace across the yellow carpet.

"Seers have true powers. How else do you explain Seer Kheldin's ability to shift the position of the windmills to perfectly capture the winds?"

The Masters of Light's observational abilities sprang to mind as well as about a dozen other nonmystical rationalizations, but Andreus held his tongue. His mother was a firm believer in the magical powers of seers, their ability to call the winds, read the stars, and therefore know the future. She loved to lecture him on the legend of the Artis root, and how it had been used for centuries to test seers. While it made for a nice story, Andreus had a hard time believing anyone could speak to the wind and call it to obey, let alone get glimpses of the future from staring at the night sky.

He believed only what he could see with his own two eyes.

But his mother had faith, especially after the prediction Seer Kheldin made before Andreus and Carys were born. Andreus had lived his entire life in fear that one of the four members of the Council that served back then would remember the prediction, made years before his birth, and take action against him. If any of those Council members shared that information, someone else could spot his secret. If he was condemned for it, what then? Andreus didn't wish to find out what darkness would come. So, outside the walls, he made sure to keep out of sight of the Council. It was how he began studying the windmills. And fortune had it, the Council wasn't the type to get their exercise walking on the battlements.

"So Lady Imogen gave you a glimpse of the future and you aren't happy with what she saw?" he asked. "That hardly seems like a fair complaint. Akin to hating the sky because it sometimes contains clouds."

"No," his mother chided as she walked to the table and poured another cup of her tea. "I'm concerned because *that is all* the girl has seen. For the last six weeks, I've asked her to give me a reading and she keeps repeating the same vision over and over. I hate to say it, but I fear your brother's intended is a fraud."

Andreus waited for his mother's next salvo, but instead of continuing to rant as she often did, she just sipped her tea as if waiting for him to speak. About what, he had no idea. Had he missed something? After several long moments under his mother's dark-eyed stare, he shifted in his seat. "Is that all, Mother?"

She put the cup down with a clatter. "Of course, it isn't. Do you not see what I am about? Your brother's marriage will put our entire kingdom in jeopardy. We are at war. If the winds fail us and the Xhelozi attack throughout the cold months, Eden will be greatly weakened and our enemies will rally their troops and advance. With Imogen's lack of skill, we won't even see the onslaught coming until they are at our gates. It is up to you to do something about it."

"Me?" He stood, pushing his chair back. "What do you want me to do? Shove her off the North Tower?"

The way she stopped and thought about it before shaking her head made Andreus shudder. "Of course not," she said. "Micah needs to understand that he's making a terrible mistake in marrying someone so weak. We have been at war with Adderton for years— with the guard fighting our neighbors, none could be spared to hunt the Xhelozi. Now we have a seer who cannot help us harness the power we require to keep the beasts away. Your brother needs to change course—before it is too late."

"Micah won't listen to me." In the last few months he'd barely listened to their father or the Council. "And even if he would, he can't remove the seer of Eden from power. Only the King has the power to order the seer's death and appoint another." Which Father wouldn't do because removing Imogen would be akin to admitting that a mistake had been made.

"You misunderstand me, Andreus." Mother walked slowly across the room and stared out the window at the darkness beyond. "I wasn't asking you to *talk* to your brother. Trust me, I've tried. No, I want you to illustrate for him his lack of judgment in a way that only *you* can."

Andreus frowned. "I'm not sure what you are asking of me, Mother."

His mother turned from the window and faced him. "I'm not asking this of you as a mother. I am asking it as your Queen. Until Micah returns from the battlegrounds, I want you to spend as much time as possible with the fair Imogen. Tell her that you wish to hear her opinions on your new designs or whatever blandishment you think flatters her most. Then use those talents my maids say you've employed on them with great success. Convince her to make a mistake your brother cannot forgive."

"Mother, you're not suggesting . . . " But she was. A mere glance at her expression made it clear. She was suggesting *exactly* what her words implied. His mother—his queen—was instructing him to seduce his brother's fiancée into his bed.

Carefully, he put his hands on the table and said, "I believe, dear mother, that you've had too much tea."

He glanced across the room at Oben, but his face was expressionless. After all these years of attending the Queen, Oben had become proficient at masking his thoughts.

Before this got any worse, which was hard to imagine, Andreus said, "I'm going to leave now and forget we've had this conversation."

"You won't forget," she insisted, crossing the room to stand at his side. "You cannot forget because I am not asking. This is a command, and if you expect the Council to allow you to continue the work you like so much, you will do as I bid. And while you do, think of what happens to our windmills if there are no winds to keep them turning. Think about the war your father has us fighting with no second sight to guide his choices. Despite what you might think, we need a seer who can help the kingdom survive." His mother took his hand in hers and looked at him with love. "Your sister and I have made so many sacrifices for you. It is time for you to repay that with some sacrifice of your own."

No. He couldn't do what she asked.

Because he already had.

Careful to keep the memories of Imogen in the windmill from showing on his face, he kissed his mother on the cheek and replied, "If that is all, Mother, I have an appointment to keep."

His mother sighed. "Fine. But we shall talk again soon, and I expect to hear that you have done what you must for the good of the realm."

When he turned toward the door she added, "I love you, you know."

"I know." He felt the same tug at his heart as always when she said those words. For all his mother's faults, she did love him. The fact that he was still here in this castle, threatening all of their futures, proved it. "I love you, too, Mother."

As soon as Oben closed the doors behind him, Andreus stopped and sagged against the wall.

Seduce Imogen.

He'd like nothing better. That night had played over and over again in his mind. The wind howling through the night. Her gentle hand on his as he coaxed a rare laugh from her. That touch was like fire that burned away the rest of the world until there was only the beating of the blades, the cranking of the gears, and her.

She was a seeress. One of the fakes that threatened his very life because of made-up predictions. Just days before she'd agreed to marry his brother.

And Andreus hadn't cared.

Her mouth.

Her skin.

Her shy voice and downcast eyes that seemed only to come alive when she stood on the battlements and looked up at the sky. Or at him.

But she was marrying Micah because Micah wanted her and what Micah wanted, he got. Andreus had wanted to hate the seeress the day she told him that Micah had instructed her not to spend time alone with him again. He'd tried to hate her. But whenever he saw Imogen standing on the battlements alone or cringing as his brother barked commands at her, he felt the same tug of desire to take her in his arms and protect her from harm.

With the Queen's sights set on her, acceptance would not be easy to come by for Imogen. If his mother didn't get what she wanted from him, then she'd employ others. Maybe she already had.

He didn't care.

He wasn't about to get involved. Imogen was just a girl. And he had lots of those. Wasn't one waiting for him right now in the stables, ready to say yes to whatever he wanted?

Andreus cast one last look at the double doors of his parents' rooms and headed for the stairs. He'd wash, change, and bring

Mirabella a present so she wouldn't sulk over his tardiness. Sulking took away from—

Andreus stopped.

The lights flickered—

and suddenly everything went black.

3

Carys sucked in air as the lights at the top of the enormous white stone staircase flickered once . . . twice . . . and then went out. For a second everything was still. Then people began to scream.

Spinning, she looked down at Garden City spread far below her and watched as the wall surrounding it, too, plunged into blackness.

"Highness, you have to get inside the castle," the most experienced of her two guards yelled as the other stood frozen at the top of the stairs. "We might be under attack. You have to go."

Attack? She squinted into the dimness as people screamed. No bells tolled to signal that the guard had spotted a foe. But if they were under attack, she had to find her brother. She had to get to Andreus.

Now.

Since she hadn't carried her stilettos with her into the city, Carys turned toward the young guard who was standing still as stone. She reached out and yanked free the knife the guard wore at his belt.

"Your Highness—"

"I have need of this. Tell no one that I took it or you will find yourself on the front lines of the war without anyone willing to watch your back."

"The knife is yours, Princess. I will tell no one. But shouldn't I go with you now and guard you?"

She doubted the boy was capable of defeating one of the stable chipmunks let alone whatever he worried was lurking in the gloom. But she admired his commitment to his duty despite his fear—of the dark and of her. "You should join the rest of the guard and check the status of the wall. Stand for Garden City as you have sworn to do and I promise you will be rewarded." The boy gaped at her as she turned and over her shoulder ordered, "Go." Then, picking up her skirts, she raced through the shadows bathing the arched entrance of the castle.

"Get inside," someone yelled as Carys shoved through dozens who were racing toward the entrance of the castle.

"Ow." She stumbled as something struck her ankle. "I order you to get out of my way," she yelled. At the sound of her voice everyone around her scattered—a distinct benefit of being a pariah—and she fought free of the crowd and headed for the stairs. A boy with a torch was in the hallway. Grabbing him by the shoulder, she led him to an alcove down the hall, took the torch, and said, "Stay here until the lights go back on. If anyone questions you, tell them you are acting on orders of Princess Carys."

Then she turned and ran through the halls that had never gone this dark in all of her years. Even when some of the lights fell in the city, the castle always continued to shine. Not today. Why?

Andreus would be asking the same thing. He would be trying to fix the problem. If he could get to the battlements, he would. That's where she'd find him. The stress and the exertion could trigger an attack he wouldn't heed until it was too advanced to hide. If that happened, it wouldn't matter if all the Xhelozi in the mountains were at the gates—they would be doomed before the Xhelozi struck the first blow.

Carys ran. Down the hall to the stairwell she knew was used by the Masters of the Light and the guard. The stairs were steep and narrow and illuminated by flickering torches. Gathering her skirts with her knife hand, she held tight to her own torch and climbed.

One flight of steps.

Two.

Three.

Four.

Until she reached the entrance to the battlements and stepped out into the darkness. To her right, men yelled. There was more shouting ahead of her. Torches glowed and flickered in the wind that began to gust harder as she hurried across the stone, looking for her twin. Where was he? Her hand holding the knife cocked back, preparing to throw at any sign of danger.

Wind pulled at the hood of her cloak. It whipped her hair into her face as she turned and squinted at the base of the windmill closest to her. It continued to pulse against the sky. Mocking the dark. Mocking her.

Then the night flickered and the light atop the highest tower began to glow. An enormous circle of white against the black of the sky shone brighter as the seconds passed.

A cheer went up from the battlements as the lights on the white walls began to blink on, one by one. Carys dropped her torch and hurried to where she could see over the white walls. The city was no longer in darkness. It was safe. The castle was secure. But what about her brother?

Carys slid the guard's knife deep into the pocket of her cloak so no one would see it in the now-bright light. The wind whipped harder as she hurried toward a group of men in gray and shouted, "Where is Prince Andreus? Have you seen him?"

The first group dropped to startled bows as they shook their heads. But an older man beyond them pointed toward several figures coming her way. Three of them were dressed in the gray robes of the Masters. The other was wearing a familiar striped cloak of yellow, white, and blue.

Dreus.

And he was smiling. He was fine.

Carys closed her eyes, took a deep breath to steady herself, then started forward. The minute Andreus spotted her, he broke away from the Masters of Light and crossed the white stone.

"Carys, are you okay?" His dark hair fluttered around his face. The wind began to slow, then stopped.

"I'm fine. I was just worried about the lights. I came up here to find out what was going on." Men hurried past with tools in hand, pulling their cloaks and robes tight against them. "Are *you* okay?" His face was red from the cold, but his breathing seemed normal. She didn't see the symptoms that normally signaled he was having an attack. Still . . .

"I am fine," he assured her. "You don't have to worry about me."

Which was a relief considering there were plenty of other things to worry about. "Do you know what caused the lights to fail?"

Andreus took a step closer, then looked around before saying, "It appears that someone deliberately cut a line to the orb."

"How? And why?" Even those working hardest to thwart the King would never want to damage the wind power system before the cold months.

"With an ax, would be my guess, and I have no idea. But whoever did it knew exactly where to sever the line in order to cut off wind power to the entire castle and Garden City. Carys . . . " Her brother's eyes narrowed. "They used the flaw in the system that I mentioned to Father months ago."

"The one that he ordered you not to disclose to anyone?"

"That one." Andreus looked back at the Masters, who were busy checking lines and gauges and a bunch of other things Carys didn't completely understand.

She did understand her father's order. And how angry he would be if he believed Andreus had deliberately disobeyed.

The weekly family meeting their father insisted on holding was never fun. Father had started the meetings when Micah was eight in order to make sure the Crown Prince was aware of the scope of a king's duties and prepared for life on the throne. Their mother was the one who insisted Carys and Dreus be included when they turned eight. Father permitted their presence but rarely involved them in the discussion, which was why Andreus had eventually started bringing his books and design maps to help him to pass the time. Carys doubted her twin realized he'd spoken aloud when he said, "That's a flaw."

But their father had heard.

"Are you interrupting your king?"

"No, Father—Your Majesty. I'm sorry. I was just surprised by something I saw on the wind power design map."

Carys held her breath as her father turned his attention to Andreus.

"A flaw, you said?"

Dreus's eyes lit up at his father's interest. Rarely did the King ask about her twin's work with the wind.

With excitement, Andreus put the design map in front of their father and explained the flaw he had found. A place in the line that, if cut, could cause all other lines in the city to fail.

"Once I mention it to the Masters, I'm sure we can fix—"

"You won't mention it to them."

"But—"

"You won't speak of this to anyone ever again," his father ordered.

"But, Your Majesty . . . " Her brother took a deep breath. "The safety of the kingdom depends on the lights on the wall."

"And on the belief that the measures *we* have put into place have no flaws. Three-quarters of the guard are fighting or have died in the war with Adderton. The Lords of the Seven Districts have sent new recruits, but they are not trained, and the Xhelozi are breeding faster than before. The only thing preventing panic is the trust that the lights will keep the darkness away. Any whisper of *flaws* will crush that trust and any hold we have on the city will disappear."

"But if we fix it—"

"Then there will be rumors of *other* flaws, problems not yet discovered, incompetence! The remaining Bastians no doubt have people here at court ready to spread distrust like wildfire. With our guard depleted, they are just waiting for the right circumstances to try once again to retake the throne. And it will not be my son who gives them their chance! Unless he has decided to take his rightful place in the guards' command? In that case, I will call the Masters of Light and discuss this matter with them right now."

Carys remembered how her brother struggled before shaking his head and saying, "I promise I will not speak of this again, my king."

"Andreus," she said, looking at the way he now refused to meet her eyes. "You didn't tell anyone about the flaw you found. Did you?" When he didn't answer, she grabbed his arm and dug in her fingers. "Andreus. Look at me. Did you tell someone when the King ordered you not to?"

"Not exactly."

"Andreus!" Carys looked around and spotted not only apprentices and Masters of Light but also members of the court and guard walking the battlements. People who had been doused in darkness were now looking to satisfy their curiosity about what had happened.

The sound of the windmills masked a lot, but now that the wind had died down, there was far less to conceal a conversation being had out in the open. "Come with me."

Making it look as though she was trying to get out of the way of the workers, Carys pulled Andreus closer to the base of the nearest tower so they stood directly beneath a massive windmill. The noise of gears and pulsing blades was loudest there, and they could still be seen. Hiding secrets in plain sight was one of the first skills Carys had learned growing up at court.

With her back to the wall and her eyes watching for those who would listen, she asked, "Tell me. How do you *not exactly* tell someone something?"

"I have done nothing." Andreus pulled his arm out of her grasp. "This is not my fault."

Which meant that he believed it was. She knew her brother. She could see the lie in his eyes.

"Dreus. There are a lot of things that aren't our fault, but we still have to deal with them." If he hadn't learned that by now, they were in bigger trouble than she suspected. "Since you *didn't exactly* tell someone about the flaw, what *exactly* did you say?"

He took a deep breath and gazed down upon the city below. "I—I asked questions. I knew they would lead to the Masters finding the flaw on their own. Technically, I didn't disobey His Majesty's command."

"Since when does Father care about technicalities?"

"Look, there was a serious problem. I wanted to help fix it. Isn't that what the royal family is charged to do? Aren't we supposed to see to the safety and well-being of the people we rule?" Andreus didn't wait for her to answer. "I thought if the Masters of Light could make the discovery on their own and bring the matter to the Council of Elders, it would look like any other action they requested permission to approve. And if they are doing a bunch of other minor improvements to prepare for winter, no one would have reason to whisper about design flaws. It's why I pushed them to run a test of the new wire I had created today."

"Today." She tried to remember the details of her brother's latest design. Something about a new wire that was somehow better at transporting wind power. "I thought the Masters were going to wait until the King returned from the battlefields before testing your design."

"They were, but when Father sent a messenger saying he and Micah were delayed, Master Triden decided we should do a trial run. That way, we would be ready to make the changes to the system as soon as Father and the Council agreed."

The Council.

Out of the corner of her eye Carys spotted the distinctive blue cloak with a deep purple V on the other end of the battlements. The V stood for virtue, and strength was the virtue represented by the District of Bisog. She didn't have to see the iron claw or the pointed white beard to know it was Chief Elder Cestrum there, questioning one of the Masters.

The Council. What could they be about in all of this?

Andreus put a hand on her arm. He smiled and said, "Look, if this was the court we were talking about, maybe I would wonder about it. But this is Master Triden and the Order of Light. They don't care about intrigue and deception. Their only concern is for the approaching cold months and making sure the lights don't fail us when we need them most."

"But there are others who work with the Masters," Carys argued. "Blacksmiths and weavers and dozens of apprentices, and not all of them are raised to the gray robes. Those people might want something."

Because everyone wanted something, and when someone coveted a thing enough, rarely did they question the price.

"I think the dark dreams you've been having are making you look for danger. The lights are working now. Things will be fine, Carys." Her brother tried to reassure her as Elder Ulrich and his red cape with black hearts sewn onto the shoulders—hearts to represent the charity of District Derio—appeared in the tower doorway to their right. His hairless scalp almost glowed against the dark and his one good eye turned toward Carys and Andreus. A moment later, Elder Jacobs, who despite his quiet, unassuming voice never quite seemed as humble as he wished people to believe, appeared beside him—his long, dark, braided hair whipping in the wind.

She thought about the outage of the lights and Andreus's test and what Larkin said about the lack of power below, and tried to see three steps ahead on the chessboard.

Andreus thought she was looking for connections because of the dreams she couldn't remember, dreams that had left her feeling so unsettled the past few months. Maybe he was right, but Carys doubted it. Someone was playing a game. The question was who, and which piece in this game were they taking aim at? Andreus? Their father? Or was it someone else?

Taking his arm again, she asked quietly, "Was your test today successful?"

Andreus grinned, transforming his handsome features into those of the boy she used to play hide-and-go-seek with. "It was. The Masters are going to watch the gauges, and if everything continues to go well, they'll replace the wire in the lines starting next week. And while they do that, they can fix the design flaw that has now been discovered and clearly leaves us vulnerable."

Carys frowned. "Father is going to think you set him up. He's going to believe you defied him, made him look weak, and are attempting to gain power for yourself."

"That's ridiculous," Andreus said. Although she could see by the way her brother's eyes narrowed that he realized it might not be. "You know I can't afford to draw attention to myself."

"I do know that, Dreus," she said as she spotted Chief Elder Cestrum watching them from across the way. "But others don't. Did you tell anyone about the test? One of your *ladies*?"

"My *ladies*, as you call them, aren't interested in talk, sister. If they were I'd be doing it wrong and further . . . " Andreus frowned.

"What?"

He turned and looked up at the orb, then took Carys by the arm and led her inside the tower. While the walls protected her from the cold, Carys couldn't shake the chill running through her. Her brother checked the stairs and whispered, "All right. There is one person I told. Max's family used to tell him that the Xhelozi came in the dark to take the children that were deformed or sickly. I told him the Xhelozi would never come for him. I thought he'd finally feel safe if he understood how it all worked."

Max. The little boy Andreus had rescued. "You told him about your new wire?"

Andreus sighed. "And the test, after he asked when the castle would start using it. But he wouldn't have said anything to anyone. I was just trying to reassure him by letting him know that the lights will always shine. The boy was scared. I know what it's like to live with that kind of fear."

"I know you do, Dreus." Too well. "But you have to be careful. Everyone has been talking about the boy."

"Because I saved him."

"Dreus, the boy doesn't understand life in the castle or the games the court plays. He doesn't know that one innocent word about you can cause us problems. You have to find out if he spoke to anyone. We have to know who is behind this. If Father thinks you've deliberately acted against him, you *will* be ordered into service with the guard."

If that happened, it was only a matter of time before Andreus's affliction made itself known, and unlike the other times, she would not be able to distract everyone before they realized what was happening.

"I'll talk with him. He's a curious boy and is probably nosing around here somewhere." Andreus turned to her and took her cold hand in his. "You should go down to the Hall of Virtues. Make sure everyone knows we aren't under attack and the world is not going to end. I'll meet you down there as soon as I have answers. Then we'll figure out our next move."

"Next move, Prince Andreus?"

Chief Elder Cestrum stood in the doorway. Carys felt her breath catch as the Elder carefully studied them both.

Smoothly, her brother said, "In assuring everyone that the city is safe and that the almost immediate restoration of the lights demonstrates that we are more than prepared for the cold months ahead. The last thing the King would want is to find unrest when he returns."

"Which is why I'm going down to circulate among the members of the court now. They need to know that I have seen the Masters of Light at work, that the wind is blowing strong, and that all is as it should be," Carys said. She smiled at the Chief Elder and added, "Would you care to join me, my lord? As you are the most respected member of the Council, your voice would go a long way to assuaging any residual fears."

Chief Elder Cestrum stepped forward and stroked the tip of his white beard with a gloved hand. "I would be happy to join you, Princess, since I'm sure your brother wants to check in with the Masters before he goes inside." He turned toward Andreus and smiled. "I hear we have you to thank for the quick fix to tonight's problem. The King might not respect those who favor brains over brawn, but the Council does. You have the thanks of the Elders, Prince Andreus."

He bowed to her brother, who took the opportunity to stride out of the door and back into the cold and wind. Elder Cestrum looked at Carys and held out his right arm. "Shall we, Your Highness?" Carys placed her hand on top of the iron claw and gathered her skirts with the other hand, then she started down the stone steps.

"Your brother is handling this crisis well," Elder Cestrum said with a small smile. "As are you, Princess. Perhaps the King and Queen have been too cautious in involving you both in more serious matters of our kingdom and court."

The chill of his metal claw beneath her fingers made her shiver as they reached the landing and continued down the next set of steps. Carys chose her words carefully as she tried to determine what Elder Cestrum wanted. "The King has reasons for the things he does, my lord."

"Yes." Elder Cestrum looked at her and nodded. "He does have reasons. Good ones. But those reasons, from what I can tell, no longer exist. From the whispers I hear from the court, you have overcome your small weakness."

Small weakness. Perhaps he thought he was being kind to make it sound so minor. Or maybe he was trying to see if she would admit to how great a vice held her in its iron grip. Even now she could feel it squeezing.

"I cannot control the whispers of the court or the will of my king, Lord Cestrum, which is good since I don't have any desire to try."

"And it doesn't bother you, Princess, to be given so little respect?"

She laughed. "Are you kidding, my lord? The less I am involved in the politics of the kingdom, the less time the leaders of the Seven Districts and their minions spend trying to wrap me up in their idiotic plots to gain power. If you're thinking I care about their respect, you have misjudged your company."

Elder Cestrum gave her a hard, calculating look before nodding.

"You're wise beyond your years, Princess."

"Since I only recently turned seventeen," she countered as they reached the next landing, "I would say that isn't a significant accomplishment."

Elder Cestrum laughed as they stepped out into the hallway and headed toward the Hall of Virtues, where the court would be waiting for news of what had happened to the wind power. No doubt tales of Xhelozi attacks had already been told. If nothing else, those were easy rumors to dispatch. If only the rest of the web being woven tonight was as obvious as—

A gong echoed in the halls, and Carys and Elder Cestrum stopped walking. Another gong sounded, followed by several more.

"The King has returned," Elder Cestrum said, starting down the hall that was already filling with people hurrying to witness his arrival. "Come, Princess. Let us greet your father."

Guard members fell in step in front and behind Carys and the Chief Elder as they swept through the halls to the courtyard. Her father would have seen the buildings go dark as he approached Garden City. He would have questions that he wanted answered, and with little time to prepare, Carys realized there was only one way to explain someone finding the flaw in the system without Andreus being blamed. *She* would confess to telling someone of her brother's finding and take whatever punishment her father chose to dole out. After years of being punished for her obstinacy, her lack of understanding, or her sharp tongue, she knew it would be severe. But she would survive it. She always had and always would as long as it kept her brother's secret safe.

Framing the words in her head, she stepped into the courtyard behind Elder Cestrum and strode down the lantern-lit white stone path to the gate of the Palace of Winds. They arrived just as a group of men climbed the final steps that led onto the plateau of the castle. The sound of the windmills pulsed. The men staggered forward under the fatigue of their trip and the soiled, heavy sacks they were carrying.

One fell to his knees, dumping his sack to the ground in front of him.

No. That wasn't a sack.

Carys raced forward. She heard someone yell her name. Hands tried to hold her back, but she shoved the man trying to shield her out of her way. There was no hiding from this truth. No hiding from the dirt-streaked material that she now realized was stitched with the crests of Eden.

Something inside her cracked and she dropped to her knees. Her stomach clenched. Everything trembled as she reached out and rolled over the body that had been dumped on the steps.

Memories flooded her. A deep voice telling stories about the War of Knowledge. A man larger than life on a throne of sapphire and gold. Hands that calmed her when she was small and scared in the dead of winter, terrified the Xhelozi would hurt them all. Amber eyes, so like hers, that she hoped one day to see approval in. Eyes that would never open again.

Carys couldn't breathe. She couldn't move. Tears burned her eyes, her throat. She couldn't cry. Not here. Not now. Not in front of everyone. Her father wouldn't allow that kind of weakness. He wouldn't forgive. He wouldn't . . .

Something was set on the ground next to her father. She blinked to clear her eyes and felt the wall holding the tears back crumble as the light her twin had helped restore shone on the bloody, waxen face.

Wind whipped her hair.

Tears slipped down her cheeks as she touched her older brother's icy hand.

The orb shone bright, but darkness had come to Eden and Carys didn't know if there was any light that could chase this kind of darkness away.

4

Unless he had gotten himself into trouble for mouthing off while serving the ladies of court, the boy had to be around here somewhere. Andreus nodded to a Master ordering apprentices to put away their tools and headed toward the back of the battlements.

He started to duck into the base of one of the windmills when he heard Max's voice call, "Prince Andreus. Did you see? Everything in the castle went dark and all the ladies started screaming. No one knew how to find candles or that they should stand still so they don't crash into things in the dark."

No. Andreus doubted they would.

"I'm betting you didn't crash into any walls getting up here."

Max straightened his shoulders despite how hard he shivered as the wind once again began to gain in strength. "Not once, Your Highness. And I came here because that's what you said I should do if ever there was an attack and the lights went out."

Andreus had forgotten he'd told Max that the safest place in an attack would be the battlements. The four-story white wall on top of the plateau made it the safest and most secure castle in Eden and in any of the kingdoms beyond the mountains or the waters.

"I heard the apprentices say you were the one who fixed the lights."

Andreus smiled at the admiration in the boy's eyes. "The Masters worked on it, too, but yes," he admitted. "I was the one who found the problem first and figured out how to rework the wires to get the lights on again."

"I knew it. How did you do it in the dark? Did you—"

"We can talk about that some other time." Andreus put a hand on Max's shoulder and steered him toward the stairs down into the castle. "Now, I'm going to ask you some questions while I walk you to your bed."

Andreus picked up the pace as several members of the guard and a few servants stopped and bowed when he passed. If his sister was right about the test and the sabotage on the lights occurring on the same day not being a coincidence, he didn't want anyone to overhear him discussing it with Max.

"Did I do something wrong?" Max glanced up at Andreus with fear in his eyes as they reached the first floor. "Did Lady Yasmie . . ."

What had the boy to do with Lady Yasmie? Whatever it was they'd deal with it later.

"No. You didn't do anything wrong," he said, realizing that Max was struggling to keep up with him. Great. Now Andreus was scaring the boy based on his sister's paranoia. Slowing he said, "I just have a few questions about people you've talked to since coming to live at the castle and whether—"

The clanging of a gong sounded in the wide hallway. When he was little the striking gongs filled him with excitement. Now they made his palms sweat and his stomach clench. "My father has returned."

"The King?" Max yelped. "I thought he was delayed at the southern battlefields. Does this mean we won the war?"

"We can always hope," Andreus said, knowing if the war had been won his father would have sent a runner ahead to make sure the army returned to feasts and music and triumph. If only. That alone would have been enough to distract Father from the rest of the Hall of Virtues business for weeks. "Run along to bed. With Father and Micah home, things will be busier for everyone tomorrow. We'll talk once things have settled down."

"All right, Your Highness," Max said with an awkward but enthusiastic bow. Then he turned and bolted down the hallway toward the servants' quarters and Andreus hurried toward the court-yards that led to the gates of the castle to greet his father and king.

He must have seen the lights go out on his ride. There would be no hiding the event. The best Andreus could hope for was that his father would be content in seeing the problem had been fixed—at least until Andreus figured out who was behind the sabotage and what their reasoning had been.

"Andreus." His mother's voice snapped behind him and he turned to watch her, wrapped in a cloak of deep red, striding down the white path. The towering, ever-present Oben was trailing silently behind her.

"Mother, I didn't expect you to come to the gates or I would have waited for you." Ever since Andreus could remember, Father insisted on being greeted when the gongs sounded his return, but Mother never once that he could remember followed that decree. Instead, she waited for Father to come find her and to beg forgiveness for leaving her behind at the castle while he went away. Whether she actually missed the King in his absence was debatable, but not as important as the charade that she performed each time he returned.

"Tonight's mishap with the wind power left me little choice but to defend you and our family from your father's wrath."

"I can defend myself."

"If that were the case, your sister would have a very different life," she corrected. "But tonight, I will make sure everyone sees their royal family together—united and confident here in our kingdom."

Andreus understood the command beneath the carefully chosen words. If Micah or Father made comments goading Andreus or Carys, he was to help his sister laugh them off. No confrontations. Not today. "Yes, Mother."

She pursed her lips and studied Andreus before taking his arm. "Oben tells me you were key in fixing the orb and the other lights so quickly."

"The Masters—"

"*You* were the hero of the night," she snapped. "The Masters failed. Their system broke down because of a mistake *they* made, and it was the Prince who recognized the problem and restored the light. That is what the Council will proclaim to the city tomorrow. And to all those who hear, that will be the truth. People will speak of how your wisdom pushed back the dark. Do you understand?"

No one would speak of the sabotage. It would be as if it had never happened.

"Yes, but the Masters—"

"The Masters know their place. Oben has already made sure they have all been suitably encouraged to hold their tongues, and any who might not have been dealt with. And tomorrow you will instruct the Masters in what you found in order to ensure this kind of thing never happens again."

Andreus pulled his cloak tighter as they approached the gate and the people clustered around it. Dozens of Eden's citizens regularly turned out to greet the King. No doubt they were right now praising Micah for the number of soldiers he had beheaded on the field of battle.

Andreus scowled. War was barbaric—and so often pointless with little achieved. So easy to applaud and glorify from a safe distance. He doubted any of his father's sycophants would cheer so loudly were they sent to the front.

Only as they approached, Andreus realized there were no cheers or bursts of laughter. Just low murmurs beneath the sound of the gong strikes announcing the return of the King.

The people near the gate soundlessly parted for them as they grew near. None could meet his eyes. He felt his mother tense beside him as the gongs went silent. When he saw his sister kneeling on the ground and spotted his brother and father staring up at the stars with unseeing eyes, Andreus understood why.

"What is the meaning of this?" His mother looked at Chief Elder Cestrum, who stood clutching his cloak with his iron claw.

"I am sorry, my queen," Elder Cestrum said, lingering on the *S* of sorry. "They should have sent word ahead to warn us . . . to warn *you* that tragedy has struck."

Tragedy.

People around him muttered as Andreus stepped forward. For a moment, Andreus could hear nothing other than the sound of his own heart beating. Not his mother, who was pointing at the bodies on the ground. Not Chief Elder Cestrum, who had stepped to the

Queen's side. Or Elder Ulrich, who had his one good eye trained on Andreus while saying . . . something. All of it was drowned out by the thudding of his heart growing faster and louder. Everything inside him tightened and ached. This couldn't be. He wanted to turn and walk away or, better, wake up because this was clearly some kind of nightmare. His father and brother couldn't be dead. Kings and princes did not lie on the palace stones dirty and cut and . . . dead.

Then Carys turned and looked up with him, her amber eyes shimmering as a tear streaked down her cheek.

That tear.

His sister never cried in public. Not when she broke her arm when they were seven. Not when their father had her lashed for one of her outbursts. Not ever. She wanted—she needed—people to believe that she could never be broken. She said shields were strong. And she believed that *her* job was to be *his* shield.

But that one drop made it real. That shield was broken now. And half their family was gone.

"No," a voice shouted from behind him. Everyone turned as Imogen, the hood of her purple cloak falling away, pushed through the crowd. "This cannot be." She staggered forward and stopped when she caught sight of Micah's body. "This is not supposed to be." She swayed as she stared at Micah's dirt-streaked face. "This is not supposed to be!"

"Imogen." Andreus stepped forward and put a hand on her arm—the first time he'd touched her since that night. He told himself it was touching her that was causing the tingling sensation in his arm. Nothing more. "Micah would want you to be strong now."

She shook her head and looked up at Andreus. Her dark eyes swam with confusion. "The Crown Prince wanted to rule. I was supposed to be at his side. I saw it in the stars."

"You saw nothing." His mother spat the words at Imogen and the seeress flinched with each one. "You are *useless*—and because of your weakness my son is dead."

Imogen pulled away from Andreus as his mother yanked her arm away from Oben, who had appeared at her side to steady her. She stepped around Imogen with a glare, then stormed toward the members of the King's Guard, who were standing not far from where the bodies lay. "How did this happen? How did my husband and son die?" Pointing to the King's Guardsmen, she turned to Elder Cestrum and demanded, "And how is it that *these* men who swore on their own lives to defend my husband and son survive while their king and crown prince were hunted like animals?"

Andreus looked at the men standing at the top of the steps just behind the bodies of his father and brother. Five members of the King's personal guard. All one hundred had accompanied the King to the battlefields along with fifty of Micah's guard and another thousand foot soldiers and knights. The foot soldiers and knights would have stayed to bolster the war effort. But the personal guards would have traveled home with the King and Crown Prince. One hundred and fifty men would have had his father and brother surrounded. And still they fell.

The men shifted and looked toward Chief Elder Cestrum and the rest of the Elders who stood behind the head of the Council.

"Answer your queen," Andreus said. Each word took more effort than the last. The tingling in his arm was turning to icy pinpricks. His heart was pounding even louder in his ears. Carys stood and came to his side, watching him carefully. Did she hear the tension in his voice? She must have. Carys had been around almost every time he'd had an attack. She knew the signs as well as he did. But sometimes the symptoms were minor.

This was minor. It had to be. He couldn't afford for it to be otherwise.

Carys stood next to him, her chin raised. Her eyes clear and determined. His sister was back to being strong. No more tears fell as she stood beside him, her back straight as a board.

"Yes," Chief Elder Cestrum said loud enough for all standing nearby to hear. "Tell your queen—tell us all—how it is that you are here instead of dead on the battlefields to the south."

Andreus tried to breathe slow and deep, but the breaths would only come shallow and fast. He pushed aside his concern as the tallest of the guardsmen, with a full, dark beard and seven stripes on each shoulder to indicate he was a member of the King's elite force, stepped forward and bowed. "My queen, it is true we failed you and our king and prince, but it did not happen on the battlefields."

"Then where?" Carys asked, stepping away from Andreus. "Where did my father and brother fall?"

Andreus forced himself to concentrate on the man's words and not on Imogen's stricken face. Or the sweat trickling down his neck and his back. Or the pain that pulsed through him with every heartbeat. Growing stronger.

"It was an ambush, Your Highness. At least a hundred of them in white-and-red livery swarmed out of the wilds of the Tempera. By the time we knew what was happening, the King had fallen from his horse and over half of our men were dead. The surprise was an advantage too great to be overcome. All but the five of us fell to the cowards of Adderton's swords."

"Impossible," Carys said under her breath so quietly that

Andreus was sure only he had heard her under the gust of wind that tugged the cloaks around them. He could see the way she studied the men who failed to see their father and brother home. Then she stared at their father and brother's bodies and frowned. There was something she saw that he didn't. He tried to focus on what that might be, but the pain was spreading and it was all he could do to not gasp aloud.

"The attackers killed the King and Prince and just happened to leave the five of you alive?" Elder Ulrich stepped forward and trained his good eye on the men.

"*You* should have died." Andreus's mother's voice cracked like a whip. "Your oath and your honor demanded that you die defending your king and your prince. *You* should have died!"

The King's Guardsman stared at the Queen, then swallowed hard and nodded. "I was at the front of the Guard when the fighting started, my queen. I wanted to die defending them. I intended to die." He glanced at Imogen, who was standing silent and sad and alone. "When I was struck down, I fell not far from where King Ulron lay on the leaves, lifeless. I wanted to rise and avenge his death, but I knew the battle was ended. Most of the King's Guard were dead. And I realized the only way to truly avenge my liege's death was to make sure that those who ordered the attack against us were brought to justice. I feigned death so I could recover the bodies of the King and Prince and bring them home . . . to you, my queen."

The bearded guardsman bowed his head. Andreus's mother started to tremble and Andreus clenched his fist as pain pulsed and grew and pulled at his chest. His knees went weak. His vision blurred, cleared, then blurred again.

No. Not now. Not today.

"Home?" his mother asked quietly. "You saved your life to bring dead men home? Your king is dead because your King's Guard forgot how to do its job." His mother paced in front of the bodies like a rock wolf studying its prey. "There is a penalty for breaking your oath."

"Surely, my queen," Elder Cestrum stepped forward, "these men have seen horrors. They can be forgiven—"

"My husband—your king—is dead. My son—the Crown Prince—is dead. There will be no forgiveness. I want their heads."

The crowd around them gasped and murmured.

"But, my lady," Elder Jacobs began. "These men have information that is vital to—"

She whirled around and stared at each member of the Council. "I don't care what they might know. The kingdom will know that an oath to the virtuous crown is the way of the light and those who break their oaths and walk in darkness will perish. Andreus will be the one who shows them. Make room for the King's justice."

"Prince Andreus does not have his sword, my queen," said Chief Elder Cestrum.

He heard his name and the words around it, but the voices sounded as if they were underwater. Muted as the world started to dim. Sweat poured down his back. His heart . . . it hurt. Gods, it hurt. He couldn't breathe.

"Carys." The word was strained and barely audible. Pain was spreading faster. Hotter. The pinpricks from before had spread. His chest was tightening. Each breath felt more impossible to take.

"Someone give my son a sword," his mother screamed. "He will show you what happens to those who do not stay true to Eden and the seven virtues."

He heard the whispered scraping of metal as it came free of a sheath. No. There was no way he could swing a blade. Not now. His mother would know that if she were paying attention. And now everyone would be watching him.

"Prince Andreus." He blinked as a blurry guardsman appeared, offering a massive broadsword with both hands. "My blade is yours."

Everything ached. His vision swam. The pulsing of his blood roared in his ears as he reached out for the sword that was bigger than the one he wore when he wasn't working with the Masters.

"Do it. For me, my son," he heard his mother command.

His legs threatened to give way. He'd never be able to lift the sword. Not now. Not with his chest barely able to take in air and his knees weak and fighting to keep him upright. But what choice did he have?

The lights were so bright. The pain of his curse dug deep into his chest.

Cursed.

The Council would see. They would remember the prediction the last seer had made. They would believe Andreus had no virtue in him. No light. They would think he was part of the darkness.

His fingers, slick with sweat, closed over the iron hilt and he willed himself to lift the blade.

"No," his sister screamed and grabbed the hilt of the sword. Carys made a show of shoving Andreus, even though her hand barely grazed him. But his sister's action had allowed him to stumble back and everyone thought they understood why.

Those gathered in front of the gate gasped as his sister took the hilt of the sword with both hands and held it low in front of her. His sister's hair whipped around her face as she yelled, "These men will not die. Not here. Not until I hear everything about how my father and brother were killed."

"That is not yours to decide, Princess," Chief Elder Cestrum said.

Carys turned toward him and stepped forward with the sword raised. Everyone watched his sister threatening the head of the Council of Elders. "I will not have the blood of these worthless men stain the ground where my father and brother lie. And do the King and Prince have no more value than trash? Why do they still lie on the ground? Do you not care?"

Andreus staggered backward a step as his sister, still holding the sword in front of her, advanced toward the Council. The crowd around him made sounds of surprise and Andreus took another small step back, then another as he fumbled to find the pocket in his cloak that held the remedy he had with him. His fingers closed around the small black vial he carried with him at all times. The remedy could never cure him. It couldn't kill the curse he was born with and had hidden every day of his life since. But it helped ease the symptoms when an attack came. He just hoped it wasn't too late for it to work now.

His fingers weren't strong enough to pull out the stopper. He had to use his teeth. Then spitting the cork seal to the side, he swallowed the horrific brew as his sister turned toward their mother with the blade still aloft. "Do you care more about the heads of these men than you do about your own king and son? What kind of queen are you?"

A crack of flesh striking flesh pulled gasps from everyone watching. Carys's head snapped back as their mother's hand connected with its target. Carys looked at Andreus and their mother struck her face again.

She was telling him to get out of sight. They would come up with an excuse for his desertion later. Now there was no choice.

"How dare you?" their mother demanded, striking out again. This time harder. Carys clenched her jaw but didn't move. "I am the one who will command what will be done. They will die."

Andreus took several more painful, unsteady steps back until he finally reached the stone wall and could use it to help him stay upright as he made his way toward the opening.

"There is no peace," his mother shouted. "Not until all who had a hand in killing my son and husband are put to death. All of them. They will pay. They will all pay." Andreus held the wall as footsteps grew closer. He watched his mother storm through the gate, followed by Oben and several members of the castle guard. He waited for one of them to turn and see him standing there sweaty and shaking and barely able to stand. But none did.

Under the roar in his ears, Andreus heard Elder Cestrum order the guards to take the sword from Carys and to put her in custody. She would pay for turning the blade toward the Queen.

Andreus wanted to defend his sister. He wanted to make sure she would not be punished for shielding him. But he knew she would never forgive him if the secret she'd protected all these years was revealed. Not when she had done so good a job of distracting the court and the Council—again.

Panting, he willed his legs to move as he held the wall for guidance toward an alcove that was hidden behind several tall bushes. But he was moving so slowly and the world around him was starting to go black. He could hear the footsteps approaching the gate. Voices were getting louder as he lurched forward toward the opening. The windmills churned high above.

One step.

Two steps.

Andreus stumbled into the opening and fell to his knees as the pressure expanded inside him. He gasped for breath as he fell forward. There was another flash of pain. Then everything went black.

5

Carys gripped the heavy sword in her hands as her mother quietly said something to Chief Elder Cestrum. The Queen then glared at Carys with a rage that took her breath away before she turned and stormed toward the gate with Oben and two members of the guard in tow.

The crowd parted for her and dropped into bows as their queen passed. Then they turned and looked back at her.

Carys held her ground and fought to keep the sword aloft. Her fear for her brother had pushed her to take action. It had given her strength to stand firm against their mother, who should have understood why Carys had done what she did.

The day Carys and Andreus were born, the seer said the Queen would give birth to two children on the same day and within the same hour. One would be pure of spirit. The other would be cursed. Seer Kheldin believed if the child filled with darkness was allowed to live a full life, the curse born with the child would sweep across the kingdom and the light of Eden would darken forever.

According to Mother, she and the midwife did everything possible to make sure none but the two of them ever knew Andreus almost died or that he struggled to catch his breath through the first week, especially when he cried. They were afraid the Council of Elders would see the seer's curse in Andreus's fragile state.

The midwife disappeared from the castle one evening two days after their birth. She was found dead, thrown from her horse while riding away from Garden City. Mother said it was the Gods' way of helping to keep Andreus safe. But the way Mother looked at Oben when she said it told Carys that the Gods had little to do with the accident. Their mother was determined to do whatever was necessary to see Andreus safe from the harm the Council and others might do to him.

How anyone could believe Andreus's condition could cause the kingdom to fall into darkness was beyond Carys. But people had faith in the power of the seers.

For hundreds of years the people of Eden had been encouraged to believe in the seers' visions and predictions that promised to keep the kingdom from harm. The stories all said it was a seer who foretold that the castle and the kingdom would fall three hundred years ago. And a seer also saw the rebuilding of the kingdom, a monarch who held fast to the seven virtues, the orb that would someday shine above the castle, and the bloody battle that brought Carys's grandfather to the throne. Belief in the seers' magical powers and the forces beyond ordinary knowledge were sacred here. As sacred as the honoring of the winds.

Kings had always had a seer to advise them because the people trusted the visions that came from the Gods. They believed in them with a devotion that scared Carys. Because she knew one day that firm faith in the seers could turn against her brother and end in his death.

But not today. From the way everyone stared, she knew that all of the castle and Garden City tomorrow would be talking about her and the sword she now wielded.

She shifted the heavy blade in her hands. Her arms were growing weary. The fear that had propelled her to act was quickly being replaced by the sorrow and shock she'd pushed to the side. Still, she continued holding the sword and stared down the Council, giving a few last seconds to her brother. Then, looking down at her father and brother's bodies, Carys let the sword drop from her hands.

Metal clattered on the white stones. The large guardsman who gave up his sword snatched it from the ground with only one hand. And the Council, led by Chief Elder Cestrum, moved toward her.

"I apologize for my outburst, my lords," she said, lifting her chin the way her mother always did. "But I am glad you agree that these remaining members of the King's Guard should be questioned. I want whoever was behind this slaughter of my family brought to justice."

It was the truth. Not the entire truth, but enough that she could say it with absolute conviction. Her father was dead. Her oldest brother cut down. She wanted vengeance against those who took their lives. Killing those who tried to defend them made little sense to her. Oath or no oath.

"My mother is out of her mind with grief," she continued. "We must not act in haste or out of anger."

Elder Cestrum pursed his thin lips together as he smoothed the white hair on his chin. "Captain Monteros," he called.

The longtime captain of the castle's guardsmen stepped forward.

"Seize these members of the King's Guard and have them taken to the North Tower. And have your men place King Ulron and Prince Micah's bodies in the chapel. Women will be sent to prepare them for the funeral."

Captain Monteros bowed slightly and said, "Yes, my lord." He glanced at several of his men, who immediately took the surviving members of the King's Guard into custody. The King's Guardsman who spoke of why they still lived looked at her, then at Elder Ulrich, then back at her and held her gaze with a fierce intensity as he passed. As if he were trying to tell her something.

"Princess Carys." Chief Elder Cestrum turned to her, and she knew before he said the words what was coming. She'd known what would happen when she'd grabbed the sword. It wasn't as if she hadn't been down this road before. Although it had been years since the last time.

With a bow Elder Cestrum explained, "You are to be reprimanded for threatening your mother's life and defying the will of the Queen. However, the Council has decided that in deference to your sorrow, you are to be given the option of submitting to your punishment now or waiting until tomorrow when you have had a chance to come to terms with your loss."

"I shall go now," she said. As much as she wanted to check on her brother, there was little she could do for him. Her punishment tonight would keep the focus on her instead of allowing people to speculate on the absence of Andreus.

"Are you sure, Your Highness?" Elder Ulrich asked as several guardsmen lifted her father and brother's bodies off the ground and began to carry them inside the castle.

Everything inside her stopped for a second. Tears began to build as the tangible reminder of her loss cut a fresh wound in her heart.

When the bodies disappeared inside the gate, she turned back to Elder Ulrich.

"I'm already in pain, my lord." She focused on the one blue eye that stared at her with great concern and the mangled, white-scarred slit of the other that could never close and yet would never again see. "Nothing more terrible can happen to me today."

Elder Ulrich sighed. "As you wish, Princess."

"Guards!" Chief Elder Cestrum clapped his hands. Two members of the guard appeared next to him. "Please escort Princess Carys to the North Tower. Captain Monteros will meet you there as soon as he can so we can all put this part of the night behind us."

As if that would ever be possible.

"Very well." She didn't wait for the guards before walking through the crowd of court members who continued to watch the drama. A few smirked as she passed. Some whispered to each other, no doubt about other times she'd walked this path and had screamed for her mother to come to her aid. After all, Carys had been doing what her mother instructed. She'd been helping her brother.

Distraction was always a good solution. The first few times when she'd dumped soup on Lord Nigel's lap, or when she'd tripped Micah's best friend Garret and he'd plunged headfirst into a fountain, people had laughed and blamed her youth. When she was twelve, her father said he couldn't expect the Lords of Eden or any of the subjects to adhere to the virtues of the kingdom if his own daughter couldn't.

"Clearly you need a lesson to serve as a reminder of what happens when you turn from the light. This is done not out of malice but out of love."

Love.

Was it love to insist your daughter be flogged while two members of the King's Guard held her down?

Yes. In a strange way it was. The world was safer when people believed justice was the same for the powerless and those in power. It was a lesson her father wanted her to learn. He'd hoped after the first instance she'd never be flogged again.

"Sorry, Father," she whispered as they reached the entrance of the North Tower. The slighter of the two guards fumbled with the door then stepped to the side to allow her to enter first.

Torches lit the inside of the tower. The kingdom did not waste the power needed for the safety of the walls on those who had turned from the light. The first floor was used for questioning and was where the Council of Elders held trials for common thieves, poachers, and those who had defaulted on their taxes. Carys sat in one of the chairs used by the Council and watched the shadows cast by the torches shift on the stone walls. Her two guards stood at the door, neither willing to look at her.

She clasped and unclasped her hands. Then Carys rubbed them on her lap as her stomach clenched. The seconds crawled as she watched the door, waiting for Captain Monteros to arrive and mete out the punishment

Everything inside her jittered and she thought about the bottle of the Tears of Midnight she'd left in her room. She hadn't thought her visit to the city would take long so she hadn't brought it with her. But it had been hours since she'd taken the much-needed sip of the drink her mother had given to her after the first time she'd been brought to this terrifyingly stark room. If only this tower had been the one swept up into the wind tunnel that struck years ago instead of the tower to the south.

But unlike the men in the cells upstairs, she'd made the choice to come here by standing for Andreus. And she'd leave once the punishment had been given.

The muscles in her legs twitched and her stomach cramped. Nerves? Need? Both?

She stood and looked around the room, feeling as if she was going to jump out of her skin. The walls seemed as if they were closing in. She needed to move.

Spotting the stairs, she said, "I'm going to go upstairs and talk to my father's men. Let me know when Captain Monteros arrives." The two guards glanced at each other and Carys started up the steps before they could debate whether she was supposed to remain on the first floor.

The first floor smelled of musty fabric and dirt and mold. That was bad. The floor above it was worse. Sweat. Urine. Rotting hay.

"Where are my father's men?" she asked the guardsmen flanking the steps.

"They are in the cells on the next floor, Your Highness," a gray-haired guard informed her. "The rest of the prisoners on that floor were moved to keep them isolated."

Ignoring the way her fingers shook as she gathered her skirts, Carys turned and climbed the stairs. The rotting smell grew stronger the higher she climbed and even worse when she took a lit torch from the staircase and started down the hallway next to the cells. Each cell had a thick wooden door with a window made of iron bars. The first two cells were empty, but a face looked back at her when she peered into the third.

"Your Highness," the man said as he stood and walked toward

the door. In the light of the torch, Carys saw the man who spoke for the other men at the castle's entrance looking back. "Your father would not want you to be here."

"There is much my father didn't want that has happened today," she answered. "I wish to know why."

"I told you why."

Not all of it. Because she'd seen her father up close, and when the initial shock faded, she had seen clearly what had killed the King.

"We both know you lied," she whispered.

"I did not lie, Your Highness." The King's Guardsman pressed his face close to the bars. "There was an ambush."

"The King and Crown Prince always travel in the center of the King's Guard."

"Yes, Your Highness."

"And that's where they were when the ambush came?"

"Yes, Your Highness."

"If my father was surrounded by his Guard, how is it that he never had a chance to grab his sword and was run through from behind?"

The first was a guess. The second was less of one. The damage to the leather tunic and the bloodstained tear in the back of his cloak were evidence enough of her theory. But it took the man flinching behind the bars of his cell to confirm fully that it was true.

Her father had been attacked in the center of men who were supposed to defend him. The only explanation for him not drawing his weapon and fighting off the enemy was that the attack came from directly behind. From his own men.

"Why?" she whispered.

The man glanced in the direction of the rustling coming from the cells down the hall. "Your Highness, you don't want people to know you were here."

"What people?" The sound of boots against stone echoed in the hallway. Someone was coming. Carys stepped closer to the cell door, gripped the torch tight in her hand, and hissed, "I will help you escape. If you tell me the truth, I will give you your life. I will find a way to get you and the others out of here."

She had no idea how, but that was less important than learning if there was someone else behind her father's and brother's deaths. If the rest of her family might be threatened. If she could be in danger.

Out of the corner of her eye she saw the freckle-faced guard emerge from the staircase. "Captain Monteros is on his way, Your Highness. He will be expecting to find you waiting downstairs."

"Then that is where he will find me," she said, looking back at the iron-barred window. The man's face had disappeared back into the shadows. But she'd return later.

She replaced the torch she'd taken and had reached the bottom steps moments before the door of the North Tower swung open and Captain Monteros appeared. Carys didn't wait for his instructions. Instead, she walked toward the area the guards used for questioning prisoners and unfastened her cloak. She would not show fear. She would not cry. Her mother had told her that in order to protect her twin Carys would have to embody the virtue of strength. It was in these moments that Carys knew her mother was right.

It took strength to unfasten the back of her dress without letting the captain see her hands quiver. It took great resolve to shift the fabric to expose her back as she pressed herself up against the wall.

"Perhaps you should talk to the Queen," Captain Monteros said from behind. "Explain that you were upset about the death of your father and brother. I'm sure she'll reconsider this punishment."

If only that were true. But it hadn't been before and today would be no different. And if she tried, her mother might not listen when she explained about the King's Guardsmen in the cells above and the truth she was certain they had yet to speak.

Carys glanced over her shoulder. While she was as tall as her brother, Captain Monteros was far taller than she. And stronger. "The sooner you begin, captain, the sooner this will be over."

"If you are certain, Highness. The Council has determined there will be three strokes." He picked up a wide, leather strap.

Carys laughed. "They *are* in a merciful mood. Do your best to be quick."

She kept her eyes open, even though she couldn't see anything with her face pressed against the stone. Closing them felt weak. Her legs trembled. Her stomach curled. She exhaled to loosen her muscles because it was worse when she tensed up. But she couldn't stop herself from flinching as she heard the whistle of leather passing through the air then . . .

Pain.

She dropped the front of her dress and grabbed the handles on each side of her head to keep from collapsing as icy hot agony pulled the strength out from under her. Her heart pounded. A whimper stuck in her throat and she braced herself as the whistle of the strap came again and with it fire as it cracked across the small of her back.

Her fingers clung to the handles. She clenched her jaw, refusing to make a sound when all she wanted to do was sob from the throbbing ache.

One more. She would survive one . . .

She gasped air, lost her grip, and slid down the wall to the musty floor as tears flooded her eyes. It was over.

Not that bad, she told herself as pain flashed and flared.

"It's over, Princess," Captain Montoros whispered. Then he raised his voice so that anyone might hear. "Your penance is served. The seven virtues have been restored."

Carys cursed under her breath. The virtues could be damned.

The biting wind was welcome when she stiffly stepped from the tower. Cold air on hot, shrieking skin. The pain was duller now than it had been only minutes ago. Still terrible, but bearable. It was amazing what a person could tolerate.

The freckle-faced guard appeared beside her.

"I'd like to be alone," she said.

The young guard looked down at his boots. "Captain Monteros told me to escort you to your rooms, Your Highness."

"Well, that's a problem," she said, wincing as she started forward. "Because I'm not going to my rooms." There were two things she needed to do first.

Balling her hands into fists, she dug her nails deeper into her palms with each step to keep herself from giving in to the pain. The cold eased the heat of the welts, but after the first soothing moments it made her huddle deep in her cloak to try and halt the shivering. Each shake of her body made her clench her teeth harder as she crossed the courtyard and entered the castle. The freckled guard followed.

Lights glowed in the halls and she willed herself to walk like the princess she was through the castle to the chapel. Inside the high arching space filled with benches and statues representing each of the seven virtues twinkled hundreds of flickering candles, symbols of the time before the virtues were the guiding principle of the kingdom.

In the front, as she knew they would be, the silhouettes of two bodies were laid on white stone benches.

"Excuse me, Your Highness." Elder Jacobs rose from a bench in the shadows near the back of the chapel, making Carys jump at the sudden movement. "I didn't mean to startle you. With the excitement at the gates earlier, I never got the chance to extend my sympathies for your loss."

"I appreciate that, my lord, but I am here to grieve and ask—"

"I am also sorry I could not intervene on your behalf." His dark skin blended into the shadows, but his eyes reflected the candlelight, causing them to appear to glow as he walked slowly toward Carys. As he moved, his long braid undulated in the shadows, making it seem almost alive. "It was a shame you had to endure more discomfort on a night filled with such sorrow. The North Tower is not a place in which a princess of the realm should ever step foot."

"If you hadn't noticed, Elder Jacobs," Carys said, "I am not the fainting type. A trip to the North Tower is never pleasant, but it didn't kill me."

"I'm glad for that. But you should be careful, Princess Carys. Just because a moth flies close to a flame and lives doesn't mean the next time it won't catch fire." He pointed a long, dark finger down at a gray moth lying on the ground. "These are dangerous times. I said as much to your brother a few minutes ago."

"Andreus was here?"

Elder Jacobs nodded and a shimmer of relief pushed aside some of Carys's aches. The attack had passed. Her ruse had worked.

"As was Lady Imogen. They paid their respects to your father and brother and left together not long ago."

"I see. Now, if you don't mind, my lord," Carys said, trying to stay still as the aching and throbbing grew, "I would like to be alone with my father and brother so that I, too, might pay my respects."

"Of course, Princess," he said smoothly. Then, with a perfectly executed bow, Elder Jacobs headed for the doorway. When he reached the arching entrance, he turned and looked at her, then disappeared, his dark, thin braid slithering behind him.

For a moment, Carys stared at the entrance, wondering at the meaning twisted in between Elder Jacobs's words. He always *played* the mediator—brokering compromise between the Council and the King, or the King and the High Lords of the Seven Virtuous Districts. But rarely did his mediations create anything other than disillusionment and dissent. What dissent was he trying to create now?

Without an answer to that question, Carys turned back toward the front of the chapel. She felt her heart tighten as she walked up the center aisle. Hundreds of flickering flames were arranged on and around the white stone bench her father's body was laid on. The soft glow of candlelight illuminated her father's face. Even in death he was handsome, with his golden hair and beard that someone had cleaned and combed so he appeared more like himself. Only now he was still. And pale. Now that the streaks of blood and dirt had been washed away, it was obvious that the man she'd always thought was undefeatable was gone.

Carys reached out to touch his cheek as she did when she was very small and still allowed to crawl onto his lap.

Ice.

And despite the new clothes they had dressed him in and the ceremonial robe draped around his shoulders, he would never be warm again. She shivered. Maybe she wouldn't be, either. Not after today.

She heard the young guardsman shift in the back of the chapel as she walked the ten feet between where her father lay and her brother.

Micah.

The next Keeper of Virtues. Guardian of the Light. Ruler of Eden.

To her he'd always looked like a younger version of their father—without a beard. Perhaps that was why they were always at odds in recent years. Both were leaders. Neither liked giving way to anyone. Now someone had forced them both to do exactly that. The question was who? Was it really the Kingdom of Adderton or had someone else orchestrated their murders?

Carys ached to bury her head in Andreus's shoulder and weep. For him. For her. For the pain streaking up her back and slowly eating away at her heart. Her stomach twisted. Her hands once again shook as she unfastened the deep blue tunic her brother had been dressed in. She tried not to look at his face as she worked. Pretending she didn't care. Even though she did.

Micah never stood up for her. He often wanted her punished more harshly for her actions. He would assert that she caused embarrassment to the crown. But he was always at her door bringing her sweets or a kind word when the punishment was over.

Spreading the tunic, Carys looked at her brother's hair-covered, muscular chest. As on her father's body, there was only one wound. A knife had been driven into the base of his throat. A place the chain shirt he wore did not cover. Carys started to roll him over, and this time she couldn't stop the moan of pain from escaping her lips and the tears from burning the backs of her eyes.

"Let me, Highness."

She hadn't heard the young guard approach and started to order him away, but she couldn't. If she spoke, she'd cry. And she wasn't sure she'd be able to stop.

Nodding, she allowed him to help her turn her brother's body.

He had scars along his back from years ago. A pink, mostly healed gash decorated his shoulder. A souvenir from his efforts on the battlefield to the south, she guessed. But the knife puncture in the throat was the only recent cut. She took each of his hands in hers. Turned them over one at a time. Calluses. Nails trimmed nearly to the quick. But no cuts or scrapes.

Micah, who trained for hours every day with his guard so he would always be better and stronger than his enemies on the field, had been struck down without evidence of his having defended himself. Maybe one of them might have been taken off guard during the attack, but both her father *and* Micah?

It seemed impossible.

The King's Guard had lied. Perhaps Adderton soldiers had ambushed them, but there was more to the story. And she would learn what that was.

"Roll the Prince on his back."

The guard did as she commanded, then started to redress him.

"I can do it," she said quietly. "I need to do it."

Her shaking fingers made it hard to get the tunic straight and fastened. The guard stood beside her the entire time. She thought about sending him away, but there was comfort in having him near. Perhaps because he was warm and breathing when she was surrounded by death.

When she was done, she leaned forward, not caring about the way her body protested the movement, and pressed a kiss to her brother's forehead. Then she turned and did the same with her father as the soldier stood silently behind her—watching.

Then Carys pulled her cloak tight around her, swallowed down the knot of sorrow and anger, and turned her back on death.

She headed to her rooms, each step more painful than the last. Twice she had to stop and put her hand against the wall. Each time it was harder to convince her body to keep moving. And it would just keep getting worse as the welts swelled and the bruises from the strap deepened.

She had to get to her rooms.

Andreus would be there. Waiting with willow bark tea and salves and cool cloths to reduce the swelling and ease the flames in her back. She would be stiff tomorrow. But it would be better with Andreus's care.

Carys made it to the doorway of her rooms before her legs gave way. She grabbed the doorframe for support as the young guard opened the door and stepped out of the way so she could walk in. A fire crackled in the hearth of the sitting room. Carys expected to see her brother in one of the high-backed blue velvet-lined chairs or at the windows that looked out onto the mountains beyond the plateau.

The room was empty. Carys looked toward the bedroom door at the far end of the room as it opened and felt her heart leap, but it wasn't her brother who appeared. Juliette, Carys's dark-haired maid, hurried forward.

"Your Highness, I am sorry for your loss. I have tea ready for you and a meal if you think you can eat."

"Tea would be fine." The mere idea of food made Carys's stomach rebel. Eating was the last thing she needed. "Has Prince Andreus been here?"

"No, Princess." Juliette moved to a table near the fireplace to pour tea. "No one has been by."

Not her mother, who knew her punishment. Not her twin, whom she had just stood up for.

Maybe Andreus didn't know she had returned.

"Juliette," she said, wincing as she grabbed hold of the back of a chair. "Ask the guard stationed outside to go to Prince Andreus's rooms and inform him of my arrival here."

"Yes, Highness." Juliette hurried toward the door. Only moments later, the maid returned. "Can I help you change into something more comfortable, Your Highness? Something softer perhaps?"

She'd heard about the strapping. Everyone must have by now. Castle gossip spread like fire in a straw hut. But even though changing into a robe that was soft and loose sounded like heaven, Carys said, "I will be fine. And you can go for the night."

Only family would see her scars. Ever.

"But . . . "

"Go."

Juliette twisted her hands in front of her, bobbed a curtsy, and promised to return in the morning. When the door opened again, Carys wanted to weep at the appearance of the guard who appeared.

"I'm sorry, Highness. Prince Andreus did not answer."

Disappointment flooded her. "He must not have returned to his rooms as of yet."

The guard looked down at the light brown carpet. "I believe he was there, Your Highness. But he wasn't alone. I heard two voices before I knocked. Perhaps that's why he chose not to answer."

"Two voices? Was one my mother?" she asked. That would explain his absence.

The guard shifted and his freckled face heated with color. "The other voice was female, Your Highness, but I am fairly certain it was not the Queen inside."

"I see." She just wished she didn't. "You can go now."

"Yes, Princess," he said with a bow. When he was gone, Carys turned and walked to the door with slow, deliberate steps. Then, summoning the last of her strength, she left her rooms and walked the length of the hallway to her brother's rooms. The guard was right about the voices inside. She leaned her ear against the door and heard sniffling and the sound of her brother's voice soothing the woman inside. Then she heard him speak the woman's name.

Imogen.

The seeress who failed to see the King and Crown Prince's deaths. The woman who Andreus watched with fascination even as he vowed to care nothing for her. And now he was with her instead of being with Carys.

The pulsing pain in her back grew stronger with each step back to her own rooms.

It hurt.

Everything hurt.

Her back.

Her heart.

Her soul.

She needed to be strong. Her father would demand it.

But he was dead.

A tear fell. More burned her throat and slipped out of her control as she closed her own door behind her. She took a few more steps as the pressure and ache and swell of sorrow broke through.

Sliding to the floor, Carys let the tears come. Tears for her loss.

Tears for the kingdom and the ever-expanding pain and the fear of tomorrow. Tears because she was alone.

Isolated.

Broken.

Tired.

She'd been fighting so long. For what? She stared at the door, willing it to open. Waiting for her brother to remember she needed him.

Her stomach twisted. Tears squeezed out, making the fire on her back burn hotter. And deep within where no strap could reach, there was an emptiness far worse than any beating she could receive. Cuts and bruises and welts she could steel herself against until they healed, but the emptiness . . . it grew wider. Deeper. Hopeless. And alone.

It took three tries to pull herself off the floor. With heavy, staggering steps she walked to her bedroom.

Her father's rumbling laughter rang in her memories.

Micah's rare smile flickered and faded.

Candlelight glowed in here. Juliette probably meant for it to be soothing. Instead, the shadows called to her as she opened the small cabinet next to her bed and reached for a red glass bottle her mother first brought to her five years ago.

"This will help with the pain," Mother said, putting the bottle to Carys's lips herself. It did. It leeched away the pain. It helped her calm the anger bubbling inside each time she took a sip of the bitter brew. Ten days after that first sip, the welts and bruises had faded, the discomfort from them had gone, but the need for the drink had grown.

"Nothing good comes without a price," her mother said when

Carys's hands shook and her insides cramped after a dozen hours had passed since her last dose. "Just a little every day is a small price for something so useful. Trust me."

Trust.

A little every day eventually became a bit more to keep the tremors and the stomach ailments and the sweating at bay. Twice she'd taken far more. In anger. In despair. She'd wanted to feel nothing and made things worse. Since then she'd been careful to take only enough to keep the signs of her body's craving at bay. After all, Andreus needed her.

She needed him now. She'd trusted he would be here for her so they could grieve together and so he could help her as she had just helped him. And he had chosen to be with someone else.

It hurt to move.

It hurt to breathe.

It hurt to think.

She didn't want to think. The emptiness was swallowing her whole. There was only one escape. She didn't care what the price was anymore.

Fingers shaking, Carys uncorked the bottle and put it to her lips. The bitterness filled her mouth as she drank deep of the potent brew that had held her prisoner to the dark for years.

So aptly named, she thought. Tears of Midnight—when the night was darkest and the pain too great to bear. When there was no light.

To hell with the light, she thought as the throbbing in her back dulled. The ache in her heart numbed and everything inside her went warm and fluid and the emptiness grew farther and farther away.

Carys dropped the red bottle. It shattered on the ground and she smiled as the weight of the emptiness inside her faded. She welcomed the darkness. And embraced the abyss.

6

Andreus looked at Imogen's tear-streaked face and couldn't squelch the ever-present desire to protect her. Long dark hair. Deep-set eyes that looked away from him each time he turned her way.

Now those eyes were filled with tears and her hands trembled as she stood in front of Andreus begging his forgiveness for her failure.

He took a deep breath and pushed aside the weakness he still felt after his attack.

Cursed.

Maybe he was.

For years he'd tried to deny it. Despite his sister and his mother working hard to hide his secret, he'd wanted to believe it wasn't real. Seers and their claims to read the future in the stars and call the winds weren't real. He'd studied the winds and the histories of the weather. He worked with the tools that captured them and powered the lights Eden depended on.

But today . . . when he lay in the alcove with his hand pressed to the gash on his forehead where he'd struck the wall as he fell, he wondered if the curse wasn't real. Thanks to his sister and the remedy, his body withstood the attack without anyone the wiser. His sister would need him once the punishment she took for him was over. He should tell Imogen whatever he needed to in order to get her to leave so he could go to Carys.

But looking at Imogen's eyes shimmering with guilt, he couldn't bring himself to escort her out the door.

"I tried to see the Queen, to explain that the stars shielded this from me, but her chamberlain told me she'd taken to her bed and could not be disturbed. And your sister is . . . busy. So I came to you."

"I doubt my mother would have been good company, Lady Imogen." She had probably already downed several cups of her infamous tea, which helped tamp down her temper, but in large doses loosened her tongue. "She doesn't deal with loss well."

"She was right to blame me." Imogen walked across the room to stare out the window at the mountain range beyond the plateau.

"You are not responsible for my father and brother's deaths," he said, crossing the room to stand at her side.

"I failed to keep my betrothed safe."

"It was the King's Guard's job to ensure their safety."

"It was mine as well. And I failed. I so badly wanted to do what was right for the kingdom. I tried to follow what I believed was right. But I was wrong."

"I'm sorry," Andreus said. While he might not believe in the power she claimed to have, he did understand guilt. "I wish I could have changed things, too. I could have ridden to the battlefields with my father and Micah. Maybe if I had, I would have seen the attackers approach. I could have helped them."

Imogen walked to him. The silk of her skirts rustled. She reached out to touch him, then just before she did pulled her fingers back. Quietly, she said, "There is nothing you could have done that a hundred and fifty men surrounding them did not try. But if I had not trusted the Guild or the vision I had telling me this would be my home, I would never have come to the Palace of Winds. Your brother and the King would not have placed their faith in me.

"I wanted to believe the vision that I belonged somewhere. That I didn't have a home as a child because my true home was waiting for me to arrive. I was foolish and Micah should have let the Council and the King replace me as seer. If he hadn't intervened—"

"Wait a minute." Andreus stopped her. "My father and the Council wanted to remove you as seer?"

Seer of Eden wasn't a job that someone just walked away from. The oath the seer took was for life.

"I didn't mean to say that, Your Highness. Micah said no one was to know. I am just upset and saying things I shouldn't. Everything will work out as it should." Imogen dropped her gaze to the ground and wrapped her arms around herself. "You should visit your sister. The Princess shouldn't be alone now."

No. Carys shouldn't be alone. Not tonight. Not after losing half their family and having to be punished for saving him. She should see for herself that she had succeeded and that he was okay. He owed her that. But what Imogen was talking about . . . a removal of a seer only happened upon the seer's death—whether by natural causes or ordered by the king.

"My sister is a strong woman. She knows where to find me if she needs me. If you need help, let me help you."

"Prince Micah said . . . "

"Prince Micah is gone." Andreus took a step forward. He put a hand under Imogen's chin and tilted her face up. "He can't protect you." Not that Micah was ever interested in protecting his betrothed.

To Andreus's eye, Imogen was just a means to an end. "But together we might be able to find a way to keep you safe. But you have to tell me what has happened that I don't know about."

She held her breath and studied him for a heartbeat. Two.

He saw the memory of that one night on the battlements in her eyes. For weeks, Andreus joined the shy, slight seeress there to help her understand the new windmill designs and the lines that carried their power to the lights on the castle and into the city below. At first her questions had been hesitant, but day after day her voice grew stronger and her words more confident. At least, with him. Andreus loved watching her come alive. He'd enjoyed seeing the smile that only seemed to appear when he came near and he wanted nothing more than to pull her close and keep her safe when she spoke of the family she'd lost when she was five. She'd talked to him quietly of how she wanted the Palace of Winds to be the home she'd never had, and Andreus recognized the same desire that he had experienced his entire life. The longing for utter safety.

Her beauty. Her passion for the wind. Her need for protection stirred him.

Then Micah and Imogen announced their betrothal and he'd felt betrayed.

It was Imogen who sought him out on the battlements later that night. To thank him, she said, for making her feel as if she was important. She took his arm and a spark passed through her touch even as the wind blew cold. Because of the chill, no one else braved the night atop the castle. There was no one to see him tilt his head down intending to meet her cheek only to have her turn. His lips touched hers and nothing else mattered. The shyness he had come to expect was gone. Suddenly she was like the wind—pulling at him.

They fumbled into one of the windmills where nothing else mattered but the warmth of her skin.

A week later Imogen found him again—this time to ask Andreus to keep his distance out of deference to his brother. Andreus wanted to ask her why she'd agreed to marry Micah, but she walked away before he had the chance. He'd told himself he didn't care. One night—one girl was nothing to him. To prove it he'd found other women to enjoy and used them to try and wedge a shield between Imogen and his heart.

Standing here with her hand in his, he admitted that those shields had never really existed. He wanted to hold and protect her now just as much as he had in the windmill that night.

"Please, Imogen," he said, taking her hand. "Tell me what I can do to help you."

Her eyes brimmed with tears. "I cannot believe after all I have done you are willing to help me. And I am grateful but there is little that you can do. I know you don't believe in the visions, my prince. Micah said you have always doubted, so there is no way for you to understand what it is like to live your life being ruled by faith. Until I came to the Palace of Winds, my voice to the wind was strong and my sight to the stars was clear. Never when I asked the stars for guidance did they betray me. But ever since coming inside these walls I have had only one vision. The Council believes the Guild lied about my abilities. That I am part of a plot against your family and the Kingdom of Eden. But I'm not. Micah told them I wasn't and he had me . . . "

"What?"

She shook her head. "He had me pretend to have a vision about a snake hiding in the forest. A few days later Captain Monteros brought back the head of a man he said attacked him while he was riding through the trees."

"Captain Monteros was rewarded for killing an Adderton spy."

She nodded. "And Micah convinced the King my vision had been true. The King took my side, but Elder Cestrum told Micah he wasn't convinced. He is still looking to replace me, and now that your father and Micah are gone, it won't be long until he finds a way to remove *my* head."

Her lip trembled and he pulled Imogen into his arms and tight against his chest.

"The Council will not harm you now. Not after what has happened already."

"You are not that naïve, my prince."

No. He wasn't. If the Council had their sights set on Imogen, Micah's death would stall their plans, but not change their minds. And after his conversation with his mother today, he doubted the Queen would intercede. More likely than not she would do whatever was necessary to see Imogen's head in a basket and a new seer installed in the Tower of Visions.

He wouldn't allow that to happen. Holding her tight, he vowed, "I will do what I must to keep you safe. Just as Micah did."

"Micah." The word was a whisper before Imogen pushed away from his chest and out of his arms.

The jealousy he'd been denying for months clawed at him. Taking a deep breath, he shoved it back. "I am truly sorry for your heartbreak, Lady Imogen."

She turned away from him and bowed her head so her hair draped over her face. "Your brother would have been a strong king. He asked me to marry him because he felt our union would make him stronger still, and I agreed because I thought it was the right thing to do for Eden. But I failed the kingdom and I can't help but think I didn't see what was coming in the stars because part of me didn't want to."

"What?"

"I should go." Imogen grabbed her skirts and turned toward the door, but Andreus caught her before she could take a second step.

"What do you mean, Imogen?" His heart pulsed. Everything inside him went still. "Why wouldn't you want to see what was going to happen?"

She shook her head and tried to pull her arm away. "I need to leave the castle. A true seer would never have let her own feelings get in the way of her visions. I wanted to care for you, brother, but he made it so hard. He knew nothing about me. Never asked where I came from or noticed what flowers I preferred. He wanted my power, not my heart, so he never cared that I had given it to another." Imogen slowly turned and lifted her glistening eyes to meet his. "Soon your mother will take the throne and she and the Council will hold me accountable for my mistakes. I deserve to pay."

"You did nothing wrong," he insisted.

"Yes, I did," Imogen said quietly. "I agreed to marry your brother, but I fell in love with you."

Andreus stood there unmoving—staring at the seeress who had visited him in his dreams for months. None of the women he'd been with since could compare. So vulnerable. Beautiful. Sad. If she truly had powers, she was as dangerous and untouchable as ever. And she loved him.

When he said nothing, Imogen dropped her hand and sighed. "I shall leave you now."

"Don't." Loss. Desire. Memories of the past. Uncertainty about the future. Duty to his family. But when she looked at him with her eyes filled with tears and regret, desire won out. He didn't want to think about Micah tonight or his father or the fact that it was safer to let Imogen walk out the door. He was cursed. He should want to protect himself. Instead, he only wanted to hold her.

His mouth found Imogen's in a gentle kiss that deepened and grew and made his body strain toward her. Her hands reached up and wove into his hair and once again there was nothing but the two of them. He pulled at the fastenings of his own clothes, then when she nodded at his unspoken question, began unfastening the ties of her dress.

Tomorrow would come and with it the grief of loss and regret. For now, he thought as she let him slip the dress off her shoulders so it pooled at his feet, they would comfort each other in the shadows.

If it damned them both, he didn't care.

Imogen was gone when he woke. A small piece of purple silk, most likely torn from the hem of her gown, was on the floor next to the bed, but nothing else spoke of the passion and contentment they'd found in each other's arms. There would be outrage if anyone learned what they had done. For him it would fade. He was, after all, a prince of the realm—the only prince now. And his interest in women was well known. He was able to take liberties with the virtues that others might not be allowed.

But Imogen . . . as a woman she was expected to hold her own virtue dear. She was also the seer and held to a higher standard still. While any who heard of *his* indiscretion would whisper about it for a day and go about their business, talk of Imogen's visit to his rooms would follow her forever.

People would think she was determined to be Queen at all costs. Others would say she had shamed her promise to use her gifts to better the kingdom. None would be without opinion and most would not be good.

And still, despite that and her fear that the Council of Elders was looking to do her harm, she had bared her soul and her body to him. He should probably feel guilty. After all, no matter what they both felt, she had been his brother's promised wife.

But he didn't feel guilty. Maybe during the funeral tomorrow, he would see his brother's body and have second thoughts, but for now his only regret was that he hadn't been awake when Imogen had left so he could assure her again that he would do whatever he had to in order to keep her safe. Imogen needed his protection and his love and he would give her both.

The second regret he had was not seeing Carys last night. She knew how to take care of herself and her maid Juliette was more than capable of helping ease any pain from the lashing she would have received.

Received . . . because of him.

Gratitude and guilt pushed thoughts of Imogen aside. Quickly, he dressed in black trousers, a black long-sleeved shirt, and a rust-colored tunic with his family's crest sewn on the shoulders. Fastening his sword at his side, Andreus considered going down to the kitchens to get some of the honey rolls his sister was fond of. Then he spotted the guard outside her rooms, ditched the idea of a bribe, and hurried down to the other end of the hallway.

The guard looked like he was barely old enough to have started training let alone be assigned to a post outside the Princess of Eden's chamber. When the boy didn't try to stop him, Andreus pushed open the door and hurried inside.

"Your Highness." Carys's maid dropped into a deep curtsy, then looked over his shoulder at the open door, which the young guard quickly closed.

"Where's my sister?"

"Resting, Your Highness. She refused to let me stay with her and had a difficult night."

Carys had been alone.

Guilt swirled as he walked to his sister's bedroom and pushed open the ornate double doors.

The room was dim. Candles glowed in the sconces next to the entrance and one near the bed where his sister slept face first on top of the bedcovers, still in the dress she'd been wearing when last he saw her. Then he saw the familiar glass bottle next to her and the shards on the floor.

She'd taken two of them.

A quarter of a bottle of their mother's Tears of Midnight should have eased the pain. Two years ago, Carys had needed a full bottle to get through the night after the last ball their father had allowed here in the castle. Andreus had known his sister was in trouble before that day. Her eyes had looked glassy. She'd lost weight so her normally thin figure appeared brittle. And even when perfectly brushed her hair had appeared dull and limp. He'd been terrified at how still she was for hours after taking so much of the drink.

After that moment, day by day she'd taken less and less until her eyes were bright again and her brain once more as quick as a flash.

He'd believed her when she said she was done needing the red bottles.

She'd lied.

Carys shifted on the bed, her hand stretched out as if trying to reach something—probably whatever was in one of the vivid dreams filled with cyclones of wind that she'd had since he could remember. She reached out again, then let out a low moan and winced with pain. He waited for his sister to wake, but her eyes didn't open. Despite the light, the Tears of Midnight had her firmly entrenched in the dark.

Slowly, he sat on the bed next to her and loosened the fastenings on her dress so he could see the punishment she'd taken for him. He shifted the fabric as gently as he could. Still his sister flinched as he examined the angry lines of raised red and purple that ran from her shoulder blades down to the small of her back. Blood was caked over a small section in the center where the strap had struck hard enough to break through the skin.

And under those painful-looking wounds were other scars. No longer red and painful, but reminders nonetheless of the curse he'd been fighting all his life. He'd tended to those wounds when she'd gotten them. He hadn't been here last night. But surely Juliette should have been.

Damn Carys and her pride.

She would not let her maid clean the cut and apply Madame Jillian's ointments to the rest. If she'd allowed that, she wouldn't have needed to be drugged into unconsciousness now. Carys should know better. She should have thought about what would happen today. Their mother would need them to help plan the funeral. She'd want to know why Carys was absent, as would the Council and the rest of the court.

Well, he'd just have to come up with a reason and hope Carys would emerge from this ready to bury their father and Micah tomorrow.

Carefully, he replaced the fabric over his sister's back and left the chamber. "Take care of Princess Carys's wounds and see no one comes in here until she's feeling up to visitors."

"But, Your Highness, the Princess said—"

"The Princess is . . . deeply asleep. She won't be aware of your ministrations." Then he turned and went to find his mother and to do his duty.

The day passed quickly. His mother was distracted as people asked her questions about which rooms to prepare for foreign dignitaries and guests who arrived from the kingdom's districts for the funeral and the coronation that would follow.

Andreus was thankful Oben was quick with a reply to the questions that everyone else found so important and Andreus had no clue how to deal with. Meanwhile, his mother seemed not to care about anything at all—not even about her daughter's absence—as she paced the dais of the Hall of Virtues, glancing every few minutes at the gold-and-sapphire throne. The only thing that seemed to catch her attention was when Chief Elder Cestrum appeared flanked by Elder Ulrich and Captain Monteros.

"Excuse me, Your Majesty," Elder Cestrum said with a bow. "I'm sorry to interrupt the plans for the funeral and your coronation, but Captain Monteros and I were just at the North Tower. All five remaining members of the King's Guard are dead."

"No. They can't be dead."

Andreus looked behind the Elder and captain and saw Carys standing with her hand on a gold pillar at the main entrance of the Hall of Virtues.

"I thought they were to be questioned before they died," Carys continued as she stepped into the hall.

Elder Cestrum turned toward Carys and bowed. "They were, Your Highness. The Council was set to interrogate them this morning. But when we went to their cells to retrieve them, we found all five of them on the floors of their cells—dead. It appears they were poisoned."

7

"Poisoned?" Carys tried to focus on her words instead of the pounding of her heart and her head. The man she talked to in the cell last night knew something more about how her father and brother had died. And now he had taken that information to his grave. "Were any of the other prisoners in the North Tower found dead?"

"No, Princess," Captain Monteros answered. "It was only the five members of the King's Guard."

"So they weren't poisoned by spoiled food or tainted water. Someone deliberately murdered these men before the King's justice could be delivered." Or before she could bargain with them to learn the truth.

Her stomach rolled. Her skin felt tight and her head throbbed. She should have taken more than just a sip of the Tears of Midnight on waking, but she would be paying the price for last night's weakness for days to come. The price would be much higher if she gave in to the desperate need for more. A little would take the edge off and keep her functioning. There was too much at stake to give in to the gnawing desire for the warmth and calm the drug provided.

"Someone must have wanted revenge for the death of King Ulron and Prince Micah and thought the crown was moving too slowly," Captain Monteros said.

"Either way," Elder Cestrum said, turning back to face the throne, "justice has been delivered. The Council will send out a proclamation letting everyone know the oath-breakers are dead. And once you are officially installed as monarch, my queen, we will want to discuss how best to retaliate against Adderton. The people will want them to pay for their crimes."

Everyone turned and looked at the Queen, who was running her fingers down the throne as if stroking a lover.

"Mother . . . ," Carys said, stepping away from the pillar she'd been using for support and across the white polished stone of the throne room. "Did you hear Elder Cestrum? The five Guardsmen have been murdered. We can't question them."

The Queen turned and locked eyes with Carys. Then, without a word, she walked down the steps of the dais and out of the hall.

"The Queen is clearly tired," Andreus said as his mother disappeared around the corner. "This has been a difficult day. I'm sure she'll deal with any other issues after the funeral is over."

"If you and your sister have no objection, Your Highness," the Chief Elder said, adjusting his tunic with his iron claw, "the Council of Elders will make arrangements to have your mother crowned as monarch immediately after tomorrow's funeral. With the war to the south and Adderton's ambush within our borders, it would be better not to wait."

"Do what you must."

"Very well, Your Highness."

The Chief Elder and Captain Monteros turned and filed past Carys, who waited for the space to clear before walking the length of the vaulted gold-and-white hall toward her brother. Each footstep echoed in the huge room decorated with murals representing the seven virtues. Above and behind the throne that Andreus stood next to was a smaller version of the orb that until last night had never been allowed to go dark.

Carys stopped in front of the dais stairs and stood watching her brother. Willing him to speak. To explain where he was last night and why he chose to abandon her when she needed him most.

When the silence continued, she asked, "How are you today?"

"Fine," he said, looking around the hall before coming down the steps, holding out his hands to her. "I'm completely fine. How are you?"

Carys looked at his hands, but did not take them. The hurt between them was too fresh, but there was no time to dwell on that. "The King's Guardsmen were not telling the truth about what happened to Father and Micah. That's why they were murdered."

Andreus dropped his hands to his side. "What are you talking about?"

"I spoke to one of them briefly last night before . . . " No. Under the calm of the drug, she could feel the pulse of the pain. She couldn't think about that now. "Father and Micah were in the center of their men when the attack happened, but both of them were killed before they had a chance to defend themselves. I was going to question him today, only now he and the others are dead."

"What are you saying, Carys?"

"I'm saying the story we were told isn't true," she whispered, looking around to make sure the room remained empty. "Or not entirely. Adderton might have been part of the attack, but there must have been others who helped set it up. Others that Father and Micah trusted. It's the only thing that makes sense."

Her brother took her arm. "You're saying members of the King's Guard killed their King? Why?"

"I don't know," she admitted. "Maybe the Bastians are maneuvering once again to take back the throne. Maybe Adderton has decided they would have a better chance negotiating peace if the two men who enjoy fighting the war were no longer in charge."

Or maybe it was someone else pulling the strings. The Council of Elders. One of the District High Lords or someone Carys had yet to consider. The list of those who wanted power was too endless to count.

"All I do know," she insisted, "is that the lights were sabotaged last night. The King and Prince return dead, and the only people who can tell the truth about what happened were murdered in their cells. Do you think all of that is a coincidence?"

"I don't know." Andreus raked a hand through his hair and paced across the gleaming white floor. "It's hard to believe that the attack and the sabotage could be related."

"Did you talk to the boy?"

"I started to. Then the gongs sounded and . . ." He shook his head. "By the time I got back to my rooms . . . I had other things on my mind."

Other things.

"I know." She held her breath, waiting for him to apologize. To tell her that they were still a team. When he said nothing, she walked past him and stared at the throne on the dais above. "Lady Imogen appeared to have other things on her mind, too. I was foolish enough to believe you'd be there to help *me*."

"I can explain."

"I'm sure you can." She turned. "But we both know there are more important things to deal with, so let's put it in the past." Far behind Andreus, she spotted someone duck behind a column and lowered her voice. "If there's someone plotting against our family we have to figure it out before it's too late. Go find Max and ask him who he's spoken with, but take care no one sees the two of you together. Last night I spoke with one of the King's Guard and today all of them are dead."

Andreus looked at her as if he wanted to say something, then sighed. "It might take a while to find Max and get him alone without anyone seeing us. Once I do, I'll let you know what I find out. You should get some rest before then. Tomorrow is going to be a long day."

Yes. She thought of the sorrow and the uncertainty and felt the tantalizing tug of need for the drink that would make it all better. Knowing she couldn't give in, she knew tomorrow would be very long indeed.

White was the color of purity. Black was the color of death. Purple the color of nobility. Her father and brother were draped in all three colors today to show death that they were pure of heart and leaders of their people as they walked through the gates of death's realm. Carys wore the deepest of purple as she stood next to her brother, also draped in the dark hue. Chief Elder Cestrum stood at the front of the chapel with Imogen. Both were dressed in white as they prepared to oversee the final ceremony of Carys's father's and brother's lives.

Which could only happen when her mother arrived.

Carys could hear the rustling of fabrics and the not-so-discreet murmurs of speculation of the court and visiting lords behind them. Their mother had not shown up to greet the Lords of the Seven Districts who had arrived throughout the night and this morning. And the farewell service for the King and Prince was supposed to have started a long time ago.

"One of us should have gone with Elder Jacobs to get Mother," she whispered to Andreus. Standing in the chapel now, it was hard to get the Councilman's words from the other night out of her head. He'd warned her about the dangers of the North Tower. The next day the five King's Guardsmen were dead.

"We were trying to make it less obvious that she wasn't here." Andreus had spent the morning once again trying to track down Max, who had gone into hiding after their discussion last night.

The boy claimed he never once said anything about Andreus or what he knew about the wind-powered lights. The way the boy answered the question and dashed off to help in the kitchens made her brother think the boy *had* bragged to someone and was worried about getting expelled from the castle.

In the meanwhile, an uproar was slowly growing behind them. The time was getting late. There was a long ride to the tomb ahead of them. Any later and darkness would be descending when they returned.

"Elder Ulrich and Lord Marksham have sent several pages to remind Mother of the time. Just breathe. We have no choice but to stay here and wait. This will all be over soon," Dreus said, taking Carys's cold hand in his warm one. "You'll see."

"Queen Betrice!" someone announced.

Carys let out a sigh of relief as she and Andreus turned. Everything inside Carys stilled as people dropped into bows and curtsies while their queen walked down the aisle in a billowing yellow dress. Her brown hair flowed loose around her shoulders. That and the smile tugging at her mouth gave her almost a girlish look—so different than the severe style she had often encouraged Carys to emulate.

"Looking serious is the only way people will treat you seriously."

Perhaps now that she reigned, Mother no longer felt like she needed to look a certain way?

Mother didn't say a word as she took her place next to Andreus, directly in front of the white stone dais where King Ulron lay with his arms crossed over his chest.

Elder Cestrum waited for the Queen to instruct him to begin. When she didn't, Lady Imogen stepped toward the Queen and quietly asked, "Your Majesty, would you like us to start?"

"Of course." Mother smiled. "Let the festivities begin."

Festivities?

Carys didn't have time to think about her mother's behavior as Imogen turned and walked to seven candles standing on gold pillars behind the bodies of Micah and her father.

Imogen stood behind the first of them and lit it as Elder Cestrum intoned, "Humility."

Imogen moved on to the next, looking strong and confident as she always did when performing her duties. So different than the way she presented herself when she wasn't acting as seer.

"Strength."

Then another—each virtue announced for each candle lit. Patience. Chastity. Temperance. Charity. Endurance.

Carys watched the candles flicker as the Chief Elder spoke of the crown's defense of the virtues and the power of the light to keep the kingdom safe. It was easier to watch the shifting of the flames than look at the faces of her brother or father. But soon the words were over and the seer and Chief Elder stood on either side of her brother. They took the edges of a cloth decorated with the symbols of the virtues and pulled it up to cover Micah's body.

Andreus took Carys's hand in his and she clung to it like the lifeline that it was. The pressure behind her eyes and in her chest swelled against the barrier the Tears of Midnight had erected as the cloth shifted over her brother's face.

The seer and elder then walked to the center of the chapel and repeated the process with the King. This time Carys forced herself to look at his face for as long as she could. To remember. And as the cloth settled over it, she vowed she wouldn't let those behind his death escape justice.

The rest of the Council appeared. In the candlelight, they lifted both covered bodies into wooden caskets and carried them from the chapel. Carys followed her mother and brother down the aisle after them and through the castle and down the steps to the city below, where they would then ride to escort the King and Prince to their final resting place.

The gongs rang again as they walked down the stairs to where their horses waited. Andreus had to help their mother mount her horse. In the blue cloak Oben had convinced her to wear, the Queen waved to the people solemnly lining the streets while the procession made its way to the main gates and then turned toward the mountains.

As she rode around the plateau toward the peaks beyond the plains Carys glanced behind her. The line of horses stretched for at least a mile. One broad face framed by red hair turned, caught her attention, and held it. Even from a distance she could make out the exact hazel color of his eyes, the wide crooked nose, and the mocking smile she'd found so fascinating when he and Micah sparred on the guards' practice fields.

Until a year ago, Lord Garret had been Micah's best friend. Then one day Carys woke up and heard he'd gone. Garret's uncle, Elder Cestrum, would only say that Garret had returned to help his father oversee the District of Bisog, and Micah refused to discuss the real reason no matter how artfully she asked. No one, not even Chief Elder Cestrum, had spoken Garret's name since.

And now Garret had returned.

He smiled to let her know she was staring. With a frown, she turned and studied the river to the south where she and her brother had played as children. She would not give in to the desire to glance behind her to see if Garret was still watching. She was older now than when she'd first felt her breath catch any time he walked into a room—his hair looking like it was on fire. Since then, she'd learned not to be impressed by thick muscles or chests as round as wine barrels. Just because something looked as if it could keep you safe didn't mean it would.

Still, she could feel him behind her as well as Elder Jacobs, who had warned her not to get too close to the flames or she would get burned. Was he referring to searching out the truth about the ambush or something else?

She rode silently, glad she had taken several sips from the red bottle to help her withstand the journey through the foothills that led to the Shadow Mountains and the majestic Tomb of Light that had been created hundreds of years before. Artisans of the past dug and carved and smoothed the stone, creating an ornate entrance to the resting place of Eden's rulers. Twenty feet inside the cave stood two large iron doors that Carys's father had had installed by the Masters of Light. Those doors could only be opened using the power from the windmill that chopped the air directly above the cave. Only the royal family and the head of the Guild of Light knew how to operate the doors. If the castle was attacked and the royal family slaughtered, the secret of the doors would stop the usurpers from desecrating those who had been placed in the light.

Their mother should have operated the doors now, but she just laughed at the idea of getting off her horse and told Andreus and Carys to go without her. Captain Monteros kept all of the mourners back as Carys and Andreus left their mother smiling in the sun while they went into the cave. Andreus walked to the left corner while Carys went to the right. It took only moments for each of them to pry up the correct stones her father showed them years ago.

Underneath her stone was a rectangular hole with wires and a pile of seemingly purposeless stones. It took Carys only a few moments to dig through the rocks and find the small, perfectly clear stone—the key the Masters had created. Carefully, she placed the stone in the space between the metal wires, while on the other side of the tomb entrance her brother did the same. A few seconds later the doors began to move. A light brighter than the sun at midday spilled from inside the cavern. Carys shielded her eyes as the guards carried the caskets inside, so that they might rest in that place, the room always bathed in the white light of virtue.

But by the time the doors to the tomb were once again closed, darkness was starting to fall.

The ride back was faster—which meant it was bumpier. Carys's still-healing wounds screamed with each bounce. But the screech that came from the mountains—and the answering call that sounded like a rusty gate being opened—made everyone turn and look behind them and had Carys nudging her horse, Nala, to go faster.

The cold season was upon them. The Xhelozi were beginning to awaken.

The sky darkened. Huddled deep in her cloak, trying to ignore the anxiety, Carys felt the desperate craving pulling at her. The procession rode out of the foothills and closer to the plateau where the orb of Eden and the rest of the lights glowed bright and promised safety.

Another screech echoed in the night. Farther away than before, but still terrifying. Carys looked over her shoulder and squinted at the mountains rising through the shadows.

Something moved near the foothills.

The Council and Captain Monteros urged everyone to go faster. The city gates and the safety of the walls were less than a mile away. Just as they reached the main entrance, a horse veered from the front of the group and circled back in the direction of the foothills of the mountains.

"Mother," Carys yelled as she wheeled her horse through the group of riders. "Mother, stop!"

"My king!" her mother wailed. Her cape billowed as she rode in the direction of certain danger. Behind Carys, Andreus shouted, but he was too far away to catch up. Carys leaned forward, pushing Nala to go faster as she glanced toward the base of the mountains and the shadows moving there. Not all of the Xhelozi would be ready to come out of their hibernation, and only once that Carys could remember did any who awoke this early travel this far from the mountains. But any that did would be hungry.

"Mother," she screamed. "Stop."

A horse from the back of the procession thundered away from the group. Her mother's horse slowed as the black stallion and the man in a dark cloak pounded toward them and Carys was relieved to see him grab the reins.

"Let me go," her mother called. "I have to go. They want me to go."

The rider ignored the words and led the Queen and the horse back in the direction of the gates.

"No! I command you," her mother screamed. "Your queen commands you!"

She kicked at the other rider and caught the horse in its flanks, causing it to rear. The rider held on to his own seat, but lost his grip on Mother, who slid off her horse and began running toward the mountains, yelling, "They're calling for me. Can't you hear it? I have to go."

The Queen stumbled on a rock and pitched forward. Oben reached her and helped her rise.

Blood trickled down Mother's face as Carys reached her.

"Mother," Carys said, sliding from her own horse while Oben tried to help his queen stand. "You're hurt. Let's get back to the Palace of Winds so Oben can stop the bleeding and get you ready for the coronation."

Her mother shook her head and pulled against Oben's grip. "They are waiting."

"You're right," Carys said. "Everyone is waiting for their queen inside the city. Oben, perhaps it would be better if you helped Mother into one of the carts for the rest of the journey?"

Oben nodded.

"No." Her mother screamed and kicked and tried to bite Oben to force him to release her from his iron grip. But he held fast as he climbed with the Queen into one of the now empty funeral carts. "Didn't you hear? I have to go."

"Get her into the city," Carys commanded the driver. Andreus and Elder Cestrum took up places behind the cart and rumbled toward the gates.

"Clear the way," Captain Monteros yelled as the gongs sounded and Carys's mother passed through the gate into the safety of the city while screaming, "Let me go. I don't belong here. You have to let me go." Finally, she stopped struggling and yelling and instead kept murmuring the words to herself.

People came out of their houses and lined the streets that were lit by the power of the wind. They were no longer somber and quiet as they had been earlier during the final procession of the King and Prince. Now they were shouting and a few young children were racing down the street waving at the procession. To them death was over and the time for the next step in the kingdom had come. It was the way things were. The way things were supposed to be.

"Long live Queen Betrice," someone shouted.

"No!" Carys heard her mother say.

Another voice took up the cheer as the streets became lined with more people looking to show their support for the new ruler.

The solo shouts grew into cheers as the procession reached the base of the white stairs that led up to the castle sitting high above.

"Long live the Queen! Long live Queen Betrice."

Andreus helped their mother down from the cart. Oben stayed a step behind. The Queen looked around bewildered as Chief Elder Cestrum took her arm and began leading her up the white stairs.

The shouts grew louder still as Andreus took Imogen's arm and headed up behind them with Carys following—watching her brother lean down and whisper something to the seer that made her look up at him with a small, secret smile.

Their mother and the Chief Elder halted on the first of the wide landings carved into the castle's long staircase entrance. Elder Cestrum turned and held up his iron claw. The crowd below went silent.

"King Ulron and Crown Prince Micah now rest," Elder Cestrum announced. "But the Kingdom of Eden continues on under Queen Betrice. Our Keeper of Virtues. Guardian of the Light. Ruler of Eden. Long may she reign."

The cheering swelled as the Queen yelled, "No. This is wrong."

"Mother!" Carys snapped as her mother pulled her arm away from Elder Cestrum. She nearly toppled from the stairs as she staggered back. The crowd gasped and fell silent. "No. No. No!" the Queen screeched. "They are calling to me. My place is with them. You can't make me stay. I will join them in the mountains."

"Your Majesty." Elder Cestrum stepped toward the Queen. "Your place is here. You will be crowned and sit upon the throne."

"Never." Hair whipping in a gust of wind, Carys's mother turned and looked out at the crowd of nobles and commoners on the street and steps below. "The only ruler is King Ulron. He beckons to all of us."

"My queen. Forgive me, but I don't understand." Elder Jacobs stepped around Carys and hurried up the steps toward the Queen. She saw him shift his gaze to Elder Cestrum, who nodded. "Are you saying you renounce your claim to the throne? Are you giving up the crown?"

"Yes. I must go! Our king calls! I must obey his command!"

People gasped and looked to the Queen as Carys hurried up the steps. "It's been a long day. We will resume the coronation after Mother gets some rest. Oben, get her inside."

"My queen . . . ," Elder Cestrum started.

"I am not your queen!" Carys's mother beamed at the crowd— her hair wild in the wind. Her voice had a singsong quality that chilled Carys to her core. "Where I plan to go there is no need for a crown." Throwing back her head, Mother laughed. Then she gathered her skirts and hurried up the steps toward the castle—her laughter still ringing in the night.

Everyone watched her go. And while Carys didn't say it aloud, others did until the whispers became louder and more persistent and filled with fear. Because as much as no one wanted it to be true, it was clear the Queen, Carys's mother—the only parent she had left alive—was mad.

The kingdom had lost a king and prince.

Now grief had taken their queen.

Who would rule Eden now?

8

"Inside," Andreus yelled as the people from the city gathered at the base of the stairs demanding answers. He could hear their fear. Gods—he *felt* it. Father. Micah. Now Mother losing her mind. It was like the darkness was mocking them even as they stood in the orb's light.

Imogen. She had been by his side, but now she was gone. He glanced up and spotted her white dress and cloak almost at the top of the stairs, far away from the ruckus below. His heart calmed. She was safe. He turned and found his sister staring down at the crowd that pushed against the line the castle guard had formed at the base of the steps.

"Carys!" His sister turned. Andreus saw the same fear and confusion pulsing through him in her eyes as she crossed to him and took his hand. "We have to get in the castle before panic makes people daft."

She nodded, gathered her skirts with one hand, then hurried with him up the enormous staircase while people shouted and screamed and cried behind them. Andreus glanced over his shoulder. He could see fights breaking out in the middle of the crowd at the base of the steps.

He listened for sounds of steel striking steel—a sign that the violence had escalated and the guards were forced to intervene. He was thankful the clash of weapons didn't come. When he reached the top, he was breathing hard, but the guards below had kept the peace.

"Are you okay?" Carys sounded strong despite the pain she must be feeling from the wounds on her back. The race up the steps couldn't have been easy for her. It hadn't been all that easy for him. He was having a hard time catching his breath, but all was normal . . . or as normal as this kind of thing got for him.

"I'm good," he said, taking her arm and leading her inside the walls she professed to hate.

"Prince Andreus. Princess Carys!" Elder Ulrich called to them as they walked across the courtyard. They turned and waited as he hurried across. "I know you will wish to check on your mother, but the Council of Elders will be assembling in the Hall of Virtues immediately and I believe you should both be there when we discuss the future of the realm."

"Immediately? The Queen is clearly overwhelmed from the death of the King and Prince Micah," Carys said quickly. "Any discussion should wait until she is back to herself and can assure everyone that she intends to take her place on the throne."

Elder Ulrich looked at them long and hard with his one good eye before quietly continuing, "The Queen has put something in motion that I fear cannot be stopped. There can be no hesitation when the future of the realm is at stake." He looked around, spotted Elder Cestrum and the rest of the Elders walking with Captain Monteros, and fell silent as they walked past. Then he turned his scarred face back to them. "The Council of Elders will be gathering in the Hall of Virtues. For good or for ill, decisions will be made. I advise you both to join us and to do so very, very soon."

He bowed, turned his clouded eye, the one Andreus found repulsive and strangely fascinating, away from them, and hurried off.

"What do you think that was about?" Andreus asked. "Elder Ulrich isn't the type to help others unless there is something in it for him."

"I don't know." Carys shivered and wrapped her arms around herself. "But we must go inside and find out. I have a feeling Elder Ulrich is right. We don't want to be late."

They hurried inside and down the wide corridors that led to the Hall of Virtues. The corridors were brightly lit and strangely empty, but as they drew closer to the throne room Andreus noticed there were more guards stationed *inside* the castle than he remembered seeing for years.

They were almost to the Hall when Carys said, "Dreus, I need to collect myself before going in to deal with the Council."

"Of course." He stopped walking and put a hand on her shoulder. Under the cloak, he could feel his sister tremble. "Carys, are you okay?"

"I'm fine." She stepped away from him and nodded. "I just need a minute to settle myself . . . alone. I'll meet you in the antechamber in a moment."

Andreus studied her flushed face and thought about the ominous tone to Elder Ulrich's words. "I'd rather not leave you by yourself."

"You had no trouble leaving me alone two days ago."

He frowned at the bitterness in the words. "Look, I told you—"

"A minute *alone*, Andreus," she said, shoving her hands in the pockets of her cloak despite the warmth inside the castle. "You owe me that."

"One minute," he said, irritated. "I'll be around the corner in case anything strange happens."

"That's fine."

He strode down the corridor alone. As he was turning the corner that led to the Hall of Virtues, he glanced back at his sister, who had moved so she was now standing near the wall with her back to him. Carys lifted her arm. Her head tilted back and he knew exactly why she'd needed the moment.

He said nothing about the drug when she reappeared. They'd deal with that later. For now, he put his arm out for her to take and together they walked into the brightly lit throne room.

"Dreus, whatever they say or do, I want you to know one thing has not changed." They walked the long length of the Hall toward the five members of the Council of Elders, who stood not far from the steps that led to the gold-and-sapphire throne. "We are a team. I promise to protect you as I always have."

Andreus put his hand on hers. "And I you, to whatever degree I am capable."

"Prince Andreus. Princess Carys." Elder Jacobs said their names in the soft voice that used to annoy Andreus's father. Father used to say Elder Jacobs reminded him of a snake that wasn't poisonous enough to kill with one bite and instead had to sting its prey and wait around for hours, hoping another creature did not come along and claim the prize as its own. Watching the man move as though he was gliding across the floor confirmed that observation. Andreus vowed to keep his father's words close as the man said, "The Council of

Elders did not expect you at such a fraught time. Are you certain your mother is in good care? Perhaps you should see to her."

"Our mother is tired, my lord," Carys said in a steady voice. "She's had a hard time sleeping since learning of the King and Prince Micah's death."

"Yes," Andreus said. "The Queen will be rested and ready to rule in time for her coronation tomorrow."

Elder Jacobs grinned. "The Council is glad to see the same affliction that struck your mother has not befallen either of you. And while we all wish for the Queen's complete recovery, her words have presented us with a problem. Tomorrow's coronation will not go forward. The Queen cannot rule Eden."

"What?" Andreus asked as his sister's fingers tightened on his arm.

"Elder Jacobs is right. By publicly denouncing the crown the Queen has legally removed herself from royal succession." Elder Ulrich sighed and shook his head. "Your mother cannot take the throne."

"The Queen was overwhelmed by her loss," Andreus said quickly. "No one can hold her to what she said outside the castle walls."

Andreus spun around as Chief Elder Cestrum and Elder Ulrich crossed the white stone floor with two pages behind them, each clutching books and scrolls.

"The Queen publicly renounced her claim to the throne," Chief Elder Cestrum said. "Unfortunately, according to the laws of Eden—the laws your father, King Ulron, took an oath to uphold— we must hold your mother to her word to prevent the kingdom from faltering."

His sister's eyes narrowed at Elder Jacobs as she strode toward him. "Elder Jacobs, as I recall it was *you* who asked my mother the question about her intent. Was it your desire to push her, in such a fragile state, to forfeit her authority as Queen?"

Elder Jacobs was about to respond when Chief Elder Cestrum cut him off. "It matters not." He looked at each of the other Elders before turning back to her. "We all heard your mother's words."

"Which were only said because Elder Jacobs pushed her into it," Andreus snapped back.

"None of us could have seen this coming, but now that it has we are bound by our duty to deal with it under the laws of Eden." Elder Cestrum looked at Andreus and then at Carys, then stepped in front of the other members of the Council of Elders. "The coldest months are almost upon us. A war is being fought and Eden has no ruler. We must see a monarch crowned as quickly as possible in order to safeguard the country and its citizens."

Carys looked over at Andreus, then back at the Chief Elder. "My brother and I are ready to do whatever is necessary to see that Eden remains safe. It is our duty and our right."

And something his sister never wanted. Neither had he. Not with the curse hanging over his head. But, if he must rule, perhaps he could do it alongside Carys. Perhaps, as always, they could share the burden.

"Sadly the Council of Elders has made a study of the laws of succession in recent days," Elder Ulrich broke in. "It appears that the circumstances of your birth make it legally impossible for us to install either one of you on the throne."

"That makes no sense." Andreus looked at his sister, who was staring intently at Elder Ulrich, trying to hear what was unsaid.

"Our blood is no less royal than Micah's and he was the acknowledged heir to the throne. How is it that the Council of Elders believes I am less acceptable than my brother?"

"There is no question that your blood is that of King Ulron, Your Highness," Elder Jacobs offered, taking a leather-bound book from one of the Council's pages. "You are a prince of the realm. Your sister is a princess. But the law is clear." He opened the book to a page marked with a piece of silk and read: "Only a successor whose right to the throne is acknowledged as greater than any other claims can be awarded the crown. If the current royal family has no successor that meets the succession threshold, the Council of Elders will legally choose a new successor with the most powerful claim to start a new line and do all that is necessary to make sure the kingdom thrives under the light."

Chief Elder Cestrum sighed. "Both of your claims are equal. Neither is greater than the other. Therefore neither meets the threshold of the law."

"Equal—because we are twins?" Carys looked at him. Her chin was raised. Her stance was defiant, but in her eyes he saw worry.

"That's crazy," Andreus said.

"I wish it was, Your Highness." Elder Cestrum took the book from Elder Jacobs. "Unfortunately, the laws of Eden are quite clear. It is illegal for the Council of Elders to allow anyone to rule who cannot be declared, with absolute certainty, to be the next in the line of succession. Since none save your mother and her midwife were present at your birth, there is no one who can give first-hand testimony as to whether you, Prince Andreus, or you, Princess Carys, were born first."

The midwife was dead. She had passed not long after their birth.

And their mother was mad.

"My brother is the eldest," his sister announced. "My mother has always said as much."

"The passage of the crown cannot be based on *hearsay*," Elder Jacobs said, his voice tinged with what was supposed to be offense but sounded more like glee. "Since neither of you can fulfill the terms of succession, a new line must be installed."

"A new line?" Carys's voice cracked.

Out of the corner of his eye Andreus saw guards appear through the side entrances of the Hall. He tried to signal his sister, but Carys was focused on the Council. "You're saying you plan on setting our family aside even though the Queen is alive and there are two children of King Ulron standing right before you? And you think the kingdom will meekly accept that? Do you believe we'll allow them to?"

"Is that a threat, Your Highness?" Elder Cestrum asked as he signaled with his iron fist for the guards to approach.

"Carys," Andreus whispered as he stepped closer to her and reached for his sword. "Be very careful."

"I'm not *threatening* anything, Chief Elder," Carys said with a calm Andreus could not help but admire considering the guards currently drawing their swords. "I am suggesting that the kingdom is already at war and there are those in the realm who believe that the Bastians living in exile are the rightful rulers of Eden. Setting our family to the side in favor of a third will only divide this kingdom further. That is chaos. I can't imagine you'd want that."

"Of course not, Your Highness. Which is why the Council of Elders is meeting tonight. We wish to determine the best way— within the laws of our realm—to install the new ruler of Eden and keep the peace. Elder Ulrich has come up with a plan that should satisfy the law and the virtues our kingdom holds dear."

"And what plan is that?" Andreus asked, anger burning deep in his throat as he tightened his grip on the hilt of his sword, ready to draw it at any moment.

Elder Cestrum smiled. "There is one successor whose claim is above all others. His grandfather fought against the Bastians. Your grandfather, upon taking the crown, declared *him* to be his successor until natural heirs were born."

Carys gasped a moment before he did and said, "You *can't* mean to put High Lord James on the throne."

James's cruelty as a High Lord was known throughout Eden. He claimed it was his duty as lord of the district that represented the virtue of strength to rule his subjects stringently. The one time Andreus and Carys had been allowed to travel with their father to visit the Stronghold, he saw from the slumped shoulders and terror-stricken faces of the castle servants how strength could easily be turned from a virtue into a vice.

"No, we cannot," Elder Cestrum agreed. "I was informed earlier today that High Lord James succumbed to illness a week ago. His son and heir, Garret, will appoint a new High Lord of the Stronghold after he is installed as King."

Garret. Micah's former best friend. Elder Cestrum's *nephew*. Andreus should have realized that's what the Council had planned. With Garret on the throne the Council, and especially Elder Cestrum, would have the kind of authority they had always wanted.

"And what is to happen to us?" Andreus asked, wondering how quickly he could slide his knife from his belt and pass it to Carys while also drawing his sword. Carys was at least as good a fighter as he was. She should be after practicing with him in secret all these years. They wouldn't be able to kill the dozen guards waiting for the Chief Elder's signal, but he and his sister would send some to their graves before they fell. "Are we to be treated like the Bastians were?"

That any of them survived the slaughter was still hard to believe.

"I think we all can agree there has been enough tragedy in Eden," Elder Cestrum said. "As long as neither of you oppose Garret's coronation—"

"Of course they will oppose it." Imogen stepped from behind one of the gold pillars into the light. She was still wearing the white dress from earlier. When had she come into the chamber? And how had she not been detected doing so? "The Council of Elders will oppose such a coronation, too," she continued, "since it not only betrays the oath you took to uphold the laws of the realm but will also plunge the kingdom into the shadows that the virtue of light cannot reach."

A guardsman drew his sword, but Elder Cestrum held up his iron claw to stop him. "The Council of Elders has made a study of the laws of Eden, Seer Imogen, as is required by the oath we took. And Garret's coronation—"

"Is premature." Imogen's white dress against the white stone of the Hall of Virtues gave her an almost otherworldly glow as she glided across the floor. She turned and nodded to the doorway of the Hall, and a young girl carrying a large black leather book with the gold seal of Eden on the cover stepped out of the shadows. When she reached Imogen's side, the seeress said, "Since taking my oath to serve the Kingdom of Eden, I have spent my days reading the histories of the land and my nights studying the winds and the skies. I've read the laws you are quoting now. But I fear in your haste to find the solution you sought, you did not consult the Book of Knowledge."

The Book of Knowledge. The history of the first years of the kingdom as recorded by Eden's first seer. Growing up, Andreus's tutors spoke of the book, but none had actually seen it. Most believed it had been destroyed when the Bastians had taken a torch to the castle in an effort to leave nothing of value for their usurpers to claim.

"Since you haven't consulted the text, I shall read it to you now." The pages of the ancient text crackled as Imogen opened it to the page she sought. Imogen read, "If two or more members of the royal family have equal claim to the Throne of Light, a series of trials must be held in order to determine the rightful heir. The Trials will be devised and administered by the Council of Elders, the designated representatives of the districts, and will measure the claimants' abilities to uphold the seven virtues necessary to wield power and avoid the temptations elevation to the crown can bring."

"You want us to compete in some kind of public contest?" Carys asked before Andreus could react. She chuckled. "No. I am happy to step aside and let Andreus rule. He understands wind power, so the Masters respect him. He's studied with the Captain of the Guard, so he understands the men he would command in battle. If I abdicate my position, his claim is greatest. There's no reason for us to have to perform as if we are street entertainers."

"Carys . . . ," Andreus started to protest, but his chest swelled. His sister had proclaimed him the worthier heir to the throne—here, in front of the Council. No other member of his family would have done so.

"Both of you have skills that would make you strong rulers, but it is not for you or the Council to choose the next defender of the light. The law demands a series of trials." Imogen straightened her slight shoulders and locked eyes with Andreus as if willing him to trust her. "It is your duty to follow the law just as it is the Council of Elders' duty to see that it is administered."

Turning back to face the Council, Imogen said, "Ever since I took my oath and began my duties as the Seer of Eden, there is one vision that appears to me when the stars are at their brightest. I see two paths stretching from Eden's orb. At the end of both paths is a crown. One path is covered in darkness. The other bathed in light. One littered with war and unrest. The other with prosperity and peace. Never has a vision been so strong or the purpose so clear. You must follow the ancient law of Eden as your oath commands of you. Only then can we be certain we have followed the path of light."

Imogen slammed the book shut. The sound rang through the cavernous room. "If you do not adhere to your oath, if Prince Andreus and Princess Carys do not compete for their place at the head of the Hall of Virtues, you will set the kingdom on a course toward war and suffering and a darkness that stretches on beyond time."

Elder Cestrum smoothed his white beard to a point as he studied Imogen. She was so calm and beautiful under the Elder's scrutiny. So unlike the girl they were used to dealing with. And it was because of Andreus. She was taking this chance—thwarting the plans of the men who wished to do her harm—out of love.

"May I have the book?" Elder Cestrum asked, holding out his iron-clawed hand.

"Of course, my lord. The page I read from is marked." She turned the book over to him, then folded her hands in front of her as the Council of Elders huddled around the tome.

Andreus tried to catch Imogen's attention, but she didn't glance his way. She kept her eyes on Chief Elder Cestrum and the rest of the

Council as they whispered and flipped pages and argued.

The seer folded her hands together as the conversation became more heated, but she never flinched or turned away. And in that moment, Andreus realized something. He couldn't compete in public trials. Not without risking the Council of Elders being reminded of his curse. If any of them saw Andreus in the throes of an attack, they would declare him unfit. They would realize Carys and the Queen knew of his affliction all along and pronounce them all traitors. A contest would kill them all.

Which Imogen had no way of knowing.

He shook his head. "I think Lady Imogen's appearance with the Book of Knowledge demonstrates how many laws govern succession. None of us knows them all." He nodded to the guards. "The people simply assume either Carys or I will take the throne; we should assure them of this. And in the meanwhile, we should thoroughly study all the laws and determine the best course for the—"

"Excuse us, Your Highness." Chief Elder Cestrum motioned to the rest of the Council, who gathered around him. As the Elders spoke in tones too muted for Andreus to make out the words, he looked at Carys and Imogen. In his sister's eyes he saw the storm of uncertainty that must be reflected in his own. The world had been yanked upside down and neither of them had any idea how to right it. Imogen's face remained assured, placid. Almost eerily so.

Elder Cestrum cleared his throat. "Delay won't be necessary, Prince Andreus. The Council of Elders is in agreement and we thank Lady Imogen for her study and guardianship of the realm's history. If it hadn't been for the seer, we might have made a grievous error that violated our oaths." The Elder smiled at Lady Imogen while, standing just behind him, Elder Jacobs glowered with open contempt.

"And we wouldn't have wanted that, would we?" Elder Jacobs drawled.

Andreus squelched the urge to shield Lady Imogen from his malice. Instead, he tightened his grip on his sword and tried to feign the confidence his sister was projecting beside him.

"I am only upholding my duty to Eden," Lady Imogen said. "I take my charge to search the stars and call the winds seriously. Without them, I can only imagine how hard it would be for the throne to keep the confidence of the people through the cold months ahead. It is important for all of us to work together to see the throne passes to the true Keeper of Virtues and Guardian of the Light. Or darkness will descend upon us all."

Smooth words covering the iron steel of a threat.

Elder Cestrum tightened his hold on the book, but his expression never wavered. After several tense moments, he nodded to the guards, who took their hands off their weapons, and Andreus let out the breath he'd been holding.

"We all serve the Kingdom of Eden," Elder Cestrum said. "Which means the Council will create a series of trials for our prince and princess to participate in that will decide the true successor to the Throne of Light. The Trials of Virtuous Succession must be designed to demonstrate the claimants' dedication to the realm and the virtues that guide it. And once the Trials of Virtuous Succession begin, the contest must continue until a successor is declared victorious or all other equal claimants to the throne are dead."

9

"Dead?" Carys stepped forward. "You wish us to voluntarily participate in a series of contests in which one of us could die?"

"I wish nothing," Elder Cestrum said with what Carys was certain was supposed to be a shrug.

Only he wasn't sorry. She could tell by the glint of delight in his eyes.

"The Book of Knowledge that our seer so kindly presented to us demands the Trials contain risks to those who would take the throne. No doubt to prove that once the new monarch receives the crown he or she has the ability to keep it. After all, the getting of power is often the easy part. It is keeping it that can prove difficult. The Council of Elders must do its utmost to make sure the person who wins the Trials has the ability to lead Eden through the difficult times ahead."

"And if we refuse this insult to us and to our father?" Andreus asked.

"Then Lord Garret will ascend the throne and he will decide how best to handle any who could jeopardize the legitimacy of his reign."

The Bastians, defeated by Carys's grandfather, were executed in Garden City in the exact spot where the Tree of Virtues now stood. Those who escaped and their heirs had plagued Eden with the threat of war ever since. Carys had no doubt the Council of Elders would advise Lord Garret to kill her, Andreus, and their mother, and the kingdom would say nothing against it.

"Prince Andreus and Princess Carys." Elder Ulrich stepped out of the cluster of councilmen with his hands raised. "I understand this all comes as a shock. None of us expected your mother's mind to collapse under the strain of this tragedy. Unfortunately, there is no turning from these unfortunate consequences. The Kingdom of Eden is depending on all of us to do our part. Can we count on your honorable participation?"

"We are the children of King Ulron," Carys said before her brother could voice the denial she saw on his lips. "Our father was the Guardian of Light and Keeper of Virtues for more than two score years. He taught us that it is our responsibility to do what is best for the realm. We would not dishonor him by turning away from our duty to Eden."

Andreus opened his mouth to speak, and Carys gave him a look willing him to trust her. Yes, she knew he couldn't compete in physical trials—ones that could result in death. The strain of whatever the Council of Elders devised could trigger an attack. If Carys couldn't help conceal it, Elder Cestrum would see Andreus's struggles to breathe and he would recall Seer Kheldin's prediction. The Council would seize on Andreus's weak heart in order to remove him from contention for the throne.

Virtues went out the window when self-interest was at stake.

But knowledge was power and right now Carys wouldn't let the

Council know that she and her brother weren't going to play this game.

Her brother frowned, but gave a slight nod before saying, "Princess Carys and I understand the importance of our duty. We will do what we must to ensure King Ulron's legacy lives on. I'm assuming the Trials will start in a few days, once the Council has time to prepare?"

Elder Cestrum waved off Andreus's assumption with his iron hand. "While circumstances surrounding the upcoming coronation have changed, the need for a quick transition to a new monarch has not. Eden needs a king or queen to secure the realm. The Council will meet throughout the night to create the rules and tasks governing the Trials that will commence at the tournament tomorrow."

Tomorrow. That gave them almost no time to find a way out of this insanity. "Do you think that's wise?" Carys asked, ignoring the dread blooming deep in her stomach. "After all, the tournament was planned to celebrate the coronation of the Queen. To use it for something else could be considered mocking the fates."

"The tournament will still celebrate the upcoming coronation, and the gathering of the court and commoners alike will give the Council an opportunity to explain the purpose of the contest between you and Prince Andreus." Elder Cestrum glanced back at the Council members, who all nodded their agreement.

All but Elder Ulrich, who stood out of Elder Cestrum's line of sight and was watching Carys with his one good eye.

Elder Cestrum turned back to Carys and Andreus. "The tournament will demonstrate to everyone that the Council of Elders, Eden's seer, and King Ulron's surviving children have agreed on this path to determining the new monarch. After so much tragedy, the people will not only be glad to have contest champions to cheer for during the tournament, but they'll be inspired to learn their prince and princess are willing to go to great lengths to prove their worthiness to wear the crown."

Great lengths. An outsider might not hear the threat in those two words, but Carys did. Especially since the Council had just made it clear their preference was to put Lord Garret on the throne.

Or most of them did. What Elder Ulrich wanted was unclear. He had warned her and Andreus about tonight's Council meeting here in the Hall of Virtues. Did he want to help them block Elder Cestrum's plot to put Garret on the throne—or had he intended to lead her and Andreus to the slaughter?

Carys stared at him, hoping to see some sort of sign as to his motive, but his expression was inscrutable.

Carys wondered. Ulrich might not be a friend, but maybe . . . just maybe he might not be a foe.

"You have a long night ahead of you then, my lords," Carys said. "And apparently my brother and I will have a long day tomorrow. So unless anyone has another book to read from, I bid you good night. Andreus, are you coming?" She gathered her skirts and paused to see if he'd heard the message she'd spoken just for him.

"You go ahead," he said with a nod of understanding. "I would like to examine this Book of Knowledge to make sure there aren't any other surprises. Get some rest, Carys," he said with his attention back on the Council. "It sounds like you're going to need it."

Rest, she thought as she spun and walked out of the chamber, *was something neither of them could afford.* Not if they were going to avoid being caught in the trap the Council of Elders were setting.

Carys headed back through the brightly lit but mostly empty

hallways of the castle to her rooms and noticed there were more guards posted than usual. Possibly because they thought they'd be enforcing the rule of a new king tonight. That alone told Carys that Captain Monteros couldn't be counted on to help her and Andreus. His loyalty clearly belonged to the Council of Elders. Perhaps she could find a way to buy his support back, but after tonight it was clear she and Andreus would never be able to truly count on him. The only people she and her brother could depend on to keep them safe were themselves.

Eyeing the guards stationed in the next hallway, Carys slipped down one of the narrow servants' corridors her brother favored, where wind-powered lights never glowed and the guard never bothered to stand. After all, why protect servants who couldn't offer rewards when there were lords and ladies with jewels and gold just waiting to be thankful?

Quickly, Carys made her way down torch-lined halls and up narrow, uneven steps to the doorway that opened nearest to her rooms. She felt a jolt of surprise followed by worry when she spotted Larkin hovering outside her door. Her friend had a pile of fabric draped over one arm and Goodman Marcus's leather tailor satchel hanging from her shoulder.

The minute Larkin spotted her, Carys's friend burst into tears.

"Quiet," Carys hissed, looking past Larkin and hoping the guards who were typically stationed just beyond the doorway didn't hear.

Too late.

She spotted the face of the same guard who had escorted her to the North Tower peer down the hall as she hurried Larkin inside her chamber. Another potential problem.

Throwing the bolt on the door, she ordered, "Don't cry. I can't afford to grieve." Larkin's sympathy would shatter her. Sadness would pull her under and make her never want to surface. Even now the red bottle called to her, compelling her toward oblivion. She had to be careful to only take enough to keep away the symptoms of withdrawal. The nervous energy and anxiety it caused in small doses was far better than giving in to the nothingness that she desperately wanted. Instead, she'd focus on anger. It felt stronger. Hotter. Sharper. Anger would help her keep the siren's pull of the drug at bay.

Larkin sniffled. Her face tensed and turned several shades of red, but after a minute or two the tears stopped. Her friend took a deep breath and in a still-shaky voice said, "I know I could have waited to bring the dresses tomorrow, but I was in the streets when you came back from the funeral procession. I heard the Queen and saw her face . . . " Tears brimmed over and streaked down Larkin's cheeks and she handed the dresses to Juliette, who had appeared at her side. When she turned back the tears were gone. "The city is swirling with rumors, none of which I can believe are true. But after I heard them, I had to make sure you were okay."

"You can see I'm fine. Andreus is, too, but you shouldn't be here."

"I want to help," Larkin said fiercely. "The rumors say the Bastians gave your mother a drug that drove her mad and that they have a force marching on the city to seize the throne from you and your brother. Others are saying the Queen is only pretending to be mad in order to make the Council of Elders think they can control the throne and that she's planning on poisoning them all in their beds."

Not the worst idea Carys had heard.

"The Queen is being tended to by her chamberlain and the castle's healers." At least, that's what Carys assumed was happening. While she was worried about her mother, she knew Andreus, the Trials, and the threats made by the Council of Elders had to come first. "Her illness has made it impossible for her to rule. Since Andreus and I are twins, there is to be a competition of sorts to decide who will be the next to take the throne."

"What kind of competition?"

"That's up to the Council," Carys explained. "And I don't want you involved with any of this. Go back to your father and tell him that you want to leave the city to travel to your new home tonight."

"Father will never agree—"

Carys grabbed her friend's shoulders. "Then you will make him. Tell him I ordered you to leave. I don't know what's going to happen, but if there is a struggle for the throne or if the rumors about the Bastians taking advantage of my father and Micah's deaths are true, there will be more trouble coming to Garden City. I will rest easier knowing that you are safe away from it all and that soon you'll be wed and happy."

It hurt to say the words, but Larkin wouldn't be safe if she stayed.

"You are my best friend. You are part of my heart—the best part. Promise me," Carys demanded. "Promise you'll return home, pack up, and leave as soon as possible. Tell your father to stay with you until you get word from me that it is safe to return."

Larkin looked down and sighed. "I promise, Your Highness." When she tilted her face up, Larkin's tears flowed once again. They streamed down her face as she struggled to find composure and lost.

Heat pricked the back of Carys's eyes as she yanked her friend into a tight hug. When she pulled back, she steered Larkin toward the door and opened it before she herself started to cry. She was going to lose Larkin to marriage anyway, but losing her *now* after so much . . . It hurt so much worse. "May the winds guide you, my friend," she said, taking Larkin's hand. "I want you to find happiness." *For both of us.*

She willed herself to let go of Larkin, then shut the door. The click of the latch made her heart ache, and Carys slid her hand into the pocket of her cloak and closed it around the red bottle.

Gods, she wanted a sip. But it was too soon. There was too much at stake to lose control. She had to change, get her things ready, and meet her brother without anyone seeing.

She considered dismissing her maid. Juliette had proved trustworthy over the last few years, but that was before information on Carys's actions had become such a highly valuable commodity. Still, Carys wasn't sure she had a choice.

"Help me out of these clothes. Then assist me into the rust dress that was just delivered," she said, knowing Juliette would expect Carys to get ready for bed instead of for another outing. If the maid had any questions about the instructions, she held her tongue as she helped Carys into the gown and did up the laces tight enough to keep the dress in place but not so tight that they irritated her still-healing wounds.

Reaching into the cloak pocket, she slid the red bottle out, then said, "Now, take these clothes to the smoke pits and burn them."

"Excuse me, Your Highness?" Juliette said, folding the funeral dress over her arm.

"Today was miserable," Carys said, walking to a small table where tea, fruit, and cheese were waiting for her. She placed the bottle on the table. "I would prefer not to keep any reminders."

When Juliette had gathered the discarded garments and hurried toward the door, Carys added, "Juliette, I wouldn't blame you if you had trouble juggling those and dropped them near the guards at the end of the hall. The cloak in particular is thick and bulky if not carried carefully."

Juliette met Carys's eyes and nodded. "I did notice that it's not particularly easy to carry, Your Highness. I will take care to make sure it doesn't cause too many problems when I take it down to the smoke pits. I'll be back later to see if there are any other items from today you wish me to dispose of."

Carys smiled at her maid's acknowledgment of the task Carys wished her to carry out. "I appreciate your loyalty, Juliette. If ever you feel conflicted about that dedication, I hope you'll let me know so I can assuage your concerns."

"There will never be a conflict, Your Highness. I shall return." With that Juliette slipped out the door and closed it behind her.

Carys moved to the door and waited several long seconds before turning the handle and opening the door a crack so she could listen to the sound of Juliette's footsteps as the maid hurried down the hall. Juliette giggled at something one of the guards said. Then she let out a small shout. A few moments later, Carys pushed open the door. She could hear the guards, but they weren't in sight as Carys slipped out of her rooms and hurried to meet her brother at the place they had always gone to when they needed to be alone.

Years ago, Andreus had discovered a door behind a large tapestry in the now unused nursery at the very end of the hall next to Micah's rooms. The wall hanging was two hundred years old, reached from the ceiling to the floor, and covered three-quarters of the wall. Iron masonry nails fixed the corners of the woven scene of the mountains beyond the castle. All around the mountains were swirling clouds and trees bending beneath the force of the wind. In the center of the biggest gust of wind was a broken crown. From what she could tell, no one knew how long the tapestry had been hanging in the room, or why an artisan created it, but it had been long enough that no one seemed to remember the door it concealed. She wouldn't have known it was there had Andreus not discovered the hidden entrance while trying to hide behind the tapestry when he was little. Whoever had hidden the entrance had done so long before she was born—long before her father was King.

Carys was relieved to see no guards were stationed in the nursery hallway. Captain Monteros must have decided there was no reason to use his men in an area where no one currently lived. Good. That meant there were no eyes to see her as she hurried into the nursery, shifted the heavy wall hanging, and slipped behind it into the darkness beyond.

An oil lamp and flint to light it were waiting on a small table Andreus had found. Striking one of her stilettos against the flint, Carys lit the lamp, lifted it to the hook in the middle of the small room, and studied the space as she waited for her brother to arrive.

How long had it been since they had come here? The last time she had been here was two years ago when Andreus insisted she try to break herself of the Tears of Midnight that had wrapped her in their seductive grip. He'd taken her into the tunnels below the castle and there she'd fought and screamed and sweated and clawed and shook so hard that Andreus was scared she'd die.

It was fear for her that pushed Andreus into giving her just the small sip that Carys begged for. Just enough to make the worst of the shaking stop and keep her stomach from cramping in a way that made her wish someone would kill her. She'd promised Andreus that she'd take a little less every day until she no longer needed the drug.

She'd gotten close so many times to breaking free of the drug's grasp, but there was always a reason to give it another day. A ball to attend. Micah pushing Andreus to take a turn on the guard's practice field. Her mother reminding Carys that it was her responsibility to protect her brother's secret no matter the cost.

Carys walked to the center of the room, pulled up the rug, and stared down at the trapdoor beneath, wishing all the usable exits to the tunnels hadn't been sealed. As children she and Andreus had used the tunnels to practice his guard drills with the sword and the bow and her with the knife. He hated how she could hit the targets dead center, one after another, while he lost his breath. Day by day, though, week by week, he got stronger and they had to look for longer corridors to set up their targets. By the time they were ten, Carys knew the tunnels below the castle as well as she knew the hallways above.

All but one of the uneven, dirt-packed corridors that ran under the castle ended at piles of boulders and rubble that stood from the floor to the ceiling. The one that didn't led to a ledge on the southern side of the plateau. From there it was an almost sheer drop to the ground. Andreus often wondered if it was the previous ruling family who had sealed the tunnels to ward off the forces wishing to take their crown and if that one lone exit was the path the surviving Bastians took when they escaped the night the rest were slaughtered. But unless they knew how to fly, Carys couldn't see how they got to the ground. There must be another unseen way out of the castle. Too bad Carys had no idea where that was because very soon they might need it.

Carys began to pace as she waited for Andreus. Could he have said something to the Council of Elders that made them detain him?

Could he have had another attack without a chance to take the remedy?

Worry had her heading for the door as the knob turned and Andreus strode in. The tapestry settled as he closed the door behind him and then several seconds passed as they both waited—listening as they always did for any sound that indicated someone had followed.

All was silent. Andreus opened his arms and Carys rushed into them. "I was afraid something had happened to you."

"I had to take the long way to get here. The guards and the Council of Elders' pages are wandering the halls more than usual."

Her brother hugged her gently, careful of her wounds, and she pressed her ear to his chest to listen to his heart. It beat fast but steady. At least that was something to be grateful for.

"Carys," he said, pulling back to look at her. "What are we going to do? I can't take part in the Trials. If I do—"

"I know," she said. "And if we refuse, Garret will be named King. Our family will be seen as a threat to his rule."

"We'll end up like the Bastians."

"The only answer is for us to leave. We have to get Mother and get out of Garden City before first light."

"Go? To where?"

"I don't know. Somewhere no one is looking to remove our heads? If we ride to the west eventually we'll reach the Fire Sea. We can get a boat and sail to Calibas."

"We'll be lucky to get out of the castle without anyone seeing the two of us. There's no way we'll be able to move Mother without detection. And even if we could, what then? Outride the guard when they discover we've gone? If we drug Mother unconscious to keep her quiet, she'll be dead weight. If not, she'll be trying to ride toward the mountains and the Xhelozi that have already woken for the cold season."

"Does it matter?" she asked. "We'll be alive."

"You will. What about me? Wherever we go, there won't be Madame Jillian."

Gods. She hadn't thought about Madame Jillian and the remedy she created at the Queen's directive. The Queen claimed Oben suffered from chest pains, shortness of breath, and prickly weakness in his limbs. She ordered the healer to create the remedy that Andreus had used for years. Andreus always had enough to see him through several weeks, but what then? Who knew if they could find another healer or one nearly as skilled?

"We can't stay, Dreus. Not without competing in the Trials."

"No. There has to be a way," Andreus said, pacing the room. "This is our home. Father would have wanted one or both of us to lead Eden—the way he did."

"The way he did?" A bitter laugh ripped out of her. "Father didn't *rule*. He did what he wanted and didn't care if innocent people were caught in the middle. He didn't bother to learn about the laws because he was the law. But now he's gone and we're stuck with laws he never troubled himself to learn about. Now that Lady Imogen has revealed them . . . "

"This isn't Imogen's fault," Andreus snapped. "If it weren't for her, we wouldn't be having this conversation. The Council of Elders would have made Garret King and who knows where we'd be. She put herself on the line and saved me."

"Us," Carys said, looking hard at her brother. "She saved us." She and Andreus were a team. The fact that he hadn't automatically thought of both of them shifted the only foundation she had. Especially after he chose Imogen over Carys two nights ago.

"That's what I meant," Andreus said.

Carys wished that were true and knew she could not push her doubts about the seer or her brother would stop listening. Carefully, she said, "I'm grateful Imogen intervened, but the truth is we don't know what her motives are or why she's given the Council leave to create these trials. There are only so many options in front of us."

"And most of them aren't options." Andreus raked a hand through his dark hair and stalked to the corner as Carys thought through their choices.

"Then there's only one thing we can do," Carys said. They couldn't escape the castle with their mother and there was no way the Council of Elders would allow them to live if Garret were crowned. "We're going to cheat."

10

"Cheat?" Andreus threw up his hands and stalked across the room. "How in the world do you intend to cheat the Council?"

"They decide the Trials we have to face, but we decide the winner."

Andreus turned. "What?"

Carys smiled. "We cheat. According to the law, the Council of Elders has to create the Trials. We have to participate in them. The winner gets the throne. But nowhere in there does it say we actually have to compete for real. If we decide who the winner is before the Trials start, we can take control of everything. That will limit the stress on you and the time the Trials take since we can make sure one of us wins most everything."

"Most?"

"No one will believe the Trials are real if only one of us wins every contest," Carys said with a burst of energy. The more she spoke the faster the words tripped over each other. "We'll make the contest look real so the Council cannot protest the results."

"But we'll still have to compete in public," he said. "You know what will happen if I have an attack."

Everyone would see that he was cursed and both he and his sister would pay the price.

"Dreus . . . "

"You should win the Trials," he said, remembering all the times he said he didn't want to rule. That he was glad not to be the Crown Prince. "Honestly, Carys. It should be you. You've studied the guards more than I have." She'd had to in order to help him. "You're better at anticipating the intrigue of the Council of Elders and the High Lords." Even if it meant stepping in front of whatever trouble was coming to keep him safe.

How many beatings had she taken in order to keep his curse hidden? She'd suffered for him. She should be rewarded. And he would spend his life hiding behind his sister.

His sister who he had seen drink from the familiar red bottle and whose hand was trembling on his arm.

His sister laid that shaking hand on his face so he couldn't look away.

"Andreus, you care about the people in the city. And they love you for it. They see your good works. Look at what you did for Max. He's alive because of you." A fierce light shined from Carys's eyes as she insisted, "None of that sounds like a person who's been *cursed*. We both have flaws. We both have strengths."

Two halves of the same whole. That's what their nurse used to say.

"Neither of us will be able to rule without help from people we trust."

For the first time, he allowed himself to think about what it would be like to sit on the throne. To have people notice what he did. To make changes without having to beg anyone to listen to his ideas. He could help more kids like Max—and help everyone understand that being sick didn't mean being cursed.

"Andreus, what do you want?"

"I don't know." He pushed past her and wished they weren't in such an enclosed space. It felt bigger when they were little. Now the walls were too close together for him to think. His heart was pounding hard and he couldn't tell if it was excitement, nerves, or the curse. "I'm scared to even consider wanting the crown."

But he was considering it. Gods. If he was being honest, he'd always wanted it. He'd just pretended that he didn't. Why wage a war for something that could never be won?

Now it could. The throne could be within his grasp and he wasn't sure if he should take it.

In the shadows, he asked the question that he'd never had the courage to voice before. "Carys. What if I *am* . . . cursed?" Always he'd denied the seers' magical powers. The wind blew with or without them. The orb glowed bright because of the Masters of Light. But Imogen believed. She believed with her whole heart that she could call the winds. He'd wanted the seers to be powerless. If he believed otherwise . . . "What if by taking the throne I destroy the kingdom and everyone in it?"

Fabric rustled and he felt his sister's hand on his back. "Have you ever considered that your fear of having your secret exposed could be the real curse? People make terrible choices out of fear of losing what they hold dear. Kings wage war and slaughter their subjects to keep their power. The Council of Elders would send us to the North Tower and see our heads displayed at the entrance of the castle steps in order to keep their authority. And you—you might turn away from ruling and making choices that might help the kingdom thrive. That fear could be what shatters the orb."

"Or it could cause an attack in the Hall of Virtues, the kingdom could be told of the old seer's prediction, and a war could be waged to remove me from power."

"It could," she agreed, and Andreus stalked away.

"So that decides it, then," he said with the taste of disappointment and frustration bitter on his tongue. Carys was being honest. He couldn't fault her for that.

But he did.

"Dreus, even if we knew for sure that the seers' predictions were real, it's impossible to know what the words mean. Remember when our tutor made us study King Perin. His seer told him water would flow across Eden and wash away that which didn't adhere to the seven virtues. He ordered all the men who worked in the fields to stop tending crops and to build ships so everyone in the castle would be able to find safety from the flood the seer predicted.

"Only it wasn't a flood." It was an earthquake that pulled apart the earth all the way to the Fire Sea. Water from the sea rushed into the void, sweeping away anything that had fallen into the crack, and people for a hundred miles around Eden suffered from starvation because men had been building ships instead of tending the land.

"And who knows if that really was what the seer predicted," his sister said, echoing what she'd often argued with their tutor. "You've said it yourself. People want to believe life isn't random. They feel safer if the seers have the power to see the future and call the winds. So they look at things that happen and find a way to fit those events around the words."

"Except that if I have an attack, we *know* what will happen. It's not magic, it's logic."

"Then we will deal with it," his sister snapped, clasping and unclasping her hands in front of her. "No matter what happens, this isn't going to be easy. I never once in my life thought I would sit upon the throne in the Hall of Virtues. I think your heart is stronger than you know. I think you would make a great king. But I will not ask you to do something that could cause you harm."

"Do you want it?" he asked. "Do you want to sit on the throne?"

Carys hesitated. Not long. Just for an instant before she answered. But Andreus heard the pause before she said, "I want us to survive."

So did he.

Andreus took his sister's hand and held it tight.

"Keep your remedy with you always, Andreus. And be careful. The Trials aren't the only thing working against us. We don't know who was behind Father's and Micah's deaths or who killed the men in the tower or why the wind power line was sabotaged. We can't trust anyone but each other."

So much happening. So many threats.

"From the moment we leave this room, we must conduct ourselves as combatants. But if I need you, I'll leave a note beneath *your* step."

His step. The loose one he never failed to trip on as a kid when he went to the battlements. "I'm going to miss talking to you, Carys."

"I'll miss you, too." Her eyes glistened. She squeezed his fingers, then pulled hers away and stepped back toward the door. "We will talk again when you are King."

And with that Carys disappeared out the door, leaving him to wait until she was long gone before he could depart as well. So he paced the room that felt smaller with every moment as anticipation and nerves began to churn inside him.

King.

Just a few days and he would rule on the throne. He would be good at it. Better than their father had been. *He* hadn't cared that High Lord James was cruel to his people. Andreus would never forget visiting the Stronghold where Lord James ruled and pointing out the dirty, starving people lining the streets of the city. His father said a strong leader did what he must to keep his people in control.

Andreus had never understood how keeping people so weak they could barely stand was a show of strength. When he was King, he'd make sure the people were better cared for.

But only if he got through the Trials without an attack. If the Council saw his curse . . .

Andreus decided he'd waited long enough. He shifted the tapestry and slipped out of the cramped, time-forgotten room and headed downstairs to his mother's quarters.

He spotted several guards and saw the way their eyes followed him as he walked through the corridors. His hand itched to hold on to the hilt of his sword.

A maid curtsied in the hall as she hurried past and gave Andreus a flirtatious look that just a few days ago he would have taken as an invitation and accepted with enthusiasm. Now he no longer had interest in what she was offering. He ignored the girl, approached his mother's doors, and knocked. When there was no answer, he yelled, "Oben, it's Prince Andreus. Let me in."

The doors opened and he hurried into the dimness. Quickly he shut the door behind him. The doors to his mother's bedroom were closed. Bits of glass and broken china and overturned chairs decorated the room.

"I'm sorry, Your Highness," Oben said. "Your mother needed quiet. A number of the Council of Elders and several of the lords and ladies of the court have come by, but I have been keeping all but Madame Jillian out. She gave something to the Queen to quiet her and encourage rest."

Which meant his mother was drugged out of consciousness. After how she'd behaved on the castle's steps, that was probably a good thing.

"Is Mother still . . . " Should he say the word? *Insane?* "Lost in her grief?"

Oben sighed. "I fear the Queen is still not herself. I saw signs of her withdrawal from this world yesterday, but I thought she'd had too much tea and was not as clearheaded as she otherwise might be. Unfortunately, today . . . "

"I know. And because of today there are things happening that will make it hard for Carys and me to help Mother through this. We're counting on you to keep her safe. Let no one but my sister and Madame Jillian through this door until we tell you otherwise."

A locked entrance wouldn't prevent entrance to men with swords who would be more than willing to shatter the door, but it would keep the Council of Elders and curiosity seekers in the court at bay.

"Of course, Your Highness. I will guard the Queen with my life."

"I know you will." Oben's devotion to his mother was something Andreus could count on even if it was often a little disturbing in its passion. If Mother ordered Oben to slit his own throat, Andreus had no doubt the man would do it. "I'd like to see for myself that Mother's okay."

Carefully, Andreus opened the door to his mother's bedroom, walked into the candlelit room, and closed the door behind him. Mother was in bed with the covers tucked perfectly around her. Her dark hair had been brushed until it gleamed and was fanned out perfectly around her pale face. The steady rise and fall of her chest told him she was deeply asleep.

Ever since he'd been born, she'd told him how strong he had to be. She'd told him he had to be stronger than anyone ever suspected . . . just as she was. Looking at her now, he resented the words he once lived by. She'd said she was stronger than everyone knew. But she wasn't.

Turning his back on her, he knelt in front of a small gold cabinet and opened the door to the remedies and potions Madame Jillian provided his mother. There were bottles of all sizes and colors on the top two shelves, but the bottom shelves were filled with black vials and bottle after glass bottle in the deepest of crimson red.

Quickly, he pulled all the black vials out of the cabinet and tucked them in a deep blue silk bag sitting on a chair nearby. His mother had always warned him to only take the remedy during an attack because too much exposure to the herbs would eventually render them ineffective for him. The idea of not being able to calm the curse when it grabbed hold had terrified him into drinking from the black vial only when it was absolutely necessary. He just hoped that there wouldn't be much need for it in the days to come.

He tied the bag and headed out the door and back to his rooms only to find Lady Imogen standing outside it flanked by two guards outside his door.

"Lady Imogen," he said, aware of the guards listening to his every word. "I didn't expect to see you here. I know today has been long and difficult for you."

"Today has been difficult for us all, Your Highness. I was hoping to talk to you about the Queen." She glanced at the men flanking her. "Would you mind if we spoke in private?"

"Please, come in." He let her pass, then shut the door behind them.

Imogen stood in the center of the room with her hair loose around her shoulders and her eyes wide with uncertainty. When the lock was turned she flew into his arms and buried her face in his chest. The feel of her body against his made everything else fade away.

Tilting her face up, he pressed his lips against hers and felt her shiver in response. He ran one hand down her hips then pulled her tight against him as he deepened the kiss. He wanted to curse the Gods when she stepped back and put a hand against his chest.

"No. The guards will be paying attention as to how long I talk with you and they report to Elder Cestrum. So I cannot stay. I just had to make sure you weren't upset with me because of what happened in the Hall of Virtues. It was the only way to keep the Council of Elders from seizing control of the throne and hurting you in that very moment. I would have told you first, but there wasn't time."

"I'm glad you showed up when you did."

"And your sister?" Imogen asked. "Is the Princess glad?"

"Carys is relieved that we aren't spending tonight in the North Tower, but she did wonder why you had never mentioned the Book of Knowledge or that law before."

"I never thought there was reason," Imogen said. "Micah was alive. Your mother was strong. I never thought my vision meant that there would be a contest between you and your sister. Not until today when the Queen . . . Suddenly I knew why there had been no visions save the one since I came to the Palace of Winds. There can be no other visions until the path the kingdom will travel down is chosen. I will not be able to see what choices must be made until the winner of the Trials is decided. I know you love your sister, but Dreus, *you* must win."

"Carys would make a good Queen," he said, putting the bag with the vials on his desk.

"I know you believe that, my prince." Imogen moved across the room and took his hands. "But there are two paths in front of the kingdom and only one of those leads to light. You are the light. You must not let your love for your sister cloud your judgment."

Great. Another vision. Only this one pulled instead of repelled. Maybe because for the first time *he* wasn't the cursed one.

"I will do my best to beat my sister at the Trials. That's all I can do." He kissed the back of Imogen's hand, then turned it over and placed another kiss on her palm. But instead of the passion he'd hoped to ignite, worry flickered across Imogen's face. She reached out and brushed his cheek with her fingertips and looked deep into his eyes.

Then she turned and hurried toward the door. She didn't look back as she slipped outside, leaving him on edge. There was no sleeping in his current state. He needed to walk off the nervous energy.

He put the sack of black vials in his bedroom in a space behind the mirror that he'd created years ago. Then he went back into the hall. A guard at the end of the corridor turned and watched as Andreus strode to the stairs and headed up to the place he felt the most relaxed: the battlements.

"Prince Andreus!" Max almost ran smack into him as he

barreled out of the door that led to the steps of the battlements. "I've been watching for you. People say the Queen went crazy and that you and the Princess might go crazy too and we'll have to have a new King. That's not true, is it? You're not going crazy."

"Much of today has made me feel as if I have," Andreus joked. But Max was taking his hands in and out of his pockets and looking at him with a stricken expression.

"The Queen isn't feeling well enough to take her place on the throne, but my sister and I are both fine."

"That's good. Not about the Queen. That's the doom. So is what happened to the King and Prince Micah. I'm . . . sorry."

Andreus swallowed down the grief those words reawakened. Today he'd heard the Council and lords and ladies from every corner of the kingdom say those words. Over and over. None of them had been as simple or sincere.

"I'm sorry, too, Max." He put his hand on the boy's shoulder and looked up at the orb shining bright against the dark of the night. A windmill churned in the shadows to the right of it. Looking at the lights reminded him . . .

"Max." He looked down at the boy. "I know you told someone about the test for my new design. You aren't in trouble, but I have to know who you spoke with."

Max kicked at the floor. "Nobody important, Prince Andreus. Honest. Just Madame Jillian when she was listening to me breathe. And some of the ladies who were bored and asked me to tell them a story. And some older boys. They said I didn't really know you so I told them to prove I did."

So everyone.

Andreus shook his head. Under the beating of the windmills, a pounding came from somewhere below.

"Come on," he said to Max as he hurried across the battlements. He followed the sound as it grew louder, until he looked over the white stone wall onto the castle guards' practice fields and saw the source of the pounding. Torches were scattered around the field, illuminating dozens of workmen and carts filled with wood planks. More carts arrived out of the darkness.

"What are they building?" Max asked.

"I'm not sure," Andreus said as he studied the scene below. Far to the left of the field he spotted Elder Cestrum and Elder Jacobs huddled with the castle's head carpenter.

When Max pointed to someone painting big wooden stumps yellow and blue, Andreus realized what he was looking at.

A game board—much like the ones his mother used when scoring the card games she and her ladies played. This one, however, only had two rows of holes.

Two rows.

Two colors.

Two players.

When his mother used the board, each point a player scored was inserted in the player's line of holes. The person with the longest line of pegs in the board by the end of the game won.

As long as no one saw his curse, he would be that winner.

He sent Max down to bed knowing he should go too. But he couldn't make himself leave the walls as he watched proof of the contest to come brought into existence.

Imogen was wrong to question whether he could trust Carys. His sister hated these walls. There was no way she would want to doom herself to spending the rest of her life behind them. And yet he couldn't forget her hesitation when he asked whether she wanted the throne. Her reaction played over and over in his head as the wind pulled at his clothes and the pounding of the hammers ticked off the seconds that were pushing him toward tomorrow and the unknown Trials that would decide their fate.

11

Yellow and blue flags fluttered high over the tournament field. Sunshine bathed the day and the wind was gentle, making the temperature warm for this time of year. Carys turned and looked back at the pure white walls of the castle that now had a large wooden board hanging high above the main entrance. Everyone had been whispering about the scoreboard that had been built overnight. Speculation flew as to its purpose and when the people would find out its use.

Soon. Far too soon. Because even with a plan to beat the Council of Elders at its own game, Carys knew how high the stakes were and how great the risks.

She turned back and squinted into the sunlight. Sleep had been hard to find last night. After hours of lying in the dark with her heart pounding and her back throbbing, she'd succumbed to the need for the Tears of Midnight.

First a little.

Then a bit more.

Until finally sleep came.

She'd needed the rest and calm. Andreus was counting on her to be rested today. She'd had no choice. And she'd been careful to take just a small sip of the bitter brew this morning to stave off the effects of withdrawal. As soon as they made it through the Trials, she would stop altogether. This time she would break the hold the red glass bottles had on her.

But not yet. For now, she'd be careful. She'd manage it.

Nala shifted under her and Carys pulled on her horse's reins as she reached the top of the hill and studied the five acres of tournament grounds set in the lowest point of the valley to the west of the Palace of Winds. The earth sloped up from the tournament field, making the competition area and the viewing grounds around it seem to be in the bottom of a bowl. The location allowed even those who were not on elevated platforms on the sidelines a clear view of the action.

It looked as though everyone from Garden City had shown up to watch the tournament. Events designed for peasants and merchants had started hours ago. People turned and waved as they noticed the parade of nobility arrive, signaling the next phase of the tournament when the most skilled members of the guard would compete. A louder cheer went up as they spotted Carys and her brother and the entourage of lords and ladies spread out behind them.

Everywhere she heard shouts of "Princess Carys" and "Prince Andreus."

Her stomach clenched as she looked up and met her brother's hazel eyes.

So many people. So much that could go wrong.

Within the fenced boundary of the tournament grounds Carys spotted younger members of the guard, and those who aspired to gain the notice of Captain Monteros and join the rank of the King's Guard, charging their horses down the list field in an effort to unseat and defeat their foes.

Far in the distance, past the lists, were the wrestling grounds and men swinging quarterstaffs, as well as an unusual-looking area that Carys could only assume was being used for footraces and maybe some kind of dueling. Closer to this end of the grounds where they were riding, men—and here and there a few women—were standing ready to test their aim at a row of archery targets.

On the southern edge of the tournament field, three viewing platforms had been erected. A blue canopy hung over the one to the left. A yellow canopy hung over the platform to the right. The center canopy was white and had the blue-and-yellow flag of Eden flying high above it.

Elder Cestrum pulled his horse in between Carys's and her brother's chestnut one.

"Princess Carys, you will be seated under the blue canopy. Prince Andreus, you will take the yellow one. I hope you will both do your best to honor the virtues today and do take care." He smoothed his white beard. "After losing your father and your brother, and after what happened to your mother, the kingdom couldn't bear another unfortunate circumstance."

Elder Cestrum snapped his reins, held tight in his clawed hand, and started forward down the sloping hill toward the viewing platforms at the back of the tournament grounds.

"Are you ready?" Andreus asked, pulling his chestnut stallion up next to hers.

Carys wished she could ask him how he was feeling, but she spotted Elder Jacobs watching them. The Elder had a black falcon resting on his gloved hand. The bird was unhooded and Carys knew it was just waiting for the Elder's command to attack. Elder Jacobs had never lifted a sword in a tournament. Instead, he let the bird he trained cause pain to others for him. She spotted Elder Ulrich, watching the bird—disdain pouring from his one good eye. Riding next to Ulrich was an elegant-looking, olive-skinned young man around her age who seemed vaguely familiar. He had a narrow, sculpted face and dark wavy hair that brushed the tops of his shoulders. But it was the seemingly careless command of his horse as he steered it around several children who came racing out of the crowd that struck a chord in her memory. This was the man responsible for catching her mother when she attempted to race back to the mountains. The unfamiliar crest on his cloak announced him as one of the foreign dignitaries who had come for the funeral and coronation.

The foreigner listened to whatever Elder Ulrich was saying, but he was watching her intently. Just as Elder Jacobs and his falcon were.

So instead of offering her support to her brother as she wished to, she straightened her shoulders and said, "I'm looking forward to winning, brother." And nudged her horse down the slope of the hill to whatever the Council of Elders had waiting for them.

Children waved and ran after her and her brother as their horses cantered past. Loud cheers shook the earth from those standing twenty or more deep around the tournament fences. Vendors darted around, selling strips of blue and yellow fabric, the colors of Eden's flag. But instead of being combined they were separate. Divided. Like the two platforms she and Andreus would stand upon.

Blue for her. Yellow for her brother.

As she looked around the spectators she spotted dozens who

must have heard what the colored bands symbolized. They were sporting yellow flags and armbands. None that Carys could see in the crowds displayed blue favors. Her brother's skill and magnanimity were known far and wide. The people already thought he was a hero. They would be excited to have him as their King.

She hadn't been flattering Dreus when she assured him he'd make a good ruler—far better than she would. She didn't have the patience for listening to the grievances of blacksmiths and merchants and lords and soldiers, didn't have the desire to fix their petty concerns with a royal decree. And when it came to the windmills—she liked the results of the powerful machines, but she had no interest in understanding how they worked or managing the Masters of Light or allocating power allotments to the city.

And even if she was willing to deal with those things, the idea of having armed guards follow her wherever she went sounded horrifying. Andreus liked attention. But every time Carys had to push herself in front to protect her brother she learned anew how painful it was to be seen—and judged. The strap hurt, but those wounds healed. It was the way everyone looked at her—as though she were unworthy of the crown—that made her want to sink into the red bottle and stay there.

People whispered.

They shook their heads, and Carys knew that even if she had not given her promise to keep her brother safe, she would still get those reactions.

Needlepoint and sitting around playing cards or strumming instruments held no fascination for her. A model of feminine decorum she'd never be. She was destined to be the royal disappointment to the kingdom. There was no point in inflicting that on the throne if there was another choice. As long as she got Andreus through whatever these Trials would be, he would keep the kingdom from passing judgment on her.

Carys pushed Nala to a gallop to the south side where the viewing platforms waited. Spectators in the back pushed and jostled to get a glimpse of the noble procession, while the others up front cheered when one of the men competing at the lists was knocked from his horse. The fallen man scrambled to his feet and raced for his sword instead of yielding. Carys didn't have to watch to know that, for the smaller man, it wouldn't end well as he faced down a much larger opponent who had ditched his lance in favor of a battle-ax. The promise of the coins or valuable weapons offered to the winners was too tempting for those in need to turn down. They'd rather risk an ax in their throats for the possibility of a better life than survive and be forced to live the lives they currently had.

The procession rounded the back of the platforms as the spectators gasped and then several long seconds of silence descended on the crowd. Quiet in the middle of the tournament meant only one thing.

Death.

The sound of cheering then resumed, signaling the body had been removed and the next contest had begun. Nobles often bet on whether or not competitors would survive the events they participated in. She wondered if they would bet on her and her brother today.

When they reached the viewing platforms, grooms came to take their horses as the Council of Elders' pages, easy to spot in their all-black attire, informed the nobles of the purpose of the yellow and blue platforms and instructed them to choose a spot on the one representing the successor they hoped would win the crown.

One by one familiar faces from the court hurried toward the platform with the yellow canopy. A few had the decency to look back at Carys with guilt, but most never bothered to glance her way as they pledged their support to her brother.

She then saw Imogen, wrapped in a snow-white cloak, blush as Andreus escorted the seer up the stairs to his platform.

Good, she thought. If the seer and the court openly supported Andreus, it would make it harder for the Council to depose him in favor of Lord Garret. Carys spotted him now, looking at her from the base of the center platform where the Council members sat. Elder Cestrum put his clawed hand on Garret's broad shoulder and said something to him, but still Garret didn't move. He just stared at her. His long red hair hung free today and in the sunlight framed his face like the sun.

Carys resisted the urge to smooth her hair or straighten her dress. She wasn't fifteen anymore and infatuated with the solidly built, skilled nineteen-year-old who had bluntly said her erratic behavior and stupors were an embarrassment to the entire kingdom. She'd admired him for speaking the truth to her face instead of whispering it behind her back and for thinking she was strong enough to handle it. But he was her enemy now, and it was clear by the way Elder Jacobs clapped Garret on the back that he was part of whatever the Council had planned for her and her brother.

Turning toward the steps to the blue platform, Carys stopped short of running smack into the same dark-haired dignitary she'd spotted riding with Elder Ulrich.

"Excuse me, Your Highness," he said with a smile that softened his sharp, tanned features in a compelling way. "I didn't mean to get in the way. Although, it seems like I am making a habit of that when it comes to your family."

"It does seem to be a skill of yours, Lord . . . "

"Errik of the House of Yarxbell, Trade Master of Chinera, and a lot of other titles my father and mother would say are necessary but mean just about nothing to those who don't live within our borders." His mocking charm should annoy her. Instead, she was intrigued by his lack of fascination with his own importance.

"Trade Master." Chinera was at least fifteen hundred leagues away, across the Fire Sea, but she had been schooled thoroughly enough on the power structure of the kingdom to know the Trade Master was a counselor to the King and empowered to speak on his behalf in negotiations beyond the Chinera border. Lord Errik appeared at most only a year or two older than herself. To rise to that position so quickly spoke either of the influence of his family or his skill. Perhaps both. "It's been at least fifty years since the last Trade Master visited Eden. And your visit was timely for my family. My brother and I owe you thanks for your interference with our mother yesterday. That habit came in useful."

"It's always nice to be of service. Although, I have a feeling you would have found a way to solve the problem had I not been so intrusive, Highness." His deep blue eyes turned serious. "I should probably get out of your way now, unless you'd allow me the honor of escorting you to your platform."

Carys shook her head as trumpets sounded, signaling that the nobility's participation in the tournament was about to begin. "I believe the High Lords and visiting dignitaries are to be seated with the Council of Elders in the center. I'm sure they'll be able to make you comfortable there."

"I find comfort to be highly overrated, Your Highness." He offered his arm. "May I have the honor of joining you?"

Normally, Carys would turn him down flat. But as much as she told herself she didn't care what people thought of her, she didn't want everyone to see her standing atop her platform at the start of these trials utterly alone.

She placed her hand on his arm and was surprised at the strength and muscle she felt there. Lord Errik was not bulky like Lord Garret or most of the guard, but there was strength in him others probably missed. She had. She wouldn't again. She noticed him studying her and said, "I trust you realize you've picked the less popular side, Lord Errik."

He put his hand atop hers and smiled. "Which makes it the far more interesting one."

There was strength in his fingers, too. And calluses that spoke of hours spent training with steel. Yes. Carys had missed much about Lord Errik in her first assessment. She tried to remedy that as they climbed the steps to the long rectangular platform, and she was surprised when they reached the top to see she and Errik wouldn't be completely alone. Eight of the young women of the court sat on wooden benches facing the tournament grounds—all girls Carys recognized as conquests of her twin brother's charms. The girls stood and curtsied when they saw her and Errik appear. They all eyed Carys's escort with interest as he walked her to the blue-cushioned throne-like chair in the center of the viewing stand. Not that Carys could blame them. Lord Errik's strong chin and angular features would catch any girl's attention.

When they reached her seat, Errik raised her hand and brushed his lips over her knuckles. Trumpets sounded and her heart skipped as she stood in front of her chair and straightened her shoulders; the people crowded around the tournament field grew quiet and turned toward the platforms.

Elder Cestrum stepped forward on the center viewing area and held up his good hand and his metal claw. Heralds stationed near the fence of the tournament area prepared to memorize his words and plunge into the crowd to make sure all who were too far away to hear learned what was said.

"Congratulations to all the tournament winners thus far. The winds blew strong for you today. I had planned to be standing in front of you now under very different circumstances. Today was to be the first of our celebrations to honor the reign of Queen Betrice. But the Queen has been struck hard by the death of King Ulron and Prince Micah and is unable to take her rightful place in the Hall of Virtues."

The crowd shifted and murmured. On the center platform, just behind Elder Cestrum, Garret turned his head and looked again at Carys. She pulled her eyes away from him and focused on his uncle as he waved off the crowd's concern. "While we are saddened that Queen Betrice cannot take the throne, we are fortunate to have two of King Ulron's children who are ready to wear the crown. Since only one can sit on the throne, starting here at this tournament we will hold a series of Trials based on the seven virtues to determine whether Prince Andreus or Princess Carys will stand as our ruler."

The crowd around them erupted in cheers. A few of them took the form of her brother's name.

When the applause quieted, Elder Cestrum continued. "He who is on the throne is required to sit in judgment of us all. It would be easy for anyone in that position of power to become prideful. But pride leads to destruction. The best kings and queens are the ones who understand humility. Today on the tournament field we will put Prince Andreus and Princess Carys's humility to the test in three separate events. In the first two events, they will compete against each other. Nobility usually competes against their peers. But today, in the third event, to demonstrate their humility, our prince and princess will also be competing with some of you who have already demonstrated skill on this field."

Surprised gasps and murmurs raced through the crowd.

Carys glanced at her brother far on the other platform. The nobility around him looked shocked at the idea of anyone from noble blood being treated as though they were the same as a commoner.

But that wasn't all. "And since Prince Andreus or Princess Carys will soon be required to pass judgment on everyone in the kingdom, we in the Council of Elders feel it is only right that the winner of each of these first three contests be determined by all of you. Prince Andreus sits under the yellow banner. Princess Carys is blue. Once a competition is over we ask that you show the colors of the competitor you feel triumphed over the challenges they faced and best embodied the virtues our kingdom holds dear."

Elder Cestrum glanced her way and smiled. Had she wanted to win it wouldn't have mattered; the crowd voting ensured that she would lose these events. Andreus was the one who saved them from darkness and the Xhelozi that could have attacked. He was the one who helped the boy who had been dying in the street. Her brother was clearly the choice of the Council to win this competition. Perhaps they were hoping they could divide her and Andreus with this obvious show of favor for her twin? If so, they were about to be disappointed.

Carys smiled back at Elder Cestrum and resisted the urge to wave.

The Elder turned back to the crowd and announced, "The first trial will be held at the archery field. Prince Andreus and Princess Carys will get one attempt at each of the three targets to show whether they have developed the skills that every child in the kingdom is asked to learn. When Prince Andreus and Princess Carys arrive at the archery field, we can begin."

"It seems I came to your kingdom at an interesting time, Your Highness," Lord Errik said quietly beside her. "Elder Cestrum doesn't appear to like you."

The understatement made her laugh. "I did warn you that you were choosing the wrong side," she said, walking toward the steps to the tournament grounds below.

"*Wrong* is subjective, Your Highness," he called to her.

She didn't look back at him, but she did smile as she walked slowly down the stairs to where two pages in black holding several bows and a quiver of arrows waited to escort her past the lists and the dueling pits to the archery station at the far end of the field. The only way she could lose today was if she won or if Andreus faltered.

Carys didn't acknowledge the crowd as she reached the roped-off area. Large wooden targets with white circles painted in the center had been set up at three different distances. The first was only twenty paces away. The next was perhaps thirty and the last was at least twice as far. Many in the guard accurately hit targets in tournaments at least three or four times that distance. Carys wasn't as skilled as they were, but her work with Andreus meant she could hit these with ease—if she planned on hitting them at all.

"Well, this should be entertaining," Andreus said as he appeared with two pages trailing behind him. "Would you like to go first or shall I?"

"Why don't you go," she said, wishing he didn't seem so pleased at the way the trial was clearly structured to favor him. If Andreus missed badly, she had to make sure she missed even worse.

"Very well," Andreus said, selecting a longbow from one of his pages and taking an arrow from the quiver before setting himself at the line of the closest target.

Trumpets sounded. Elder Cestrum stood at the edge of the middle viewing platform. The rest of the Elders were behind him as he announced, "One arrow at each of the three targets. When the trial is completed, we will ask you all to signal which of our successors won this round and will be awarded a point on the scoring board on the castle wall. Now let the Trials of Virtuous Succession begin."

The trumpets blared. People all around shouted and stomped their feet. They waved banners of mostly yellow. Andreus took his place in front of the shortest distance and raised his bow.

The arrow flew true and thunked into the center of the target, making the audience cheer. Carys picked out a bow of her own and set herself in front of the target. Her accuracy was greater than her brother's. This was a fact generally acknowledged by both of them and proven by their hours together in practice. She would normally hit dead center. Instead, she took a deep breath, held it, and let the arrow fly so that it thudded into the knot she spied in the wood on the left side of the target.

Andreus looked at her with a frown as the crowd applauded her effort.

Did he want her to look a fool and not hit the target at all?

He turned his back on her, walked to the next target, notched the arrow and let it fly. Center again.

The cheers were louder. She heard her brother's name shouted as she stood at the marker, drew her own weapon, this time picking a spot at the very top of the target to hit.

The arrow stuck exactly where she'd intended. More polite applause for her attempt as her brother stepped to the final distance. His arrow flew through the air and landed several inches to the left of the center circle he'd aimed for.

"Miss," he said under his breath as he stalked by her with his bow and she took her place at the line.

Drawing the bow, Carys eyed her brother's arrow sticking out of the target, then the center circle.

She sighted her target and let the arrow fly.

Thunk. It skewered the small yellow flower that sat at the bottom of the left leg of the stand. She turned and met Andreus's eyes to let him know that she had hit exactly what she'd aimed for.

"What are you doing?" Andreus asked.

Handing her bow to the page, Carys looked toward the center platform where the trumpeters were again playing. "Only what's needed," she answered.

Elder Cestrum waited until the crowd was quiet then asked, "Who among you awards the point for the effort in archery to Princess Carys?"

More cheered than Carys had expected, but it was nothing compared to the thunder of approval and waving yellow banners that followed the announcement of her brother's name.

Andreus beamed and executed a flourished bow to the crowd, causing them to cheer anew.

When the audience quieted, Elder Cestrum announced, "And

the winner of the first point of the Trials is Prince Andreus. For the second event of this tournament, Prince Andreus and Princess Carys will receive quarterstaffs and assume their places in the fighting pits."

"What? He can't be serious," Andreus said, quiet enough that only Carys could hear.

They had passed the fighting pits on their way to the archery field: a fenced-in section that had been wetted down so the dirt was now thick and sticky. In the center of the mud, standing four feet high, were two square platforms big enough for a person to take a small step forward or to the side. Anything more would send the person stumbling to the wet dirt below. Which was the idea. The platforms were close enough for the fighters to wage combat. For the novice fighters, the first to be knocked off his platform was the loser. The more experienced fighters often continued fighting if the fallen didn't yield. Those fights typically ended in death.

The crowd murmured in confusion. Did the Council truly mean for the royal family to be seen . . . striking each other? It was unprecedented. Elder Cestrum held up his iron hand for silence. "The competition will end when only one competitor remains on his or her platform."

So it was true. They were to physically spar with one another. Andreus looked ill. As well he should. No one would look with approval on a man who willingly knocked a lady down for sport.

Carys smiled. She had to hand it to the Council for creating a trial that would cause both her *and* Andreus to lose favor with the crowd. They'd succeed in that aim, unless Carys did something to change things.

"Excuse me, Elder Cestrum," Carys yelled and everything went silent.

"Yes, Your Highness?"

"Are you and the Council of Elders requesting that I strike my brother?"

Elder Cestrum frowned at her choice of words. "Do you wish to refuse the task, Princess?"

"I'm just wondering why no one allowed me to do this before," she said with a smile. "It would have simplified my childhood."

The crowd nearest to her laughed.

Elder Cestrum glared. Feeling a burst of satisfaction, Carys took the offered quarterstaff from a page and without waiting for her brother strode toward the fences that marked the boundaries of the fighting pit.

Andreus stepped beside her holding a long, thin wooden staff like the one clutched in her hand. The quarterstaff was something Andreus had never needed to work with in his required guard training, so it was a weapon neither of them had attempted before.

Carys removed her cloak and handed the heavy fabric to one of the pages, then walked to the entrance of the fighting pit. She could feel every eye on her. Everything inside her jumped and itched and yearned for a drink of the Tears that would replace the churning feeling inside her with a warm calm. As her feet sank into the muck, she wanted nothing more than to lose herself in nothingness. But she climbed the planks nailed to the side of the dirty platform and stood atop it with her shoulders straight. The crowd quieted.

Dreus took his place and the trumpets sounded.

Elder Cestrum's voice boomed, "Let the second contest of the Trials of Virtuous Succession begin."

Andreus looked at her with concern as he bent his knees and turned the long stick in his hands. Carys didn't give herself or her brother time to think. She flipped the stick so she was holding it parallel to the ground and lunged at her brother. He deflected the blow, hopped backward and almost took a dive into the mud. She poked the quarterstaff at him again. This time he smacked his own stick against it with more force than she'd expected, which made it easy to make it look as though it was the blow that made her stumble to the side and fall off the platform. Her boots squished into the mud. She tried to grab onto the platform to keep herself upright but the quarterstaff she'd kept hold of sent her off balance and she went down to her knees.

The mud was cold and clammy and oozed around her legs, encasing them in muck. She waited for her brother to jump off the platform and help her up, but the crowd was stomping their feet and shouting his name. Carys had struck first. Andreus had no choice but to strike back, which meant the people could still cheer for their hero.

Really, it was almost too easy.

Plunging the end of the quarterstaff into the mud, Carys pushed to her feet. The bottom of her dress was heavy with muck, but she pretended it didn't matter as she slogged out of the pen and handed the quarterstaff to the page, who gave her a look filled with pity. Was he sorry for her because of the mud or because she was going to lose again? She wasn't sure it mattered. Pity was the last thing she cared about.

The trumpets sounded as Elder Cestrum called for another demonstration of support to determine the winner. Carys steeled herself for silence when her name was called out, but this time there were more shouts in her favor than before. And she saw several blue banners wave in the crowd, but the yellow overwhelmed them in numbers and, again, Andreus was declared the winner. Now he was two points ahead. She wasn't sure how many were required to get across the scoring board in the Council's twisted little game, but Andreus would reach that goal soon.

Elder Cestrum wasted no time in moving on, announcing, "The final contest in this first trial of humility will be an obstacle footrace. Prince Andreus and Princess Carys will run alongside six of the victors of contests held earlier today. A sack of gold will be presented to any competitor who reaches the finish line first, and the Council will ask for the final show of support for Prince Andreus or Princess Carys to award one last point for this first trial."

The six other runners in this race were waiting for Carys and her brother when they arrived on the other side of the tournament grounds. The obstacle footraces often were run by men and women both, so Carys wasn't surprised to see that two of the people chosen to run were young girls, streaked with dirt and sweat from their earlier competitions. They were wearing dresses that fell just above the ankle, which gave them better mobility. Smart. Carys itched to cut the muddy bottom half off her own gown, but it wasn't her goal to win or to scandalize everyone watching.

The other four competitors ranged from young boys to muscular men who were twice her age. All but one of them looked at the ground or out at the crowd—anywhere but at Carys and Andreus. Clearly, this race with the royal family made all but the man with several missing teeth and a scar down the side of his face uncomfortable.

The blare of the trumpets meant it would all be over soon.

Carys caught her brother's eye as they walked to the starting point and tilted her head to the side in a silent question that he answered with a smile. He was feeling fine. No tight breathing. No tingling in his arms. No curse, which was a relief. If they could get through this footrace without his heart seizing, they'd be able to get through anything the Council threw at them.

Carys took her place at the starting point, next to her brother and a boy of maybe thirteen, for the race that took up almost half of the tournament grounds. The obstacle footraces were always one of the most popular events since a person didn't need to bring a weapon or have any specific skill in order to compete. And the obstacles meant being the faster runner didn't necessarily make you the winner. It was often the fastest who raced headlong into obstructions without studying them first. Depending on the nature of each one, the result could be life-threatening.

Careful and clever often won over brute strength and fast feet. Carys had always enjoyed the obstacle races more than watching armored guardsmen smack each other with lances at the lists. Of course, that was when she didn't have to worry about her brother running across the tournament grounds toward near-certain, impulsive doom.

"Let the third event of this trial being," Elder Cestrum called, and the heralds blasted their horns again.

"Be *careful*," she yelled to Andreus. Too late. He bolted with the others down the path marked with bales of hay and fences.

Carys raced behind her brother, who had pulled ahead of all but one of the other competitors. While she intended to lose, she had to stay close enough to Andreus to intervene in case he grew weak or, more likely, he misjudged the challenge set before him. She picked up her heavy, mud-caked skirts and awkwardly leaped over a log, then steadied herself before climbing over several more piled across the length of the path a few feet away. Andreus and the two young boys were disappearing over a shoulder-high stack of rocks when she heard a shout from farther up the trail. She cursed at her unwieldy dress as she searched for footholds and pulled herself up atop the wall of logs. On the ground to the left side she spotted the man who had cried out trying to escape from a spike that had impaled his foot when he landed on it from above.

"Watch out for spikes," she yelled to the two girls and one of the men who were coming behind. From their slow pace, she doubted they were interested in risking the wrath of a future ruler by winning this competition, which meant they would probably be fine.

Wiping her forehead, Carys hurried past the injured man and headed down the path toward the water pit her brother was jumping over. Andreus landed with a splash near enough to the other side that he didn't get very wet, with a boy and the man with the missing teeth hot on his heels. The boy yelped as he crashed down in the water a foot from the edge and scrambled to the dirt beyond. When Carys reached the water she saw the long, thin undulating black streaks in the water and the scaled head that rose above the water and then plunged back in.

Water serpents. A bite from them caused numbness that would fade after several days. Anything more would cause far worse damage.

Carys lifted her skirts and raced to the edge of the pond where the distance from one side of the water to the other was only three feet and leaped across. Distantly she heard the crowd cheering and wondered what was happening up ahead. Worried that she could no longer see her brother, she pushed herself to go faster.

Her feet pounded the path as she hurried around a pile of hay bales, passed the boy who had been ahead of her, and spotted why the crowd had been cheering. Andreus had leaped over a flaming pile of coals and was now streaking toward a line of flags three hundred lengths in the distance that signaled the end of the race.

The man with the missing teeth jumped over the pile of hot coals, and was now running twenty yards behind Andreus. He was fast and looked as if he was trying to win the Council's promised prize, but her brother was faster. She pushed herself harder and was about to jump over the coals when she saw it.

A knife. The man with the missing teeth had pulled a knife out of his pocket and was taking aim at her brother's back.

"Andreus!"

The crowd. The distance. He couldn't hear.

Carys dashed over the hot coals. She tripped over her hem as she fumbled for her pockets. Larkin's design was true. The long, sharp knives came from their hiding places. The man slowed his pace and lifted his arm to throw as Carys used the motion she'd practiced so often in the underground passages and let the stilettos fly.

Andreus crossed the finish line and the first stiletto bit into the base of the man's neck. The second sank into his back just before he fell to the ground.

12

The cheers.

The excitement.

And it was for him.

Sweating and panting hard, but refusing to slow down, Andreus had crossed the finish line. He held up his arms to acknowledge the spectators when he heard the first scream. In the crowd beyond the field, he saw people pointing. Everything around him went silent and he looked back to see what the problem was.

Carys was standing just past the fiery coals obstacle. He felt a spurt of relief when he realized she hadn't fallen into one of the traps. Although smoke was billowing up from the bottom of her dress. Was that what the people were shouting about?

Then he saw the man lying on the ground twenty lengths from the finish line. Blood oozed from the familiar silver stilettos sticking out of his back.

For a second it was as if nothing moved. Then chaos erupted.

Several guardsmen leaped over the fence separating the racing path from the spectators and hurried toward Andreus, swords drawn. Another grabbed a bucket that was being handed to him over the fence and sent the water splashing onto Carys.

Carys screamed at the man to let her by, shoved past him, and raced down the course toward Andreus.

"Are you okay?" she shouted above the din.

Andreus looked around at the crowd, at the guardsmen, at the other five runners who were standing near the fiery coals appearing as stunned as he felt.

"What did you do?" he shouted at Carys, trying to understand what was going on. One minute he was winning the footrace—and not because of anything his sister did to help him. It was his victory. His alone. The other competitors were racing for gold. But as hard as they ran, he was the one who crossed the finish first.

Growing up, he'd watched his brother victorious on this very field. He'd listened to the cheers and saw how the girls ripped fabric from their hems to offer as favors to their champion. He'd seen Imogen's eyes glow each time Micah sent a strong competitor to the ground. Even if she hadn't loved Micah, she'd cheered him as if he were a hero.

Today Andreus was the hero.

In crossing the finish line, he realized how much he wanted the crown. How much he wanted to see Imogen watch him with glowing eyes and to hear the people of Eden cheer for him.

Now the cheers were gone.

"He had a knife, Andreus," Carys said. "He was trying to kill you."

"Kill me?"

Captain Monteros climbed over the fence and the crowd quieted as the head of the castle guard slowly walked to the fallen racer. He picked up the blade lying on the ground next to the dead man and turned it over in his hand several times before sliding it into his belt. He then grabbed hold of the silver stiletto handle, put his foot on the man's back, and yanked the knife free. He did the same with the one buried in the base of the fallen attacker's neck.

No one made a sound as Captain Monteros examined both of the weapons for several long seconds, then looked up at the center platform and nodded to Elder Cestrum. Captain Monteros wiped both stilettos on his cloak and walked to where Andreus and his sister stood.

"Princess," he said, turning the silver weapons so that the handles were pointed toward Carys. "I believe these belong to you."

Carys hesitated for several long seconds before closing her hands over the stilettos.

"Your brother owes you a debt of gratitude," Captain Monteros said loud enough for those standing close to the fence to hear. "I spotted the man's intent a second before your blades took him down. Had it not been for your excellent throws the Prince would certainly be dead."

Andreus's chest tightened and his heart pounded harder than it had while he was running.

"It was luck, captain," his sister quickly said. "And the fates that guided my blades to protect the heir to the throne!"

The Captain of the Guard smiled and flicked his gaze to the stilettos that Carys held with such command. "That is the kind of luck I would very much like to have. Truly, your skill is most impressive, Highness. Where did you learn to throw so well and why is it that no one has spoken of your abilities?"

Carys glanced at Andreus and he could see fear. This time it wasn't of a blade that might kill him, but of a secret being revealed. A secret that would lead people to ask questions.

"I taught her," he said, straightening his shoulders as if unconcerned that someone tried to put a blade in his back. "She used to watch me practice throwing and asked to learn. Since Father didn't think girls belonged fighting with steel, we practiced in my rooms."

"Andreus lost a lot of pillows and more than a few vases and mirrors," Carys said.

"You must be quite a teacher, Prince Andreus." Captain Monteros smiled. "Once the Trials of Virtuous Succession are over, I would be honored if you would come demonstrate your style to the guard trainers. Our guardsmen would benefit from your tutelage."

"Of course," he gulped. Trapped by his own lie.

Trumpets blared. Chief Elder Cestrum stood on the center platform, waiting for the crowd to settle down. Standing just behind him was Elder Jacobs with his black falcon perched on his gloved fist and most of the other Elders. Elder Ulrich, however, was standing far to the side in what looked to be an intense discussion with Lord Garret.

After a moment, Elder Cestrum spoke. "I am certain I speak for all of us when I say that I am relieved Prince Andreus is unharmed after this dramatic footrace. Captain Monteros has verified the would-be assassin is dead. The guard is watching for anyone else who might be so brazen as to hurt our Prince or Princess, and I promise all of you that we will hunt down any who may have plotted with this attacker and the Kingdom of Adderton to once again strike at the very heart of our kingdom. They *will* pay for their actions."

A swell of approval rang through the tournament grounds. As Elder Cestrum waited for the sounds to abate, Andreus noticed his sister slide the stilettos into slits on either side of her mud-stained dress. She had never mentioned that she carried the stilettos with her. And she certainly didn't say they were on her person today.

The Tears of Midnight, and this. Two secrets now she had kept from him.

"The next trial," Elder Cestrum announced, "will be held later tonight in the castle. Prince Andreus and Princess Carys will entertain the court, the visiting dignitaries, and winners from today's tournament at a ball."

He saw Carys stiffen. She hated the public pageantry of balls where her every word and gesture were judged. It was at the last ball two years ago that everyone had become aware of her need for their mother's drink.

This next trial was designed to give Andreus the clear advantage.

"But before we can move on to the next trial, we must complete this one," Carys pointed out. "A winner has not been chosen."

Elder Cestrum scowled. "Quite right." He cleared his throat. "I ask the audience once again to pledge support to the successor they believe won."

Andreus straightened his shoulders as Elder Cestrum called his name, grateful for the guard standing close in case any other attack came.

Yellow banners waved for him. People shouted his name. But perhaps not quite as loudly. They must be more subdued because of the assassination attempt. He had almost died. He could appreciate that.

"And who here at this tournament supports Princess Carys for her efforts in the final event?"

The words were barely out of Elder Cestrum's mouth when the crowd roared. Strips of blue fabric were hoisted into the sky. People stomped and waved to Carys, whose mud-streaked face looked pale as she turned in a circle while the tournament spectators chanted her name softly, then louder.

His sister hadn't won the race, but she'd won the event by saving his life.

So he did the only thing he could do. He applauded, too.

He forced himself to smile and to praise his sister's skill, but he couldn't help the spark of resentment that flared.

He was supposed to be ahead three to nothing on the enormous scoring board above the steps leading to the entrance of the castle. Instead, there were two yellow pegs in the board that had room for ten pegs from one side to the other. Beneath his two points was one peg painted bright blue. For Carys.

When he arrived at the white steps that led to the castle, Andreus handed his horse's reins to a groom and hurried over to help Imogen climb off her horse.

"Your Highness." She looked over her shoulder then back at Andreus with eyes filled with warning. Behind her Elder Jacobs stood next to his horse with the hooded falcon on his arm, waiting to dismount. "I failed you. I should have seen the danger. After Micah's death, my visions have been blocked by my sorrow. I promise that I will not fail you again."

She curtsied deeply. He reached down, took her hand to help her up, and felt her squeeze his fingers tightly.

"I have news. I will come to your rooms as soon as I can," she whispered as she rose. Then she turned, gathered her skirts, and hurried off into the crowd. When he lost sight of her, Andreus headed up the steps. While there were guards all around, he would feel better when he was inside the castle walls.

His would-be assassin could have been part of the same plot that killed his brother and father. If the man had succeeded—

"Prince Andreus," a voice yelled from up above. "Prince Andreus, you're okay."

Max. Andreus looked up and saw the boy barreling down the steps toward him. A guard stepped in front of Andreus and put a hand on his sword.

"It's all right. I know him," Andreus said as the sweaty, panting boy gave the guard a steely-eyed look and then bolted to Andreus's side.

"They're saying someone tried to kill you," Max said, eyes wide with worry. "I heard that you were winning all the events at the tournament and that you even knocked the Princess into the mud and then when you were running the footrace a man tried to kill you just like someone killed King Ulron and Prince Micah."

Clearly news of what happened at the tournament had run ahead of his return.

"But they failed, Max, and in doing so revealed themselves. Now the castle guard will be on high alert. Whoever would wish me harm, it seems, has lost their chance." Andreus put his hand on the boy's shoulder and urged him to walk up to the castle where they could speak without half the court trying to listen in. But as confident as he sounded, he couldn't help looking at everyone he passed as they reached the top of the steps and headed through the castle's arching entrance. Could any of his subjects have something to do with the man with the knife? Were they plotting his death?

"Sebastian said that Princess Carys pulled swords out of thin air and saved your life," Max reported. "But I told him that wasn't possible because no one can make a sword come out of the air. Not even Lady Imogen."

"No one can pull weapons out of thin air," Andreus confirmed as he veered away from several castle workers who were glancing in his direction. "But someone *can* pull stilettos out of hidden pockets and kill someone by throwing them with a great deal of skill. Which is what Princess Carys did to save my life."

"Wow." Max stopped walking, put his hands on his hips, and cocked his head to the side. "My sister Jinna could hit a rat with a rock at fifteen paces. I wonder if she could learn to do it with a knife."

The sad, wistful sound that crept into Max's voice as he spoke about the sister he hadn't seen in a year struck Andreus. Max knew that even if he saw his older sister again, their parents wouldn't want her to speak to him. They believed he was cursed.

"Maybe someday you'll find out," he said to Max.

Then Andreus allowed himself another thought. Maybe if things worked out the way he and Carys planned, Max's parents would be happy to have a son who had the ear of the King. Maybe they would welcome him back with open arms. He glanced down at the boy. "Isn't there something you should be doing instead of talking to me?"

"I was helping carry water to the Hall of Virtues for the fountains they built for the ball, but after I spilled a bunch on Mistress Violet, she screamed at me to get out of her sight so I came to find you."

"Well, I'm pretty sure there is something else you can do to help out." As fond as he was of Max, Andreus didn't want him hanging around when Imogen arrived. Max was too curious and talkative.

And Imogen's position was perilous. By short-circuiting the Council's plan to replace the ruling family with another, she may as well have drawn a target on her own back. Andreus would do nothing to further draw the ire of the Council. The idea of losing Imogen when she had finally admitted she was his was unthinkable. Andreus would not take the risk.

Max scrunched up his face with concentration. "I guess I could bring water to the Princess' rooms. Although someone probably already did that. Ladies don't like being dirty and she was really dirty after the tournament. She looked unhappy, but the lord walking with her into the castle didn't seem to mind."

Lord? Carys had done her best to reach the castle before anyone else. "What lord was walking with the Princess?"

"I don't know his name," Max said. "But he looked like a devil."

"A devil?"

"I know you said devils aren't real, but I saw a picture once and the huge man's black cape and red hair looked a lot like it. Devils are the doom."

Devils certainly were the doom. But so was the only man Andreus could think of who had red hair and might be hurrying after Carys.

Garret.

Carys used to be fascinated by Micah's best friend. After that last ball, Garret had stayed nearby her chamber. When she finally woke, he stormed into her bedroom to tell her how stupid she'd been. Andreus had tried to get Garret to leave, but he'd pushed Andreus away and shook Carys hard, telling her she had no right to throw away her future. Carys had slapped him. Because she was shaking and weak from the Tears of Midnight wearing off, the strike had little force behind it. Garret had actually laughed at her, and when she pulled away from his grasp, he didn't go to assist her when she fell backward onto her cushions.

"You are too important to throw your life away, Carys," Garret had said, standing over her. "Your father and Micah might be blind, but I understand the person you are meant to be. Don't disappoint me." Then Garret turned to Andreus. "I will hold you responsible if she ends up like this again. And you will not like the consequences."

Andreus had put his hand on the hilt of his sword, but before he could draw it, Garret turned on his heel and left. Even though Garret loomed over half a foot taller and weighed a good six stones or so more, Andreus would have welcomed the opportunity to duel his brother's best friend. He'd always despised him. His sister said it was jealousy that fueled his dislike. And perhaps she was right. Their father had treated Garret as though he were better than Andreus and made Andreus watch when Micah and Garret sparred on the training field.

Jealousy, Carys told him, had always made him overreact.

Perhaps that was why he felt the same need to pummel Garret now. Why was he here in the castle? The Council of Elders wanted to put him on the throne instead of Andreus. Was he measuring for new draperies, certain that all would end the way the Council intended?

Maybe Garret was behind the tournament attack. Eliminating Andreus would put him one step closer to the throne. And if Garret could convince Carys to marry him, the entire kingdom wouldn't just accept his authority, they would celebrate it.

"Max! Before you go, did you hear anything that the devil-looking lord said to my sister?" he asked.

Max shook his head. "The Princess was walking really fast and the devil man was calling for her to wait. But she didn't. She went inside the castle. I didn't see him after that."

Good for Carys. She always possessed a will of iron.

But that will was straining, Andreus thought.

The Tears . . .

"Instead of helping with the ball," he said to Max, "how about you help me with something instead?"

The boy's eyes lit up. "Do I get to work with the windmills?"

"No." He'd forgotten that he needed to check in with the Masters to find out if they'd learned anything new about the sabotage. "It's not the lights. I'd like you to find Lord Garret—the devil—" he said at Max's blank look. "Once you find him, I want you to follow him for as long as you can without drawing his attention. Then let me know where he went and who he talked to and whether he spoke to my sister."

"You want me to be . . . a spy, Prince Andreus?"

Andreus winced at Max's enthusiasm. The stakes in this game were higher than the boy could fully comprehend. "What I want you to be is careful. Stay out of sight and make sure you have something in your hands—an errand you will say you are running if anyone questions you. If you think for a second anyone is watching you and wondering why you're hanging around, act as though you got lost in the castle and get away from there. These are dangerous times, Max. I don't want anything to happen to you. So, if you don't want to do this, I will understand."

"Will this help you win the Trials and become King?"

"I think so."

"Then I want to do this. Your sister is good with throwing stuff, but you should be King. And I won't get caught. I promise."

"See that you don't," he said, then told Max to come to his rooms as soon as he learned anything. Leaning down, Andreus pulled the boy close. Max leaned into him for a moment then started to wriggle and Andreus let him go. With a flash of a smile, Max bolted off to play spy.

Sending Max to trace Garret's moves was risky, but Andreus knew nobles rarely noticed servants going about their work. Even if Max was spotted, Garret would most likely assume the boy was avoiding work and shoo him back to the Hall of Virtues to help with the ball preparations.

The ball.

Andreus looked up at the sun that was no longer shining as brightly. They only had a few hours before night arrived and with it the ball that the Council of Elders would somehow turn into a trial. As much as he wanted to check on the lights, Andreus knew he had to prepare. Winning the Trials had to be his first priority. The sooner they were over, the sooner he would be King and be able to get to the bottom of whoever was responsible for the damage to the wind power, track down anyone else involved in today's assassination attempt, and see to it that he and Imogen were never threatened by the Council of Elders or anyone else ever again.

Andreus headed for his rooms. For most of his life he'd been worried about dying, but it had always been the curse that made him fear his own mortality. Now . . . he had no choice but to compete. No choice but to keep trying to win no matter who might want to kill him in the course of the Trials.

His valet had a bath waiting for him when he arrived. Andreus instructed the man to put out clothing for that night while he walked to a chest next to the fireplace and pulled out a recently sharpened dagger. Placing it on the edge of the tub of water, Andreus dismissed the valet to bathe and dress and wait for Imogen on his own.

A knock at the door came when he was starting to dry himself off. Wrapping a towel around his hips, he yelled for whoever it was to enter and closed his hand over the knife.

Imogen slipped into the room, closed the door, then looked down at the floor instead of at him. Her embarrassment at catching him undressed charmed him even as her worried expression filled him with dread.

Crossing the room, he put his hands on Imogen's shoulders and asked, "Are you all right?"

She nodded, then looked up into his eyes. "All of Eden could have lost you. I could have lost you." She stepped into his arms and pressed her hands against his wet back.

"I'm fine. I'm right here with you." He tipped her face up and pressed his lips against hers—first gently, then more insistently as the feel of her against his skin lit a fire in him. Nothing else mattered but the way she made him feel—like he was already a king. Like there was nothing he couldn't do as long as he had her.

"We cannot, Andreus. We have no time."

He didn't need time. He just needed her.

"Andreus. My prince," she panted then shifted back so there was space between her body and his while still keeping her warm hand on his chest. "The ball will start soon. There are things I have learned and you must know. I came upon Elder Ulrich speaking with Captain Monteros. They were speaking about the knife the man used to try and kill you."

"What about the knife?" he asked.

"It had a maker's mark on it."

Andreus didn't see why that was such a big deal. All of the blacksmiths in Garden City had a mark they used to identify their work. Adderton metal workers would follow the same custom. "That should make it easier to track down where the attacker came from."

"That's the problem. They know the mark and where it is from." She shivered and looked up at him with worry bright in her eyes. "It was made by the blacksmith here at the Palace of Winds. The attacker was not sent by the King of Adderton."

The words took his breath.

Was the assassin from here? From Eden Castle—his home? Did someone in the court wish him dead?

"Do they know anything about the attacker other than where his knife was made?" he asked, pulling away from Imogen so she didn't see the fear that shivered up his back.

When Imogen didn't speak, he turned back. "Imogen? Is there something else I should know?"

"Captain Monteros isn't sure whether the rumor he's heard is correct. He is not certain . . . "

"About what? Tell me."

"No one from Garden City recognized the attacker, but one of the guards says he remembers seeing the man speaking to someone near the tournament grounds fence during the first trial. A woman. The guard recognized her as someone who comes often to the castle with her father to make dresses for the ladies of the court."

A girl who made dresses for the court. A memory tugged at him, of a dark-haired girl's tear-streaked face and his sister's smile when she played with the girl and the irritation he felt when he realized his sister cared for the girl almost as much as she did for him.

"According to the guard, the girl gave the assassin the knife. They are searching for her now and . . . " She stopped and shook her head.

"What?" he asked. "What else are you not telling me?"

"Elder Ulrich said two guards accompanied someone from the castle to the girl's shop in the city just a few days ago." Imogen ran her hand down his chest and stepped closer to him as she looked up into his eyes. "That person was Princess Carys. Your sister."

13

"Princess . . . "

Garret's voice chased her into the castle, but Carys didn't stop walking. Servants moved to the side and dropped into curtsies as she passed. Many couldn't hide their surprise at her appearance. She wanted to put them in their place for not remembering that she was a princess and they were supposed to show respect. She wanted to slap them for their wide eyes and snickers and their horror at the fact she'd killed a man right out in the open.

But there hadn't been horror, had there? Not from the crowd. After she'd slain the would-be assassin they'd cheered her name. Carys had won a point that she was never meant to win—and that made this all worse.

Now the Trials would go longer. And the future she ached for, one away from this castle where she could finally find peace, was a tiny bit further out of reach. She needed to be smarter and faster if she wanted to finally get away from the scheming and thirst for the power that came with the throne. She shivered. Her body felt too heavy and too cold to think.

She needed the Tears. They would help her focus. She had to get to her rooms.

The attacker.

The stilettos.

Her brother's shocked expression.

The man lying dead on the dirt-packed ground—dead by her hand.

The cheers and the gasps of the people.

The way Captain Monteros looked at her as if understanding she had a reason for not only learning to wield the stilettos, but to hide her skill.

All of it jumbled together amidst the overwhelming *need*. The bottle was in her pocket. She just had to be alone.

Her breathing became ragged as she attempted to outpace the two guard members, including the one who had accompanied her to the North Tower, trailing behind her. Watching her.

In the castle, there were too many servants, too many guests in the halls for her to brave pulling the red bottle from the pocket of her cloak.

One sip.

Only one terrible, blissful drink.

That would be enough. It would.

She shivered in her cloak, feeling as though the chill of the wind outside was traveling through the halls with her as she headed up the stairs. When she got halfway, she stopped and listened to make sure there were no footfalls from above or below.

Nothing. Only the beating of her heart as she pulled the red bottle out of her pocket and uncorked it.

She took a small drink. The bitter taste made her wince. One more swallow, just in case the amount she had just consumed wasn't enough to pull her body and mind back from the heavy, sweating, fear-filled state that had been creeping up on her since the blades left her hands and everyone saw her secret. They would wonder why she had special pockets to store weapons. They would want to know what a princess living in a castle surrounded by the castle guard was so fearful of. They would ask questions and in learning her secrets they might learn her brother's and she would have failed at the one thing that had purpose in her life.

She started to tilt the bottle again. Just a little more. It would make it easier to hide the secrets. It would make her better at helping her brother.

No.

Carys forced herself to pull the bottle away from her lips and put the stopper in the bottle's throat before shoving it deep in the folds of her cloak. What she took would be enough to get her through the ball. She paused a moment, her back against the stone castle wall. Already she felt lighter. The throbbing in her head was clearing.

Ignoring the guard posted at her rooms, Carys shut the door behind her and wished she didn't have to go out of it again today. But she did. And she had to be ready for whatever came. Andreus was counting on her.

Juliette hurried to greet her. If her maid was shocked by the stilettos Carys pulled out of her pockets before she allowed Juliette to assist her in removing her muddy clothes, she didn't show it.

"I have a rose oil bath waiting for you, Your Highness, and Miss Larkin delivered several items along with your dress for the ball."

"Larkin was here?" Carys had ordered her to leave the city.

"Yes, Your Highness. Not long ago. She was wearing the dress of a noble lady. When I asked her what was wrong, she told me to tell you that she would be waiting after the ball at the place that you spoke of with her father—and that until you speak not to trust the stars. I couldn't make sense of it. Do you think she's gone mad with the same illness that struck the Queen?"

Carys felt her pulse jump. Larkin wasn't crazy. She had a warning for Carys. Something that she had to tell her in person. A warning about the person who looked at the stars—the seer Imogen.

They would meet in the stables. After Carys knew what the problem was, she would fix it.

The warmth of the Tears swept over her and all of her muscles seemed to melt at once. Carys allowed Juliette to wash the mud from her hair and her body before answering a knock at the door and receiving a message from one of the Council pages.

"The Council of Elders will send an escort for you in two hours, Your Highness, who will bring you to the Hall of Virtues."

Two hours. Just two hours before the next trial. "Did you see Lord Garret of Bisog in the hall?" she asked as Juliette helped her into a red silk robe. He had seemed insistent on talking to her, and it wasn't typical of Garret to be dissuaded so quickly from something he was interested in. Perhaps he had changed since his time away from Garden City, but Carys doubted that.

"I heard several mention Lord Garret's return to the Palace of Winds, Your Highness, but I have not seen him."

So he was waiting for another time to corner her. She would have to be ready when he did. Had the attempt on Andreus's life today succeeded, it would have put Garret one step closer to the throne—which was part of Elder Cestrum and the Council's plan. But was it Garret's? Could he or his uncle have been behind today's attack?

She hoped not. But there were too many sinister occurrences

in the castle for her to dismiss the idea that this was the case. The sabotaged power lines. The death of her father and brother. The poisoning of the only guards who knew what had really happened on the King and Prince's trip back to Garden City. Carys was certain some if not all of the people behind these events would be in the Hall of Virtues tonight, smiling and dancing and waiting to stab her or Andreus, literally, in the back. She had to learn who posed the greatest threat and what they wanted. Andreus would take the throne, but that wouldn't remove those who wished to cause them harm. Power was a prize too many wanted and would do almost anything to have.

Normally, Carys cared little for the primping ladies like her mother enjoyed before public audiences. As long as her hair was brushed and the dress Juliette selected didn't make her feel like she was wrapped in a tourniquet, Carys deemed her appearance acceptable. But today she knew it was imperative the Council of Elders believe she was making a true effort to win the Trials and the crown. Otherwise they might think about her knife throwing and wonder why it was she had no skill with a bow. After all, aim was all in both of those pursuits. The Council had to believe this contest was real. She had counted ten pegs across on the tally board that hung on the castle walls facing the city. Her brother needed to gain eight more without raising suspicion over the Trials' legitimacy. Which meant letting Juliette brush her hair until it shone, then sitting for what felt like forever as her maid twisted and reworked the styling before weaving diamond-, citrine-, and sapphire-jeweled pins into the intricate braids and curls.

Finally, Juliette declared her hair perfect and went to the wardrobe to pull out the dress Larkin had delivered for tonight. It was silvery blue and nothing like the ones her mother liked Carys to wear. When the light hit the fabric, it glowed like moonlight. And when Juliette fastened the gown and Carys turned toward the mirror and examined how she looked in the dress with the deeply scooped neckline, flowing sleeves, and shimmering skirt. Tears pricked her eyes. In Larkin's hands, she was as close to beautiful as she would ever be. She wished she could give Larkin a farewell gift to match this one.

Thanking her maid, Carys asked Juliette to stop by the Queen's quarters to check on how she was doing. Once Juliette was gone, Carys carefully cleaned her stilettos until they glistened like the jewels in her hair, and then slid the silver blades into the sheaths hidden in the seams of her dress. The weight of the stilettos against her thighs was reassuring as she paced the room, waiting for the escort the Council of Elders would send. Normally, Carys would have defied their wishes, but they were in control of the Trials and her brother and her fate. Openly challenging them was a bad idea.

Waiting was something Carys was bad at, and in the isolation of her rooms with only the rustle of her dress and the anxiety building inside her to keep her company, the minutes dragged by. The red bottle she'd stashed under one of the pillows on the settee called to her. She didn't need another dose. Her hands were steady and her mind remained clear. Still, she couldn't help pulling the bottle out from where she had hidden it and turning it over in her hands.

She pulled the stopper out of the bottle then put it back in a dozen times as need warred with common sense. If given another minute, need might have won, but a knock at the door had Carys sliding the bottle back into hiding before opening the door to find Garret waiting on the other side.

His red mane of hair looked almost like licks of fire against the black of his tunic. His nose looked more crooked than it had before. He had fought hard since he had left the Palace of Winds, and knowing Garret's power, she was sure he had won. His eyes met hers and the intensity of the gaze and the strength of his large shoulders and arms pulled at the girl who longed for someone to shield her—a girl she never had been allowed to be.

Garret bowed. "I have been sent by my uncle to act as your escort, Your Highness. I hope you don't mind."

She should have known Garret would be the one Elder Cestrum sent to find her. The fact that she hadn't immediately seen that possibility set her on edge. "Should I mind?" she asked as she closed her door behind her.

"I shouldn't think so," Garret said, holding out his arm.

She smiled, then turned and headed down the hallway toward the steps, leaving Garret to catch up. Once he did, he quietly said, "There are a great number of people who have done you harm over the years, Your Highness. I have never wanted to be one of them."

"Is it any wonder I find that hard to believe, Lord Garret?" she asked, glancing at him. "Plotting with your uncle to seize the throne from my family would do me considerable harm."

"I had nothing to do with my uncle's scheme."

"Of course not." She laughed. "It was loyalty to your fallen king that made you ride your horse into the ground to get here so quickly."

"It was loyalty to you." Garret reached out and grabbed her arm. She pulled back, but he held fast and stepped close as he said, "I am not your enemy, Your Highness. You are the reason I left the Palace of Winds in the first place, and whether you choose to believe it or not, you are the reason I have returned."

The sound of stringed instruments drifted down the hallway. The ball was beginning. "If you think I will let you use me in order to climb the steps to the throne, you are sadly mistaken, Lord Garret."

"You will find, Your Highness, that I am the only person in Eden who has no interest in using you for personal gain." He tightened his grip on her arm. "Unlike my uncle and your father and Micah, I understand how important you are."

"Because I might become Queen."

Garret studied her for several heartbeats. "You still don't know you are so much more."

He let go of her arm, but she could still feel the heat of his touch as he stepped back and began walking down the hallway. "The ball will be starting and your guests are waiting, Your Highness. I need to deliver you safely to the Hall of Virtues."

She hurried to catch up with him and spotted her brother in the antechamber that the royal family used during formal occasions to wait for their entrance to the Hall.

"I must leave you here," Garret said, not crossing the threshold of the antechamber. "May the winds guide you until we speak again, Princess."

With a bow he turned on his heel and disappeared out the door.

Once she was certain Garret had truly gone, she turned to her brother. Andreus was eyeing her with suspicion. "Lord Garret was sent by his uncle to escort me here. He is trying to make me believe he has no interest in the throne."

"And do you believe it?"

"Of course not," she said. But there had been something in the way that he spoke that made her wonder if there was more to his purpose. "But there might be value in making him think I do."

Father always said to keep your friends close and your enemies even closer, mainly so that they couldn't see the dagger until it slid into their gut. "It couldn't hurt for *you* to appear to be friendly with him as well," she suggested. "Elder Cestrum might start questioning whether Garret has changed allegiances, and sowing uncertainty in the Council can only help us get through these Trials and secure the throne."

"You mean help me secure the throne."

"Of course." Carys frowned at the way Andreus stood looking at her. His posture was stiff, formal. She sensed doubt. "Do you think I have changed my mind about wanting you on the throne? Andreus, it's not my fault you didn't get all three points today. I had to defend you."

"I know," he said, taking her hand. "I'm sorry. If it weren't for you I wouldn't have to worry about the Trials or the throne. I'd be in my grave instead. I'm having a hard time thinking about that or the man who . . . tried to kill me."

"But he didn't kill you," Carys said, squeezing his hand. "And tonight you will charm everyone at the ball and win whatever contest we are given." He looked handsome in his gold-and-black doublet. With his shining dark hair and sword at his side, he looked as if he stepped out of a storyteller's tale.

"You're right," he said with a small smile. "I have to concentrate on tonight. We both do." He dropped her hand and stepped back to look at her. "You certainly look lovely. That dress isn't your typical style. Who made it?"

She glanced down at the dress and back at her brother, who was eyeing her with an intensity that made her shiver. "Why do you ask?" The only interest her brother ever displayed in women's attire was assessing how quickly he could get ladies out of it.

"I'm sure the seamstress will be in great demand after tonight. I am certain people will want to seek her out. I might even want to have a conversation with her myself."

Her brother's words set her on edge. "Andreus, what's wrong?"

"Nothing."

"I know you." Almost as well as she knew herself. "There is something bothering you. If it is Lord Garret, I promise you—"

Trumpets blared. A page appeared in the doorway and bowed. "The Council of Elders has asked me to bid Your Highnesses to join them in the Hall of Virtues."

"Very well," her brother said, offering Carys his arm. "Shall we?"

Her stomach tightened at Andreus's tense smile as she placed her hand on his arm and walked with him at the measured pace their mother long ago taught them was appropriate for ceremonies. They crossed through the corridor and reached the white stone arch and massive gold doors that led to the Palace of Winds' throne room. The trumpets sounded again, the guards pushed open the doors, and Carys and her brother started forward.

Every face turned toward them and everything went silent as she and Andreus strode into the room. They'd walked this path together at formal events dozens of times in their lives. Always they had entered before their brother Micah and their mother and father— side by side—together. Then they had been the opening gambit. The ones who announced more important, more powerful members of the family were on the way. The court used to pause for them before they continued whatever they were doing. Now everyone was completely still as they once again walked shoulder to shoulder into the spectacularly lit hall.

Orbs of colored lights were everywhere. Hanging from the ceiling. Attached to the pillars. On the wall behind the dais. And the throne was lit in a way that made it appear as though it glowed with the power of the sun. Carys glanced at her brother. His eyes stared at the throne as if mesmerized by its beauty.

She couldn't remember seeing the throne ever look so beautiful—perhaps because she was used to seeing her father sitting there. Maybe that was what made Andreus watch it with such intensity now. Maybe he too was feeling the pull of memories that clawed at her heart.

Pushing away the mental picture of her father, Carys looked around the Hall as Andreus led her through the crowd to the dais. A group of entertainers stood off to the left. Some held musical instruments. Others were carrying flaming torches they would no doubt juggle and perhaps swallow to the delight of the nobles. But now, all was still. The hundreds in attendance were dressed in the finest silks of every color of the rainbow. Carys was used to seeing judgment in their eyes. Never good enough. Never beautiful enough. Never adhering to tradition in the way they believed she should.

They judged her for her lack of care in their frivolous pageantry. And she judged them right back for their investment in it.

Now, though. Now, she sensed something different.

Each member of the court wore bands of colored fabric, tied around their arms, or wrists, or pinned to their lapels.

Yellow strips of silk, as far as she could see. Yellow for Andreus.

But . . . there were also blue bands. More than those of her brother's castoffs who had joined her on the viewing stand. More than Lord Errik, who was standing not far from the Council of Elders at the front of the Hall. A strip of light blue set off against the dark blue velvet of his tunic. For every two yellow bands, there was at least one of hers. In this room where she had so often been condemned for her behavior, the show of approval cut through her resentment and warmed her.

When they reached the front of the Hall and turned to face the crowd, she could see the tightening around her brother's mouth. His eyes met hers for a moment, and even through the haze of the Tears of Midnight she felt the accusation burning through her.

Trumpets began a new fanfare and Elder Cestrum stepped forward to address the crowd. "The Council of Elders and Prince Andreus and Princess Carys welcome you to this ball and the second of the Trials of Virtuous Succession. We thought it was fitting to hold the trial for temperance here, in the place where it is most needed. Strong monarchs must have control over their actions, thoughts, and feelings—especially when seated on the Throne of Light with the fate of our kingdom in their hands. Now the Council will bear witness to the actions of Prince Andreus and Princess Carys during this evening of celebration. The successor who demonstrates the best control over his or her actions will be awarded with a point on the scoring board."

Elder Cestrum turned to Carys and Andreus and smiled. "Let the festivities begin."

With that, the musicians began to play and an acrobat bent forward, performed a handstand, and then began walking across the white stone floor on his hands.

"That's the contest?" Carys asked. "Temperance. How do you judge that?"

Elder Cestrum glanced over to where Garret stood not far from the steps leading to the throne, where he was speaking with Elder

Ulrich. When he turned back to Carys, his smile grew even broader. "Any way we wish to, Your Highnesses."

"I am certain the Council will not be disappointed with me, Elder Cestrum," Andreus said, giving his sister a look. "Now, if you will excuse me, I see Lady Lillian. She must be heartbroken by Mother's illness. Perhaps a dance will raise her spirits."

Andreus crossed the room to the woman in question. Their mother's friend put her hand to her chest and looked ready to cry when Andreus offered his arm and escorted her onto the floor. Soon they were gliding around the center of the Hall with what seemed to be all of the court nodding in approval.

When the dance was finished, Andreus gave the woman a charming smile and then asked another, older member of the court, instead of the younger girls he typically favored, to dance. *Tempering* his behavior, Carys thought. Well, that gave her an idea.

Carys strolled into the crowd that she would normally avoid and spotted three of the girls who had been on her viewing platform earlier today. All of them had bands of blue on their arms and several had their hair, two of brunette and one of bright red, tied back at the neck in the simple style Carys had worn during the tournament instead of the elaborate twists and turns those in the court normally wore.

"Princess Carys," the redhead stammered as she and the others performed hasty curtsies. "Is there something we can do for you?"

The nervous glances the girls exchanged made Carys aware once again of how out of place she was in court. All three of these girls had grown up here at the castle. Carys had known them all of their lives and still they viewed her as a stranger. Well, that was going to change now. Smiling, Carys said, "I was hoping you might be willing to show me how to have fun at one of these things. I fear I'm out of practice."

The redhead looked too stunned to speak, but the taller of the brunettes—Carys thought her name was Lady Shelby—smiled and said, "We'd be honored, Your Highness. How about we start with the entertainers? I'm not sure if they throw knives as well as you do, but we can ask them to try."

Carys laughed and suddenly the other girls lost their worried expressions and included her in their chatter as they wove through the room to where half-dressed acrobats were walking on their hands and doing flips on the hard, stone floor.

When Carys admired one performer's skill aloud, the other girls rushed to praise him as well.

"Anyone can do that. It's not that special," a man called.

Carys glanced around for the source of the words and smiled when she spotted a young man holding a goblet of wine, standing with a bunch of his friends.

"I could easily walk on my hands," he said to his laughing companions.

Carys turned to the girls. "I'll be right back."

She made her way over to the young man.

"Excuse me," Carys said, "What is your name?"

"I'm Lord Trevlayn, Your Highness," he said with a grin that told her the drink in his hand wasn't the first he'd had. "At your service."

"I couldn't help but overhear you say that you can walk on your hands. Is that true?"

"Well, I think so, Your Highness. I mean—"

"Excellent! We would all like to see you show your skill. And any who succeed will be rewarded with a dance with one of my ladies."

The blond lord's friends slapped him on the back. One took his drink and the acrobats that had been performing stepped to the side to allow the braggart a chance to display his abilities. Left with no other option, the lord put his hands on the floor, hesitantly kicked his feet up, and fell back to the ground with a thud. His friends burst into howls of laughter. The young lord pushed himself up off the floor, scowling, and started to stalk off the floor. But one of the girls with Carys, a petite, curvy brunette, stepped forward and said, "I believe you can do it, Lord Trevlayn."

Carys smiled at the earnestness in the girl's face. Clearly, she had interest in Lord Trevlayn beyond this moment. Which made Carys like the drunken fool a bit more. "Yes, Lord Trevlayn. You didn't give it your best effort," Carys agreed. "Try in earnest and I believe I can get Lady Michaela to award you with a dance."

Lord Trevlayn puffed out his chest, wiped his hands on his legs, and gave it another try. Everyone gathered around the entertainers cheered as his feet reached toward the ceiling, hung there for a moment, and then suddenly toppled over. Others in the ballroom began to wander over as Lord Trevlayn's friends decided to try the feat. Bets broke out on the sidelines among some of the younger lords and ladies as the boys kicked up their feet and sprawled on the floor, spilling drinks and eliciting shrieks and laughter from the gathered ladies. The older members of the court looked outraged. Finally, the shortest of Lord Trevlayn's friends managed several steps on his hands—feet flailing in the air—to great cheers. When he stood upright again, the young ladies batted their eyes at him while his friends snatched goblets off a passing tray to lift in his honor. When they were done toasting him, they all turned to Carys and lifted their glasses again.

"To Princess Carys and the Throne of Light."

They offered her a glass, from which she took a polite sip, as they all turned toward the throne and held their glasses aloft. Her head was spinning from the audacity of her actions—disrupting the formal ball, encouraging the young members of court to break free from their rigid roles. It was the very opposite of temperance. Her sense of triumph at the stern expression she saw on the faces of the older members of the court was fantastic. She spotted Andreus standing with Elder Cestrum and two of Eden's High Lords. When he glanced her way, she waited for him to nod—to acknowledge her efforts to help him—as he always did when she stepped in front of him and took the worst of what this castle had to give.

But the look he gave her was dismissive, and panic flared.

Something had changed between them. Suddenly and dramatically, things had been altered.

But how? And why?

No. Andreus was just *acting* as if he were upset with her. That was their plan all along. He would win the Trials and together they would do what they had to in order to keep him safe and Eden secure.

The young lords and ladies moved through the crowd toward the dancing area. When one of the ladies offered to stay with Carys instead of dancing with the boy she clearly favored, Carys said she would join them on the dance floor soon and headed off to find the perfect partner. Someone who might be willing to continue her show.

She spotted him lounging against a column near the front of the Hall and headed toward him, ignoring several members of the court who tried to catch her attention along the way. Errik straightened and gave a deep bow as she approached.

"Lord Errik," she said with a smile. "Do you by chance like to dance?"

He cocked his head to the side and studied her—his deep blue eyes gleaming in the bright hall. After a moment, he gave her a small smile. "All Trade Masters like to dance. We have to since the Kings and Queens we visit feel obligated to throw balls for us. How about you, Princess Carys. Do you like to dance?"

"I despise dancing," she said with complete honesty. "Perhaps that's why I'm so bad at it."

"Honesty makes an already lovely woman far more beautiful," he said, taking a step toward her. "But I find it hard to believe the Princess of Eden is a terrible dancer."

"Are you calling me a liar, Lord Errik?" she asked.

"No." Lord Errik's dark eyes met hers. "I'm asking you to prove it."

The musicians started a new song and Carys held out her hand in a way a lady would never do to a man. "When you can no longer walk, my lord, I ask you to remember that you have only yourself to blame."

"I consider myself warned, Your Highness," he said as he took her hand and strolled with her through the crowd of nobility and tournament champions, all of whom seemed to be watching her.

Growing up, Carys's free time had been spent running guard maneuvers with Andreus so he could execute them flawlessly the first time during drills. If he only had to do them once, the chance of an attack was less likely. As a result, Carys never danced. She barely knew how. And today, she didn't care.

She laughed as Errik took her in his arms. He was handsome and told her she was beautiful, and if she knocked him over during the dance it would get her and Andreus one step closer to their goal. She would make a fool of herself; she was determined to do so.

The music was fast. Errik's hands were warm and his expression amused as they moved between the other couples on the floor. Several of Carys's new friends smiled at her and Errik as they twirled by. Carys tripped as Errik spun her around and then laughed as he pulled her against his chest to keep her from stumbling into the couple dancing next to them.

"I fear, Highness," he said, "you weren't lying and neither was I. You are lovely."

Her arms felt loose, and the harder she tried to think, the more her thoughts scattered. No doubt the Tears of Midnight were having their effect, flowing through her blood. Or maybe it was the warmth she felt with her hands pressed against Errik's chest, knowing that she should move away and yet having no interest in doing so. Still his words made her frown.

"Do you doubt your appearance, Highness?" Lord Errik's smile vanished. "There are hundreds of people here today who would tell you how lovely you are."

"Nobility never tells the truth to those with more power than they have. It's the unspoken oath they take."

"Then I guess I will be the one person you can count on to tell you the truth about yourself," Errik said, moving into a dance hold again and spinning her gently around the floor.

"Well, you've already said that I am a terrible dancer. Since we've only known each other a matter of hours, I fear there is very little truth you can tell me."

"Oh, I wouldn't say that." He smiled and whirled her around. This time she didn't stumble over her feet as the music grew faster and Errik held her tighter. "After all, I saw the real you at the tournament today. Many of us did, but I might be the only one who will tell you what those of us truly paying attention saw."

Errik slowed their dance and she fought to clear the haze from her mind and focus. "The real me? I fear your truth telling has come to an end."

"If you say so, Your Highness." He spun her as the music came to a stop and executed a bow. When he came up, he met her eyes with his. "But anyone who draws and throws two stilettos accurately enough to kill a man from over fifty paces would have more than enough skill to hit the center of a target with an arrow at half that distance."

"Sheer luck," she said with a shrug as though his words didn't make her heart pound and her hands sweat.

"Perhaps." Lord Errik gently put his hand on her back and guided her off the dance area toward the men juggling torches. The crowd cheered as they tossed their torches to one another and then back again.

Leaning over her shoulder, Lord Errik pointed to the entertainers as if showing something to Carys, but in her ear said, "Once you left the tournament, I walked over to the archery area. A shooter would have to be quite skilled to hit the notches at the edges of the target with precision."

"You give me too much credit, Lord Errik." She forced a laugh as the crowd gasped at the jugglers, who had added more torches to their act and were throwing them back and forth. "You seem to forget that with the final shot I missed the mark altogether."

"Much to the dismay of the flower you skewered. While most people had eyes on the targets, I was watching *you*. *You*, Highness, missed so that Prince Andreus would win."

Her stomach jumped and Carys looked around to make sure no one else heard Errik's damning words.

Easing away from the crowd watching the fire throwers, she said, "Truly, Lord Errik, you give me far too much credit."

"I am giving you more credit than you would like," he said, taking her arm and steering her away from the edge of the dancing area. "Those are two different things." Andreus was speaking with Elder Cestrum, Elder Ulrich, and several High Lords. Elder Ulrich looked her way. He followed her movements with his good eye while in the bright lights of the Hall the white filmy scar across his other eye appeared to glow.

"Unfortunately, I am not the only one who saw what you wished to hide. Others now realize you have secrets, Highness. Some may want to use them—use *you*—to their advantage. Others might want to bury those secrets altogether. I'm sure you realize this is a dangerous game you're playing."

"I'm not playing," she insisted. "And I don't need a man to explain my position to me, Lord Errik."

Errik looked to where Elder Ulrich was still watching both of them. "Unfortunately, no one on your Council of Elders agrees." Errik took her hand and lifted it to his lips. He kept it there for several long heartbeats as he looked into her eyes. The heat of his mouth on her skin made her shiver. Or maybe it was the words that he spoke when he let her hand go. "Be careful of your next steps, Highness. There is more than one game being played in Eden. And unless you win them all, you may find yourself removed from the board."

Without a backward glance, Lord Errik disappeared into the crowd. A moment later Carys heard someone scream.

14

Andreus stood with two of the High Lords and their ladies, but only half listened to the conversation swirling around him as he watched his sister move through the crowd. She was making a fool of herself with the entertainers and the young lords and ladies who normally she studiously avoided.

The rowdy laughter and cheers were certainly *not* a show of temperance. But then he saw one of the girls tie a band of blue onto Lord Trevlayn's arm, and he wondered if Carys's motives were really so clear.

"Your sister looks beautiful tonight, Prince Andreus," Elder Jacobs said softly as he came to stand at Andreus's side.

"Yes, she does," Andreus agreed, even though it was a word he'd never used to describe his twin. But tonight with the jewels in her hair sparkling and her dress glowing in the wind-powered light, Carys commanded attention from men and women alike. Her appearance unsettled him. After the tournament today and Imogen's revelation about the origin of the knife, he realized the one person he thought he knew better than any was really a mystery to him. Carys always told him that they were a team. That she was happy not to have to have secrets between them. That she was content blending into the background with him.

She'd obviously lied.

He studied his sister as she beamed while those surrounding her lifted their glasses and toasted her. He saw the way her eyes turned and stared at the throne sitting empty at the front of the Hall. And he knew Imogen was right. That Carys wanted the throne as much as he did and she was playing a dangerous game in order to get it.

"I don't remember a formal occasion where the Princess had so many friends surrounding her." Elder Jacobs turned his dark, intense eyes on Andreus. "Or a time where you were so interested in hearing from the High Lords about their districts."

Carys always said the Elder of Mulinia—Eden's District of Temperance—reminded her of a serpent. Andreus had never agreed more as the man's words oozed together in an almost hypnotic way. Clearly, he wanted something, but Andreus wasn't sure what that was. He chose his words carefully as he said, "My father and Micah preferred I keep my interest in the running of the kingdom to myself. As for Carys—" Andreus frowned as Carys strolled across the hall toward a man he vaguely recognized from the funeral. "I guess she is taking advantage of their interest in her now that she has a chance to gain the throne." He thought for a moment. "She certainly seemed to like the attention of Lord Garret. I guess she has the Council of Elders to thank for that."

"The Council, Your Highness?"

"It was the Council that ordered Lord Garret to act as her escort to the ball tonight."

Elder Jacobs stared at Andreus for several beats, then said, "I fear you are mistaken, Prince Andreus. The Council as a whole ordered no such thing. If we had, it would have given the appearance of favoring your sister in the Trials."

Andreus seethed. "If Carys were to win the Trials, the Council of Elders could arrange for her to marry Lord Garret. That would help you achieve your goal of putting him on the throne."

"That was Chief Elder Cestrum's goal, Your Highness. My goal is to serve the realm, and Eden is best served when we adhere to the law. When I agreed to support Lord Garret as the next ruler, I believed it was the only option for keeping Eden whole during these troubling times." Elder Jacobs looked around them, then quietly added, "Personally, I was relieved Lady Imogen provided us with another option and have been delighted that you are having such success with the Trials thus far. There are some on the Council who feel the Princess would allow them to gain more power in the kingdom, but you and I both know she is not the ruler this kingdom needs."

"And I am?" Andreus shook his head. "I find that hard to believe after what almost happened in this very hall."

"A mistake," Elder Jacobs admitted. "We all make them. I supported the Chief Elder's choice of successor. You comforted a vulnerable young lady after the tragic loss of her fiancé."

Andreus stiffened. "I don't know what you're talking about."

"Of course you do. You'll find I make it a habit to discover all I can about those I wish to make my enemy . . . or my ally."

"And which one am I?"

"I would have thought that was obvious. Elder Cestrum still wishes to put his nephew on the throne despite his nephew's unexpected reluctance, but I have come to understand the error of that choice and believe that you, Your Highness, have a chance to do great things *if* you have the right people at your side. Your father was at odds with the Elders, but I could convince them to work with you. As representatives of the districts, the Council of Elders wields a great deal of power with the High Lords and the common people. Influence a smart man could use—if he were to win the Trials and become King. Perhaps a smart man could figure out how to tap into that influence even before the Trials' end to guarantee that he wins."

Andreus went still as he studied Elder Jacobs, who was watching the dance floor as though the words he spoke were of little importance. For a second he wished Carys were with him. *She* would be able to untangle everything Elder Jacobs had said, and all that he hadn't. If Elder Jacobs knew about Imogen and their relationship, how much else did he know? Could he know about the curse? Carys would be able to read into the hidden meanings of the words. She'd be able to tell him if she thought the Elder suspected Andreus's affliction and was simply toying with him, or if his offer of the crown and the support of the Council were real.

If they were, the crown would be his no matter what his sister's plan. The Council and the districts they represented would bend knee and follow him without question. He would be a stronger King than his stubborn father was or his intractable brother ever would have been.

He looked at the throne as it gleamed bright as the sun on the dais and heard Imogen's voice playing in his head as she warned him to beware of his twin. Of the desire for power that had taken hold in Carys even as she pretended to be working to hand that power to him.

"Your sister is clever, my prince," Imogen had said while buried in his arms. "She understands that the love of the people holds more power than any crown. By killing the man she sent to attack you, she has gained the support of those who once looked upon her with doubt."

He shook his head, hating that he worried whether what Imogen said was true. "If Carys had wanted to win the throne she could have just let the man kill me. Instead, she killed him."

"And in doing so gained the admiration of everyone watching. Just yesterday they were calling *you* their hero, but now even though she is losing the Trials, the Princess is all they talk about."

The court had spoken about her, too. And all with fascination.

"I am sorry, my prince, but I fear your sister has turned against you. If she knew about us I would say it was jealousy that has caused her to do you harm. After all, she is your twin. She feels she has a claim on your heart. Who knows what other lengths she might go to keep it?"

He didn't want to believe that Carys could be involved in the attack against him, but the more he thought about it, the more he recalled the way she assumed that if she truly competed, she would win the Trials and the throne would belong to her. She wanted the throne, but once he'd objected to her plan for him to help her gain it, she pretended to have no interest.

And then there was Carys's reaction to learning that he had spent the night with the seeress instead of waiting for his sister to return from the North Tower. His sister had acted as though he'd betrayed *her*. But *she* was the one who was guilty of betrayal. She was the one who with her secrets and now her jealousy was intent on harm.

The stilettos, the Tears of Midnight, and Carys's ball gown—and its possible connection to the seamstress Captain Monteros was searching Garden City for—proved louder than words that his sister was skilled at hiding things from him. He had been a fool to take his sister at her word. Imogen's assertions made sense and her worry for him was real. He should have paid attention to the doubt he felt when Carys promised her interest in the crown was only to protect him from his curse.

But he would also be a fool to take Elder Jacobs at his word now. And he was done being anyone's fool.

"After your support of Garret, it would be hard for a smart man to trust you at your word, my lord."

Elder Jacobs smiled. "That is not only true, it is wise. Trust is earned and I would like us to trust one another. I find the virtue of temperance fascinating. I suppose I had no choice since I grew up in Mulinia. But I believe I would be intrigued by the complexity of the virtue even if I had not. So much of temperance is about *not* giving in to one's most passionate emotions and impulses. That sounds so simple, but I find the virtue of temperance to be a double-edged sword. Don't you?"

Andreus waited for the Elder to make himself clear. "Because temperance can cause inaction. It can also cause confusion. You see, it is easy to understand how a person should not give in to emotions like anger, but it is harder to see that temperance applies as well to the desire to forgive—and to gain approval from those around them. Especially if a person is King. Kings cannot give in to their desire for affection when they have been betrayed. That is when strong action is required. A definitive line must be drawn in the sand so people know it cannot be crossed."

"Are you saying you don't believe I can draw that line?"

"Me?" Elder Jacobs shook his head. "No. But there are others on the Council who have . . . concerns."

"What kind of concerns?" Andreus demanded.

"Your lack of enthusiasm for your training with the guard, your willingness to work with commoners on the windmills, and your fondness for the boy who you rescued make many wonder if you are weak. A kingdom this large must be ruled in part by strength—a strength your sister showed at the tournament today. The Council and the kingdom know that she will deal swiftly and permanently with any who seek to injure the kingdom or the crown. I fear by tomorrow the Council will be tailoring the Trials to ensure they can award points to Princess Carys. Unless, of course, you do something to change their minds."

Two lords and their ladies walked over to extend their sympathy to Prince Andreus.

He clenched his fists at his side, but smiled and thanked the nobles for their kind words. Then, he apologized for needing time to confer with the Elder about an important and private matter.

"Of course, Your Highness. Please tell the Queen she is in our thoughts."

He assured them he would even though he knew he wouldn't. As far as he knew his mother was still in a drug-induced stupor. He hoped she would stay that way until he could secure the crown.

If the Council was turning toward Carys, it meant they were once again seeing Andreus as second best.

He wouldn't let them. Not this time.

Once the nobles were out of earshot, he turned back to Elder Jacobs and asked, "Do you have a suggestion as to how I might change those minds? I would be happy to speak to each of the

Council members if that would gain their support."

Elder Jacobs sighed and quietly said, "I fear words will not do much good. You see, many on the Council believe you are not capable of tempering your desire for approval in order to instill fear, which is a tool all effective kings must be willing to command. The court and the commoners alike must know you are capable of punishing those who do you harm or there can be no respect for the crown. Without that respect the kingdom will falter. The Council of Elders is waiting for a demonstration that you can instill fear. I have assured them you will not disappoint. If I am right, the Council will shift their allegiance to you. You will be declared the winner of all the trials, for appearance's sake, and the throne will be yours."

Andreus glanced back at the gold-and-sapphire seat on the dais behind him. Still studying the glistening throne, he heard Elder Jacobs say, "I expect you will not let me or the kingdom down tonight, Your Highness." And with that, Elder Jacobs strolled into the crowd.

As others approached to curry favor and offer their sympathies, Andreus looked around the room for Imogen. She had to be warned that Elder Jacobs was aware of the two of them. Elder Jacobs's words felt like a threat. If Andreus didn't take advantage of the Elder's desire to be an ally and rally the Council to his side, then the Elder had made it known that he had the tools to be a very dangerous enemy.

He would not lose Imogen or the throne that Carys promised would be his, and he fought to bite back his frustration each time a new noble stopped to talk with him as he moved around the Hall searching for the seeress.

"Your sister is not at all acting like your mother would," High

Lady Rivenda sniffed as she looked to where Carys was standing—closer than she should be—to the man she had been dancing with not long ago. "I had heard she had overcome her . . . difficulties. Clearly, not."

"My sister is just feeling the stress of this terrible week, my lady," he said, automatically defending his twin. When he realized what he had done, he changed tactics and offered, "It has been difficult for us all. I guess you can't blame her for resorting to whatever offers comfort."

"She is lucky to have a brother who is so understanding," Lady Rivenda gushed. "I am so sorry for your losses and wish you luck in the Trials. My Lord Wynden and I are rooting for you." She pointed to the yellow jewels she wore and Andreus smiled before extricating himself from the conversation.

Where was Imogen? Her worries about Carys's jealousy pulled at him as he spoke with several other lords and ladies, several of whom wished to introduce him to their daughters. Then he spotted Imogen speaking with Elder Ulrich and he couldn't help but smile. Lady Imogen's gown of rich yellow, a public pledge of her belief in him, made his entire being swell with pride. She was his. Micah might have wanted her, but Imogen loved Andreus. Just as he had loved her from the first. He would do whatever it took to give her the home she always yearned for as a child. If that meant—

A scream scraped over the music and the laughter. Then another.

Reaching for his sword, Andreus looked around for the cause as Captain Monteros and several of the castle guard emerged from the crowd with a screaming young man in tow.

"Leave me go. I just wanted to see what a ball was like. I didn't cause no harm."

The crowd parted and the Council of Elders appeared at the base of the dais in the front of the Hall. Elder Cestrum nodded at Captain Monteros as he grabbed the boy and threw him to the white stone floor. Andreus stepped toward the front of the room and saw his sister appear on the other side. The man she had danced with was at her shoulder as she watched the trembling youth sprawled face down on the ground.

"Excuse me, Elders." Captain Monteros bowed. "My men captured this thief inside the Hall."

"I ain't no thief. I was just told—"

"Silence, boy." Chief Elder Cestrum stepped forward. "This is a serious charge. Captain Monteros, do you have proof this boy was in fact stealing in the Hall of Virtues?"

Captain Monteros nodded to one of the guard members standing behind the protesting youth.

"I saw him," the guard said. "He cut a purse off a lord's belt. That's when I grabbed him."

"I have the purse right here, my lords," Captain Monteros said, holding up a small, black velvet bag. "It belongs to Lord Nigel and proves without a doubt that the boy is a thief."

"I am not!" He pushed himself to his knees. Fear shone from his eyes even as he straightened his shoulders in defiance. It reminded Andreus of Max the first time he woke up in Madame Jillian's quarters and saw a prince standing over him.

The Hall that had been filled with music and laughter seconds ago was silent as they waited while Elder Cestrum and the Council spoke in hushed tones to each other. When they turned back, Elder Cestrum said, "The Council has decided to leave the decision as to the boy's guilt and his punishment in the hands of Prince Andreus and Princess Carys. The successor who pronounces the punishment that we the Council feel serves best will see his or her sentence carried out and will be awarded an additional point. Would Prince Andreus and Princess Carys please step onto the dais?"

Elder Jacobs glanced at Andreus as he moved past the other members of the Council and walked up the four steps to stand next to the Throne of Light. For a moment Andreus could picture his father sitting there, Micah standing at his side. The image was gone as he turned and watched his sister reach the top of the dais. Her eyes were filled with concern as she looked down at those on the floor of the Hall.

"Princess Carys." Elder Cestrum pointed with a black iron finger at the boy kneeling on the ground. "This boy has been accused of stealing the purse of a High Lord in the Hall of Virtues. What punishment would you command be carried out to see that he and all others in the realm understand the severity of this crime?"

Carys looked at Andreus. Then she stepped down from the dais and crossed to the boy on the ground with his defiantly raised chin and terrified eyes.

"What is your name?" she asked.

It took the boy two tries to say, "My name is Varn, Your Highness."

Carys cocked her head to the side and calmly asked, "How did you come to be in the Hall of Virtues tonight, Varn?"

The controlled way his sister spoke was the essence of temperance. Concerned, Andreus glanced at the Council, who were watching Carys intently as the boy on the white stone floor explained, "A man said there would be food here. He told me I could come. So, I did because I was hungry, Your Highness."

Andreus could see some in the crowd shift with impatience, but there were others who clearly believed the boy's simple declaration and felt sorry for him.

Carys frowned and whirled toward Captain Monteros, her voice louder as she demanded, "Captain, how is it this boy was allowed into the castle, let alone the Hall of Virtues?"

Captain Monteros stared at Carys. "He must have snuck past the guards at the gate, Your Highness, and—"

"How many guards did you post at the entrance?"

"Dozens, Your Highness."

"And they all are aware that my brother, their prince, was attacked by an assassin on the tournament grounds?"

"Of course, Your Highness."

"And yet this boy, who looks as if he hasn't bathed in weeks and hasn't eaten a real meal in at least as long, managed to gain access to the castle, wander dozens of corridors to reach the Hall of Virtues, and venture inside without any of the castle guard seeing him?"

A gasp went through the crowd as the significance of Carys's words became apparent. Captain Monteros's eyes shifted behind Carys to the Elders.

She didn't wait for his answer. The bottom of her dress rippled and tendrils of hair blew around her face as she spun to face the Council. "If the guards Captain Monteros trained cannot be trusted to keep Varn and others who are uninvited out, how can I trust the word of the one who spoke against this boy tonight?"

"Are you saying the boy is innocent?" Elder Cestrum asked.

The room held their breath as Carys said, "Did I say that, my lord, or are you putting words in my mouth? Perhaps my maid can get you a dress to wear so you can just pretend to be me."

Carys's angry words made everyone in the room mumble—with surprise or disapproval, which Andreus could not tell. The Chief Elder's eyes narrowed. If he wasn't angry with his twin, Andreus would have applauded the insult. As it was, he was glad for the lack of control she was currently displaying. Certainly, a loose tongue was the opposite of temperance. Her words were coming faster and faster, and he could see the way she trembled. Most people would think it was because she was so upset, but he knew better. He recognized the signs of the Tears of Midnight losing effectiveness.

"You wish to know what I think?" His sister turned back to look at the boy, who appeared more terrified than when this began. "I believe there are many in this room and this castle who are to blame. This boy is but one of them. And it would be unjust to punish one without punishing them all. A week in the stockades in the center of Garden City for the guards who failed in their duty will make sure they don't do so again. As for the boy—since there was no one concerned enough to tell him he could not enter the castle, my verdict is that he is to go free."

The guard members standing behind Captain Monteros exchanged nervous glances.

The youth started to scramble to his feet, but Captain Monteros grabbed his shoulder and pushed him back down. "I don't believe you are done yet, boy," Captain Monteros said, standing over him. "Prince Andreus has yet to give *his* verdict on what your punishment should be."

Elder Cestrum nodded. "Yes. Prince Andreus. Your sister has given us a fascinating view of what her reign as Queen would look like. Publically punishing the guard is a . . . unique choice. Now the Elders and the court here in the Hall of Virtues would like to hear from you. What ruling would you give this young man for his crimes?"

All eyes turned to Andreus. He pretended not to feel the weight of their expectation as he studied Varn huddled on the floor. Andreus had no doubt as to how the boy got in the castle. After his discussion with Elder Jacobs, Andreus was sure that this "theft" was designed by the Council as part of the Trials. The boy was here because the Council wanted him here. The guards let him through because that had been their orders. Did the boy cut the purse Captain Monteros was holding off a lord's belt? The boy had no knife that Andreus could see. If he had one, surely the guards would have taken it and shown it as another sign of the boy's guilt.

His sister was right to say the boy should be set free, at the very least given a minimal punishment for this "crime." But Andreus knew that was not the ruling the Council wanted—not the ruling he was supposed to give. Not if he wanted to convince them that he was strong enough to set aside his desire for approval and do what the kingdom needed. That he could draw a line in the sand that others knew could never be crossed without serious retribution.

Micah used to say their uncle had been right to want to lead a force decades ago against Adderton for their sheltering and support of the living members of the Bastians. Their uncle claimed King Ulron was weak for not hunting the last of them. He said strong men removed the head of a snake if they truly wished to ensure its death.

Instead of striking down Adderton and the Bastians, their father ordered the guards to seize their uncle for what he claimed was a plot against the crown. Not long after, Father took the advice offered by his brother and removed the snake's head. No one after that dared to call King Ulron weak.

Now the Council was looking for that same strength—from him. As long as Andreus could convince Elder Jacobs and the rest that he was his father's son, the crown would be his. His sister's bid to bring the Council to her side would fail. Imogen would be his Queen and Carys would accept her new place in his life—or he would deal with that, too.

But first he had to cut the head off this snake.

"I understand my sister's desire for mercy. It is only human to be swayed by a tale of hunger and a sad face. A strong ruler cannot act out of pity, but must instead think of the law." Andreus glanced down at the boy—Varn—whose defiant pose was gone now. Instead, he seemed to be pleading for help with his eyes.

Andreus's resolve trembled like the innocent boy in front of him. He thought of Max and for a moment wondered if Varn and Max could have known each other on the streets of Garden City. What would Max think after hearing that Andreus had passed judgment on a boy who was in essence just like him? Would he still believe Andreus was his hero?

Andreus pulled his gaze up and found Imogen standing not far behind the boy in the crowd. To keep her safe, he must be King. To be King, he must prove to the Council he was strong. What was one life when compared to all the others he would help as King? One life against hundreds of thousands.

And really, the boy was here in the Hall of Virtues. He must have known that when he walked into the castle and came through these doors he was doing something wrong. Still he came. For that arrogance the boy deserved to pay a price.

Keeping his eyes firmly on Imogen's face, Andreus straightened his shoulders and said, "This boy stole a purse. Thefts must be punished. If they are not, it only encourages others to incite trouble in our city and the kingdom. The punishment for theft is the loss of a hand."

"But I didn't do it, Your Highness," the boy cried. "They—"

"Silence," Andreus snapped. "By interrupting you have shown clearly that you have no respect for the lords of this land. Not only did you steal a purse, but you used a weapon to do so."

"Andreus," Carys said.

He could hear the concern in his sister's voice and he shoved it to the side. Thinking of the throne sitting just behind him, he walled up any pity he felt for the boy and instead focused on the way everyone waited for him to continue. High Lords hung on his every word. The Council of Elders and the guard were waiting to act as he ordered. Terror made the boy on the floor shake.

They all watched him as he had always seen people look at his father. He was no longer the one who guarded a terrible secret—no longer the one that was cursed. He was the one with power.

"To allow you to walk free would be a signal to all of Eden that attacking a lord is allowed."

"But I didn't—"

"Andreus!"

He wasn't listening to his sister or the boy. He felt the power of the throne calling to him as he said, "For the crime of attacking a lord with a knife, stealing from him, and open disrespect to the throne, I order this criminal put to death."

Elder Cestrum stepped forward. "The Council agrees with Prince Andreus. The boy is to be taken to the North Tower, where he will be executed as the Prince of this land has decreed."

"No," the youth said, shaking his head at the same time Carys yelled, "Andreus! What are you doing?"

The lights flickered in the hall. The shining orbs hanging from above began to sway as Captain Monteros yanked the boy to his feet and shoved him toward the two guards.

"It wasn't me," the boy shouted. "Your Highness. You have to believe me. It wasn't me!" He pulled himself free of the guards' grasp and came racing toward the dais. His hands were clasped in front of him—begging for mercy.

"I didn't do it," Varn shouted. "Please, Your Highness. Please—"

Light flashed off the steel in Captain Monteros's blade as it slashed through the air.

Andreus heard his sister scream.

The lights flickered again. Captain Monteros's sword bit into and through flesh. Blood spurted like a fountain, staining the white floor. Shrieks rang through the room and then went silent as the boy's body crumpled to the ground and his head landed with a thud and rolled toward the dais.

When the Chief Elder stepped forward and declared Andreus the winner of both the ball and the extra trial, putting him two points closer to the throne—closer to the power he had just wielded— Andreus knew he should be horrified by what he had done.

The boy was dead. His words were the sword that killed him.

He had crossed a line he had never thought he would cross.

Regret bubbled up inside him. But when he saw Imogen's understanding expression and saw Elder Jacobs nod when he met his eyes, Andreus shoved it back down instead, focused on the rush of strength and control. That power was what he wanted. That power would let him destroy the curse that had controlled his life since the day he was born. Once he had the throne, the "curse" would be no more and the people he had always feared would realize they should now fear him.

No, he would not regret his choice.

A glance at his sister shaking and sweating as she looked up at him with horror told him exactly what line he had to cross next.

15

Her head rang. Her heart pounded. Everything inside her screamed as she remembered the way her brother stepped in front of the Throne of Light with the dead body lying below him. There had been a smile on Andreus's lips as Elder Cestrum spoke, but Carys couldn't make sense of the words. Nothing made sense. The world was spinning. The lights above swayed and Carys felt a swirl of air pull at her skirts while she stared at the blood spread across the shining white stone floor.

A boy. No more than twelve or thirteen.

Just a boy.

"Princess, wait," a voice called to her as she hurried down the corridor—away from the Hall of Virtues, and her brother, and the senseless death he had brought to an innocent boy.

She didn't want to talk to anyone. Not after what had just happened. She couldn't stay and smile and act as though nothing was wrong while her brother accepted congratulations for his victory and Captain Monteros supervised his guard picking up the headless body and carrying it away.

The blood on the white stone floor would be cleaned. In mere minutes, maybe even right now, people would be dancing atop the spot where the boy had begged for his life and lost it. And her brother would smile and dance with them.

She couldn't think about Andreus and what he had commanded in the Hall of Virtues. Her brother wasn't heartless. It was the reason she thought he would make a great ruler. He believed in compassion. She had been certain he would do what was best for the kingdom.

Instead he struck a blow to the foundation of her world. She couldn't stay in the Hall and she couldn't go back to her rooms. Not yet. Not with the image of her brother's satisfied smile playing over and over in her head. If she returned to her rooms now the need to drown those images with Tears of Midnight would be too strong for her to deny. It was everything she could do to keep herself from heading for the stairs and giving in to that desire.

Soon.

First, before the Tears blissfully chased the world away, she had to get to the stables. If Larkin had been hiding there for hours, there had to be a very good reason why. And if it was about Imogen, Carys needed to know exactly what that reason was.

She turned down a torchlit hallway, hoping to discourage the person following her. The footsteps behind her stopped. Then they started again . . . faster and getting closer.

Putting her hands in her pockets, Carys grabbed the handles of the stilettos, drew the blades, and turned.

Lord Errik stopped in his tracks and put his hands up in the air. "I apologize for startling you, Princess."

"Don't you know it's a bad idea to pursue a lady who doesn't wish to be followed?" she asked.

"In my experience, most ladies who are being pursued want to be caught. Clearly, Princess, you aren't most ladies." When she didn't lower her weapons, his expression turned serious. "After what just happened with your brother and the attempt on his life earlier, I was worried about you being alone in these halls. Eden doesn't appear to be a very safe place right now."

No. No, it wasn't. "I appreciate your concern, Lord Errik, but I assure you, I can take care of myself."

"As we all learned with your excellent demonstration today," he agreed, stepping forward. "But your eyes can only see what is in front of you. Even the most skilled warrior has need of someone to guard his back."

"I thank you for your concern, Lord Errik, but my back is just fine." At least it always had been because her brother had guarded it as she had guarded his. Now . . . now, unless she could change the path he was on, she would be on her own.

"Please, if you'll allow me." He lowered his hands and stepped forward.

"Why?" she demanded. Lowering the stilettos to her side, Carys said, "A good Trade Master would be careful not to take sides until a new ruler is on Eden's throne. And if you truly believe I'm trying to lose, you should be in the Hall of Virtues still, with my brother."

"A good Trade Master understands that it is impossible to partner with kingdoms that are at war with other countries or themselves. And even if that wasn't true, I believe in fair play. It is clear there are a great many people in this castle who don't. The fact that you're losing isn't going to alter that. It might even make it worse."

"Andreus was only doing what he thought he must tonight," she insisted, working to convince Errik of what she had been trying so hard to make herself believe.

"The Prince did what he thought would get him what he wanted. He made his choice and you made yours." Errik looked down at the stilettos in her hands and then back at her. His tanned skin looked richer and his features sharper in the flickering torchlight. He stepped forward until he was less than an arm's length from her. "I'm an outsider, which means you have no reason to trust me to take your part. But as strong and determined as you are, I don't believe you can do this on your own. I am offering to stand at your side."

She stared into the intense darkness of his eyes and felt the pull of his offer. Offering her trust was offering Errik power over her. Power was dangerous. Look at what it had already done to her brother. But Errik was right in saying that she needed someone to watch her back.

Still, she asked, "And if I refuse your offer, my lord? What then?"

Errik smiled. "Then I hope I'm better at dodging those stilettos than the man earlier today, because I have made the decision to keep you safe—at least until I have the opportunity to teach you how to dance."

The words, the look on his face, the nearness of his body made her heart pound harder and her stomach jump. And she didn't have time for either.

"I have to go," she said, stepping away so she could slide the stilettos into her pockets.

"Will you allow me to escort you back to your rooms," Errik asked, "or shall I just hang in the shadows and allow you to pretend I'm not here?"

Yesterday, she would have said no. She would have commanded him away. Yesterday, her brother was on her side. Now Andreus was a different person and she needed to trust *someone*—before these trials and the people involved in them took him away from her forever.

"I'm not going to my rooms," she admitted. "There is something I have to do in the stables first."

Errik ran his eyes up and down her body and raised an eyebrow. "In those clothes? I'm going to have to teach you more than dancing, Highness. Have you ever heard of the word stealth?"

A half hour later, Carys had exchanged her shimmering blue gown and jewels for a dark gray servant's dress that was a size too big and a matching gray cap under which Errik insisted she shove her distinctively colorless hair. Since there weren't any pockets in this dress, Errik found a basket of dirty laundry for Carys to shove her stilettos into in order to carry them with her.

"Aren't you going to change into servant's attire, too?" she asked.

"Of course not." He smiled. "My job is to be noticed. If there's a demanding noble around no one has time to notice the servant scurrying through the halls before him."

"I never scurry," she said, heading into the hall with the basket balanced on her hip. The late hour meant there were fewer people in the castle corridors. She kept her head tilted down as she hurried to exit the castle. She needed to get to the stables before Larkin decided she wasn't coming.

The chill of the night made Carys wish for a cloak as she crossed the castle's courtyard, passed through the exit, and went down the narrow steps that led to the royal stables. They had been constructed on a wide ledge on the side of the plateau between the castle and Garden City with a slope that allowed the horses to easily get to the ground below. Lights on the castle walls glowed bright in the night. Carys could hear Errik's voice echoing behind her as he boisterously spoke to everyone he passed.

By the time she reached the stables, the hands on duty knew

there was a noble on his way and gave Carys barely more than a quick leer before she passed into the grand structure that smelled of hay and manure. Horses nickered. Hay crunched under her feet. The dim glow from wind-powered sconces lit her way as she headed toward the ladder that led to the hayloft where Carys, Andreus, and Larkin spent hours playing over a decade ago.

A stiletto clutched in one hand, Carys reached the loft. No wind-powered lights graced its walls, and Carys squinted into the shadows as she moved carefully deeper into the hayloft.

"Larkin?" she whispered, clutching the stiletto tight. Hay crackled in the corner and Carys turned in that direction. Nothing there. She whispered Larkin's name again and jumped as something else rustled in the loft.

"Larkin?" Two stacks of hay moved and Larkin appeared. "Thank the Gods," Carys whispered, hurrying forward toward her friend, who was wide-eyed and pale. "Are you okay?"

"I worried that your maid wouldn't give you the message or that you wouldn't understand where to come or that I wasn't hidden well enough and someone might have seen me." Fear colored Larkin's voice and her eyes were bright with tears.

"What is it? You can tell me—whatever it is."

Larkin nodded and swallowed hard. "I know you wanted me to leave town and my father and I planned to, but I wanted to bring you the dress I'd been working on for you. The tournament was over and everyone was returning by the time I reached the castle with the garments. There were rumors about an attack at the tournament and I wasn't sure if someone would question me coming to the castle, so I went through the maze paths in the courtyard that lead to the kitchen gardens." She paused to breathe. "It was there I heard

Lady Imogen's voice coming from around the corner. I started to go back the way I came. But that's when I heard her tell someone not to worry. That Prince Andreus already was hers in ways Micah never was and once you were killed he would rely on her even more. She said that once the appointed time came for the true King to take the throne, Prince Andreus would be far easier to kill than Prince Micah and King Ulron had been."

For a moment Carys couldn't breathe. The words slammed through the haze that surrounded her and the truth dawned. "They killed Micah and my father."

"I believe so, Highness. I should have left and found the guards and brought them there to hear them speak, but I didn't know who to trust. And I was too scared to move."

Carys was certain had Larkin left she would never have brought the guard back in time. Even if she had, after the part Captain Monteros and his men had played in tonight's trial, there was a chance he was part of Imogen's plot. If that were the case, Larkin wouldn't be standing here to tell her tale now.

"You did the right thing. Did the person Lady Imogen was speaking with give any clue as to his identity?"

Larkin nodded. "His voice was low and quiet and I think I heard him say something about a visit to the North Tower, but I can't be sure." Larkin took a deep breath and looked Carys square in the eye. "But I am sure she referred to him once as Elder and that he is on the Council."

The Council that was running the Trials—the Trials that would end if one of the twin heirs to the throne won or ended up dead.

"She said her visions told her they would triumph. That the orb would crack and the winds would sweep in a new ruler to sit on the

Throne of Light. Just as they planned."

A new ruler. Did that mean Andreus, or someone completely new?

It had to be Garret. Or was it? He had wanted something when he talked to her today, but it felt as though he wanted something from her personally, not just the crown.

Carys's head spun. Her legs tingled, spots appeared in front of her eyes, and she grabbed the stack of hay bales for support.

"Are you okay, Highness?" Larkin rushed forward to take her arm.

"I'm fine," she said as the lightheadedness faded. "It's you I'm worried about. You have to—"

They both jumped at the sound of footsteps in the stables. Carys's heart hammered against her chest as the footsteps stopped near the ladder. Then whoever was below began to climb.

"Behind me," Carys hissed, ignoring the weak trembling of her legs as she lifted her stiletto and prepared to throw.

"Should I be concerned that you're making a habit out of aiming that at me, Highness?" Lord Errik asked as his head and shoulders appeared. Carys lowered the stiletto with relief. Before she could ask why he had abandoned his job as a distraction, he said, "We'll have to talk about your penchant for sharp objects later because unless I'm mistaken, this lady is the clever seamstress the guard believes was part of today's plot to assassinate the Prince."

"What?" Larkin gasped as Carys said, "That's ridiculous."

"I would tend to agree, but the guard won't find my point of view all that compelling. From what I could learn in my quest to play irritating nobleman, they have sealed the gates under orders from the Council of Elders and are searching every house in the city in order to find her." Errik turned toward Larkin. "I fear, my lady, you have made an enemy who wishes to see you dead."

Imogen. She must have seen Larkin in the courtyard or perhaps she simply learned of Carys's secret friendship and was using Larkin against her. "You have to get out of the city."

"How?" Larkin asked, panic clear on her face. "With the gates sealed, there's no way out."

And eventually the guards would search the stables. If they found her, Larkin's time in the North Tower would last only long enough for the Council and Imogen to organize her execution. Larkin couldn't stay here. She couldn't leave the city. Carys only knew of one place Larkin could hide where the guard would not know to look.

She studied Errik and wished she knew more about him. He was handsome. Clever. Determined. And he pulled at her in ways she hadn't expected or wanted to think about. But could he be trusted?

Her stomach clenched. Her legs felt weak again, and she put a hand on the hay to steady herself as she weighed her options and realized she had none. If she wanted to keep Larkin alive, she would have to trust Errik with another secret.

"You have to hide until they have called off the search, and I know a place where they won't find you."

Quickly, she told Larkin about the hidden room behind the tapestry and the passages in the plateau under the castle. "Errik will have to escort you there. If Lady Imogen and anyone on the Council are behind this, they will have people looking for me in the hope that I'm helping you." Putting her in the North Tower as a coconspirator for the assassination against Andreus would certainly guarantee her brother gained the throne.

"There's no way the guards are going to let me into the castle looking like this," Larkin said.

Damn. Larkin was right. Her pulse pumped. "There has to be a way to get you in."

"There is," Errik said. "Where's your ball gown, Highness?"

"In the basket below, but it won't fit Larkin."

"It doesn't have to fit," Errik said with a smile. "Go back to the castle, Highness. I pledge my word, I will see your friend safely hidden away."

She had no choice. Carys took her terrified friend's hand and said, "Do as Lord Errik bids. He'll keep you safe until I can find a way out of this for you."

"And my father, Your Highness?" Larkin asked. "What about him?"

Goodman Marcus. She hadn't thought that far ahead. Now that she had, a cold dread settled into the pit of her stomach. "He doesn't have the same connection to me that you do, and he didn't hear what you heard. He should be safe . . . for now." They would throw him in the North Tower when they couldn't find Larkin, but they wouldn't kill him. Not if they could use him to draw his daughter out of hiding. But the image of the kindly, thin man with his warm voice and gentle hands in those cells pulled at her. She was a princess, a member of the royal family of Eden, and yet she couldn't be more helpless to prevent his suffering.

Swallowing down the knot of tears, she said, "Worry about getting yourself to the hidden room first, and I'll be thinking of ways to get you out of this. I promise." Even though she couldn't. Not now. Maybe not ever. And if she didn't come up with a way to defeat the treachery in the castle, everyone she cared about would end up dead.

Carys turned quickly toward the ladder so Larkin wouldn't see the frustration and tears flooding her. Errik followed close behind. When they reached the bottom, he handed her the other stiletto from the basket and took her arm before she could leave.

"I will help your friend into hiding, Highness," he said. "But you must know she will never be safe. The Council and your seeress have branded her a traitor. They will continue the hunt for her for years if necessary in order to demonstrate what happens to those who defy the crown."

"Then what?" she hissed as anger heated the hollowness inside her. "You think I should just let the guards have her and be done with it?"

"No, Highness." He reached up to her face and brushed away a tear that she hadn't realized had fallen. "But you might want to consider other options. When a battle is being lost on one terrain, sometimes an army must draw back and find new ground to fight on." He stared into her eyes for several long moments, then said, "I will get word to you when the package is safely delivered." He took the dress out of the basket, put her stilettos back in, and shoved a bunch of hay on top before handing it to her. "Now, Princess, you should go."

She hurried back to the castle the way she'd come, shivering as the wind gusted. The windmills seemed louder with every step. A guard stopped her at the gate and pulled her cap off her head to check the color of her hair.

Carys held her breath and tightened her grip on the basket as the man walked slowly around her. Sweat trickled down her neck and she tried to guess how long it would take for her to reach inside the basket and pull out the stilettos if it came to that. Finally, he gave her backside a squeeze and told her to come to the guardhouse after her kitchen duties.

"Me and my friends will pay you well for your time."

Carys bit back the angry words that sprang to her lips and instead smiled. "I'm worth more than the few coppers you have in your pockets."

"Name your price and if you prove you're worth it, we'll pay it."

"A lord once said I was worth a sack of gold." She smiled. "But I'll take a sack of silver since you asked so nice."

Swaying her hips, she hurried away from the guard. Then, ditching the basket behind a hedge in the courtyard, Carys jammed the cap back on her head, clutched the stilettos at her side, and kept her face tilted down as she passed servants and nobles stumbling back to their rooms after the ball.

Nowhere did she see Imogen or any of the Elders. Nor her brother. She would look for him after she changed and steadied herself. She needed just a bit of the Tears to stop her thoughts from tripping over one another.

When she reached her floor, she plucked the cap off her head, shook out her hair, and then walked around the corner as though her attire were typical. A young guard was stationed outside her door—the same one who had walked her from the North Tower. He glanced at her gray gown but said nothing as she let herself into her rooms and sagged against the door after it closed behind her.

Larkin's scared warning.

The boy's head falling with a sickening thud onto the polished floor.

Andreus's expression of pride when he was declared the winner.

Errik's warning and his smile.

The images swarmed in her head. Her fingers shook as she unfastened her dress, jumping when the fire in the hearth crackled and when the wind howled outside her window. Everything in her tensed and clenched as she pulled a simple-to-fasten dress out of her wardrobe and slipped it on. Then she knelt down next to her wardrobe and dug in the back with unsteady hands for the red bottles and the answer to the anxiety that was getting worse with every passing minute. She needed more of the Tears. Just a little would make it better—smooth everything out so she could find a way out of all of this for her and her brother, as she had always done.

Only when her hands opened the small panel at the back of the closet and she reached inside, she felt nothing.

Carys pushed herself to her feet. She grabbed armfuls of fabric and threw dresses to the floor until the wardrobe was empty and there was nothing blocking her view to confirm what she already knew.

The red bottles she needed were gone.

16

Andreus turned the empty red bottle over in his hand, then set it next to the line of other bottles on the table before going back to the window and closing it.

Perhaps he should get rid of the bottles so Carys would be forced to wonder who was responsible for taking them. Rarely did he deliberately provoke her anger. After all, he had always needed her to work with him to protect his secret. His curse.

Now that Elder Jacobs was bringing the Council to Andreus's side, he didn't need Carys to protect him anymore.

Still he stared at the bottles, marveling at how far they had come in only a week. Carys working to orchestrate an assassination attempt. Him ordering an innocent boy put to death.

The boy.

Andreus shook his head against the memory of the blade slicing through Varn's neck. The sounds the head and the body made when they hit the floor.

Those sounds proved he was strong, he told himself. They proved he would be a king people feared and respected and would not cross.

He shifted his gaze from the bottles toward the bed where his mother slept before stepping out of the dim room and into the light.

Oben stood and asked, "Did the Queen stir at all when you spoke to her, Your Highness?"

"I'm afraid not, Oben," he said with a sigh. "Whatever Madame Jillian gave Mother has her in a deep sleep."

Oben shook his head and clutched his hands together. "Your mother seemed more lucid the last time she was awake. Madame Jillian was hopeful that this last dose would clear the rest of the darkness from the Queen's mind and return her to us as she was before the King and Prince Micah died."

"I hope that is true, Oben," Andreus said, turning for the door. "You will send word if my mother's condition changes?"

"I will, Your Highness. When it does, the Queen will be glad to hear you and so many others have come to spend time at her side."

"Others?" he asked. "What others?"

"Several of the visiting dignitaries and High Lords have come to ask after the Queen. I have refused them all, but at one point I stepped out and when I returned Elder Ulrich was exiting the Queen's room. He apologized for not waiting for me to allow him entry, but insisted it was of the utmost importance for him to see the Queen's condition for himself."

Andreus stilled. "Did he tell you why?"

"Only that it had to do with the Council's duty to the safety of the realm."

"Did he stay long?"

"Quite a while, Your Highness, and he spoke with her. I thought I heard the Queen's voice while he was in there, but Elder Ulrich swore she never woke." Oben shrugged. "I must be hearing things."

Or not. Andreus looked back at his mother's closed door. "What did you imagine you heard?"

"Nothing really, Your Highness. Elder Ulrich was speaking too quietly for me to make out the words. There was only one I thought I heard clearly."

"What word was that?"

"Curse. Not long after that Elder Ulrich came out of the Queen's room looking disturbed."

As Andreus was now.

Could his mother have been talking in her drug-addled sleep and let loose Andreus's secret? The possibility haunted him as he walked back to the Hall of Virtues, his hand on the hilt of his sword in case someone was hidden in the shadows. He almost hoped someone did attack. After years of living in fear of having his curse discovered and being slaughtered for the crime of being born, he was glad to face enemies he could see and kill.

The true question for him now was whether his sister was one of them.

The Hall of Virtues was empty and dark except for the throne, which was sitting in a round pool of light. All signs of the ball and the trial that had taken place here were gone.

"Prince Andreus?"

He turned and spotted Max standing in the arched doorway and smiled. "I guess you received my message. Come in." The boy nodded and took several hesitant steps into the room instead of racing forward as was his typical way. "You must be tired," Andreus said. "You're normally in bed by now."

Max shrugged and looked down at his shoes.

Andreus walked toward the boy. "Is something wrong, Max? Are you feeling all right? Have you had trouble breathing today?"

"I had a . . . " The boy frowned. "*Asode*?"

"An episode?" Andreus asked, and the boy nodded.

"On the battlements. One of the Masters called for Madame Jillian and she had to leave the girl she was helping that was dying. She made me drink something even worse and yelled at me for being out in the cold air. She says cold is bad for me and that she warned me not to go on the battlements until it was warmer and said if I did it again I'd have to come help her tend to the sick, which I don't want to do because the girl she was helping was the doom. You should have seen her face . . . "

From the look on Max's, Andreus was glad he didn't have to. "You shouldn't go on the battlements anymore."

"But I had to tonight," Max insisted. "The Lord devil man went up there and you told me to watch him."

"Lord Garret was on the battlements?"

Max nodded. "He had the Masters show him where the line to the orb was cut and asked a lot of questions that I couldn't hear, but I got close enough to hear him ask who was on the battlements before the lights were sabotaged."

"What did the Masters say?" Andreus had meant to ask them that question himself, but then his father and Micah's bodies were brought back and the Trials happened and he hadn't had the chance. There was something about the timing of those events, when he considered them together, that made him nervous.

Max screwed up his face into a mask of what was probably intense concentration. "The Masters said they were in their quarters when the line was cut, but the apprentices assigned to the watch said

Lady Imogen, Elder Ulrich, and Captain Monteros were all on the battlements near the orb tower before the darkness came."

All three often walked the battlements. Imogen to call the wind and study the stars. Captain Monteros to check on his guards and watch the mountains for the Xhelozi. And Elder Ulrich to talk to the Masters about their work on the windmills and the lights.

"Did Lord Garret say anything else?"

"He asked if anyone had seen Elder Jacobs."

"Elder Jacobs? Why?"

"He didn't say, Prince Andreus. And I couldn't hear the Master's answer, but I think he nodded his head and Lord Garret left. I was going to follow him like you told me to, but I couldn't breathe and that's when they called for Madame Jillian. But I did follow him before and heard him talking to Elder Cestrum. They were shouting so I could hear what he said."

Whatever it was must have been intense since Max was white-faced and looked as if he was ready to bolt out of the Hall at any moment. "Tell me."

"Elder Cestrum told Lord Garret that he was going to do his duty if he wanted to or not, and Lord Garret said it was clear Elder Cestrum had lost control of the Council and that there was more than one way to power. They had tried it Elder Cestrum's way and now they were going to follow Lord Garret's plan."

"Did Lord Garret say what that plan was?"

Max shook his head. "The Chief Elder called Lord Garret a fool to give up power so easily, but Lord Garret said that his uncle was just like Prince Micah—that they thought there was only one kind of power. But Lord Garret knew there was power beyond the throne that none of them could see."

"Is that all?"

Max swallowed hard and shook his head. "He said his uncle should be careful in playing both sides and that at some point he'd have to choose and he hoped his uncle chose the right side."

"And what side was that?"

"I don't know, Prince Andreus. Honest."

"That's okay, Max," Andreus said. While much of Garret's conversation with his uncle was a mystery, the part about not doing it Elder Cestrum's way was clear. Garret was no longer counting on the Council of Elders' plan to sit him on the Throne of Light. Garret had another plan, and Andreus was betting it involved his sister.

"Did I do a bad job?" Max asked with wide eyes that shimmered with tears. "I'm sorry I got sick. I promise I won't next time. Honest. Can I go now?"

Andreus put a hand on the boy's shoulder and felt him tremble. "Max, what's wrong? Did something happen when you were following Lord Garret today? Did you see something that scared you?"

Max looked toward the front of the Hall at the throne shining in the light, and Andreus realized what the boy saw.

"Did you come into the Hall during the ball?"

Slowly, Max nodded his head. "Madame Jillian said I should rest, but I wanted to do a good job and all the lords and ladies were in here."

"And you saw that boy die."

"There was a baker's son my sister used to play with named Varn," he said quietly.

Pity and guilt stirred. "Max, there are laws that have to be obeyed. When laws are broken, the King has a duty to punish the lawbreakers. Now it's time for you to go to bed. It's late and I'm sure

Lady Yasmie will have lots of chores for you tomorrow."

"Yes, Your Highness." Max gave a careful bow before running out of the hall.

"You are good with children, my prince."

Andreus grabbed at the hilt of his sword and spun around as Imogen stepped out from behind the throne. She was still wearing her dress of yellow, but her hair that had been pinned and sculpted now flowed freely around her face.

The smile she gave him made her even lovelier as she patted the seat of the throne and beckoned for Andreus to join her. "I had heard you had rescued a sickly boy off the streets and brought him here to the castle. Everyone in the castle and in the city below was talking about your kindness, which is the same kindness you showed to me when I first came here and felt so alone."

Andreus took Imogen's soft outstretched hands in his. "I scared him . . . the boy I rescued."

"He will come to understand why you had to do what you did," Imogen said, leading Andreus to the Throne of Light. "And now he will think twice if he ever considers crossing you. A king cannot afford to associate with those who could be persuaded to betray."

"Max would never betray me."

"Perhaps not willingly. But he is a child and there are those who might take advantage of that."

Andreus thought of the sabotaged lights and Max admitting he'd told a number of people about the test Andreus planned to run. The boy was enthusiastic and friendly. Both were endearing. Both could, if Max wasn't careful, be deadly in a place filled with people so intent on wielding influence.

Imogen reached up and placed her hand against Andreus's cheek.

"Is there any doubt as to why my heart was yours from the moment we met? You looked at that young boy and saw past his sickness to the potential within. And believed that your kindness will be repaid with loyalty."

"And you don't?" he asked.

"Micah was hungry for power, but he studied the histories and he understood that for kings kindness is a tool, like any other." She took his hand and led him to the throne. "And it is most used by one who has shown he is willing to evoke fear. Micah always liked to remind me of the vision I feigned and how there were men willing to speak of their part in making it come true if I ever dared cross him. Fear mixed with kindness is unsettling and powerful."

Andreus tightened his hold on Imogen wondering what other things his brother had done to cause her fear. "You should have told me what Micah was doing."

Imogen shook her head. "It was my choice to stay quiet just as it is my choice now to see how you wield your own power. Tonight you proved willing to use the fear and strength the crown bestows. Once you are on the throne, you will teach the Council and your subjects that they will bend to you or break. Once they learn that lesson, you can show them the kindness you have always shown me. Before then the people and your enemies will see any sign of mercy as weakness. Your father understood that. It was why he had no choice but to have your uncle killed."

"My uncle committed treason."

"That's what your father said." She put her hands on his shoulders and gently pushed him down until he was seated on the Throne of Light. "The truth is what the man who sits in this chair wishes it to be. You belong on this throne, my prince. The kingdom needs you to stay safe. I need you."

He let those words settle over him, washing away some of the doubt he felt at the look he'd seen in Max's eyes and the guilt that lingered after emptying his sister's bottles. Had he not known how she would suffer, it wouldn't bother him. Or if he knew for certain she had betrayed him . . .

"You still look troubled, my prince."

Andreus took her hand in his. "Do you know if they've located the seamstress seen talking to the assassin?"

Imogen sighed. "Captain Monteros sealed the gates, but so far no sign of her has been found, which is a shame."

"Do you think she would implicate my sister in the plot?"

"I doubt it. But you said the girl was someone you both knew when you were younger. The fact that your sister has kept her association with this girl a secret from you demonstrates how important she is to the Princess. That kind of affection is a weakness you could exploit to your advantage with the Council . . . and the people of Eden."

Andreus thought of the row of empty glass bottles. "We don't need the girl for that. My sister has more than one weakness."

"I hope you are right, my prince. I saw the way she looked at the throne tonight. She is not winning the Trials, but she has made choices that have captured the hearts of many of the people, and once they hear of tonight's trial and the choices she made, more will flock to her banner."

"That will never happen." Especially not after tomorrow, he thought. "Carys will break."

Imogen placed her hands on his knees. "My vision still shows two paths before the kingdom—not one. You have to take care even if you don't believe."

"It's not that I don't believe." It was that he couldn't. "I've seen too many decisions based on visions that turn out wrong."

"Visions are the Gods' ways of sending us warnings to pay attention to the future. Seers are trained to report only what we see in the stars. But many seers seek to find power beyond their visions, giving meaning to that which the stars gave none. You may not believe in them, but that does not mean they aren't real." Standing, Imogen held out her hands. "Come with me to the tower. I can show you the stars that are guiding your way."

He rose from the Throne of Light and looked down at the sapphires that glowed with an almost hypnotic light.

"Come, Prince Andreus, you can tell me what you have done to keep Eden safe from the path that leads to darkness and I will check the stars to see if they have changed their message."

"I doubt I will be able to concentrate on the stars, my lady," he said, running a finger down her face. "Not with your beauty distracting me."

She laughed, but took his hand and wove her fingers through his. "Is it any wonder that I fear your sister's jealousy will try to take this from us?"

"Carys cannot hurt us," he assured her. "Trust me."

17

They were gone.

Carys stared at the wardrobe as if she could will the bottles to reappear. Her head spun. The bottles had been here earlier. They should be here now. But they weren't, and Carys could only think of one reason why they would be gone.

Andreus.

He must have realized she had lied about the Tears of Midnight. Part of her wanted to believe he wasn't the one behind this—that it was the Council that had figured out her secret. Because Andreus knew what happened when her body craved the drink. He'd sat with her when she shook and sweated and screamed at him that she was dying. He held the bottle to her lips when he could no longer bear to see her suffer.

But that was the brother who needed her to act as his shield. The brother she saw in the Hall of Virtues tonight no longer wanted her aid, and this was his way of telling her that they were done.

Gods.

Carys rubbed her temples and tried to think. The welts on her back were already beginning to throb. Not terribly, but the wounds whimpered when she moved. By the start of the next trial tomorrow evening, it would be worse. Which is what her brother was counting on and something she couldn't let happen. Andreus needed her even if he didn't realize it anymore. She had to warn him about Imogen before Imogen had the chance to destroy Andreus the way she did Father and Micah, or before she could find and hurt Larkin.

Larkin. Fear gripped Carys anew as she wondered whether Errik had gotten her friend to safety. If not, the guards would be talking about her capture, as would Andreus.

She could feel the guard following her with his eyes as she walked down the hallway to her brother's door. No one answered when she knocked, and the door was locked. She shook the handle several times and banged on the door again, calling her brother's name, wanting to warn him with one breath and desperate to find the bottles with the other.

When the door remained bolted, Carys pushed away and headed downstairs, asking guards she passed if the traitor had been captured. They all said no, which made Carys sag with relief as she slipped into her mother's sitting room and found it blazing with light from every corner. Not a shadow remained. Maybe Oben thought the light would chase away the darkness the Queen was fighting the way it kept the Xhelozi from the walls.

"Your Highness, is there something I can do for you?" Oben asked as he hurried to greet her.

"I came to see my mother," she lied.

"The potion Madame Jillian gave her has pushed her into a deep sleep."

"I will only be a moment," she assured him as she opened her mother's bedroom door and quickly closed it behind her. Here there was darkness. Her mother lay on the bed with her eyes closed. Candles flickered on the far end of the room as Carys quietly knelt, opened her mother's small cabinet, and reached inside.

"You won't find them."

Her mother hadn't moved, but her eyes were now open. White orbs among the shadows, looking at her as she said in a singsong voice, "He was already here." Her mother pointed her finger to the desk beneath the window and Carys bit back a scream as she saw the red glass bottles all lined up perfectly in a row as if waiting for her.

Taunting her.

Carys reached for calm as she walked to the bottles and knew what she would find even as she picked each one of them up and held it to the light.

Empty. Not a drop left.

She wiped her hand under her nose and hurried toward her mother's cabinet even though she knew what she would see.

"I thought I could fix it."

The cabinet was completely empty.

"He took them. Perhaps I should have stopped him, but I didn't. I have stopped it for as long as I could. It is time and soon everyone will know. The winds will come from the mountains. The orb will break. The Xhelozi are calling. Can't you hear them?"

"Mother. Please," Carys said as disappointment sliced through her soul. Her mother was no better. Still, she begged, "I need your help. Imogen was part of the plot to kill Father and Micah. She has to be stopped. You have to help me stop her."

"Nothing can be stopped. He thinks taking the bottles has

stopped something, but he's wrong. And now he'll know. They'll all know."

"Know what, Mother?"

Her mother's hair was wild, but her eyes were clear. Her face was dead calm as she looked into the shadows. "I wanted to protect your brother so I hid what I knew. But I was wrong."

"This is about the Council and Imogen, Mother," Carys snapped. "This isn't about the curse."

"Of course it is," her mother whispered. "Only I got it wrong. I thought your brother's sickness was the sign of the curse."

"I told you . . . "

"But it is not." Her mother stared her dead in the eyes. "The Tears of Midnight weren't to control your pain. I couldn't care less about your pain. I made you drink it to control the curse in *you*."

Carys stepped back and grabbed the cabinet as she shook her head. "That's not true, Mother. Andreus is the one who has the attacks."

"Is it any wonder I believed those were the signs? But I was wrong and the Xhelozi are calling." Her mother sighed, fluffed her pillow, and lay back down. Smiling, she pulled the silk covers over herself. "When you crack the orb of Eden, they will destroy us all."

Mother was still crazy, Carys told herself as she watched the Queen close her eyes. Her expression was tranquil and she refused to speak or look at Carys again despite Carys's attempts to rouse her.

The *words* were crazy. Carys wasn't cursed. She had spent her entire life shielding her brother. She had been told it was her duty to see him unharmed. Two halves of the same whole—only she had been born normal while he was not.

"Did the Queen awaken, Your Highness?" Oben asked, but

Carys pushed past him without answering and went out the door.

Cursed.

She shivered and wiped a line of sweat off her forehead as she walked quickly through the halls. Every guard she passed, every footstep she heard, made her speed her steps.

Cursed.

Was she?

Her father and brother were dead. Her mother was crazy. Her brother had turned against her. Larkin was hiding in the darkness below the castle in fear for her life. And soon she would begin to lose control of everything as the need for the red bottles kicked in.

Madame Jillian made the Tears of Midnight for the Queen. She could make more, but it took at least a week to distill the drink and the healer had delivered a batch to the Queen just days ago. Which meant there wouldn't be any new Tears of Midnight ready for days.

Desperation clawed at Carys. She had to tell Andreus before Imogen made her next move. She had to get him to meet with her.

That's when she remembered their plan and headed back to her rooms to write Andreus a note begging him to speak with her. Since Larkin was in the hidden room behind the tapestry of the nursery, Carys picked the battlements at dawn. No one would think twice about Andreus wandering the battlements that early and the sound of the windmills would conceal their conversation.

Her eyes were heavy and her back was sticky with sweat by the time she returned from sliding the note into the step she and Andreus had agreed on. The guard standing at her door stepped forward as she approached. "Excuse me for disturbing you, Princess," the young guard said, looking at her shoulder instead of her eyes. "But one of the foreign dignitaries dropped by. He asked me to give you this."

The guard held out his hand. In it was a red rose with parchment and a white ribbon wrapped around the stem.

"Thank you." She started to turn away. Then looked back at the guard who had been her shadow for the last several days. "What is your name?" she asked.

"Graylem, Your Highness." He raised his eyes up to hers.

"I believe I owe you a knife," she explained, seeing as how she had no idea where the one she took from him was.

"That's not necessary, Princess."

"Necessary and right are not always the same thing." She shivered. "I will make sure you get it as soon as possible."

Turning, she went back into her room and threw the bolt. Now she could shiver and read the note on the flower without pretending she wasn't sweating. With uncertain fingers, Carys untied the white ribbon and unfurled the small piece of parchment.

I look forward to our next dance. Let me know where and when. —Errik

She staggered to her room and sat on the edge of the bed. If anyone else read the note, they would think it was a flirtation instead of a signal. Lord Errik had gotten Larkin safely to the passages and was waiting for Carys to decide the next move.

Why? He was clever and attractive and had no reason to be putting himself on the line to help Carys. Which meant he wasn't to be trusted. After years of teaching herself not to be close to or to trust any save Andreus and Larkin, Carys found herself helpless to block the desire to lean on him.

Whatever his motives, he had kept Larkin safe. For now. Errik had been right when he said that would only last for so long. Carys had to convince Andreus of Imogen's treachery. Once he realized the plots against him, Carys should be able to make him understand that Larkin was an innocent fly in Imogen's—or someone she was allied with's—web. Because there was more than just Imogen at work here. No matter. She had plotted against their father and brother and arranged their deaths. For that alone, Carys would make her pay.

Holding the flower, Carys lay on the bed. Her eyes were heavy, her body craved rest, but sleep wouldn't come. Her brain raced. Her heart pounded. The more she tried to sleep, the worse her stomach churned and her muscles tensed.

Her back throbbed as she shifted positions. Just a sip of the Tears would fix everything. The sleeplessness. The aches in her body and her heart. Just one drink.

She tossed and turned and rose from the bed and paced, looking out the window every few minutes, waiting for the sky to lighten—terrified that Andreus would not be on the battlements when she arrived. Even more scared that he would turn away from her if he did come. If so, she wasn't sure what she would do. The Andreus at the ball was not the one she had known all these years. Or maybe he was. Maybe she didn't know him the way she thought.

*Maybe*s spun in her head. Every muscle in her tightened. Sweat trickled down her neck as she paced in front of the window and watched the stars shift in the sky. Shadows moved on the mountains. Faint screeches in the distance made Carys pull her arms tightly around herself until the sky finally showed signs of lightening.

She changed into another of Larkin's creations—this one a deep red. When she swiped a brush through her hair at the mirror, Carys's white skin next to the color of her dress reminded her of the ball last night. Red against white. Blood against stone.

Wrapping a dark gray cloak around her, Carys spotted the rose on the bedcovers and slipped the flower into one of the pockets of her dress so it rested next to the stiletto. With one hand wrapped around the blade in her pocket, she headed to the battlements to meet her brother.

Or not.

The battlements were empty. Windmills creaked and pulsed and pounded as they churned the air. The orb glowed bright on the eastern tower. Two guards stood near the front of the battlements, looking off in the distance for signs of trouble. They glanced at her but said nothing as she paced the stone walls and waited.

She pulled her cloak closer to ward off the chills going up her spine even though the early morning was still. No breeze blew as she held her breath and looked around the battlements. Once she thought she saw something move in the shadows, but Andreus never appeared.

The dark sky faded to light gray. If her twin was going to come, he would have been here by now. He must not have checked the loose step for the note she had left. She refused to believe that no matter what he had done, or how thirsty he was for the power of the throne, he would ignore a desperate plea for them to meet and discuss who was behind their father's and brother's deaths.

Carys decided to check the step to prove he hadn't received the note. Perhaps he had and had left a reply explaining why he couldn't come. Carys turned and saw Imogen standing in the doorway of the southern tower. The seeress's dark hair fluttered around her as she stepped onto the battlements and headed for Carys. As she grew closer, Carys spotted a piece of parchment in Imogen's hand.

"Good morning, Princess," Imogen shouted above the thumping

of the windmills. "I hope you had a good night. Your brother certainly did. When I left him, he was sleeping soundly, which is why he never had a chance to find the note you left for him. He had actually been thinking of leaving one for you, which is how I knew to look under the step. I'm glad I did or you would be left standing here alone. Is there nothing worse for a lady than to be left waiting for a man? Even if the man is her brother."

Andreus had told her about the notes. What else had he spoken about? A whip of wind pulled at Carys's cloak. "You sound as though you speak from experience. I didn't know you had a brother."

Imogen stepped closer. "There are a great many things you don't know about me, Princess. Yes, I have a brother. I have not seen him since I came to Eden to study with the seers when I was five. But I think of him every day."

"Came to study?" Carys asked. "I thought you were from the District of Acetia." And timid. They all thought her timid. But this Imogen wasn't the same one who stood beside Micah and flinched if he said something unkind. This was the Imogen from the Hall of Virtues with the Book of Knowledge in her hands and a plan on her lips. Only Carys hadn't seen that. She'd been too concerned about the Elders and Garret and had only worried that her brother was letting passion rule his head. And that worry—the jealousy of his choosing Imogen over her—had made Carys blind to the truth that was standing in front of her now.

The wind howled and Imogen—frail, fragile Imogen—stood strong as a tree as she yelled, "I'm disappointed in you, Princess. A person can say they are from anywhere if there is no one to contradict them. My family admired the power of the seers and the trust they command. They wished their daughter to be one of them. And here I am Seer of Eden and soon to be wife of Andreus, King of Eden, Keeper of Virtues."

"My brother does not believe in your supposed power." Everything churned inside her. "He has spent his entire life hating the Guild and their seers."

"Your brother says a lot of things, but at his core he wants approval. He ordered the death of that boy in order to gain the support of the Council. He bends on his disbelief of the seers to please me." Imogen smiled. "He said he destroyed the thing *you* needed to make it through the Trials, and yet while he slept, I found this."

From her pocket, Imogen withdrew a red glass bottle. Without thinking, Carys lifted a hand and took a step toward it.

Imogen pulled it back with a frown. "You only gain it if you give something to me."

Carys couldn't take her eyes off the bottle in Imogen's hand. Imogen was the enemy. She'd had a hand in killing Micah and Father. But the desperate ache inside Carys pushed down the anger at these truths. It was there. Carys tried to hold on to it. But the bottle called to her. Just a bit of it and she would be strong. She would be able to defend her brother against this woman. If she could just get the bottle . . .

She hated herself as she asked, "What do you want, Imogen?"

Imogen stared at the red bottle while turning it in her hand. "I'd heard about your troubles when I first came here. Micah said Lord Garret used to annoy him by telling him he needed to help you get control over your need for whatever is inside this. Lord Garret said if Micah didn't intercede, it would lead to the downfall of Eden." She smiled and Carys shivered as the wind grew stronger around her. "I guess I'm glad Micah didn't heed his friend's warnings or we might not be standing here now."

"What do you *want*, Imogen?" Carys repeated as yearning and loathing tugged inside her.

"I want the seamstress who aided your brother's attacker. She was here in the castle earlier and now the guards cannot find her. Where is she?"

"I don't know. Why don't you check the stars?" Carys said, forcing herself to look at Imogen's face and not at the bottle just out of reach.

"You don't want to refuse me, Highness." Imogen stepped forward, bringing the bottle closer. "Once Andreus is King, the three of us can work together to make Eden strong."

"Work *together*?" Everything inside her tightened as Imogen shifted the bottle so now it was held casually in front of her. Just two or three steps forward and it would be in Carys's hands. "Like you worked with my brother Micah? It's because of you that he's dead."

Imogen sighed. "I was right! You have spoken to the seamstress. But it doesn't matter."

"You had my brother and my father *killed*."

Imogen sighed. "You give me too much credit. Micah is the one who killed your father. He thought he'd convinced the King's Guard to come to his side. Only many of the men had been well paid to take a different side, and they struck once the King had fallen. Poor Micah never considered the possibility of his own death. I'm sure it came as a great surprise when his own guard shoved a blade into his neck. But there is no one to say I had anything to do with it."

Carys's heart pounded. Wind swirled. The bottle called to her even as anger simmered and fought to break free. "There's me."

"You?" Imogen laughed. "The drug-addled princess who is so

desperate to win the throne that she will say anything?" Imogen stepped forward again.

The bottle was closer still. An arm's length away.

"How many hours has it been since you had your last dose, Princess? Is it the wind making your eyes water and your hands shake, or is it the pain of not having this concoction? We don't have to be at odds. You have been treated poorly by everyone here in the Palace of Winds—even your precious twin has betrayed you."

Another step closer. The windmills turned faster—louder—as the wind howled.

"You owe your brother nothing, Carys. Let him win the contest, and play at King until the *true* ruler of Eden claims his throne. When he does, I can see that you rule at his side."

Imogen held out her hand. The red bottle balanced in the center of her palm. "Your brother doesn't care about you or you wouldn't be looking as though you can barely stand. Take the bottle, Carys, as a promise that we will work together."

No. This was wrong. Rage burned even as Carys stared at the bottle. She could take the bottle and still tell Andreus what she knew. There was nothing stopping her. But this was all wrong.

Imogen lifted her hand so the bottle was in front of Cary's face. Just a breath away. Impossible *not* to look at.

Wait—

Carys shifted her eyes down and saw the blade in Imogen's other hand coming toward her.

Carys stumbled backward as Imogen lunged, the bottle shattering on the ground as the knife caught Carys's cloak. The sound of the thick fabric ripping under the thunder of the windmills rang loud in Carys's ears. She jerked herself backward toward the battlement wall. Imogen careened forward, caught herself, then turned as Carys pushed her hair out of her face and glanced toward where the guards should stand.

They were gone.

The wind howled harder.

Imogen moved forward with the knife pointed at Carys.

Frantic, Carys fumbled for the stilettos inside her dress, but her hands shook and the wind whipped the cloak she was wearing. She couldn't find the openings. Couldn't reach where they lay. She dove to the side as Imogen charged, caught her foot on a stone, and crashed to the ground.

Pain sang in her hands and knees as she pushed herself up and tried again to find the stilettos. Where were the pocket openings? She glanced over her shoulder. Imogen was advancing again. Carys rolled onto her back to kick at the tourniquet cloak that limited her movement.

"You should have taken the bottle, Carys. You could have drunk it all. It would have been easier that way."

Carys got her legs free and pushed to her knees as Imogen charged. Pockets. She had to find—

There.

Her hand slid into the slit in the fabric as Imogen's knife bit the air, slashing toward her.

"No!" Carys screamed.

Wind gusted again with a strength that should have knocked Carys onto her face, but she fought to stay on her knees as Imogen was pushed off balance. The seeress stumbled to the side and grabbed the wall, righted herself, and started forward as Carys's fingers wrapped around the metal hilt of the stiletto. Imogen charged against the wind as the stiletto slid from the sheath.

Wind whipped Carys's hair in front of her eyes. She was almost blind as she sent the stiletto flying forward.

The windmills pounded the air. Her heart raced in her chest as she shoved her thick mane out of her eyes.

Imogen's beautiful face was crumpled in shock and pain.

The seer reached for the stiletto sticking out of the center of her stomach as she fell to the ground.

"No." Carys scrambled to Imogen and looked down into her glassy eyes. "Tell me now. Tell me what you know! One of the Elders is working with you. Who is it? You have to tell me who!"

"I should have known." Imogen stared up at Carys and weakly pulled at the blade. "The stars are never wrong."

The devil with the stars. "Tell me which Elder helped kill my brother and father and I'll get Madame Jillian," she promised as she looked at the blood oozing out of the seer. "She can heal you. Tell me!"

"The power. The winds. I thought it was me, but it's you." Imogen coughed. "And you don't know."

"Know what?" It didn't matter, she told herself. "Who is helping you, Imogen?"

"You are the dark path. You will shatter the light with your power." Imogen coughed again and a line of blood trickled out of her mouth. "You'll destroy it all."

"Imogen," Carys yelled. No. Not yet. "Imogen, you can't die. You have to tell me who else is trying to kill my family."

But the seeress's chest no longer rose and fell. Her eyes were wide as they looked up at the sky. The Seer of Eden was dead.

And Carys had to get off the battlements before the guards

returned and saw. Andreus. He would—

Something raced out of the shadows. Carys grabbed the stiletto. The winds began to swirl again, but the figure didn't run toward her. Instead it darted toward the entrance to the East Tower and turned for just a second before racing down the stairs.

It was the boy. Max. And Carys was certain where he was running to. He was going to tell Andreus that her hands were stained with blood.

18

Andreus smiled at the note as he finished getting dressed in Imogen's rooms.

Went to call the winds and study the stars. Didn't want to wake you.

If she had woken him, Andreus certainly would have tried to convince her there were other things to do this morning than walk the battlements looking at the sky. But he knew she wouldn't have been dissuaded no matter how much he pleaded. She spent hours searching the skies each and every day. On the mornings he worked with the Masters of Light he could count on seeing her on the battlements with her eyes fixed on the heavens. Perhaps it wasn't a surprise that he had found more and more reasons to spend additional time working on the lines. He had wanted her then like he had never wanted anything else.

Now she was his.

Just as the throne would be his.

He hadn't wanted his brother and father to die. Part of him

feared his coronation would be tinged with guilt. But as Imogen told him as he lay next to her, the death of the King and Micah came at the hands of the Kingdom of Adderton. Once the crown was on his head, he would call on the High Lords to send more men to his banner. There they would avenge their fallen king. Andreus and his army would crush Adderton. He would show them and all other kingdoms what happens when faith is broken with virtue and light.

He hoped his sister would learn that, too. He wasn't sure how long it had been since she had last taken the Tears of Midnight, but it had been long enough that she would now show signs of her body's need for it. Her muscles would be aching. Her stomach cramping. He knew from the last time she went through the withdrawal that she wouldn't be able to eat. It took great efforts to get her to take tea or water as she sweated and shook and screamed from the pain.

He remembered the glassy look in her eyes—the agony. He wished things could be different. But she had made her choices and he had to make his. And really, wasn't he helping Carys? Once the Trials were over, she would no longer be bound by the drugs that held her in their thrall. Then she would have another choice to make: to stand by him as he ruled or to be banished to another kingdom as the wife of a foreign lord. Imogen said he might have to exert more force upon her to bring her to heel, but the seeress didn't know his sister the way he did. She only wanted the freedom to live her life as she pleased. They would make peace.

In truth, Carys had served him for their entire life. She would do so again because he was all she had.

Gongs echoed as he turned the key to unlock his rooms. The same gongs that signaled the return of the King or the attack of the Xhelozi. Only there was no King and the sun was shining, so the gongs should not be ringing at all. Andreus put his hand on the hilt of his sword. He turned and started toward the steps just as Max burst into the hall. "She's dead," he yelled. "The Lady Imogen."

Andreus went cold. "What are you talking about? Did you hear someone say that?"

"No, Your Highness. I saw it. I stayed up all night so I could follow the devil man and I saw the Princess and Lady Imogen on the top of the castle. They were fighting. Princess Carys threw a knife."

The battlements. Where Imogen had said she was going to go to look at the stars. She'd gone up there to search for a vision that would help him.

No. The boy got it wrong. Imogen wasn't dead. His sister couldn't have—*wouldn't* have—killed the only woman he had ever loved.

Pushing past servants and members of the court who were wandering the halls in confusion at the sounding of the gongs, Andreus raced through the castle and up one of the sets of stairs that led to the battlements. The footsteps sounding behind him said Max wasn't far behind.

She wouldn't be up here, he told himself as he burst through the door onto the battlements. But he stopped as he saw dozens of people looking down at something on the stone walkway. His heart pounded as he stood, unable to move.

Elder Ulrich turned his scarred face toward Andreus. Others noticed him and stared as he stood, not wanting to get closer. Not wanting to see.

But when Chief Elder Cestrum and Elder Ulrich stepped to the side, Andreus had no choice. He saw the hair first. Dark, long curls blowing in the breeze. Hair that he could still feel brush his chest as she leaned over to kiss him.

He forced himself to move closer. Some of the Masters of Light watched him with sympathy. Members of the court who had found their way upstairs whispered as he reached the circle around the body of the woman he loved.

His chest tightened. Everything went numb.

Imogen. Her skin, normally a rich shade of tan, looked pale next to the streaks of blood that traveled down her still-beautiful face. So lovely that it seemed impossible she was dead. But her chest no longer expanded with life, and the blood pooled around her from the wound in her stomach told him, beautiful or not, Imogen was gone.

He fought to breathe, but the air was gone. Something inside him broke and he dropped to his knees next to the future he had dreamed of. She had been his. *Everything* was supposed to have been his. If he closed his eyes, he could still hear her voice warning him that he couldn't let the scream clawing at his throat free.

Imogen had warned him that his sister would exact revenge for what he had done. As angry as he had been with Carys, he couldn't believe she would do something to truly hurt him. She had vowed to always protect him.

Gods. How could she do this?

"I'm sorry, Prince Andreus," Captain Monteros said. "The guards never saw him, but we recovered a knife like the one used by yesterday's attacker. I am having men sweep the city and the castle now. We will find the assassin."

"It wasn't an assassin." His throat was so tight he could barely speak.

"What did you say, Your Highness?" Elder Cestrum asked.

Andreus swallowed hard and forced the words out. "It wasn't an assassin who killed Lady Imogen. It was my sister."

Captain Monteros and Elder Cestrum exchanged a look as

people whispered around him. "We understand you are upset, Your Highness," Elder Cestrum said, stepping toward him. "But there are no signs that your sister was here. The guards never saw her."

"He did." Breathing was like fire. Still, Andreus forced himself to rise and turn toward Max, who was standing at the entrance to the tower. Pointing to the terrified boy, he said, "Max told me he was here when Lady Imogen died and that it was my sister's hand that held the blade."

Captain Monteros stepped toward Max. "Come here, boy." Max's eyes were wide and fixated on Andreus as he approached the Captain of the Guard.

"Tell me what you saw," the captain commanded.

Max looked down at the ground and said something that was hard to hear over the beating of the windmills and the whispers of the onlookers.

"Louder, boy," Elder Cestrum snapped.

"I saw the Princess on the ground. Lady Imogen was over there. Then the Princess took out one of her knives and threw it and Lady Imogen fell."

Captain Monteros looked back at Elder Cestrum and shook his head. "My guards never reported seeing Princess Carys up on the battlements."

"The boy has no reason to lie," Andreus shouted. "He knows what he saw."

"Or he knows what he believes he's supposed to say." Lord Garret stepped forward from the crowd. He looked down at Imogen's too-still body and shook his head.

"Are you calling the boy a liar?" Andreus asked.

"I think the *boy* will say what he believes will help you secure the throne," Garret said. "From what I hear, he owes you his life. Perhaps he believes he can repay that debt by giving you the throne."

"I don't need anyone to *give* me the throne. It belongs to me."

"Perhaps you are right," Garret said, looking at Max. "But Lady Imogen's death will not help you gain it. I am not sure what this boy thought he saw, but the truth is that I was with your sister at first light this morning."

The noble behind Garret gasped and Andreus looked at Max, who had his eyes lowered to the stone beneath his feet.

"And while I appreciate your desire for justice, I am curious," Lord Garret continued. "Why do you think Princess Carys would have reason to kill Lady Imogen?"

Andreus looked down at Imogen's motionless body. Anger whipped through him as he said, "Carys was jealous of her. She hated how much my family loved her." How much *I* loved her, he added silently. "Captain Monteros, I order you to seize my sister and take her to the North Tower."

Andreus had weakened Carys by emptying every red bottle in the castle. He had taken something vital to her, and she had struck back—just as Imogen had said his sister would. Now Carys would pay.

Captain Monteros looked at Elder Cestrum and the rest of the Elders.

"What are you waiting for?" Andreus yelled.

The windmills pounded.

The air swirled.

Imogen's hair—her beautiful, glistening hair—fluttered in the breeze.

His heart strained and ached as it pounded harder. Demanding vengeance.

Elder Cestrum sighed. "I am sorry, Your Highness, but you are not the King. The captain cannot follow your command."

"You had no problem with him following my command last night." Andreus kept his shoulders straight. The curse pulled at him. The burning in his chest made him want to double over, but he refused to give in. No one would see it. Carys would not win.

Elder Jacobs stepped forward. "The word of a lord who has taken an oath to the King weighs more heavily in our laws than that of a commoner who might be encouraged to say what he believes will gain him reward. One who seeks to be King should understand that. The captain and the guard will hunt down the true attacker. Meanwhile the Lady Imogen will be taken to the chapel and honored as her service to the kingdom demands."

Elder Cestrum and Elder Urlich turned toward Captain Monteros. Carys's foreign dignitary faded back and headed off to one of the northern exits. The gathered nobles whispered to each other as if it was settled. Nothing was settled. He was to be King and they would listen to his commands.

"Wait . . . " His throat was too tight for the word to have any force. He had to get out of here. He had to relax so the symptoms of the curse would fade. But he couldn't bring himself to leave her.

"I admire your dedication to the woman who was to marry your brother, Your Highness." Elder Jacobs stepped next to him and lowered his snakelike voice. "But I fear many will start to wonder if you have other motives for demanding the justice you seek. More . . . intimate reasons that might not seem as virtuous should they come to light."

Andreus pulled his eyes away from Imogen's face and looked at the Elder. "That sounds like a threat."

"No, Your Highness. It is a warning from one who would like to see you take the throne in strength. And I would be a poor ally if I didn't mention that if your . . . involvement with Lady Imogen comes to light, it will not take long for speculation to begin about whether you had a hand in your brother's death."

"I had nothing—"

"Of course not, Your Highness. But there are those who would see your involvement as a sign of disrespect for the Crown Prince, and your desire to punish your sister as an indication that you don't want to have to compete anymore for the throne." Elder Jacobs looked at Lord Garret, who was speaking with Elder Cestrum, then back at Andreus. "The next trial is at dusk. If it is vengeance you wish, there will be opportunities for you to take it then."

Elder Jacobs held his gaze for one second . . . two . . . three. Then he turned and walked back to Imogen's body. Everything inside Andreus ached for her. He wanted to kneel on the stone beside her and gather her body in his arms—to warm her against the cold wind and the flakes of snow starting to drift down from the sky.

But it was getting harder and harder to pull in air. His left arm tingled. The attack was worsening.

Elder Cestrum would see it.

Andreus would lose the throne and the chance to see his sister pay for what she had taken from him.

So, he forced himself to turn his back on Imogen's body, nodded for Max to follow, then retraced his steps—each harder to take than the last—to the stairs leading down into the castle. Pressure built in his chest. When he reached the staircase, he took several steps down to make sure he was out of view before leaning his head against the cold wall. Tears swelled, pushing against his throat. He pounded his fist against the wall as his heart strained harder to burst free.

"Prince Andreus? Are you okay?"

No. The attack was getting worse. And while he trusted Max's loyalty, he couldn't let the boy see him struggle.

"Sir, you look unwell. Maybe you should sit?"

Andreus pushed away from the wall and told Max, "I'm fine, just upset." His ears rang. He took a step forward—

—then everything went black.

Max's face swam before him. The boy's fear-filled eyes widened as he saw Andreus move. Immediately the boy rushed to help Andreus get to a sitting position.

"Your Highness, are you all right? I wanted to get Madame Jillian, but I didn't want to leave you alone."

It was then Andreus saw the small knife in Max's hand and the alcove he was currently sprawled in. He couldn't have been out for more than a moment, but the boy had pulled him into the protected space and was prepared to defend him against any attackers.

Andreus ruffled Max's hair. This boy was special. His soul was made of the seven virtues and Andreus had to protect it—had to see threats coming and head them off the way his sister—

The way he couldn't for Imogen.

She would want him to take care of the boy. He owed her that.

"Max, there's something I have to tell you. Until the Trials are over, it is better for anyone close to me to stay out of sight. Once I win the throne, everything will be back to normal. Do you understand?"

Max bobbed his head. "Yes, I—"

"Good. Now, go."

Max bowed, started down the stairs, then turned back. "I don't want to work on the windmills no more." With that he darted off.

Andreus put his hand on the wall and took deep, even breaths to try to slow his heart rate and encourage the attack to ease. He took the steps at a slow pace as the straining muscle pounded . . . but not as hard. The attack was easing. As long as he rested, he could encourage it to fade entirely.

The desire to storm through the castle, find his sister, and wrap his hands around her throat was strong. He could taste the need for vengeance. But he forced himself to walk slowly and to breathe with deeper and deeper breaths even as his frustration over the deliberate pace simmered.

His chest still ached, but breathing no longer set his chest on fire by the time he stepped into his hallway. He looked at his door, then strode down the hall past the guard standing watch and pounded on the entrance to his sister's rooms.

When she didn't answer, he shouted her name and demanded she face him. Elder Jacobs wanted Andreus to wait before making Carys answer for her crime, but Elder Jacobs hadn't loved the woman Carys had struck down.

"Carys!"

The door opened, but instead of Carys or her maid, the irritating foreign lord stood blocking the threshold. Lord Errik was it? His hands were supported by the hilt of his sword, the tip of which was resting on the ground in between his feet.

"Move out of the way." Andreus reached for his own sword.

The lord casually shook his head, but tightened the grip on his weapon. "The Princess doesn't wish to be disturbed. She needs rest. There's some kind of important event planned for tonight. I think you might have heard about it."

Rage churned. "I am heir to the throne of Eden! I command you to let me pass."

Lord Errik cocked an eyebrow. "You do that well. If and when you become King, I am sure I'll obey you with appropriate speed. Until then, Your Highness, I will stay right here."

He itched to draw his weapon. "You dare mock me?"

"I dare a lot of things that my family wishes I wouldn't," the lord said, his voice calm but his body tense—coiled—ready to strike.

"Your family is going to be sorry when I am King and you are made to pay for this disrespect."

"My family might not agree with your assessment. But I would most certainly be sorry. Just as I am sorry that you have suffered so many losses this week."

Was he referring to Imogen? Andreus drew his sword. "Do you think I care for your sympathy?"

"Not in the slightest." The lord shifted his weight and gripped his blade with a casual efficiency that, despite his anger, gave Andreus pause. "However, I offer it, as well as this: I know more about Lady Imogen and her interest in the Palace of Winds than you or anyone in your family ever has. She is not what you thought she was."

Andreus lifted his blade. "Don't speak of her to me. How would a Trade Master from Chinera know more about Eden's seer than those who actually knew her?"

"A Chineran Trade Master wouldn't know anything. But I do. Do not make me strike you down over someone as trivial as her."

Andreus shifted his grip on the sword. His hands were sweating.

His chest still ached. He wanted to strike down the arrogant lord in front of him. He had chosen his sister's side. Why? She was unliked. Spurned by nearly all who crossed her path. What did she promise him? Andreus wondered. She must have promised something. How many other dignitaries had she also made assurances to in order to secure their support?

Whatever she offered them would be meaningless when the Trials were over. And then—*then* he'd teach this foreign-born lord to be wary of whose name he found in his mouth.

"Very well," Andreus said, sliding his sword back into its sheath. "I will let my sister *rest*, as you call it. But give her a message for me—will you?"

"Of course, Your Highness." The lord bowed, but never took his eyes off Andreus.

Andreus looked past the lord, toward the doors to Carys's bedroom. "Tell my sister that I look forward to seeing her on the battlements tonight. I plan on permanently resolving this matter there."

He dressed with care in black pants and boots and a deep yellow doublet that Imogen would have admired. She'd wanted him to look every inch the King she believed him to be. In the pocket of his black cloak was a lock of Imogen's hair tied with a ribbon of white. She'd looked so peaceful on the chapel dais—almost like she had when she slept beside him. Seeing her that way—keeping a piece of her with him during this trial—would give him the strength to do what he needed to do.

Elder Cestrum, Lord Garret, and several of the Masters were on the battlements when Andreus stepped from the stairwell into the cold air. He couldn't help but look at the spot stained with Imogen's blood. Then, tearing his eyes away from the place where she lost her life, Andreus looked to the front of the battlements that overlooked the city. There, Elder Cestrum stood between two platforms. One was yellow. The other blue. Neither had existed when Andreus was here earlier. Each had ropes attached to them that stretched up and over the castle's white walls.

Andreus strode across the stone, accompanied by the sound of the windmills that he'd always loved. The Chief Elder turned toward him as the Masters hurried to inspect some wires and metal cones that Andreus hadn't noticed before. They were used to spread the sound of the gongs throughout the castle and to the base of the steps in the city to warn of a Xhelozi attack. The Masters had improved the design of magnets and wires and coils that were powered by the wind over the last decade. Andreus had been drawing out some new improvements himself, but had never found them to be as important a task as the wind-powered lights.

"Prince Andreus." Elder Cestrum stroked his white beard to a point as Andreus approached. "I trust you have recovered from your trying time this morning."

Recovered? From losing Imogen? Elder Cestrum, too, would feel his blade when all was over. "I am ready to do my duty and participate in the next trial."

"As soon as the Princess arrives . . . " Elder Cestrum shifted his focus. "Ah, there she is. Once the Masters tell me they are ready, we can begin."

Andreus shifted to look at his sister, who was walking slowly with the foreign lord at her side. Her hair was pulled off her face, her skin paler than usual. Even from here Andreus could see the glassiness in her eyes and the pain that each step caused her. His mother's

Tears of Midnight suppressed pain. So perhaps it wasn't any wonder a body that had been used to feeling nothing for so long would interpret each step as something filled with agony.

Despite the lift of her chin and her straight back, Andreus could tell his twin was suffering. He looked back at the dark blood stain on the stone and any residual guilt faded away. Imogen must have suffered before she died. It was good his sister would, too.

As she called his name, he turned and headed toward the platforms. He would not let her manipulate him with her slippery words. He'd made a choice. This would end. And it was going to end today.

Elder Cestrum beckoned to them both. "This trial will test two kinds of strength: the ability to inspire your people to follow you, and the physical strength it takes to lead them when it is time to fight. You each will step onto your designated platforms and inspire the people in the city below with your words. When the speeches are done and a point awarded to the one who the people display their affection for, a gong will sound, signaling it is time to use the rope ladders to climb down the wall to the steps below. The winner will be the one who safely reaches the bottom first."

Andreus stiffened.

"You can't expect the Prince and Princess of Eden to climb down this wall," the foreign lord shouted as he stepped closer to Carys. "They could die."

The wall was over forty feet tall. Snow was falling from the sky. Darkness would soon be upon them, and the curse could show itself when he was too high up for anything to help him. And then, yes. He could lose his grip and die on the stone below. But so could Carys.

"Each day a monarch rules on a throne is filled with risk," Elder Cestrum said with a smile. "My nephew assures me he could make the climb down without falling. Of course, if the Prince or the Princess want to refuse, they can nullify the Trials . . . "

And Garret would end up on the throne.

Andreus stepped to his platform, turned toward his sister, and said, "I am happy to prove that I am my father's son. I will do what it takes to win and keep my throne."

"You can't," the foreign lord shouted to Carys above the pounding of the windmills.

Carys stared at Andreus for several long seconds and said, "I have no choice."

"Very well." Elder Cestrum looked to the Masters standing next to the blue platform. "Are we ready?"

The Masters nodded.

"Good. Then Prince Andreus and Princess Carys, I ask you to take your places. Prince Andreus will speak when the first gong sounds. Once he is done, Princess Carys will begin. Two gongs will signal the start of the physical part of the trial. All of us on the Council will be watching from the bottom. I wish you the best of luck."

With that Elder Cestrum headed for the stairs. Lord Garret stopped, leaned down and whispered something in Carys's ear, then lumbered behind.

Andreus stepped closer to the battlements and could hear the noise of the crowd that had been masked by the churning of the windmills. The square below the steps was filled with people, as were the streets and the rooftops. A cheer went up as they spotted his face, which helped quell the nerves he felt as he ascended the four steps that led to the top of the yellow platform.

His stomach lurched as another cheer went up and he looked at the rope ladder that was affixed to an iron rod in the middle of the platform and then disappeared over the battlements. Which is exactly what he would have to use. He was used to looking down from the height of the wall, but *climbing* down it . . . The Council was right about one thing—it was going to take a lot of strength to overcome the fear of stepping over that edge and even more determination to make it to the ground with the temperature dropping and the snow falling around them.

He turned to his sister, who was struggling to unfasten her cloak. The foreign Lord Errik stepped forward to help her, but she shook her head. The cloak finally fell away and Andreus stared at her with surprise.

His sister was wearing pants. Black and fitted and something their father would have had her flogged for if she had made an appearance in them while he was alive. She was wearing a white-sleeved tunic that hung just below the black belt at her hips, from which both silver stilettos hung. But it was the fitted vest—half deep blue, half yellow—that was the biggest surprise. Not just her color. But both of their colors. The colors of all of Eden.

Shaking off any assistance from her foreign friend, his sister walked stiffly to the platform, took a deep breath, and one step at a time made it to the top.

Despite the cold she was sweating. And when she looked at him and held his gaze, he could see the pain swimming in her eyes as she yelled his name.

"You will pay for what you have done," he said as the Master hurried around the platform, checking the system that would carry his and his sister's voices, amplifying the sound for all to hear.

"Imogen had Micah and Father killed," his sister shouted. "I left a note asking you to meet me so I could tell you what I'd learned, only she came instead."

"You can say anything. She is not here to defend herself anymore. Because of you."

A gong sounded, cutting off whatever else his sister might have tried to say to sway him. Adderton was to blame for Micah and Father's deaths. If Carys thought her tall tales were going to harden his heart toward Imogen, she was wrong.

Refusing to look at his sister, Andreus stepped closer to the edge of the battlements so he could look down at the people below.

Taking a deep breath, Andreus angled himself so his words would travel into the iron cone the Masters had suspended above the platform. Then, hearing Imogen's words about what a King should be echoing in his memory, he said, "For years I have worked beside the Masters of Light on these walls. I chose to study the windmills and the power they bring because I wanted to help keep Garden City safe. And that is what I want to do as King: keep Eden safe. I will lead the Masters in new ways to ward off the Xhelozi. I will insist the guard seek out their dens in the summer and cut each one of them down until there is no longer anything to fear from the mountains. And with the aid of the seven High Lords and the virtues their districts represent, I will see that the war with Adderton is won. The orb of Eden will shine more brightly than before as a symbol to all kingdoms of what is possible when the seven virtues are heeded and the people walk in the light."

A cheer went up from below. Pride swelled inside him.

The people were his. It was always so. And so it would be. He would sit on the Throne of Light by nightfall.

19

Carys waited for her brother to look at her. She needed another chance to explain—to warn him in case something happened to her—but he kept his eyes forward and she knew one thing was certain as she blinked back the tears. She'd lost him. Imogen's poison thoughts had rooted themselves in Andreus's brain. And her death had insured they flourished.

Gods.

The ache in her heart mirrored that of her body. Every muscle screamed from a need she couldn't fill. She wiped her wet palms on the pants Larkin had created and delivered along with the ball gown last night. According to Errik, Larkin said she'd made the outfit as an expression of her faith in Carys. It was Larkin's way of showing that she believed Carys was as good as any prince or king.

Only the desperate need to warn her brother, Larkin's and Errik's faith in her ability, and the willow bark tea Juliette encouraged her to drink gave Carys the ability to climb out of her sweat-soaked bed where nightmares plagued her every time she closed her eyes. Her face bloody and unrecognizable. Her brother with his sword raised. A wind cyclone like the one from when she was twelve barreling down the mountains, destroying everything in its path. Ready to destroy her.

Errik asked no questions about her *illness* and refused to leave his post in her solar even when she ordered him away. He said nothing to her about her brother, even though she heard Andreus's voice yelling from the next room.

Imogen.

She had taken the secret of her coconspirator's identity to the grave and in death had turned the person who Carys depended on against her.

The wind swirled around her. She flinched. She could swear she could hear it calling to her, which wasn't possible. It was the illness from the withdrawal that made her think the wind was whispering— asking her to set it free.

"Princess Carys," one of the Masters near her platform said. "It is your turn to speak."

She stepped closer to the edge of the platform—to the threshold of the battlements—and her stomach rolled as she looked down. So, she pulled her gaze up and kept her eyes on her brother as she tried to decide what to say. She was supposed to speak to the people. And she would. But it was her brother's stony face and the love that had caused her to shield him all these years that pulled the first words from her.

"I have always tried to be strong. I've done my best to stand by you in my way—the only way I know. Am I perfect?" She laughed. "Gods no. There is no one in this kingdom who would believe me if I said I was. I have said the wrong things, unsettled people with my choices, and have often been seen as . . . unpleasant. The one thing I have done right in my life is love you."

Tears swelled. Her legs trembled beneath her. The wind swirled.

"I will never be perfect. I will make mistakes just as you have. If you give me a chance and believe in me I will learn from them. Our arrangement, this way we live, cannot be sustained. We strain too hard at our predetermined places, our prescribed roles. We want more. We deserve more. We should be freer to choose the path we desire.

"That desire for freedom—to speak, to live, to feel as I choose— is perhaps what has made me who I am. Made us what we are. But no matter what we *are*, I dream of what we can become. When this trial is over, all I know for certain is that I am supposed to be at your side. It is my fate to stand in front of you, to shield you when the darkness comes. My life has been pledged to you since the day I was born, and no matter what you decide—I *will* be here for you. I will reach with you for that better way, for freedom—a freedom that we may share—until the day I die."

Her shoulders groaned as she straightened them. Then she braved a look down at the mass of people standing silently beneath her and realized her words—all the phrases she had just spoken to her brother—also belonged to them. *They* were the people who stood in front of the lords when a battle began. *They* were the ones who were flogged while those above them were set free. She understood them. She *was* them. Now she wanted them to understand her.

"No matter how these trials end, my heart is yours. My life belongs to you. I am Princess Carys . . . daughter of Ulron . . . Keeper of Virtues and Guardian of Light. He might be gone, but the commitment of his blood runs true. I give you my oath." She glanced at her brother. "Even if I am pushed away or pushed down, no matter how bloody or beaten I might be, I will rise and fight again. Because I will be fighting for you."

Her brother stared straight ahead. No one—nothing below the battlements—seemed to move. It was as if everything was frozen in time. Then Carys saw banners of blue in the center of the crowded main square lifting up toward her. Then more. Blue near the front of the square. Blue from people lining the streets snaking through the city.

She blinked back the tears blurring her vision as the blue banners began to wave and what sounded like her name floated up on the wind. Louder. Then louder still, telling her that they had heard the truth of her words.

Her stomach cramped. Every step she took made her muscles weep, but as much as she wanted to sink to the ground she would fight—for her brother's soul, for her people.

She braved a glance at her brother as the next set of gongs sounded. He didn't bother to look her way as he moved to the edge of the platform, got down on his knees, and took hold of the top of the hemp ladder in his hands. He reached back with his foot, found a foothold, and shifted backward onto the top of the wall. With the next move his legs went over the battlements.

A cheer went up from the people below. Then only his head was visible. Finally, Andreus spared a look at her. There was hatred there. Not just distrust. Not just betrayal. Hatred. As if she was the curse he had waited his whole life to kill.

Then he was gone and Carys had to follow.

Swallowing down a metallic taste in her mouth, she inched

forward and carefully lowered herself to her knees. The braided hemp ladder was narrow and was shifting back and forth in the wind. Flurries of snow landed on the platform next to her as she shivered from cold and terror.

She was scared. Never before in her life had she known this kind of naked fear. Her palms sweating, her body weak, and hundreds of feet between her and the ground. She was unlikely to survive this trial. But there was a chance she would. And that was how she convinced herself to wipe the moisture from her hands and grip the ladder as her brother had already done.

Wind gusted snow into her face and pulled her hair. Her heart pounded hard and fast against her chest. This was just like playing on the ladders in the stables, she told herself, trying to forget that she fell off those ladders when she was seven and broke her arm falling from eight feet up.

She tested her grip, then tested it again, before backing up to the edge of the battlements. Gritting her teeth, she slid her leg over the edge to search for a foothold.

A cheer from below floated up as she found one, held her breath, and forced herself to lower her other foot over the edge. The narrow platform shook as a gust of icy wind tugged at the hemp rope. She clutched it tightly and leaned against the wall, knowing she had to move. The longer she was on the rope, the weaker her aching muscles would become. Fear screamed to go slow, but she knew that would kill her. So she used the fear and the sound of the blood pounding in her ears to drive her all the way over the edge.

Her foot searched for the next rung and found air. She closed her eyes tight and squeezed her fingers so the hemp bit into flesh as she felt nothing beneath her. The rope had to be there.

Yes. Sweat trickled down her neck as she found the rung and slid her foot onto it.

Don't think, she told herself. Just go and don't stop.

Facing the white wall she had always hated, she clenched her teeth against the pain in her arms as she shifted her foot and lowered herself down the ladder. One rung. Two. Never looking down. Never letting more than a few seconds go by before feeling for the next rung, or the icy knot in her stomach would overwhelm her and she wouldn't be able to move at all.

One foot on the next rung. Move one hand. Next foot. Then the next hand, tightening her grip when she couldn't find the next foothold for several seconds. The rungs weren't evenly spaced. Some were over a foot apart. Others were just inches. Each time her foot found a rung she let out a sigh of relief before her insides once again clenched with fear.

The snow fell harder. The wind blew, turning her fingers to ice and making it more and more difficult to grip the braided rope. Her arms trembled as she lowered herself down another rung. Her calves cramped and Carys bit her lip with the new wave of pain. Gods help her. Her body wasn't going to be able to hold on much longer. She had to go faster.

She found the next rung. Then the next as the crowd cheered.

The cheers sounded louder than before. She had to be getting closer.

Wrapping one arm around the rope to give her scraped, freezing fingers a rest, Carys braved a look downward. Still over half the distance to go. Glancing to her side, she could see Andreus fifteen feet below. His ladder dangled two arm lengths away from hers. He was reaching down toward his leg. Were his muscles cramping from the cold? Or was it something worse?

If he had an attack up here . . .

Carys wiped the dampness from one hand on the sleeve of her tunic, gripped the ladder as tight as she could, and resumed her descent, determined to catch up with her brother. He might hate her, but he would hate the idea of falling to his death more.

She descended two more rungs. Then two more, flexing her fingers each time, trying to make sure she could still hold on. She ignored the spasms in her arms and the pain shooting up her back. She leaned her head against the coarse hemp and choked back a sob as a tremor shook her body, making the rope ladder swing.

Keep going. She had to keep going.

Carys lowered herself down another rung. Below her, Andreus didn't appear to be moving.

"Dreus!" she yelled, blinking against the snow. "Are you all right?"

Her fingers closed around the next rung. She stepped down, then down again until she was even with her brother. "Andreus! What's wrong?"

Her brother looked up at her. "My boot. I can't get it free."

Stuck—fifteen feet above the stone below. Her own fingers were barely hanging on. His would be stronger, but the cold would eventually make him lose his grip.

From here, she couldn't see his boot well enough to tell what the problem was so she clenched her jaw and forced herself to move several feet lower. Squinting into the swirling snow, she spotted the problem. A piece of hemp had come free from its braiding and had caught on the ties to his boot.

"I'm going to cut you free."

"What?" he yelled.

She wrapped her right forearm around the ladder and drew the stiletto from her belt with her left. "Don't move," she yelled.

Oh Gods. She swallowed hard and leaned to her left, pulling herself away from her own ladder so she could reach the one Andreus was on. Her left foot slipped and her stomach lurched and she hugged the ladder and found her footing again.

She closed her eyes, took a deep breath, and ordered herself to try again.

Swallowing hard, she shifted her weight and leaned toward her brother again. The snow fell. The air was still as she held her breath and tried to reach the rope that was keeping her brother from continuing his climb. "Can you move?" she yelled.

"What?" he yelled back.

"Kick your foot away from the ladder so I can cut the rope that's holding you."

He looked down at her for a long second, then gave a slow nod as she braved leaning a little farther. Her arms shook. Sweat streamed down her back as she shivered and told herself not to worry. She could do this. She'd get her brother free and make it the next twelve feet to the plateau's surface.

Andreus kicked his foot away from the rope and the ladder began to sway.

"Again," she yelled, judging the distance and the angle like she would a target she wanted to hit with her blade. Andreus followed her command. The movement sent the ladder an inch closer to her. Then another as it swayed on the wall.

Carys could hear the gasps from the crowd. Her heart pounded as the coarse hemp dug through the fabric of her tunic and into her arm, which was beginning to weaken more. If she didn't want to fall, she needed both hands to hold on.

She judged the sway of the ladder as Andreus kicked his boot again and slashed with her blade knowing it was the only shot she had.

The blade caught the rope, but not enough. It was still attached to Andreus's boot as she grabbed her own ladder and hung on for dear life.

Out of the corner of her eye, she saw her brother kick again, trying to break the rope's hold on him. She heard him shout something. Then out of the corner of her eye, she saw his boot a second before it slammed against her hand.

She let go.

The stiletto dropped from her hand.

Her feet slipped and suddenly there was nothing beneath her.

She dangled from the rope by her forearm and desperately reached for a rung with her left hand when another blow struck the side of her head.

Pain swirled. Lights flared behind her eyes and her forearm slid down . . . then free.

A scream clawed her throat as she fell. The air around her swirled harder, then harder still, pushing her toward the wall—toward the ladder—as her fingers tried to grab hold of something. Anything.

The crowd below jeered.

Her hand latched onto a rung, jerking her arm, stopping her descent before her fingers slipped again.

Only this time she didn't fall. The wind swirled under her feet—keeping her from falling long enough for her to grab the rungs one more time and find the loops with her feet.

All at once, the wind stilled completely, as though it had been sucked into the windmills. She willed herself to hang on for the next rung. And the next. And one more, until finally, she crumpled into the snow on the ground.

Everything inside her clenched and screamed and pulled and trembled as she tried to rise but couldn't. Not even when she heard her brother step from his ladder. Not even when she heard him whisper that next time she wouldn't get so lucky.

She heard Lord Errik calling to her—asking if she was okay. Garret crouched in the snow a few feet away and held out his hand and she shook her head.

No. She had to get up on her own. The people had seen her fall. They would see her rise. She would show them—show her brother— that she would always get back up as she promised. She needed them to see it so they would remember.

Placing her scraped, raw hands into the snow, she pushed slowly to her knees. Then, using the ladder, she pulled herself to her feet and sound exploded around her.

Blue banners waved against the snow and the darkening sky. People cheered and stomped and called her name.

Her brother's eyes burned as Elder Cestrum pointed up to the scoring board on the wall where two blue pegs were being lowered in. Behind the board, atop the highest tower, the orb of Eden glowed bright.

Trumpets sounded and the people fell silent as Elder Cestrum stepped forward and announced, "The trial of strength is complete with Princess Carys as our winner. While I am sure they are tired and would like to rest, monarchs often do not have a chance to rest in between decisions that must be made. Duty always calls and they must have endurance to answer that call. Tonight, Prince Andreus and Princess Carys will demonstrate that endurance. For this trial, they must travel to the Majestic Tomb of Eden. The Council has hidden the crown of virtue in the tomb. The one who finds the crown and safely returns to the castle will win. Your attendants have prepared your horses. Good luck to you both because this trial begins now."

Now.

Tears slipped down Carys's face.

The crowd shouted their encouragement as Andreus raced toward the large staircase.

Carys could barely take a step. Her head pounded. Her arms throbbed. And she was cold. So very cold as she willed one foot in front of the other—as fast as she dared.

The wind began anew. It pulled at the strands of her hair, which had come free from its binding as she squinted down to the bottom, where her brother was already mounting his horse. She couldn't beat him in this challenge. She wasn't sure she'd even be able to survive it.

The cold.

The pain.

The way her legs trembled beneath her, telling her no matter how much she willed them she would soon no longer be able to stand.

The darkness and the mountains where the Xhelozi hunted.

And Andreus who had tried to send her crashing to her death. She had survived his anger once. Unless she could outthink him, she wouldn't be able to survive another attack.

She wanted to lie down, to give in to whatever her fate would be if she did so. But the blue banners kept her standing. She closed her eyes and took a deep breath, thinking about the Trials. Then she stiffly walked down the steps to where Errik stood waiting.

"Your brother tried to kill you," he said, draping the cloak she'd discarded earlier around her shoulders. "If you follow him out of the city he'll try again, and there will be no one there to stop him."

"I know," she said, marshaling her strength before looking deep into eyes that warmed her more than the cloak she now wore. Putting her hand over his, she leaned into his touch. "I have to go, but I need your help."

He stared at her as if memorizing her face, then leaned close and placed a gentle kiss on her lips. "Ask of me anything."

The sounds of the crowd were all around her, but as the snow fell harder it felt like she and Errik were alone. She should be angry that he'd kissed her in the open, but she was glad for the moment. Because that moment might be the last bit of tenderness she ever had.

Stepping away from his touch, she looked out at the city and shivered. An image from her nightmares flashed before her eyes: a bloody face. Whose?

Quietly, she said, "If my brother comes back and I do not, there is something you need to know and there is something I need you to do."

20

Wind whipped Andreus's skin. The falling snow and setting sun painted streaks of pink and purple speckled with white. The crowd lining the road waved and bowed. Here and there he saw a banner of yellow, but the majority had turned blue.

For Carys.

It seemed impossible that she had reached the ground safely. He'd watched her lose her grip and plummet. She should be lying on the flagstones at the foot of the battlements—broken. Beaten.

But then the wind had—

What had it done, Andreus? he chided himself. *Had the winds come to slow Carys's fall? Had they protected her—come to her call?*

No. It was preposterous.

No matter what had actually occurred his sister reached the bottom intact.

And part of him—a part he hated—had been glad.

It was a momentary weakness. One Imogen had worried about.

Well, it was the last time he'd be that weak. After this trial, Andreus's subjects wouldn't raise Carys's banner again. Imogen deserved justice and Andreus needed to prove that he was the man he'd promised her he could be.

He glanced back as he passed through the main entrance of the city. Carys wasn't there. But she would get on her horse and ride to the tomb. His sister didn't give up unless someone made her.

Tugging on the reins, Andreus turned his horse toward the mountains. The trek to the tomb of the Kingdom of Eden's rulers had been a two-hour journey when they'd escorted his father and brother to their resting places. Without the wagons and the stately pace he should make it in half that time. Cole had been exercised by the grooms regularly. Andreus was sure he would be able to make the journey in good time. Unless, of course, the snow that was thickening with each passing minute slowed them down. The swirling white made it harder to see as the sun disappeared from the sky. And as the sun sank, the temperature dropped.

Andreus shivered and urged Cole to return to a gallop as they moved toward the mountains and away from the safety of the illuminated walls behind him. The faster he traveled, the faster he would get back to the lights.

A screech filled the air and Cole slowed his gait. Andreus held his breath and reached for the sword he'd taken from a member of the guard before riding out of the city.

There was another screech—like a rusty hinge being opened.

The Xhelozi were awake and coming down from the mountains to hunt. If he wasn't careful, he would be their prey.

His horse's pace slowed to a trot as he turned toward the southwest. Andreus looked behind him for a glimpse of his sister. The dark and the snow made it impossible to tell if she was back there.

He would deal with her later. For now he would focus on completing this trial so his subjects would have something to cheer.

"Come on, Cole," he said, blowing warm air onto his hands before clutching the reins. "We have to move."

Cole's hooves pounded the ground. Andreus ignored the tightening in his chest as he pulled the cloak snug around his body. Every few minutes, Andreus looked back to Eden's orb shining like a beacon above the castle to make sure he was going the right way.

A gray fox darted out of a distant grove of trees. Normally the darkness would shield it from view, but against the white of the snow the fox was easy to spot. Just as Andreus would be if anything on the mountains was watching.

Cole was tiring. Andreus slowed him to a walk. If he didn't the horse would be too spent to race back to the castle after Andreus succeeded in the trial.

The snow continued to fall. His breath turned to smoke in front of his face. The mountains grew larger as the ground under Cole's feet shifted from grass to dirt and stone.

Almost there and still no Carys behind him.

The pulse of the tomb's windmill filled the silence as he reached the entrance and dismounted.

His legs buckled and he grabbed the saddle for support. The trek down the wall and the hours in the cold had taken their toll. But he'd be fine. He would endure as he was supposed to. And he would win.

He took a deep breath and stiffly led Cole into the entrance that, unlike the tomb beyond, had no wind-powered lights. Good thing the small stones he needed to connect the windmill power to the door were smooth and easy to find by feel next to the other rough rocks.

Massive steel doors rumbled. Light flooded the darkness,

blinding him as he stumbled forward into the tomb.

Death filled his nose. Rotting decay that he gagged and choked on. He forced himself to look around the first of the series of chambers that made up the tomb. In the center of the largest of the stone rooms was a small but perfect replica of Eden's orb, surrounded by seven stone statues depicting the seven virtues. At the foot of each statue was the vice one must overcome to achieve the light. Benches carved into the walls were covered with dusty shrouds. These crypts housed the very first of Eden's royal families.

Andreus threw off the shrouds. Beheld the bones they hid.

None of those long-dead rulers had the crown he sought. He would have to go through the passages that wound underneath the mountain range.

The smell of death grew stronger the farther he traveled in the dim light. Shadows pursued him as he peered into each burial shelf carved into the walls. But as much as he hated the enclosed spaces filled with death, he was grateful for the lack of wind and snow.

The jagged stone floor slanted downward as he retraced the steps the guards would have taken to lay his brother and father to rest. There. The gold-and-sapphire crown caught the light. It was sitting on top of his brother's shroud as though to remind him that it was Micah who was supposed to be King.

Andreus laughed. The Elders were toying with him. Only it wouldn't work. Micah was stuck rotting in here and Andreus was going to rule.

He grabbed the crown, turned, and went back through the passages. First at a walk. Then at a run. He wanted to get back to the castle with the crown that was rightfully his.

He crossed into the cold darkness of the entryway, activated the doors, and watched them slowly close, blotting out any light. When the grinding of the gears ceased, Andreus attached the crown to his belt and then walked toward Cole. The horse was shifting restlessly. He nickered and blew out air and Andreus patted his flank to settle him.

He heard something shift. Andreus went still. A rock skittered across stone. Something was moving behind him in the darkness.

Carys?

Andreus reached for the sword on his belt and drew it slowly, trying not to make a sound. The metal whispered its release from the scabbard. Cole's hooves clattered on the ground as he started forward. Ready to be off.

Slowly, Andreus turned and squinted into the shadows in the cave, but he could see nothing. Feeling foolish, he grabbed the pommel of the saddle and was pulling himself up when the sound came again.

He glanced behind him and that's when he saw it. Claws. Teeth. Thick gray scales across the chest. White fur. Long arms on the narrow but terrifyingly tall and powerful body.

Xhelozi.

Cole jerked forward. Andreus almost lost his grip and slid sideways. His heart pitched with his body and fear spiked hard as he pulled himself up, dug his heels into Cole's side, and yelled, "Go."

A loud screech came from his left as the horse raced out of the cave and onto the slick, snowy path. Cole reared as another rusty cry echoed in front of them.

Oh, Gods.

Andreus raised his sword and urged Cole forward. The horse balked, but Andreus dug his boots deep into the horse's flanks as another screech cut through the night. Behind him. To the side. In front. Cries came from everywhere as they raced forward through the darkness. Away from the mountains. He had to get back to the castle and the lights.

A shadow darted out of the trees. Fire raked across his leg as something slammed into the horse from the side. Cole whinnied and reared. Andreus clutched the pommel with one hand and swung with his sword. The blade struck flesh. A shriek of agony cut through the air, making the horse rear again. Andreus lost his grip and slammed to the ground. Hoofbeats raced away from him.

Another screech came from somewhere to his right as the thing in front of him snarled.

Dark liquid stained the white fur on its arm. It snarled again and leaped forward. Andreus scrambled backward and rolled to his side as the creature landed on the spot he'd just vacated.

He lashed out with his blade and connected. Then he clambered to his feet and hobbled to his right. The monster turned back toward him with teeth bared and hooked claws extended.

Blood trickled down Andreus's left leg. He could barely put weight on it. The creature reared back on its powerful legs and sprang.

Andreus dropped to the ground and rolled under the attack, swinging the sword as hard as he could. The blade bit into the Xhelozi and sliced across the midsection. The air shook as the thing screeched.

Through his panic, triumph flared. Andreus scrambled to his feet, balancing all his weight on his right foot, and lunged at the wounded creature. It snarled and started to rise just as his sword punched into its chest, sending the Xhelozi back to the ground. He pulled out the sword and stabbed through the mass of white fur and scales again. The Xhelozi gurgled once. Then, for a moment, every-thing went silent.

Finally, Andreus braved a look at the leg cut by the Xhelozi's claws.

Blood. He leaned on his sword to help him balance as blackness swirled in his eyes and the world went in and out of focus. Three deep gashes running from just below his knee to halfway down his calf oozed and bubbled with blood that spilled onto the white of the snow.

A rusty cry came from the left. Then one from behind.

Close. They were close. And he was surrounded.

He ripped off the bottom of his tunic and tied the swath of fabric tight around the wound.

Another cry. This one somewhere to his right. As if they were hunting him in a pack.

He clenched his jaw as he limped away from the dead Xhelozi and whistled for Cole. But there was no time. Could he hide from them? Maybe. There were stories travelers told of surviving the Xhelozi by burying themselves in the snow. It supposedly concealed their scent and the heat of their bodies. But Andreus wasn't sure he believed those tales, and even if he did, the bandage on his leg would only help for so long. He had to get back to Garden City.

Leaning on his sword, Andreus licked his lips and whistled again. He sagged with relief as he heard a whinny from somewhere over the hill. It took him four tries to pull himself onto the stallion. Twice the Xhelozi calls made the horse buck, but he held tight to the reins and eventually pulled himself on as a tall shadow appeared in the trees to his left.

"Go," he said, leaning over the horse's neck. Cole bolted forward like an arrow out of a bow. There was a snarl behind him. Then another, followed by a grinding metallic shriek. The Xhelozi were giving chase.

Andreus looked around the white landscape, trying to get his bearings. The castle was to the northwest. The fastest route was the foothills and meadows he had come through the first time, but those were mostly out in the open with no place for him to take cover. The forest was straight ahead. The Xhelozi might give up the chase in there.

Blood trickled down Andreus's leg as he headed for the tree line.

Cole dodged over hills and around massive trunks, never breaking stride. Andreus glanced behind him at the shadows that were darting in between the trees. From the left. The right. The Xhelozi smelled his blood. They weren't giving up and Cole wouldn't be able to keep up this pace for much longer.

Andreus angled the horse toward the high riverbed that had yet to freeze over. There was a path—not easily seen and fairly steep—behind some rocks not far from here. He and Carys used to scare their nurse by hiding there safe from sight. Maybe the same trick would work now.

Cole plunged into the icy water and splashed across the wide riverbed. Andreus looked over his shoulder. He could hear them calling, but they were still deep in the trees.

He urged Cole up the embankment and then around the rock formation he remembered from his childhood. The horse picked its way up slowly. Too slowly. Andreus was certain they were going to be found and in the tight path, caught between stone and dirt, there would be no escape.

Finally, the horse crested the incline. Andreus bit back a shout of victory, nudged the horse forward, and heard a soft nicker.

Turning, he spotted Carys's brown mare tied to a low, scraggly bush. The horse shook snow off its head and Andreus looked for his sister. If her horse was here, she had to be as well.

Footprints. He could follow them and pass judgment here for what she had taken from him. The Council might speculate, but no one would know that he was the one who struck her down. It would all be over then. The Trials. The betrayal. The pain of knowing all these years she'd been biding her time until she could betray him.

"Carys?" he said quietly. "Are you there?"

A screech answered him and it was close. Just over the rocks. Then another.

He didn't have time to track his sister. He'd let the Xhelozi do it for him.

Andreus brought his sword down on the rope tethering Carys's horse, grabbed the mare's reins, and urged Cole forward.

Both horses shot through the night.

There was quiet.

Then the night was split open by a soul-breaking scream.

Carys.

The scream of agony raked through the night again. The wind gusted. Snow swirled. Andreus felt the pull to reverse course. To save his sister.

He turned his back instead.

The screams rang in his ears—louder until they were drowned out by the cheers as he made it through the Garden City gates.

The gongs sounded, welcoming him home.

His head rested against Cole's neck; he cared little what the people watching him thought. He desperately held on while the horse limped down the icy streets. The shouting and cheers grew louder as more people came out of their houses. He saw a pall come over them as they noticed the second horse walking beside his—and his leg that left a trail of blood as he went.

People called his name as he reached the main square and the base of the castle's steps. He held tight to the pommel of his horse as he pulled his injured leg over the saddle and slid off. His legs buckled. He clenched his teeth and refused to go down to the ground. Instead, he hung on to the saddle to keep himself upright. He was King. He would not be seen on his knees. Not after all he had done.

Lord Errik shoved his way around the Elders. "Where is Princess Carys?" he demanded.

"I don't know," Andreus rasped. "The Xhelozi were chasing me and I found her horse as I was fighting my way back to the castle. I couldn't see her anywhere."

Lord Errik grabbed Carys's horse, leaped onto it, and wheeled to gallop down the street before Andreus had finished speaking.

Andreus scoffed. If the Xhelozi left anything for Lord Errik to find, he would find it too late.

The snow stopped falling as Andreus fumbled with cold, blood-stained fingers to pull the crown from his belt. Finally, he presented it to Elder Cestrum.

"The Prince needs a healer," the Chief Elder yelled as he took the crown from Andreus's hands. "Captain Monteros, have your men get a stretcher to bring him to the castle."

The guards arrived. Carefully, they helped him onto the stretcher. As they ascended the steps to the castle, Andreus kept his eyes on the scoring board and watched as a yellow peg was added to the board.

He had won.

He was the King of Eden.

Madame Jillian was at the top of the steps when he arrived. She ordered him carried to his rooms so she could treat the leg, which had gone numb. Then it burned as she drained the wound. She gave him what she could for the pain and sent someone to the Queen's rooms for Tears of Midnight to dull the rest.

Andreus laughed. It wasn't funny, but he couldn't stop laughing even when the healer wrapped the wound and warned him the leg might never be the same again.

Then the gongs sounded and his laughter stopped.

Carys was back.

That couldn't be. He had heard her cry out. The Xhelozi. She couldn't have survived.

The healer tried to push him down, but he forced himself to his feet and ordered his valet to bring him his cloak.

Two members of the guard helped him limp to the courtyard. His heart pounded harder with every painful step and his chest tightened. Still he urged them to go faster until they reached the courtyard. Moments later Lord Errik appeared in the entrance of the gates with what must be Carys in his arms. Even in the bright wind-powered light it was impossible to tell.

Her clothes were in tatters and there was blood. So much blood. But the hair—almost completely white in this light—was unmistakable.

Elder Ulrich followed behind Lord Errik, telling him to slow down.

"No," Lord Errik yelled, cradling Carys's disfigured body close to him as he ran. "She was still breathing. There could still be time. Send for a healer."

The Elders asked everyone to assemble in the Hall of Virtues to wait, but as they all turned toward the castle door, Lord Errik returned. Anger and blood colored his face. Andreus held his breath as he waited to hear the words that would end this.

The wind gusted, making it almost impossible to hear the words that Andreus had been waiting for.

"You are too late! Princess Carys is dead."

Pain flared again. Andreus's legs trembled under his weight. He limped back to his rooms before he passed out. All the while, the castle shook as the people rang the air with four words.

Long live the King.

21

"I have to see her," Andreus said, trying to stand.

Light streamed through the curtains of his bedchamber. The seven members of the Council of Elders stood at the foot of his bed.

"You need to let me put this splint on your leg," Madame Jillian said, holding out what looked like a small circular cage. "The poison from these cuts is still festering. The numbness and lack of muscle control might never fully fade."

"When will I be free of this contraption?" he asked.

"I don't know."

"You don't know? Then who does?" he demanded. "Kings must stand on their own two feet!"

"No one I have treated ever fought the Xhelozi and lived, Your Highness." Madame Jillian bowed. "But I am working on a solution."

The only man she knew to fight the beasts outside the walls and survive. Andreus smiled in satisfaction. The Elders had heard. They knew now the kind of king they would be dealing with. Soon, songs would be written about the strength of King Andreus who single-handedly faced down the Xhelozi.

Elder Cestrum cleared his throat. "The Council of Elders has arranged for your coronation to occur tonight. There are decisions about the war that need to be made and can only be made by our King."

Andreus rose from his bed and Elder Jacobs offered to accompany him on his walk to his sister's door. "I must warn you," the Elder said softly. "The Xhelozi were not as kind to your sister as they were to you. The Princess suffered."

Screams echoed in his memory as he opened the door.

Her body lay on the bed. Andreus took one step into the room and froze.

Her face was gone. Someone had smoothed and brushed his sister's white blond hair around the series of gashes and scrapes crusted with blood and gore. In one place, the cut went so deep Andreus was certain he could see bone.

His stomach lurched and Andreus grabbed the doorframe for support as his legs threatened to give way.

His sister was dead.

Her screams clawed through his mind.

"Would you like a moment alone?" Elder Jacobs asked.

"No." He stepped back from the bedroom and shut the door, but the screams continued. "No, that won't be necessary."

"Don't feel bad, Your Highness," Elder Jacobs said, taking Andreus's arm. "Your mother had a hard time seeing your sister as well."

"My mother was here? How is she?"

"She seemed much improved."

He thought of their mother's attempt to get to the mountains when she first lost her mind. Perhaps he was not haunted. Perhaps hers were the screams that had met his ears. "Did she cry out when she saw Carys?"

"No," Elder Jacobs said with a frown. "She laughed."

Heavy.

Arms. Legs. Everything was heavy. And tired. And so cold. She shivered and cried out in pain.

Then she remembered she wasn't supposed to cry out.

"You're going to be okay."

Errik had said that to her when he found her near the river, wedged deep in between three large boulders buried behind a grove of wintergreen trees. Scared. Cold. Heartbroken. Bleeding from the scrapes on her face and arms, heart racing from the screams of the Xhelozi. The scraping of their claws along the rocks. The snarls when she was certain they smelled her. And the wind that shifted the snow and the trees until she heard Errik's voice calling to her.

He spoke of the plan for their return as he slashed her clothes and cloak. He ran his hand along the scrape on her jaw. Then across her cheek. Finally rubbing his thumb against her lip before gently gathering her aching, bruised body in his arms. The Xhelozi calls echoed against the snow. Errik held her closer with each cry. Finally, the sounds were gone—the monsters pulled back to the mountains where they belonged—and Errik slowed the horse. He pressed a soft whisper of a kiss on her lips before lifting her off the horse and drawing his knife for the second time.

The duck's blood was warm and sticky and made her want to scream as he smeared it over her face along with strips of the inside of the bird. The smell made her want to gag, but she told herself not to move—not to make a sound. She drank the thick sleeping draught he offered to her and clung to his soft encouragement as they rode toward the gates.

The wind whispered.

Then she sighed as darkness enveloped her.

And now, Larkin's voice soothed her as a wet cloth passed over her face.

"Keep your eyes closed just a little while longer."

Carys wasn't sure she could open them even if she wanted to. "Lord Errik," she whispered. How long since he'd brought her here to the nursery where Larkin had been waiting?

"Don't worry. It'll grow back, Your Highness."

"What will?" She trembled as the wet cloth passed over her face.

"Your hair."

Water trickled nearby.

The cloth ran over her cheeks and forehead and eyelids again. Carys remembered Larkin helping her undress before wrapping her in a blanket and Errik saying he needed her hair. There was a servant who had died—disfigured. With Carys's hair Errik was certain he could make the dead girl pass for her.

More tinkling water and finally Larkin said, "You can open your eyes now."

Even though she was clean, Carys could still feel the blood caked on to her lashes. She slowly opened her eyes and looked up at the shadows on the ceiling of the hidden room. Then she gazed into Larkin's dirt-smudged face. "Maybe instead of washing me, you should use some of that water on yourself."

Larkin smiled. "Be glad you didn't see your reflection, Highness. You were a fright."

"Good. That was the idea." She lifted a hand to her head and laughed as she ran her fingers through the hair that barely brushed the top of her ears. "How do I look?" she asked, hating that she even cared. She wouldn't normally. But when she thought of the way Lord Errik had kissed her . . .

"You don't look like a lady," Larkin said, putting a glass of water into Carys's uncertain hands.

"I've been told that not being considered a lady is a compliment." She smiled and waited for Larkin's grin in return.

"That it is. But lady or no lady, we are going to have to get you dressed. Since Lord Errik required the use of your other clothes, I instructed him to bring me these." She motioned to a stack of men's garments piled nearby. "I figured Prince Micah didn't need them anymore. They won't fit as well as the others I made you, but we can work on that."

Carys struggled to rise. Larkin moved to help.

By the time she was dressed in trousers Larkin had hastily altered and a gray tunic, Errik strode through the door. He stared at her for a heartbeat as she sweated in her ill-fitting clothes and then gave a deep bow. Then, flashing a smile, he said, "I'm happy to report, Your Highness, that you are officially dead."

"She was a kitchen maid," Errik explained as he opened the trap-door and threw the bag of supplies he'd assembled down into the darkness. "Your healer was caring for her until two days ago when she died."

Carys slid her stilettos into her belt, then wrapped her arms around herself to ward off the chill and sank down on a wooden crate. So much death.

"She had no family here in Garden City." Errik turned to her.

"And she will get a princess' funeral instead of a pauper's grave, Your Highness. You can feel good about that."

There was little she felt good about right now. In an hour her brother would stand on the dais in the Hall of Virtues. The crown would be placed on his head and he would be surrounded by people who would be working to destroy him and Eden. The Council. The Captain of the Guard. Garret. Who knew how many or who would take a knee and swear an oath they intended to break.

And for the first time she wasn't at her twin's side to help. She clenched her fist and felt air flutter her hair. A draft. It was just a draft.

Only, she knew deep inside her that it wasn't.

Her mother had said *she* was the curse. That she had given her the Tears of Midnight to keep the curse at bay.

But the curse was not evil—not like she had thought.

It was power.

Carys heard the wind, and the wind heard her.

She could call it to her aid.

She had done so on the battlements against Imogen. It had saved her on the wall.

And it had driven back the Xhelozi when they surrounded her on all sides.

Now there was nothing standing in the way of Carys's power. Nothing except Carys herself.

A few days. A few weeks. The pain of the withdrawal would stop. She would be stronger. She'd learn to focus her power, figure out who was trying to steal the crown and she would return here to the Palace of Winds—where she now knew she belonged.

"Do you still believe you need to speak with Lord Garret? If so, you should let me bring him here to you." Errik knelt next to her.

"No," she said, forcing herself to stand. Dust swirled in the small room. "I will handle Garret myself. There is something else that I need you to do."

Andreus stood in the Hall of Virtues' antechamber where he and Carys had waited before their entrance to the ball. Now three days later, he was to wear the crown. His first command would be to take the scoring board down from the walls. He didn't want anyone to remember his sister had even had a claim to the throne. *He* had won. *He* was the King.

He paced across the small room to practice walking with the black iron contraption Madame Jillian had affixed to his leg. The rods were heavy and felt awkward, but now when he walked into the throne room, he would be doing so without any assistance.

Alone.

His chest tightened.

"Excuse me, Your Majesty." Max pushed aside the curtain and took a hesitant step inside. The boy was dressed in a hastily altered velvet tunic of yellow and blue and was to be given new rooms to go along with his new status as king's squire. He should have been delighted, but Max still showed fear in his eyes around Andreus.

It would fade, he told himself. Just as the ache Andreus felt for Imogen would disappear—just as, weeks from now, he would no longer remember Carys's screams.

Max shuffled his feet. "I am s'posed to tell you that the coronation is about to begin." Then with an off-balance bow, he darted back through the curtain to take his place near the front.

The trumpets sounded.

Andreus's heart thumped.

The curtains parted.

The tightening in his chest grew.

He took a deep breath and walked slowly through the high-arching entrance of the Hall as everyone—the court, the visiting dignitaries, and the Council of Elders—stood. He limped down the center aisle and those who watched dropped into low bows and curtsies. Elder Cestrum stood to the left of the throne. Andreus tried not to look at the empty space on the right where the Seer of Eden should have stood. Instead, he kept his eyes fixed on the crown. It sat glittering on the throne—waiting for him.

Elder Cestrum placed the polished crown on his head. It was heavy and dug into his scalp. He straightened his shoulders to appear triumphant, but couldn't help but picture the crown as it looked when he first handed it to the Elder—stained with blood.

One by one the Elders knelt before him to offer him their oaths of fealty, followed by the High Lords, Captain Monteros, and the members of the court. The names and faces ran together, but the lack of one stood out to him.

Elder Cestrum's choice for King. Lord Garret.

Carys slipped out of the shadows as Lord Garret passed by the alcove in the empty corridor and pressed the point of her stiletto into his back. She dug the tip into his flesh as he reached for his sword—drawing blood to show she was serious.

"I'll take that." She slid his sword out of the scabbard as Lord Garret turned his head so out of the corner of his eye he could see her face.

"You—you're not dead."

"No. But you might be soon." She dropped the sword to the ground and kicked it behind her. "Tell me who on the Council is plotting to take the Throne of Light from my brother."

"Are you looking for allies or enemies?" He shifted so his hazel eyes could meet hers. "Your brother tried to kill you, Highness. We all watched him strike you on the wall."

"He didn't succeed."

"Do you know why?" he asked, his eyes intent on hers. "I do. I know how you stopped your fall because I was there on the battlements when the wind tunnel appeared. I watched your mother's man strike you on the head at her command and watched as the wind tunnel faded into the sky. And no tunnel has appeared in the sky since your mother gave you the drug that is making it almost impossible for you to stand now."

She shook her head. That's not what she had been told. She'd been hit with a piece of the windmill which had been broken and tossed by the wind tunnel. Seer Kheldin had made the wind appear. He had been the one who sent it away.

Garret drew closer. "I'm not your enemy, Princess," he said. His red hair blew in a sudden draft and he smiled. "You have never believed me, but I wish to help you. That's all I've ever tried to do."

She lifted her blade as sweat trickled down her face. "Prove it," she said. "Tell me what the Council is plotting and I'll let you live."

"I could do that," Garret said leaning forward. "But I won't. At least not yet."

"I hate to break it to you, Garret, but I am a little pressed for time."

He smiled. "I'm sure you are. With everyone in the Hall of Virtues, now is the perfect time to sneak out of the castle. I'll make you a deal. I'll tell you what I know . . . if you take me with you."

Everything in her went still. "With me? Why?"

"Because I know who you are." He stepped closer. "And I know what you are meant to do."

The crown was heavy. The deep blue robe Elder Cestrum had placed on his shoulders was hot. He took deep breaths to quiet the straining he felt in his chest, then called the Elders over.

"Tell the High Lords I wish to see all of them tomorrow. Now that I am King there is a war to be won and they will help me win it."

"I'm sure the High Lords will be happy to give their advice, Your Majesty." Elder Cestrum nodded.

"I don't need their advice," he spat. "I just need their men. Their own regions will be better defended when Adderton is brought to heel. My father and Micah must be avenged. And we must prove to all the kingdoms—and the Bastians who many still support—that we will not tolerate those who do not walk in the light."

"We will tell the High Lords you require their presence, Your Majesty," Elder Ulrich said, stepping next to Elder Jacobs. "If you are certain that is the path you wish to take."

"It is," he said, remembering the night he and Imogen made these plans. She might be gone, but her words and her love would guide him from the grave.

"You can't be serious," Errik said as Garret followed Carys down the trapdoor to the stairs below.

Pain flared in her legs. She leaned against the wall and explained, "Garret has information about the Council that I need for when I return. And about . . . my past. He's coming."

"Are you certain you will return, Highness?" Errik stepped forward and put a hand on her arm. "You could leave Eden and all its problems behind. You could be free of this place . . . forever."

She thought of her brother—seated this moment on the throne, mistakenly believing he was in control. She thought of the people of Garden City who had watched her struggle and raised their banners to honor her fight that so mirrored their own.

"I have no choice. When I am stronger, I will come back to Eden and fight against all who would bring it down—whether it be Adderton, the Council, or someone yet to be uncovered."

"What about your brother?" he asked gently. "Do you believe he will welcome your return?"

He wouldn't have a choice. The rules of the Trials guaranteed it.

"My brother can wait. We have to go."

"With Garret." Lord Errik sighed.

"Jealous, my lord?" Carys asked.

Errik stepped forward, touched his fingers to her cropped hair, and said, "Not yet. Now follow me."

"I'm not sure I'm ready to climb down the plateau," she said, thinking of the sheer drop and the wind . . . the wind that she had no idea how to control. She would learn. She had to.

"No climbing will be required of you this time." Errik's expression was unreadable as he said, "I know a way."

"What way?" she asked. She'd been through these passages hundreds of times. She knew them better than anyone.

Or so she thought as he held the torch aloft and led her through the dark, cold passages to an opening that had never been there before. She was not sure of much right now, but of that she was certain.

Before she could ask how he had discovered the opening he said, "The others are waiting. If you wish to stay dead, we must go."

With each step through the narrow space she felt more unsettled about what the hidden passage meant and how he had discovered it. When she stepped out of the passage and found herself safely at the base of the plateau where Garret and Larkin waited with the three horses Errik must have brought here, she wondered again why he was helping her.

He refused to meet her eyes as he helped her onto a chestnut-colored mare. But his touch was warm as he handed her the reins and asked if she was ready to ride.

Secrets. So many of them. Errik's. Garret's. The Council's. Mother's. Hers.

She would uncover them all, she thought as she clutched the reins tight in her hands and nodded. "Let's go."

The wind whipped harder as the horse took her farther away from the battlements she'd always despised. Looking up at the white stone walls, Carys vowed to return. No matter what Errik's true agenda was or what Garret wanted from her, she would come back. Nothing would stop her. And when she did, the game the Council and her brother thought had ended would begin again.

Only when next they played, the game would be on her terms.

ACKNOWLEDGMENTS

My name might be on the cover, but there are a great number of people who have contributed to the creation of this book. I owe huge thanks to my family, especially my husband, Andy, my son, Max, and my mother, Jaci, for putting up with my crazy hours and my desperate need for caffeine and popcorn, and for always telling me I'm going to get to THE END on the days when I'm convinced it will never happen. I love you!

This story would also certainly never have existed if it weren't for the fantastic vision and enthusiasm of the HarperCollins team and editor extraordinaire, Kristen Pettit. Kristen—thank you for letting me take this story on unexpected twists and turns and for trusting that when I jumped off the cliff it would all turn out okay. Also, a big shout-out to Elizabeth Lynch for her fabulous patience and humor, and to Jennifer Klonsky for her encouragement. Deep gratitude goes to Emily Rader and Martha Schwartz for making me look like I know what I'm doing; and join me in giving thunderous applause to the incredible artists Toby & Pete (I can't draw a stick figure!) and designer Jenna Stempel for the best cover ever. (Feel free to stop reading so you can admire their work again. It's amazing!) And to the entire PR, marketing, and Epic Reads teams—you guys rock!

And they don't make enough Peanut Butter Twix for me to appropriately demonstrate my gratitude to the amazing Stacia Decker. You are not just my literary agent, you are my sounding board, my biggest cheerleader, and the one who keeps me sane at two o'clock in the morning when I'm desperately trying to make all the pieces of the story fall into place. Thank you for taking a risk on me years ago and for being there every step of the way. I can't wait to see where this journey takes us next.

Also, a huge bouquet of thanks to all the booksellers, librarians, and teachers who work tirelessly to put the stories young readers need into their hands. The work you do is so important. You aren't simply creating readers, you are opening up new worlds and changing lives.

And last, but most importantly, I want to say how grateful I am to the readers who have spent hours with me and my characters. A book is like a duet. It requires two—the author and the reader—to bring the story to life. Thank you all for turning the pages and for making the stories sing.

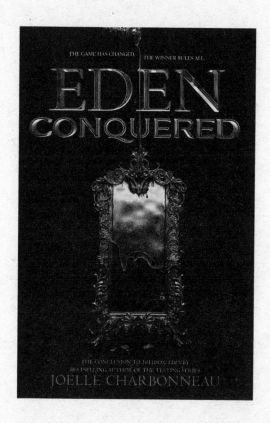

1

Something whispered.

Carys stared at the hills surrounding her traveling party. Nothing moved. The only sounds were the crunch of the snow beneath her quivering horse's feet and Garret's irritated voice as once again he insisted they were going the wrong way.

No branches rustled on the trees that dotted the landscape. The air was still.

But Carys heard whispering.

The wind. It was calling.

She shivered, wiped the trickle of sweat off her forehead, and burrowed deeper into the coarse gray cloak that Lord Errik had wrapped around her on their escape from the Palace of Winds. The biting cold both inside and out had made the first several days a blur of bone-aching pain, a desperate fight to stay on her white and brown mount. The voices of Lord Errik, Lord Garret, and Larkin grew increasingly angry. All three felt they knew what was best for Carys, after all, now that she was dead.

Carys would truly *have been* dead if her twin had gotten his way.

Years of drawing punishment onto herself—diverting attention from Andreus and his secret should have ensured their trust was unbreakable. She had always been there for her brother. Defended him. Yet, when it most mattered, he had abandoned her.

She clutched the reins tight in her hands. The whispering inside her head grew louder.

The trees rustled. Her horse danced beneath her as a branch snapped and fell to the ground to her left.

"We need to go faster," Lord Garret complained from atop his limping gray mare. "Someone could be following the tracks we're leaving in the snow."

"No one is following us," Lord Errik countered. "We traveled in that stream to ensure there were no tracks. Or maybe you forgot that's why the horses are so worn. If we push them to go any faster, they'll give out and we'll be stuck traveling on foot. Something I'm certain you have never done in your life."

"If you had found better mounts instead of these plow nags, we wouldn't have to worry about them giving out."

More arguing. It got them nowhere.

"Next time I have need to steal several horses without raising suspicion from the guard and anyone else inside the city, I will have you take the lead. You're lucky you even have a horse. You, Lord Garret, were not supposed to be a part of this journey."

"Garret." The word scraped her dry throat. A breeze tickled her neck.

"I'm here because Princess Carys wishes it."

"You're here because Princess Carys had no choice but to bring you," Errik snapped, then shook his head. "Of course, Lord Garret, if you are feeling tired of this journey you have only to say the words and . . ."

"Call him *Garret*." Carys straightened her shoulders. "*Only* Garret."

Despite the effort, her voice still sounded weak to her ears. But it was stronger than yesterday and stronger still than the day before. Six days in all had passed since the Kingdom of Eden was told of her death, thus ending the Trials of Virtuous Succession. Prince Andreus, being the only "surviving" competitor, was now the occupant of the throne.

Her twin was now his majesty King Andreus. Guardian of Virtues. Keeper of the light.

And she was nothing.

She was outside of the confines of the walls that surrounded Garden City and the Palace of Winds, but she was still not free. Not the way she had once dreamed. Instead, she could feel the pull of the walls and the people inside them growing with each mile she put between them. Calling her back to face the darkness.

Calling her back to bring them the truth.

"What did you say, Princess?" Larkin called.

"I said that Errik should call him Garret." Carys tugged on her reins, bringing her trembling mount to a halt. "Titles command attention." People—especially commoners—notice them for fear of the consequences if they don't. "I can't risk word getting back to the Palace of Winds that there are nobles traveling the roads with a mysterious girl. No one must know I'm alive."

No one. Not until she discovered who in Garden City had killed her father and older brother and was plotting against Andreus at this very moment.

She shouldn't care about Eden or her brother anymore.

She knew it marked her as weak that she did.

Her twin had tried to kill her. He intended for her to die and probably celebrated now that he thought she had breathed her last. She hated him for that. She wanted the Gods to strike him down for turning against her—against the trust they had forged in the womb. And still . . .

Carys pulled her cloak tight as Errik and Garret brought their horses to stop. Larkin struggled to bring her own mount under control. The mare bucked and pranced before finally coming to a halt fifteen-feet away from the others. As someone who typically rode in the cart alongside her father on trips, Larkin never had need to learn how to do much more than sit a horse. Carys would have to teach her childhood friend that she had to take control if she wanted the horse to follow commands. Just as Carys would have to take control now.

Her brother had weakened her body and soul. She had no choice but to follow Errik and Garret away from the Palace of Winds if she wanted to stay alive and gain the power to return. Now the Tears of Midnight she'd relied on for so many years were almost purged from her body. Her body was still pained and weary, but she would be stronger than before when she saw her brother again. She would be free of the drug's cursed withdrawal. She would do whatever it took to make that so.

"I am sorry, Your High . . ." Errik stopped himself. He shook his head, causing the gray hood to slide off and down his back. His dark hair fluttered. He gave a slight smile that warmed his rich brown eyes. "*Carys*. You were right then and you are correct now. You are not only in danger from those in Garden City, but from the company you keep until your return. Any threat to that safety must be swiftly dealt with."

"I am not a threat to . . . Carys," Garret snapped. His red hair gleamed in the dying light of the sun. "If I were, do you think I would be here with you now trying to help her get away from my uncle and the rest of the Council of Elders? I could have remained in the Palace of Winds and helped my uncle to gain more power or gone home to take my place as High Lord of Bisog. Instead, I'm risking my title, my lands, and my life out here in the cold on this nearly crippled horse."

"If you'd like to go back to Garden City, I won't stop you," Errik said with a laugh. "But I will insist you leave your much-maligned steed."

"And leave her with you? I have waited too long and worked too hard to leave her in the hands of someone . . ."

"Quiet!" The word echoed through the trees. Carys's cloak billowed. Another branch snapped in the wind.

Her mount danced anxiously, and she yanked on the reins.

"I'm sorry, Your . . . Carys." Errik's eyes caught hers and held them. "It was not my intent to upset you. I know you aren't feeling well."

"I'm fine." Her head rang. Her back throbbed from the lash marks that had yet to heal. More than anything she wanted to find a place to curl up and wait for the pain to end—both inside and out. "I would be better if you stopped bickering like children." And if the whispering at the edge of her thoughts would stop. The whispers compelled her to listen, but spoke no discernable message. It pushed at her mind as her frustration built. She felt as if she were going crazy.

Seers talked of calling the wind. Of having the power to bend the air to their purpose. To travel on its back. To compel it to level armies.

While she was growing up, Seer Kheldin claimed to have stopped a wind tunnel from destroying Garden City and the palace. It was a tale so heroic it was akin to the children's fables of seers from hundreds of years ago. But in none of the stories about the seers did they speak of *hearing* the wind. Of feeling the pressure of the element in their mind and its urgency and . . .

"I didn't start it," Garret said. She frowned at him, and he let out a chuckle. "Sorry, I couldn't resist. Andreus used to say the same whenever Micah and I stumbled upon you and he squabbling. Do you remember?"

Micah's stern expression and Dreus's answering grin echoed in her mind. The memory clamped onto her heart and squeezed. She shook off the sorrow that threatened to pull her under.

"Andreus never liked anyone believing he'd done anything wrong," Carys said. "He still doesn't."

"That's something we can use to our advantage when you return to the Palace of Winds to claim your rightful place on the Throne of Light," Garret said. "The sooner you return, the better it will be for the kingdom. We need to start gathering forces."

"I hate to admit this, but Garret is right." Errik frowned. "If you do plan on returning, we will need to start planning for that moment. I know you are still weakened from the competition, but each day that passes will increase your brother's confidence and power."

And each passing day would give whoever had been working with Imogen the chance to stab Andreus in the back and take the throne. The seeress was dead now, but in the months she had exerted influence in the Palace of Winds, she had fooled them all. Because of her, Carys's father and oldest brother had paid with their lives. Andreus had paid with his heart.

Whatever Imogen had set in motion, Carys had to stop. Otherwise, there would be no way to avoid a war that would tear Eden apart.

"Then that settles it," Garret said with a nod. "We will ride to Bisog."

"There is no way Carys is going to Bisog." Errik laughed.

The whispering grew louder. Swirling through her head as the men faced each other. Her anger built with each accusation they hurled at one another.

"The houses in Bisog are bound by oaths to the High Lord of the district," Lord Errik argued. "Now that my father's dead, they are sworn to me. I will take control of their guardsmen and lead them into Eden under the princess's banner."

Her heart pounded. The wind pushed against her chest, drowning out the words.

"And once she's in your district surrounded by your swords, you'll take control of Carys as well. Over my dead body."

Garret reached for his sword. "That can be arranged."

"Stop!" She shouted as Errik drew his sword. Fighting each other about who could be trusted—when she didn't know if either could be.

Wind gusted and swirled on the top of the hill in front of them. And that's when she saw them. Six men on horseback with steel brandished, cresting the hill and bearing down toward them.

"Run, Larkin!" Carys unfastened her cloak so she could reach into the pockets of her gown. The wind caught her cloak and pulled. Her fingers closed around the hilts of her stilettos. Errik and Garret moved in front of her with their swords drawn, ready to fight the four charging men.

Carys cocked her right arm back to throw when she heard the twang of bows. She lifted her eyes, and spotted two of the men at the top of the hill notching new arrows in their longbows. They fired again—in the direction Larkin had run. Urging her horse forward, Carys picked her target and let one stiletto fly. Despite the cold and her weakness, her aim was true. The man dropped the bow in his hand as the stiletto buried its long, sharp point deep in his neck.

Steel scraped against steel not far from her. Someone let out a war cry that ended abruptly. Carys couldn't turn. She kept her eyes on the man before her—who had just let another arrow fly.

"Look out!" Errik shouted as his blade slashed through one attacker.

A horse screamed. She heard Garret call to Errik as she drew back the other blade and let it fly. The wind gusted. The stiletto missed the attacker's throat and dug deep into the hollow of his cheek. Carys saw his eyes widen just before he fell from his horse.

"Carys!"

She turned. Her friend was standing under a tree. Her horse was nowhere to be found. Garret fought with one of the two remaining brigands on the ground. Two others were dead by Errik's hand. The other attacker was still mounted and thundering toward Larkin. And Carys had no other weapons with which to protect her friend.

Wheeling her horse, she urged it forward, desperate to reach Larkin before the man with the sword.

Then Errik was there atop his own horse. His steel flashed. The man clad in brown and gold parried, then looked up at Errik's face and shouted, "It's you!"

The attacker dropped his blade to the ground just as Errik swung his sword again and buried it in the man's neck.

"Larkin," Carys yelled, sliding off her horse. She caught her friend in a tight embrace before pulling back to look at her. "Are you okay?"

Larkin swallowed hard as she nodded. "I'm fine." She looked down at the ground near where she'd been standing. At her feet were several arrows—their shafts cracked in two. "I thought I was going to die. But—none of the arrows hit me. They just . . ." She looked at Carys with wonder. "It's like they just stopped. They're broken."

Anger swirled in Carys's thoughts. Then it was gone. She shook her head and wrapped her arms around herself. "The arrows must have been in the cold for too long. The shafts must have splintered."

Errik cocked his head to the side and studied her before sliding his bloody sword into his sheath and dismounting. "Bad luck for them. Good luck for us."

"I'll take that kind of luck any day," Garret said, crossing to Carys and Larkin. Not once did he look at the men whose blood was draining into the snow. He pulled off his cloak and draped the thick garment around Carys's shoulders. "But you and I both know we have another force to thank for our lives." He whispered in her ear, "We have much to discuss, Your Highness." A shiver went up her spine as he turned to the others. "And our luck continues because these men are no longer in need of their horses. Would you care to join me in taking charge of our new mounts, Errik?"

Errik smiled. "Lead the way."

The minute the two were gone, Larkin stooped down and picked up a broken arrow shaft. Fear filled her face. "This wasn't luck. Was it, Carys?"

A lie sprang to Carys's lips. After years in the Palace of Winds, surrounded by people scheming to gain influence and power, speaking untruths with conviction was, for Carys, akin to breathing. But this was Larkin—someone who had her own life turned upside down just because she dared be Carys's friend. Larkin should, at that moment, have been traveling to her wedding. Instead she was on the run.

Carys owed her the truth, even if it meant scaring her even more. Hearing the stories of the powers of the old seers was one thing. Seeing them—*living* them was quite another.

Carefully, she said, "It wasn't luck, but I . . ." She felt the confusion inside her build anew. The whispers returned. She clenched her fists, and her breath caught in her throat. The trees bent and she pressed a hand against her stomach—and took a deep breath to clear her mind. "I don't understand what's happening. The wind is . . . in my mind. It saved my life during the trials, but I don't understand what it is or how to control it."

Or if it could be controlled. Stories claimed that it could, but her brother hadn't believed the seers had this kind of power. His faith, for lack of a better word, rested only in what he could see with his own eyes and test with his own mind. He convinced her the stories were complete fabrications. She never studied them. She had no idea what wisdom they might hold.

"You're scared," Larkin said.

It wasn't a question, but Carys nodded anyway. "Since the trials, I've heard voices I can't comprehend. I keep thinking I'm going crazy because I can't understand what they say. The wind cannot speak.

Not to me. I'm not a seer. So how can this be?"

"How do you know?" Larkin asked. "What makes you believe it's the wind that calls to you?"

"How could it be anything but? How could I mistakenly believe I had some kind of affinity?"

Larkin gave her a long look. They didn't discuss Carys's secret, but it sat between them just the same. The Tears of Midnight and all they had done to her, body and mind. Larkin held out a broken arrow shaft. "I don't know what is happening, but I believe there is a reason for it. Just as there was a reason for us becoming friends."

"Maybe . . ." Carys frowned as Larkin slipped the broken shaft into her pocket. "I'm just grateful you are safe. And as long as we get you to your betrothed and his family in Acetia, you will stay that way."

Acetia was far to the north, but if they found a group of merchants, it might be possible . . .

"No," Larkin said firmly. "Your brother is convinced that I was involved in a plot to assassinate him. If he hasn't learned of my betrothal yet, he will soon. How long do you think Zylan and his family would live if they protected me?"

"Then I'll find somewhere else for you to hide until it's possible for you to be reunited with him. You are not going to be safe if you stay with me."

"I did not become friends with you because it was *safe*," Larkin snapped. "And winner of the Trials or not, you are my Queen. Whether you wish me to or not, I will stand at your side and defend you with my last dying breath—as I know you would do for me and for the rest of Eden." As if to prove it, Larkin dropped into a deep curtsy and in a voice filled with certainty said, "Your Majesty, I pledge myself to your service. When the night is darkest, I promise to be a light to help you find your way."

Tears pricked Carys's eyes. The words weren't the typical ones spoken to swear fealty, but the passion behind them sealed the vow as certainly as if it was said in the Hall of Virtue before the Throne of Light. Yet, they made clear Larkin's intent to be her champion. To be, in her own way, a knight in Carys's service.

Swallowing the lump in her throat, Carys took Larkin's arm and helped her stand. "I'm supposed to vow that I will never ask you to betray the seven virtues of our kingdom. But considering I'm going to return to Garden City in order to unmask traitors and take the throne, I'm not certain I can do that."

Larkin stood and gave a hint of a smile. "I'd be happy to push your brother into a dung heap if given the chance."

"No offense," Carys said, feeling the anger that had been growing with every passing day vanish like smoke. "But that's something I might have to do myself."

Larkin nodded with mock sincerity. "As you wish, Your Majesty. Would you like me to retrieve your stilettos?"

"I have already done so," Errik said, sliding off a chestnut brown stallion and starting toward Carys. "But feel free to take anything else from our fallen friends that you think we might have use for."

As Larkin hurried off, Errik pulled the long, silver blades from beneath his cloak. "Things might not have gone so well for us had the bowmen not been stopped so quickly. It's a relief to be traveling with one so skilled."

Carys looked down at the blades then into the handsome face of the foreign dignitary who had helped her when she needed someone to trust. And she *had* trusted him, but that was before he assisted her escape through the tunnels below the Palace of Winds.

He should never have known about the tunnels' existence. How had he discovered the passage out when she, who had spent so much of her childhood roaming those lost tunnels, never had? Her body's craving for the Tears of Midnight had made it impossible to demand answers before. But she was growing stronger, and now that the danger had passed, she could see the attack on them with greater clarity.

"Are you feeling all right, Your . . . Carys?" Errik asked stepping closer.

In the distance Carys saw Garret speaking to Larkin as her friend examined another of their enemy's bows. "I'm . . . not sure." Carys wrapped her hands around the hilts of her silver weapons and took them from Errik's grasp.

"Is there something I can do?" He took another step forward and put his arm around Carys's shoulder. "You must be tired."

Carys leaned against him, felt the warmth of his body relax against hers. Then she pictured the man Errik had killed. A man who laid down his weapon because he recognized Errik.

She took advantage of his ease and jabbed the point of a stiletto into his side. His body went still as she quietly said, "I'm tired of the people I trusted with my life lying to me. So it's time to tell me how you found the escape tunnel under the Palace, and after that you will explain how you knew the man you just felled."

"Carys, you have to trust me . . ."

"No." She dug the tip of the stiletto through his shirt and felt him gasp as the steel pricked his flesh. "I don't. But you did aid me in my escape so I will allow you to explain. You are not a Trade Master."

"No. I am not from Chinera."

"Then where? Who are you and how did you come to the Palace of Winds?"

"Technically, I have no true home. My family has shed blood, broken oaths, spurred others into war and betrayed one another to regain the power they believe is rightfully theirs."

"You speak in riddles."

"I speak the truth." He paused. "I grew up in the castle of Dragonwall, but it was never my home."

"Dragonwall. You mean *Adderton*?" The kingdom to the south had been at odds with Eden since long before Carys was born.

"There is more." He sighed heavily. "What was left of my family took refuge in Adderton a hundred years ago when they fled through those same passages that carried you to safety. *My* ancestors fled—while their brothers and sisters were being slaughtered by *yours*. My name is Lord Errik of the Family Bastian."

Bastian.

Carys's head spun. Her great-grandfather had cut down the Bastians in order to be King. The Bastians had sworn revenge against them at all cost and had, through Eden's last fraudulent seer, killed her father and brother and turned Andreus against her. If given the chance, the Bastians would kill him, and her, too.

Her cloak fluttered as she turned. "I will do you the honor of looking you in the face as I dispatch you for this treachery."

"There is no treachery. If I wished to betray you, Carys, I could have done it long before now. I could have left you to die as your brother did or killed you quietly when you begged in your sleep for someone to end your pain. I am not like my cousin, the seer. Imogen came to reclaim the throne for my family. I am not with them. I want none of that."

Don't listen, she told herself. Kill him now. But his words and his face held no fear, no sign of deceit, only conviction. It stilled her hand from spilling his blood then and there onto the frozen ground.

"What do you want?" she demanded. "If not the throne, why did you come to Eden?"

"I came hoping to find a way to make peace. Instead, I found something more important." His eyes met hers and held them fast. "I found you."

TURN THE PAGE TO READ
JOELLE CHARBONNEAU'S NOVELLA

INTO THE
GARDEN

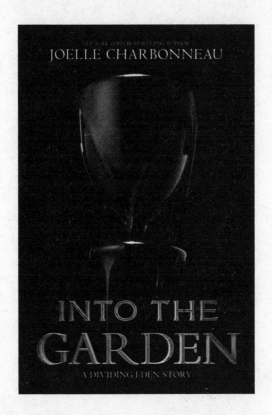

1

"Lady Betrice," Seer Zachar called. "Come in, please."

Betrice hesitated outside the door to the head seer's dwelling.

Lady. Betrice's heart clenched. She hadn't been referred to as *Lady* Betrice since her first steps into the Village of Night.

Almost two years ago she was escorted through the winding paths that snaked throughout the village and the enormous hillside to this very building, which had looked to her like little more than a wooden shack. It was not the kind of place anyone of importance lived in—or so she was taught. Yet, the Seer charged with supervising the training of every potential oracle who stepped through the boundaries of the village lived exactly here. In the small, square cabin no bigger than any others scattered around the base of the hill.

Everything about this place had turned out to be different from Betrice's home in Grace City where the buildings were made of stone and her uncle's windmills made water run and lights glow for all who resided in town. Everyone in *her uncle's* part of the kingdom in the district to the north focused on gold and influence. In this part of Eden, they were focused on the stars.

Here no one schemed over money and power. They knew their fortunes were already written.

And here no one forced her against the wall of her room with a hand over her mouth, daring her to scream. Here, she was blissfully alone.

"Seer Zachar." She took a halting step from the dwindling light of the day into the sparse space. A scroll of a star chart was unfurled on the wooden table nearest the hearth. A fire crackled despite the early summer warmth. Considering what tomorrow was, she could only think of two possible reasons for her to be standing here. One of them left her too cold for any fire to warm.

She bowed her head for the customary show of respect, then forced herself to look directly into his dark eyes as she would have never dared do with her High Lord uncle. To the seers, everyone in the Village of Night were equals because all, no matter talent or age or influence, were seekers of truth. More than anything she wanted to be equal and have the control of her own life that equality would bring.

"You wished to speak with me?"

"A runner from Derio arrived today." He sighed. "He brought a missive from High Lord Xavier."

Her legs trembled under the flowing white she wore. Her uncle hadn't forgotten the approach of her sixteenth birthday—and that tomorrow she would be considered a true woman. Her time in the Village of Night was up. He was calling her home as he had sworn to do. And when he saw her again . . .

"I request the Artis root test," she blurted out. "I believe my place is here."

This was the home she wanted. She could be a seer if they just gave her more time. The recurring nightmare that had brought her here had to mean something more than sleepless nights.

"High Lord Xavier said he was sending an escort and that you should expect them tomorrow. You are to return to Derio when they arrive." Seer Zachar held out the scroll that was clenched in his brown, wrinkled hand.

She backed away from it like it was a snake preparing to strike. "But, if I take the test and pass . . ."

"You will not pass," Seer Zachar said gently, but she felt the slap as surely as if he had struck her. "Lady Betrice, we both know you do not have the talent to be seer."

"But my dreams—"

"Are not signs of second sight or skill with the elements." He turned and shuffled toward the fire. "They are just terrible dreams, albeit more vivid than most. I believe they are echoes of a vision you were born with. Perhaps the talent runs in your bloodline. That may be why you were given this one repeating vision that haunts your sleep. But you have worked with our guides and sat under the stars for almost two years. Your mind has not opened."

"But please, I have to try." She rushed forward, her hands clasped in front of her. "Some students of the stars take years before they unlock their talent. I just need more time."

Her mentor didn't understand. She had to stay. She *needed* to stay. She would rather take the Artis Root test and fail than to once again be under her uncle's control.

Her hands shook. Her heart beat faster and faster as Seer Zachar fiddled with the small scroll—her uncle's seal embossed on it in red and gold wax. "Please," she begged.

"My dear, if I thought time was the key to unlocking your ability to calling the winds and read our reflection in the lights above, I would keep you here as long as necessary. My authority is such that the High Lord could not compel you to leave my tutelage and protection. But I cannot willfully deceive the High Lord. And he is calling you home."

Grace City was not her home. It would never be her home.

Betrice clenched the scroll tight. She tried to breathe deep to find the calm seers taught her. But the churning inside grew stronger. Her throat tightened, making it impossible to speak. She was powerless in all things—as she always was. She had no talent. No power. She was nothing.

Seer Zachar placed a gentle hand on her arm and waited until she lifted her eyes to meet his once again. "When you first arrived, Seeress Neri said you would not stay. She was right as she so often is.

"Betrice, if you were to remain here, your future would be no more than an echo—a sound whose source had long disappeared. You are not meant to be one who quietly listens to sounds of the past. You are meant to leave the Village of Night and find your true voice."

What voice?

She had none.

She was a High Lord's ward. At his disposal. His thing to use and throw away.

She shuddered. If her dreams hadn't scared him so badly, he wouldn't have let her go in the first place. And he had warned her what to expect when she returned.

"Please," she whispered. Tears fell. She tasted the salt in them and sobbed as she placed her hand over his and squeezed with desperation. "Let me take the test. Let the Gods decide my fate. Whatever they choose is what I want. Whatever their choice, it is better than . . . what would be."

She'd seen three aspiring seers take the Artis Test under the glow of the stars. Each time an aspirant drank the tea in view of the entire village. All three collapsed in the center of the Star Wheel. Only the first and the third rose again, and passed the test.

The second had claimed everyone passed the test no matter their skill and demanded his right to prove his belief. He paid the price. The man never took another breath again. Betrice had helped bury him on the other side of the great hill.

"Lady Betrice, you have never officially been one of our society," he said, taking his leathery hand out of her grasp. "You have been allowed to participate in training without pledging yourself to our order as a favor to the High Lord of Derio. It is not your right to request the Artis Test. As of now, you are no longer required to wear the white of our order. The clothes you brought with you have been returned to your dwelling. If I remember correctly, they were quite lovely."

She started to plead again, but before the words passed her lips Seer Zachar turned his back and moved toward the fire.

"Lady Betrice," he quietly said, "I look forward to seeing you one last time in the circle tonight at the calling of the stars. Perhaps the lights in the sky will have something to say to you before you leave the Village of Night."

Betrice recognized the orders as surely as if it was a command given by her uncle or the king. No matter how the seers said that everyone here was equal, the lie was clear. Seer Zachar wielded power over her life much as her uncle did. She was simply a pawn.

The smallest piece on the chessboard and the one that everyone used to their advantage. The one sacrificed without a thought should a better opportunity come along.

Without another word, she walked out the door.

A breeze tugged at the hair she had tied at the nape of her neck. Was it a natural draft, or was someone calling the wind right now?

Betrice glanced around, looking for Haymin. He spent almost all his waking time atop the hill, preparing for his test. All the seers said he would pass. He was important.

Haymin would get to stay here in the village, as would all the others. Day after day they would walk the paths through the grass and flowers that snaked around the enormous hill of the Seers and stare at the sky searching for signs of danger without ever looking at the ground with concern for their own safety. Why would they? Guards from the seven districts patrolled the Village of Night to keep the Seers of Eden safe.

The seers and their skills were worth protecting.

A mere girl was not.

Lifting her flowing white skirts, she hurried down the paths that led to the cabin she shared with three other students of the stars. Seer Zachar said the escort from her uncle would arrive tomorrow. If she did not wish to go with him, she would have to leave today.

Soon it would be dark. She would have to work fast. The calling of the stars would commence once night had fallen. Seer Zachar had already informed her that he would notice her absence. Betrice would have to make her preparations now and slip away after the daily ceremony ended, when the seers and aspirants moved off to their own favorite locations to gaze at the heavens until the sun rose again.

None of the girls she shared her dwelling with were inside

when she arrived. All three were likely finishing their studies. The belongings Betrice had brought with her from Charity Keep were, as promised, lying on the narrow cot she had been assigned on her first day.

Holding up one of the gowns with its elaborately decorated corseted bodices, she realized how much taller she had gotten. And the necklines would most certainly fit a bit differently now than they had then. But she didn't want to put them on. The gold and silver beading and rich fabrics would immediately mark her as a member of Eden's nobility. A noble woman traveling alone would be memorable and an easy mark for anyone untrustworthy. In attempting to escape one terrible path, the last thing she wanted was to stumble onto another.

She folded the finery carefully before stowing each piece in the travel bag someone had placed at the foot of her cot. She would have no money of any kind when she fled the Village of Night. The gowns would have value if she could locate a buyer for them.

Beneath the clothes she found it. The signet ring suspended from the gold chain.

Betrice picked up the heavy iron ring that had once graced her father's callused hand. Two swords crossed above a bird standing in the middle of fire. When she was little, her father told her the phoenix was part of his coat of arms because their family always rose from the flames.

No matter how desperate she became, this she would never sell.

With shaking hands, she slipped the thick chain over her head. The weight settled on her chest, and she blinked back tears, wishing more than anything her father hadn't died delivering a message to the king. Had he lived . . .

No. Thinking that way wouldn't help her. She had to keep moving.

It took almost no time at all to pack her things. Her drinking cup. The silver brush set that had belonged to her mother. The gowns from her days as a lady as well as two of flowing white that she had grown accustomed to wearing here. A thin gray blanket. The blue and silver beaded slippers were too small, but they, too, might be able to fetch a price if—

The door opened and Kiara, the most recent addition to the dwelling's inhabitants, skipped in. Her red curls bounced and her smile was bright when she spotted Betrice.

"What did Seer Zachar want?" Kiara asked as her eyes went to the bag on Betrice's cot. Her smile disappeared. "Is he sending you away? Are you going away like Jichard?"

The tremble in Kiara's small voice made Betrice want to sink to her knees and weep. "No one is sending me away," she lied. "And this isn't like Jichard." The boy had shown great talent, but one day was simply gone. Whatever he had seen in the stars had caused him to flee. The seers looked for him for days. Betrice would have no one from the village looking for her. "My family has summoned me home. Since I don't have the same kind of talent you do, there is no reason for me to stay."

"But we're your family, too." Kiara sniffled.

"That's why I'll never forget you." Betrice turned her back on the girl's glistening eyes, picked up the slippers, and began to shove them into the leather travel bag.

"What are those?"

"These are the shoes I wore the day my carriage came through the gate. I didn't get to wear them after that. Could you imagine me trying to walk up and down the hill in them?"

"No," Kiara giggled. "But they're pretty."

Yes, they were.

Betrice looked down at the shoes and made a decision. "Help me pull the curtains." She lit several candles from the one that was burning on the table near the hearth, then hurried to the window closest to her and pulled the cord so the heavy covering dropped to obscure the light. Across the small cabin, Kiara did the same.

Kiara then turned back toward Betrice with expectation shining on her face.

With night falling, no one would question the darkening of the windows. Everyone was required to pull their curtains before the calling of the stars so no light other than that provided by nature could obscure the view. And now no one would chance to see when Betrice held out the slippers to her small friend and smiled. "I'd like you to have them."

Kiara reached out, then frowned. "But they're yours." The girl carefully put her hands behind her back. As if the temptation to touch would be too great if she didn't.

Betrice shook her head. "They are too small for my feet now. I'd like you to have them. They'll help you remember me even if you won't be able to wear them." She held out the slippers again.

"I can wear them when I sleep." Kiara giggled and reached out for the glistening shoes. Betrice's fingers brushed the girl's, and Kiara's eyes went wide before going blank. Kiara's face drained of color. She was completely still. Then she blinked, and the color returned as she looked up at Betrice.

"You had a vision?" After two years in the Village of Night, Betrice knew what a seer's trance looked like.

She wasn't supposed to ask. It wasn't her place. But Betrice had to know. "What did you see?"

Kiara bit her lip and scrunched her nose. "I don't know. I'm not good at this yet. It all went so fast and I haven't learned how to remember it all. But I saw you."

"Me." Betrice's breath caught. "What about me?"

Kiara shook her head and clutched the shoes to her chest. "I don't know. There were children and a bad storm. Wind and betrayal. There was also death and a gold throne and darkness and love."

"Love?"

Kiara nodded. "I saw a flame. One that will burn hotter than the sun and change the Kingdom of Eden forever."

They both jumped as bells sounded. Kiara dropped the slippers and scrambled to grab them back up again.

"I have to go. I'm supposed to help carry the food for the calling." Kiara jammed the shoes under her pillow. She flashed Betrice a smile before hurrying out the door.

Love.

Hope flared in Betrice's chest. Kiara was gifted. Everyone spoke of her great talent and her lack of ability to control it. *Love.* Could it be? But there was no way that vision could come true if Betrice went to live in her uncle's Keep. Maybe the vision meant that her plan would succeed.

That this time, she would truly get away.

All doubts about striking out on her own fled as Betrice grabbed her saddlebag. She would hide it behind some rocks on the hill. Going back down the path to the village early during the calling of the stars might draw someone's notice, which she could ill afford. But no one would question her going to her favorite secluded place on the hill to meditate. She'd collect her bag then and slip off into the night.

The sky was smoky gray. Figures dressed in white were trekking up the path to the top of the hillside, toward a stone arch that led to the circle. Betrice clutched her bag and veered to the west side of the hill, looking for the group of stones she had so often sat on when she needed to think.

There. She quickened her steps as the gray of the night quickly turned to black. The bell would ring again soon. She had to hurry.

Betrice dropped the bag behind the largest of the rocks. Then she turned on her heel and raced back toward the path lined with Foxfire mushrooms. Now that it was dark, the fungus glowed a pale, ghostly green. The light wasn't bright, but it was enough to guide the way for Betrice and the others hurrying to join the evening ceremony.

She put her hands on her sides and worked to catch her breath as she walked through the archway into the stone circle. Foxfire glowed here in the circle, too. The moon shone brighter still as Betrice found a place to stand and waited with her heart pounding off the seconds. Each moment that passed was one closer to her leaving this place of safety to set off for . . . where?

Her mother had grown up in the district of Orgo. Her father always said her mother was a perfect example of the humility that was nurtured and flourished there. But while there might be someone who fondly remembered her mother's family, Orgo was the northeastern most district in the kingdom. Getting there on foot—alone—seemed impossible. Even in summer when the Xhelozi were hibernating in the mountains. Irae and Bisog were closer, but Adderton was nearer still. King Adham had begun to talk to Adderton ambassadors recently. Tensions were easing between the two kingdoms if one was to believe the reports of visitors who came to the Village of Night. A girl from Eden might be more welcome in the neighboring kingdom now than when Adderton first sheltered the remainders of the Bastian family.

The Kingdom of Adderton had been a refuge for the Bastians after they were struck down from the Throne of Light. From that moment on, every resident of Eden was taught to consider the former ruling family as traitors—enemies. Betrice's uncle had risen to his position as High Lord because of his backing of the current king in the battle against the Bastians. The Bastians' refuge would be the last place her uncle would look to find her.

Excitement and anxiety mixed together as she made her decision. She would head south—despite the stories her father had told her, stories of the creatures that roamed the marshes and abandoned villages there.

They were only stories, after all. Yarns spun about a no-man's-land created by a war long ceased. If no one dared to settle the land, there would be no need to war over it. And if men from both kingdoms feared the land, they would not settle it again.

Betrice had convinced herself. Her chosen path was the right one. She turned her attention with ease when the bell rang again.

One chime for the wind they strove to harness. Then one each for the rain, earth, and fire—elements seers in other parts of the world could control. Then finally four more strikes of the bell to appeal to the stars. With each toll aspirants and seers alike turned to the east, then to the south, to the west and finally north.

When the sound of the last bell faded, Seer Zachar spoke. "The lights above have shined from the first day of this world. They have watched forests grow, waters go dry, mountains collapse, and worlds shift. They are the keepers of the past, present, and future. Tonight, we call on them to shine bright as we open our minds and hearts and search the skies for a glimpse of the wisdom they keep. Blessings on all who seek the truth. May your search be fruitful."

"Blessings on all who seek." She added her voice to the others, giving the practiced response.

The bells sounded again. Once it was quiet, everyone moved toward the center of the circle. There, sustenance waited to see them through the night. At dawn, the seers and aspirants would take to their beds until noon arrived and time for study began once again.

Betrice's stomach rumbled. She would need strength. That meant she needed food.

Quickly, she wove through the others, keeping her gaze lowered, fearing her plan would show in her eyes. She slid two apples and a small hunk of cheese into her pockets, then grabbed a loaf of bread. Her hand hovered over the table as she thought about the darkness beyond the boundaries of the Village. It might be hard to find food. But if she took more, people would notice. She would just have to have faith she would find more food once she was on her own. After all, didn't Kiara's vision tell her she would succeed?

Her stomach rumbled again. The woman next to her laughed and handed her a piece of chicken, which Betrice took with a smile of thanks. Biting into it, she hurried across the stone circle and stepped through the archway.

"Lady Betrice." Seer Zachar's voice made her stop in her tracks. Did he know?

He couldn't, she assured herself. Stay calm, smile, and it would all be okay.

Betrice turned and the smile died on her lips as she saw two men dressed in leather and steel standing in the moonlight behind Seer Zachar. Even in the shadows she could make out the crest of Derio on their chests. The escort had arrived earlier than the message had said. Her uncle had trapped her against a wall—again.

2

She pulled back the curtain and peered out the window. The other three were in their cots asleep. One of Kiara's hands was under the pillow, touching the beaded slippers she'd hidden there. But not everyone in the Village of Night was asleep.

Betrice shifted the curtain back into place as two boys in white trudged past—heading for their cots. She knew from experience they had probably already been sleeping somewhere on the hill. Most nights the stars—even those here at the Village of Night—did nothing more than twinkle in the sky.

Seer Zachar had blocked her escape when he insisted Betrice join him in one last meal and invited the three men to join them. But now, as everyone finally took to their beds, she might have another chance to slip away from the village and her guards.

One of them was familiar to her. He was the head of the High Lord's sentinel and completely loyal to her uncle. The other was taller and younger, new to her uncle's service or she would have remembered his unusual height, his dark hair, and his almost stone-like demeanor. He stared at her as Master Zachar explained to the men about the nightly ceremony they had just missed and asked for news beyond the Village gates since rarely did anyone who wasn't invited come to this remote area. When Seer Zachar gave her leave to meditate for the rest of the night, the young guard insisted on escorting her to a place on the hillside not far from where she'd hidden her bag. He then moved to what he called a reasonable distance and watched her every move.

So instead of fleeing along the back of the hillside, she pretended to contemplate the stars while coming up with another plan. Kiara's vision firmly in her mind, Betrice shifted the curtain again and this time no one was outside.

Quietly, she picked up the bag she'd had Kiara retrieve and slipped out the door.

Everything was still. It would be hours before everyone in the Village of Night would rise for the day. Swallowing hard, she kept her eyes fixed firmly on the trees far to the east of the village. She was halfway there when she heard a twig snap and whirled around.

The taller of her uncle's men from last night stood fifteen paces behind her, outlined by the early morning sunlight. Thick, dark curls framed an angular face that was younger than she'd assumed. He appeared to be only two or three years older than she, and his expression was just as unreadable as it had been in the light of the stars.

"Are you following me?" she asked.

The man wearing her uncle's coat of arms looked at the bag that dangled from her hands. "My lady, I took an oath that I would see you safely to Charity Keep. I do not take my oaths lightly."

"And I do not take being followed like a common street thief lightly."

A hint of a smile appeared on his face and lit his dark brown eyes. "Lady Betrice, if you were common there would be no need for me to follow you." He gave a slight bow. "Our Captain gave orders that we were to set out for Derio as soon as you awakened. He'll be delighted that we will get so early a start. As you remember, it is a week's ride back to your home."

No matter how long it took, it would never be long enough.

"Would you like to continue your walk, Lady Betrice, or should we find the Captain and tell him it's time for us to be on our way?"

The way he looked at her bag told her that he knew she wasn't just on a walk. He had her trapped. For now.

"The sooner the better," she lied. "I appreciate you coming to escort me home, Guardsman—I'm sorry." She smiled up at him. "I don't know your name."

"Oben, my lady." He bent slightly at the waist and bowed his head before looking back at her with eyes that no longer showed any humor. "Oben Tyndale of Lussuria, although it has been years since my family called it home."

"Did they decide they preferred a different virtue to emulate?" Not a surprise considering her uncle and his men appeared to go out of their way to break Lussuria's virtue of chastity at every turn. Oben and his family were no doubt like them.

"No, Lady Betrice," Oben said flatly. "They died." Before she had a chance to apologize or offer her sympathies, he said, "I will show you where Captain Tarak and the rest of the escort are waiting."

He matched her stride as they walked. A neat trick considering Oben was almost two heads taller than she and his legs seemed twice as long. If she ran, he would most assuredly catch her with ease despite the mail shirt he wore. It was something that she would have to consider, she thought as they crossed the colorful tall grasses around the village toward the main gate.

"Your uncle must care for you a great deal," Oben said as they climbed a small hill.

She tensed. "Why do you say that?"

"Why else would he send a dozen of his best-trained swordsmen to act as your escort?" They reached the top of the incline and he pointed to the gathering of men dressed in black leather, red capes, and steel. Several were already on horseback. A quick count said Oben didn't exaggerate. Eleven men, some faces horribly familiar even at a distance, were waiting near the gate. Oben brought the count to twelve. All to make sure she was delivered straight into her uncle's roving hands.

"And he also sent you an age day gift." Oben pointed to a beautiful white mare tethered not far from the group. The leather saddle and halter gleamed like bronze in the sunshine.

She was now sixteen. Old enough by law to wed and bed. And this time, he would not stop himself when he barged through her chamber door.

"Lady Betrice," Captain Tarak bowed so she could see the bare spot in the center of his ash-blond hair. When he stood back up, his eyes settled on her chest, and he smiled. "High Lord Xavier will be gratified to hear how eager you are to return to Charity Keep. He will also be delighted to see that his pretty ward has turned into a lovely woman."

She fought to smile as she shivered.

"Would you like help with your horse, Lady Betrice?" Oben asked.

Gratefully she nodded then hurried to the cream-colored mare. She could feel Oben's eyes on her as she tried to pull herself into a seated position. Her father had taught her how to ride when she was little, but after he died, her mother insisted that they both ride in carriages on the rare occasions they left the confines of Charity Keep. Once her mother died, Betrice never left the keep's stone walls until she traveled to the Village of Night.

There was a snort from someone behind her when she boosted herself up, failed to reach the saddle and ended up back on the ground. The snickers turned to full-blown laughter when she failed again. Captain Tarak's laugh was loudest, and she lowered her head so they couldn't see the color heating her cheeks.

"I can do this."

"Get a better grip on the pommel and don't hesitate before pulling yourself up."

She jolted at the hushed words spoken amidst peals of snide laughter. It was Oben. He was holding the horse's bridle, staring straight ahead as though he had never spoken at all. Taking his advice, she put her foot in the stirrup, stretched up and grabbed the pommel as firmly as she could, then pulled herself up onto the white horse that hadn't so much as shifted a hoof.

Oben handed her the reins and waited for her to get a firm grip on them, then turned to store her bag onto the back of the saddle before heading to his own mount. It was then that Betrice saw the dozens of figures dressed in white standing shoulder to shoulder at the edge of the village. Together they each placed one hand on their heart, then lifted the hand up to the sky. A farewell from the only home she had wanted—the one that had rejected her.

Captain Tarak yelled, "We ride."

Betrice dug her heels into her mount and hung on for dear life as she passed under the stone archway etched with constellations. Captain Tarak rode in front of her. Several men brought up the rear and the rest were positioned twenty feet on either side of her horse. In the center of men carrying broadswords and bows, there was no escape. She worked to stay on her horse as they traveled the King's Road through the district of Irea, the southwestern most district of Eden and the district representing the virtue of patience. A week of riding to the northeast would take them to the heartbeat of Eden—Garden City and the Palace of Winds. Instead they headed north where her uncle waited to control her life.

They rode hard. The hills and flowers gave way to scraggly trees that grew taller and thicker and the road narrower. The men didn't talk much at first. But their chatter grew as they continued to ride. She listened to them brag about rock wolves and fanged foxes they'd gutted or how the bones that they had broken on the practice fields sounded when they snapped. Some boasted about how many Bisog men they had bested in recent raids. And more than one man yelled to Captain Tarak that he must be setting a fast pace in order to get back to the warm bed of his new wife.

Oben said nothing. Not a word of banter or bragging as they rode or when they stopped for food and rest. He silently appeared when it was time for her to remount her steed in order to hold the horse steady. The only time he spoke was when she asked, "Oben, does my horse have a name?"

He paused before saying, "Her name is Snow, my lady."

By the end of the first day, Betrice never wanted to see Snow again. Her entire body ached, but as tired as she was she couldn't just go to her blankets and sleep. Instead she pretended to be fearful of every snap of a tree branch and asked if members of the escort would be standing guard throughout the night.

"Are you scared, Lady Betrice?" Captain Tarak asked, amusement coloring his voice as he tethered his horse to a tree. All the other men were busy tending their own mounts and setting up camp.

"It's not that," she said, looking off into the forest and biting her lip. "It is just that I have gotten used to knowing that someone will be awake until the last star disappears from the sky."

"You can rest assured there will always be someone keeping watch to make sure no harm comes to you," Captain Tarak said, turning his back toward her to survey the men.

The hilt of a knife protruded from the opening of his pack. Quickly, she reached out, grabbed the knife, and hid it in the folds of her gown. "That is a tremendous comfort. I cannot imagine being out here on the road alone." She hoped soon she wouldn't have to imagine it. She would live it. She just needed to find the right moment, no matter how much each animal howl or shriek in the night made her shiver deep in her bedroll.

By the third day her muscles were still sore, but she was able to mount Snow on the first try and didn't have to hang on for dear life as they rode. But she was sure to bite her lip, clasp her hands to her chest, and let out small yelps whenever someone else came into view on the road. By the time they reached the northern Irae plains filled with wheat and corn, she was fairly certain her escorts believed she was the least-brave female in any kingdom.

This allowed them to relax their attention to her when they made camp for the night. A girl so scared would never run off into the darkness alone.

Oben was the exception. She'd studied him as he rode, but his

long, sharply featured face was still unreadable. All she knew was
that he never drank the way the others did and always insisted on
taking first watch. Each time he stood in the shadows as others slept,
she'd seen him turn and study her and she could swear he watched
her even when he himself appeared to be asleep since he sat up each
time she made the slightest movement in the night.

Buried deep into her blankets on the forth night, she listened
as one guardsman talked of an inn in a town called Jule where they
could spend tomorrow night. "The food and wine tastes terrible, but
the bar maids don't."

Several men laughed.

"We won't be stopping in Jule or any other town until we reach
Derio," Captain Tarak said quietly. "You'll all have to wait for service until then."

"I don't see why we have to go without a little fun just because
Lord Xavier has an itch he's wanting to scratch," a gruffer voice said.

"I will arrange for you to personally tell Lord Xavier that you
think having a bar maid scratch your itch is more important than
arriving back in time to guard King Adham when he comes to celebrate Prince Ulron's betrothal and the peace treaty with Adderton."

She gasped. The King and Prince were coming to Charity Keep.

Swallowing hard, she listened to the men shifting around the
fire and strained to hear their conversation. For a long time after
Captain Tarak's words, there was silence. When the men began once
again to speak, it was in murmurs too quiet for her to hear.

She waited for Oben to take first watch and fought sleep until he
woke the next to look for danger. When he turned to his own sleeping place, he did so without looking toward her. And when she sat up
in the darkness, he stayed quiet in his bedroll. His strange interest in

her seemed to have faded. With that last obstacle out of the way, she vowed that tomorrow night she would make her escape.

Her sleep was fitful and filled with images that made her jolt awake but faded before she opened her eyes. Each time she went through the meditation exercises the seers had taught her to keep the nightmares at bay. Still, the next day she found herself wishing she could just curl up and sleep as the summer sun beat down while they rode. More than one guard complained about the heat. Betrice said nothing, but was grateful when Captain Tarak took pity on them all and led their party off the King's road toward the forest to the northeast.

The cool shade of the trees was a relief. Captain Tarak led them at a slower pace than they had traveled on the open road. Between Snow's rocking gait and the cool shadows, Betrice's eyes were growing heavier. The men behind her laughed and she jerked her head up before she could be pulled into sleep. She shook her head and out of the corner of her eyes noticed the reflection of the sun glinting off metal.

Before she could scream a warning, there was a twang and an arrow buried into the back of the blond guard riding ten feet in front of her. He made a gurgling sound. Her uncle's men shouted warnings. The scrape of swords being yanked from scabbards rang in the forest as the blond guard toppled off his horse to the ground. Then the world went wild.

Men charged from the trees carrying their swords. Snow reared and Betrice clutched the reins for dear life. An arrow streaked a breath away from her head. She screamed and squeezed Snow's flanks with her thighs.

Snow darted forward. Betrice grabbed a fist full of the horse's mane as a man in black leather came charging from behind a tree with an ax. Suddenly, one of her uncle's men was there. A sword bit into the attacker's neck as Snow stormed past. Metal clanged against metal behind her as she dug her hand into her pack, trying to find the stolen knife.

Grunts and screams and the whoosh of arrows filled the air and Betrice gave up searching for the blade and instead leaned over Snow's neck and urged the horse to go faster. Snow's hooves thundered on the packed dirt. Blood pounded in her ears.

"She's getting away!" a man yelled.

Betrice looked over her shoulder. At the edge of the fighting, one of the attacking men pointed toward her. Another grabbed the reins of a riderless horse, mounted it, and wheeled in her direction.

"Go, Snow. Go." The horse thundered over the uneven ground, leapt over a fallen log, and Betrice slid dangerously to the left, clutching desperately to the pommel. The horse jumped again. She squeezed her eyes shut and pulled herself back to the center of the saddle. In her chest, she felt every impact of Snow's hooves as the horse ran without any guidance. Betrice had none to give. Their only hope was to keep going.

A tree branch struck Betrice in the face. She yelped and hung on as Snow continued to run.

Finally, after what felt like an eternity, the horse slowed and came to a stop.

The forest was eerily still. Breathing hard, Betrice dug back into her pack and came up with Captain Tarak's knife. Clutching it, she turned from side to side watching for the man on the horse to emerge from the shadows.

Snow trembled beneath her. Or maybe it was her own shaking

she was feeling as tears, fear, and the vision of a sword plunging into flesh threatened to pull her under.

She blinked back the tears, swallowed hard, and stroked Snow's neck with her free hand. That's when she saw the drops of red on Snow's white mane. Blood. The tree branch had cut her face. A small price to pay for being alive.

And free.

The thought struck her as she slid down from Snow to the mossy earth. In her desperation to get away from the attackers, it hadn't occurred to her that she had in one fell swoop stayed alive and fled from her uncle's men.

Only now Betrice wasn't sure what to do. She had no idea where the closest town or farmstead would be, and the attackers could still be in the forest looking for her. So she did the only thing she could do. She took Snow's bridle and led her forward. Whatever was ahead of them couldn't be worse than what she had left behind, and it certainly would never be as bad as what was waiting for her if she returned to Charity Keep. The minute she walked through that gate, she would be trapped—surrounded by people whose lives were dependent on the High Lord's whims and desires. With both her mother and father gone, no one would care that the High Lord's newly-of-age niece was what he desired or that he would use force to take what he believed belonged to him.

After all—she was his ward, and unless he married again, she was his heir.

Betrice spotted a narrow stream and led Snow to it. Kneeling beside the horse, Betrice dipped her cupped hands in the water. Never had anything tasted so wonderful. She drank again, then noticed her shifting reflection in the water and bit back a horrified laugh. There was a jagged cut on her right cheekbone, dried blood and dirt on her face as well as twigs in her hair. All in all the epitome of a lady.

Leaves crunched behind her. She froze and held her breath as a man with a sword appeared in the reflection of the water.

Her throat went dry.

Her heart hammered and she did the only thing she could think to do. She lurched forward, determined to run. Only her foot caught on her dress. Legs tangled, she landed in the stream with a splash. Flipping onto her back, she scrambled against the bank and looked up at the man on the other side, not sure whether to be relieved or to scream.

Oben had found her.

3

"You're unharmed," Oben panted. For once his expression wasn't stone-like. Despite the scrape on his jaw, he looked relieved. It was then that she looked at the rest of him.

His pants were torn. There was a long gash on his leg oozing blood, and his mail shirt and hands were coated with gore.

"You're bleeding." She scrambled up out of the stream and sloshed toward him even as everything inside her screamed at her to run. Now that Oben was injured, she most certainly *could* outrun him, but she wasn't going to get far in a waterlogged gown and shoes and with no supplies. As much as she wanted to break free of her uncle's control, this was not the time to announce her intent.

Snow tossed her head as Betrice pulled herself up onto the bank. The cut on Oben's leg looked worse up close. It was at least six inches long, and the flesh around it was jagged. "You should get off that leg so I can look at it. That cut looks bad."

"I've been hurt worse," he said, not moving.

"We need to stop the bleeding," she insisted, stifling the urge to roll her eyes.

"We need to get moving. It's my job to get to you to safety."

"I doubt you'll be able to do that very well if you pass out or bleed to death," she shot back. "But I'm willing to let you if that's your wish."

Oben looked over his shoulder. Nothing moved. The only sounds were the rustle of the trees, the soft rush of the water and their two horses' gentle breathing.

"Very well, Lady Betrice," he said, stepping toward her. "As long as it can be done quickly. It's not safe to stay here any longer than we must."

She looked deep into the forest and swallowed hard. "Fine."

She leaned down, picked up the blade she'd dropped in her scramble to get away, then walked toward the guardsman as he lowered himself to the ground. Kneeling next to him, she stared at the torn, bleeding flesh. She gagged and panic bubbled inside her. When she was little and she'd fall and scrape her elbow, her father would always tell her the blood made the injury appear worse than it really was. She hoped that was the case now.

Quickly, she hacked at the hem of the richly decorated blue dress she had worn when she arrived at the Village of Night until she pulled a large swatch of it free. She then did as the healer did in Charity Keep, dipping the fabric in water and worked to clean the blood and dirt from the wound.

"We don't have time for niceties," Oben said, gritting his teeth.

"This will just take a minute." She turned and rinsed the fabric into the stream them handed it to Oben. "Here, you finish cleaning the blood away from the cut. I'll be right back."

Before he could object, she stood and hurried over to Snow to fetch a blanket from her bedroll. A few more stabs of her knife and a lot of ripping and she had something with which to manufacture a bandage. Oben was looking over his shoulder, with one hand resting on the hilt of his sword, when she lowered herself next to him again. No pain showed on his face. The guard really did seem as if he was made of stone.

Betrice wished she felt half as sturdy as she cut away the material around the raw, bleeding tear in his flesh. Then she shifted his leg and began to wind strips of blanket around it as tight as she could to stop the bleeding. Oben grimaced once, but never took his eyes off the forest behind them. Was he expecting her uncle's men to appear or the attackers intent on finishing what they started? Since neither was a good option as far as she was concerned, Betrice worked faster.

"That should hold until there's time to do a better job." Betrice turned toward the stream and plunged her hands in, relieved to wash away the blood. When she finished, Oben was standing near the horses, his eyes continuing to watch the shadows between the trees.

Despite his injury, Oben still held Snow's bridle while Betrice mounted. Then he pulled himself onto his horse and headed northwest. Oben said nothing as they rode side by side, but she could tell he was on alert since one hand held his reins while the other rested on the hilt of his sword. Remembering the way the men suddenly attacked, she put the knife in her lap—just in case. But the only movement in the trees was that of rabbits and birds. No one seemed to be coming. They were alone.

When Oben slowed their pace to a walk, Betrice wiped a damp lock of hair off her neck. She quietly asked, "What happened back there? Do you think Captain Tarak or any of my uncle's men . . ." She tasted fear as she remembered the arrow plunging through leather.

"I know some of them are dead, but Snow ran and I didn't see what else happened. Do you know if anyone survived?"

Worry flickered across Oben's face and then was gone. "I don't know, Lady Betrice. At least three of our numbers and a half dozen of theirs were dead before I gave chase to the man who was riding after you. But Captain Tarak has come out of worse fights than that with barely a scratch. If I had to bet, I'd wager he made it through. And if he did, several of the others probably did as well."

"I'm sorry you lost friends today."

"I fought beside them. That doesn't make them my friends."

She waited for a minute for Oben to continue. He didn't. His stony silence had returned.

"What happened to the man who was chasing me?" she asked. "Do you know who he was? One minute he was there, the next he wasn't."

"From the style of knife you are currently wielding, I would guess the man was from Adderton and was too busy looking at what was in front of him to notice me coming from behind."

Betrice blinked and started to correct him about where she had procured the knife, but stopped as Oben said, "When the man finally did see me, it was too late for him to defend himself."

She swallowed hard and said the only thing that came to mind. "Thank you."

His dark eyes met hers. "Are you thanking me for killing a man?"

"No," she answered as she stared back. In that moment she realized how captivating his face was. Not handsome. His features were too long and sharp to ever be considered traditionally appealing. But there was strength of purpose there that was . . . compelling. "I'm thanking you for saving my life, Oben."

"I pledged to return you safely to your uncle, Lady Betrice," his deep voice echoed in the quiet of the trees. "I do not break my oaths. Ever."

Her gratitude faded at his reminder of their cross purposes. She turned her eyes in front of her and once again they rode in silence, watching for anything that might jump out of the shadows.

The sun was fading when they reached the edge of the forest. Betrice urged Snow forward, glad to be free of the trees and underbrush where enemies could hide, but Oben reached out, grabbed the reins, and brought both horses to a halt.

"Why are we stopping? I thought we were trying to get out of these trees."

"We should make camp in the woods and strike out fresh in the morning."

"But might there be men still in the forest looking for us?"

"If there are, they'll have an easier time finding us in the open," Oben explained. "The stone-covered embankment will make it harder for anyone to find us after the sun sets and the Devil's Moth I saw will keep even the hungriest rock wolves at bay."

He shifted on his stallion and she realized that he was sweating—a lot more than he had been when the sun was at its highest. And his face looked paler than it had before. His skin was deeply tanned compared to hers, but now it looked brushed with ash.

"Fine," she said. "Let's go back and set up camp."

Oben wheeled his horse and headed back the way that they'd come. His shoulders were square. His back was straight, but his jaw was clenched tight as he swayed in his saddle. Something was very wrong with him.

Worry swelled and she batted it away. Just because Oben seemed unlike the other men who served her uncle didn't mean that was true. Her uncle chose soldiers who were ruthless and ambitious and willing to do anything he asked—especially if it made them feel more powerful. Wasting concern on someone like that was pointless. It was better to hope he'd pass out or die so she could take whatever food and supplies he had and flee without fear of pursuit. Unfortunately, as unsteady as Oben looked, he kept upright on his horse with his eyes continuously looking for danger as they settled into the spot he'd scouted.

It only took minutes, but every one of them felt like hours to Betrice as she watched sweat drip down Oben's face. She waited for him to pitch forward into the dirt even as she admired that he didn't. Finally, she dismounted and hurried to him, as he slowly eased himself to the ground.

"You're not well. Let me help you," she said, grabbing his arm.

"I can make it to the rocks by myself."

He tried to pull his arm away, but she held fast. "You could, but why when I can help? Or would you rather end up with your face in the dirt than accept a lady's aid?"

"I don't need anyone's aid," he said, but this time he didn't push her away as together they walked toward the stream. He stumbled down the rocky slope, but somehow stayed standing as they reached a small, mossy area surrounded by rocks and squat bushes. Between the stones, brush, trees, and nearby water, she understood why Oben wanted to camp here. It was secluded and if they didn't have a campfire, they would be almost impossible to spot in the dark.

Oben swayed.

"Sit and rest."

He shook his head. "First, I need to tether the horses . . ."

"I'll move the horses. You sit," she ordered and spun on her heel before Oben could object.

She led the horses to a mostly secluded spot not far from where Oben was sitting and tied each to a squat tree then removed the travel bags. It took several trips for her to get Oben's packs and his sleeping roll to camp. She untied his blankets and spread them out, then helped Oben onto them.

"I need to look at your leg before darkness falls."

He shook his head. "My leg is fine, my lady."

"If your leg is fine, why does it look like you're going to pass out?" she asked, hoping that he would do just that.

"I've lost blood. I haven't eaten since first light and . . ."

"And what?" she prompted. Was there another injury he hadn't told her about?

He sighed. "I haven't slept more than an hour or two for the last few days. The lack has made me sluggish."

"Why haven't you slept? You had first watch every night."

He shifted back on his elbows and closed his eyes. "Rocks are not the most comfortable of bedmates."

"And dishonesty is not a quality I find entertaining."

"Very well," he said, his eyes still closed. "I promised your uncle you would be safe on your journey back to Charity Keep."

"You said that before."

His eyes opened, found hers, and held them. "What I didn't say, Lady Betrice, is that I feared not all the men understood that alive was not the same thing as safe. They are, after all, your uncle's men."

"And you're not?" she laughed. She had to laugh. If she didn't she'd scream. The High Lord and his men were capable of anything. One might be evil, but another, by feigning ignorance, was equally insidious. "I thought you gave my uncle your oath. Why would you do that if you don't approve of his leadership?"

"I sold the service of my sword to the High Lord, but I am not like him. I am my own man and I have my own reasons for the things I do. Many of them have nothing to do with the High Lord or his interests." He grimaced as he leaned back against the rocks behind him. His face was flushed and his eyes blurred with fatigue. "Could you please bring that small pouch to me?" He pointed to where she had set his travel bags.

That he didn't even try to get the bag himself spoke volumes of Oben's pain. Wordlessly, she retrieved the black leather sack from his travel bags and placed it in his clammy hands. He winced as he struggled to untie the cords. Betrice reached over, but before she could help, the bag was open and Oben had pulled a bottle from its folds. He uncorked the dark brown vessel and took a drink. Almost immediately, his shoulders relaxed. The creases in his forehead smoothed and he let out a sigh of relief. He put the cork back in the bottle and held it out for her to take.

"Lady Betrice, would you put it back with my packs?"

"What is it?" she asked.

"I told you I've been hurt worse," he said softly. "When you are dealt pain, you have to find a way to stand up when you want nothing more than to fall."

"And this helps."

"Sleep will help more." He tugged at his mail shirt, then sighed. "I should not ask this of a lady, but could you assist me in getting this off?"

"Of course." She put the bottle back where she found it, then knelt next to Oben and looked at the shirt made of metal links. "Can you lift your arms over your head?"

He did, but it took effort. She grabbed the sleeves of the shirt and pulled up as hard as she could. Oben grunted as she tugged the heavy metal shirt up and over his head, then stumbled backward when it and the fabric shirt that had stuck to it suddenly came off him. She dropped it to the ground and wiped her hands on her dress before turning back. "Feel better?"

One look told her Oben wouldn't be answering any time soon. He was leaning against the rocks with his eyes closed. His breathing was even. His lips parted—asleep. Whatever was in that bottle must be really powerful if he was able to use rocks as pillows. If she wanted to make her escape this was the time.

Oben was injured, but he wasn't her responsibility. His sword was near his hand. If anything attacked, he would survive—or not.

Assuring herself that she had no other choice but to leave now, she headed to Oben's packs to look for spare food or anything else that might aid her in the days ahead. She found some nuts and dried meat, an extra waterskin and a length of hemp rope and shoved them in her own pack as she considered her poor luck that Oben was so tall or broad. Even if she had a tailor's skill, it would take forever to make his garments into something that wouldn't draw unwanted attention, so she stuffed his clothing back in the bag and closed the flap. That's when she spotted what looked like a large iron locket next to the bag and opened it.

Inside was a miniature of a lady's face. Even in the falling darkness she could see the similarity of features between the artisan's depiction of the dark-haired lady and Oben. And on the opposite side of the locket was a flame etched in the silver. She held the miniature closer to get a better look at the woman and recalled Oben saying his family was dead.

Carefully, she slipped the miniature into the folds of the clothing in Oben's pack to ensure its safety and jumped as a wolf howl cut the night. Snow tossed her head and shuffled her hooves. The stallion nickered as another howl echoed in the darkness. This one was from the opposite direction. Betrice stood and held her breath. Her heart hammered as she looked into the darkened forest for signs of the animals that had made the sounds.

Her father always said wolves preferred to avoid humans, especially in summer when hares and red squirrels abounded and made for easier prey. Rock wolves, however, attacked anything that strayed into their path. Oben must think the vicious animals were nearby to have insisted on returning to camp near Devil's Moth. Rock wolves would not venture near areas where the purple-flowered plant grew.

Unfortunately, cuttings of the plant did not seem to have the same effect. Whatever properties chased away the wolves only worked when the plant was whole. If Betrice was to run now, she would have to brave the darkness and whatever roamed it without the protection of the plants—or Oben.

Quickly she washed her own cuts in the stream and changed out of her ruined gown into one of her seer gowns of flowing white. She reached for her bag and flinched as something screeched in the night. Oben moaned.

That's when she noticed his scars. The lines were long and lighter in color than the rest of his skin. She ran her finger gently over the one on his shoulder. The scars were long healed. How old was he when he got the first of them? Surely younger than she had been when her uncle had come into her room flanked by his men and ordered her maid to leave. She placed her hand on her throat remembering the nick of the knife on her skin. The mark was barely visible, but she felt it every day. What did Oben feel after getting these?

I've been hurt worse, he had told her.

Yes. He had.

I am my own man, he also swore to her.

Deep inside, she longed for those words to be true. Clearly, as a boy he had endured great pain. As a man, he had pushed himself to exhaustion to see she remained untouched by those who were charged to see to her safety. None of her uncle's other men had been concerned about her as more than a means to an end. Yet, Oben seemed to be. He was the first one in a very long time who wanted to shield her from harm.

She thought of the woman in the miniature, the flames etched on the opposite side and Betrice's breath caught in her throat.

Fire.

Her heart leapt as she knelt next to Oben and stared at his face that even relaxed in sleep looked both hard and strong. In her vision, Kiara said there was fire. What if Oben was that fire? And even if not, surely the boy who received these scars would understand why she could not return to her uncle. It was clear he had been in her uncle's service at Charity Keep long enough to know the truth of what she would face. A man with these scars who went sleepless for her would not want to deliver her to someone who would do her harm. And maybe, just maybe, if he was the man she hoped she wouldn't have to face the rock wolves prowling the night alone.

Oben moaned again and she put her hand on his shoulder. He relaxed immediately under her touch. Heat spread from her stomach through the rest of her. A wolf howl sounded and this time when she shivered it was with yearning instead of fear.

She retrieved Captain Tarak's knife and returned to her place beside Oben's sleeping form. She would stay with Oben for now and protect him through the night as he had protected her. If the fire meant nothing, she could always get Oben to drink from the bottle again and slip away.

The breeze fluttered her hair. The water trickled in the stream as she stared into the shadows fighting the urge to sleep. She would not give in to the pull. She would not—

Faces appeared in the darkness.

A man with a beard screamed at her. Blood oozed from a hole in his stomach. Another man clutched his throat as blood streamed out. Then behind him others appeared. An army of wounded and dead coming through the trees. Arms extended. Weapons dripping with blood.

The bearded man lunged.

A blade caught the light as it plunged toward her, and she scrambled backward and screamed.

4

Betrice bolted upright and struck out with the knife in her hand. "Stay away from me. Get away!"

The blade raked across flesh. She slashed out again as a hand clamped over her wrist and pushed her arm down to the ground.

"Let go of the knife," a man said quietly even as his hand squeezed hers hard. "Lady Betrice, it was just a dream."

A dream.

She blinked and the face in front of her changed. No more beard, no rictus of anger and blood.

Instead, there was Oben, outlined by early-morning light. She hadn't had the nightmare in over a year. Not since mastering the seers' meditation technique. The men . . . the blood . . . her knife striking flesh had felt real.

"Oh Gods." She saw the streak of red running down Oben's arm. The blade she'd been holding dropped with a thud to the ground. "I'm sorry," she said, looking for something to stop the bleeding. "I didn't mean to hurt you."

She trembled and pulled her eyes away from the blood as the nightmare played inside her head.

"It's just a nick." Oben put his hand on her arm and looked into her eyes. "Your scream, however, nearly killed me. I thought you were being attacked."

"I was. In my dream." She shook her head. "You must think me simple for waking you for nothing more than a nightmare. I'm no better than a small child."

"Children have nightmares about what they fear, but have never seen." He reached out and brushed a finger against her wet cheek, wiping away a tear she hadn't even known she'd shed. "Our dreams echo those things we have witnessed. The evil that we know exists. The attack yesterday, on the road, was not an easy thing for one who is not a swordsman to see and live through. It would be a wonder if those images didn't invade your sleep."

Betrice shook her head. "It wasn't that." She paused. "I've had the same nightmare ever since I can remember. The seers taught me how to keep it at bay. The dream was the reason my uncle allowed me to go to the Village of Night in the first place. I was trying to keep watch last night to make sure you were safe and—I must not have focused my thoughts properly."

"*You* were keeping watch for *me*?"

Gods, how asinine that must sound to a man trained to kill. A girl pretending as though she could fight off real-life attackers in the night with nothing but a knife and her ability to scream. She pulled her legs up to her chest, wrapped her arms around them, and looked down at the ground.

"You have my thanks, Lady Betrice."

"I don't know what you have to thank me for. It's obvious I

didn't do a very good job."

Oben's fingers cupped her chin and gently tilted her head up. "It's been a long time since anyone felt the inclination to stand between me and harm's way." His eyes were no longer stony. There was a softness and warmth there she hadn't seen before. And in his voice a kind of wonder. The same she felt when she realized he had forewent sleep to make sure the other escorts didn't forget their manners.

"You didn't lie to me when you said you have received worse injuries," she said quietly "Last night, I saw the marks you bear."

He dropped his hand. "I don't regret the marks I wear, but I will cover them if you find them repulsive. Many ladies do." When she didn't answer immediately, Oben struggled to get to his feet.

"No," she blurted, realizing she had been staring instead of answering his concern. "You don't have to cover your scars."

The moonlight had only given her a small glimpse of the ones on his back. But looking up at him now in the early light of day, she saw that those weren't the only ones Oben bore. Raised marks decorated the front of his shoulders and his muscular chest.

Tears burned the back of her eyes. So many wounds. They no longer bled, but how so many could ever heal was beyond her. But it explained the taut, defined strength of the rest of his body. Anyone who had been that injured would certainly find a way to prevent injury again—to himself or any he allied himself with.

Quietly she said, "My father once told me that scars are symbols of braveries large and small. A body without scars belongs to someone too scared to live." She glanced down at the line of blood on his arm. "I'm just sorry that I have added to your wounds, and that I woke you so rudely. I promise I won't fall asleep on my watch again." Standing, she added, "I'll find something to eat before we break camp."

Snow nickered as Betrice dug through her bag and came up with some dried beef and two apples and a small swath of the blanket she'd used to bind the gash on Oben's leg. She filled a waterskin at the stream. By the time she was done, Oben had already stowed her bedroll and pack on Snow and was starting to stow his own.

He turned toward her and winced. "Those who might look for us will be searching near the roads leading northeast toward Derio, so we will ride to the west before turning north. I want to put distance between us and anyone from yesterday's attack. Hopefully, we'll find somewhere to get supplies. I'd rather not waste time hunting unless we need to. The fewer delays we have, the faster I can get you back to Charity Keep."

The hope that had bloomed inside her when she remembered Kiara's vision faded. Oben was still taking her back to her uncle. Scars and lack of sleep did not make him any less her uncle's man, even if he was different from the rest. She had to keep that in mind and find a way to use it to get what she wanted: a life where she had control—of what she did and where she went and what people did to her. That determination burned like a fire within her.

She took the waterskin from Oben and drank. Oben turned to grab the last of his packs and grimaced.

"Do you want the bottle that helped you sleep last night?" Betrice asked.

"That won't be necessary," he said. "The pain is manageable."

She frowned. "But if you have something that stops pain, why would you choose to suffer at all?" Did this mean he wouldn't take it again? If not, she might have to find another way to gain an opportunity to flee.

Oben hefted the last of the packs onto the stallion. "Because pain that is hidden sometimes causes more harm than good."

"That sounds like something Seer Zachar would say if he didn't know the answer. Rubbish."

Oben looked down at her and laughed. "You are not as you seem, are you Lady Betrice."

She stiffened.

"I mean no offense, my lady."

"I am not your lady," she said, crossing her arms over her chest. "And I find being mocked with laughter always offends, do you not?"

"That was not my intent." He took a step toward her and she fought the urge to step back. "I only meant that when we started this journey you were more like a rabbit—quiet and seemingly afraid of your own shadow. Only now . . ."

Oben stopped and considered her again. She straightened her shoulders in the silence to make her feel as if she was not so small next to him. On the inside, she cringed. After fleeing the attack and with Oben injured she'd forgotten all about the ruse she'd been playing at to make her escort let his guard down.

"And now what?"

He smiled. "And now, Lady Betrice, I am thinking you are less of a rabbit and more of a fox."

If she were more foxlike, she would have left last night. Now she could either retreat into her ruse, or test whether Oben was the fire in Kiara's vision after all.

Straightening her shoulders, Betrice said, "I cannot return to Charity Keep."

"Where will you go? Back to the seers?"

She pictured the Village of Night as it would be right now. Peaceful. Without fear. Gates open to all with talent. And she . . . she was not talented enough to belong. "No." Her heart hurt to admit, "I am of no use to them."

He frowned. "So where did you plan to go?"

"Adderton," she admitted. "I heard some of the men mention Prince Ulron's betrothal to one of their princesses. I thought since . . ."

"Adderton is no place for you, Lady Betrice." Oben tightened the straps holding the packs. "Prince Ulron is not married yet, and until the wedding takes place Adderton still has a bounty on the head of anyone from Eden who strays inside their border. If someone in Adderton discovers who you are, you'll either be dead or lucky enough to be ransomed back to your uncle."

"Lucky? You have no idea what awaits me there!" Betrice snapped, but Oben interrupted.

"There are many in Adderton who have vowed to help the Bastians retake Eden's throne. Capture of a High Lord's niece would be a great victory for their cause."

"Then I'll go somewhere else."

"Where, Lady Betrice? Anyplace you go you will be ransomed back to your uncle once you are discovered."

"Then I won't be discovered."

"Are you that good a hunter with simply a knife? Or do you plan to steal weapons and whatever else you need to survive? You do know the punishment they mete out for convicted thieves?"

She clutched her wrist. "If I lose a hand, then so be it. I won't return to Charity Keep." She started toward her horse and found Oben blocking her way.

"I have to take you back to your uncle."

"And if you do, I'll end up dead."

"Your uncle does not wish to kill you."

"No. He wants to force himself on me in ways worse than before I left his castle. No one will stop him because he is a High Lord and I am in his charge. He has already put a knife to my throat in front of his men to demonstrate that I am powerless and to warn me that I would have no choice but to submit to him when I became a woman."

The memories of the moment washed over her. The blade had pricked her neck. A drop of blood had run down her skin as her uncle slid a hand under her skirts. His fingers on her inner thigh. Inside, she screamed for help. But the only ones watching were her uncle's men.

And they had laughed.

They had egged her uncle on.

But her uncle had stopped. He leaned close to her ear and whispered that she wasn't yet ripe. He would wait because it was far better to pick fruit when the time was right.

Oben's striking face blurred as she fought to keep the tears from falling. "My uncle doesn't wish me dead, but if he has his way, I give my oath to you that I will kill myself. Remaining with him would be a fate worse than death."

Oben stepped toward her and she had to tilt her head up to see his face. It was filled with emotions she did not understand. "Lady Betrice," he said quietly. "Death is never the answer. Where there is death there can be no vengeance."

"I don't want vengeance." Betrice turned on her heel. "I want you to let me go."

"I can't!" He grabbed her hand and held it, but it was the anguish in his voice that made her listen. "I gave my oath to your uncle, but even if I hadn't I would still return you to his keep. Because I *do* want vengeance. Now, it is all that I want."

The anger in his voice made her turn and stare at him, transfixed by the power he radiated.

"I have made only one other oath in my life—to my grand-mother. I promised her that I would avenge my parents' death and bring down those who had a hand in it. I cannot let those who destroyed my family go unpunished."

She looked down at the strong hand that held hers and thought of her own parents. The king had already arrested and put to death those who had killed her father. Her mother had died in childbirth not long after, along with Betrice's brother. Whatever vengeance and justice Betrice could hope for had been delivered.

Still. "I don't understand how presenting me to my uncle will help your cause. Do you think he'll give you money? If so, you are mistaken. Gold is not something my uncle parts with willingly."

"No amount of gold could buy my loyalty."

"Then what could you possibly think you will get?" she asked.

"The King. He will be at Charity Keep when we arrive." His fingers tightened on hers. "He has requested that several of the best trained of your uncle's guard be gifted to his service. According to Captain Tarak, any who escorted you safely across the districts to Grace City would be among that number. It was the reason so many volunteered to ride."

"You plan on leaving Charity Keep." Oben would escape her uncle's authority and she would be trapped in hell.

She tugged to free her hand, but Oben held fast. A storm of emotions swirled in his eyes.

"My mother was beaten and killed in front of my father because he refused to tell the guards how members of the deposed royal family escaped Garden City. My father was then beheaded at the top of the stairs leading to the Palace of Winds, while my grandmother fled with me in her arms." His face went stony and cold. "The people who killed my parents are in Garden City. If I am going to uphold the oath I took to my grandmother, I have to be in Garden City, too."

"Then why not just ride there? Today! I'll go with you." She had blurted out the idea without thinking it through, but it made sense. "No one will expect me to flee to Garden City. After yesterday's ambush, my uncle might even think that I am dead. No one will be looking for either of us."

"I cannot." There was regret in his voice, but conviction on his face." I will become a member of the King's Guard. I will be trusted by he who sits on the Throne of Light and I *will* get justice. It is what I have dedicated my life to. It is what I have to do."

Regicide. That was what Oben meant. His plan was to kill the king. She heard resolve in Oben's voice, and in his eyes she saw something more. Fire. One she not only understood, but was drawn to like a moth. He was an orphan like she was. He had faced tragedy and pain and instead of running from it, he used the flames of his agony to forge himself into a weapon.

Panic swirled. She had no talent to see into the future or call the winds. She had no family to protect her. Even if she slipped away from Oben, she would need to steal and get help from others in order to survive. The flames in his eyes told her he would follow her to the ends of the earth if he had to in order to drag her back to her uncle and fulfill the oath he'd sworn. He would see his plan through to the bitter end, even if in doing so he would upend the kingdom, become a traitor to the crown, and send her into hell.

"I am sorry, Lady Betrice."

Was he? If so, she had to find a way to use that regret—to take his fire and turn it into a weapon for herself. "If you are truly sorry, will you answer a question?"

"I will answer whatever you desire to ask."

She cocked her head to the side. "Do I have your oath?"

He did not hesitate for even a heartbeat before saying, "You do."

"Then tell me, Oben—how did you come by your scars?"

Now he did hesitate. "Some of the scars I earned while training. Others like the one I will have from yesterday's attack I gained in battle."

"But not all of them," she countered, walking around so that she was now facing his back. Snow nickered as Betrice placed a finger on one of the raised marks as she did last night when he was sleep. She heard him suck in air as she slowly traced it down to the small of his back. This scar was lighter than the others. Longer healed. "This scar was not earned in battle. Neither was this one." She placed her hand on a slash of white on his left side.

Quietly, Oben said, "After we fled Garden City, my grandmother became the housekeeper for an aging Lord in Lussuria. The Lord took an interest in my education with both reading and the sword. I excelled at both, unlike his own son, who was far older and had long abandoned his studies to spend his days in taverns, waiting for his father to die. I still don't know how the son learned that my father served the Bastians as head of the King's Guard. Perhaps he overheard my grandmother telling me stories when she tucked me into bed at night. After his father died, the Lord's son came to my room and told me he knew about my parentage. He threatened to tell the High Lord that we had information on the whereabouts of the Bastians if I didn't take off my shirt and kneel against the wall. He whipped me with a scourge, then warned me that he would do the same to my grandmother if I revealed what he had done."

A scourge.

She placed her hand on another scar. Oben had lost his family and instead of the safety he thought he had gained, found pain. She knew the ache of loss and the darkness of rejection when you thought there was no hope.

"That was not the last time he beat me," Oben said quietly. "But after a while, he used his fists. My grandmother was helpless to do anything but discover how to make the drink for me that is in that bottle. The Tears of Midnight blocks out many things—including pain—as long as it is used carefully."

The stream gurgled. A bird sang.

Betrice walked around to stand in front of this man who had suffered so much. A knot lodged in her throat, and everything inside her ached. "What happened to the Lord's son," she asked.

"I was twelve when my grandmother died," he said, staring out into the forest. "Two days later, the Lord's son rode with his friends to hunt. None of them ever returned."

5

Betrice pictured Oben striking down the man who had whipped his flesh. Satisfaction chased away the fear that had gnawed at her since the minute Seer Zachar told her she was leaving the Village of Night. Because Oben had been in darkness and had made his own light. He had found a purpose and control where there had been none. He had become his own flame.

"He was a lord of the realm. Killing him was a crime."

"His death was justice," she snapped.

Oben nodded. "Justice and law are not necessarily the same thing. If a lord or lady were to speak of my acts to the King, their word alone would be enough to have me put to death."

Betrice stilled. Her heart hammered hard and fast. She was a lady. And Oben had just put his life in her hands.

"You could have lied to me," she said. "I would never have known."

"I gave you my oath."

And by doing so he gave her the power she desired. He could not give her control over her own future, so he gave her something else. Control over his. The heat of it flowed through her like nothing had before.

She could hardly breathe as she stepped forward and placed a hand on his warm chest. "So I will give you my oath. I will not betray your trust."

Oben calmly nodded, but she could feel his heart as it pounded harder and faster in his chest. The power to gain vengeance wasn't the only one she had. "High Lord Xavier will be expected to dote on the King while he and the Crown Prince are in residence," he offered. "That gives you some time to plan."

For what he didn't say, but as Oben walked to her horse to hold the reins, Betrice knew if she was going to forge a future out of fire, she couldn't rely on Oben entirely. She would have to spark the flame herself. And whether he knew it or not, she thought, climbing into the saddle, Oben had just pointed the way.

He glanced at her as they galloped, as if he expected her to steer Snow in another direction at any moment, but she kept her back straight and her eyes forward while they crossed the miles to the Derio border. They spoke of inconsequential matters when they broke from their ride, and after they finished their evening meal, Oben handed her the bottle of Tears of Midnight and suggested she drink from it.

"The cut on my face doesn't cause me pain," she said, even though she was curious about the drink after seeing its effect on Oben the night before.

"The Tears blocks many things—pain is only one of them. The drink quiets visions," Oben said, pressing the bottle into her hands. "It is powerful. It should not be used often. But for tonight, it will keep your nightmares away."

The drink was bitter and made her gag, but it did what Oben promised. No bloody faces or reaching hands plagued her during the night. The following day, her body was rested and her mind clear to think as they galloped. The pace made conversation nearly impossible, which was good. It allowed her to focus on the things she had learned on her return home—about Oben's plan, Captain Tarak, the King's visit to Charity Keep and the knife. She was exhausted every time Oben found a secluded area to make camp and had little energy to do more than eat before she took to her bedroll. But each night Betrice found her meditation skills less calming than the last and herself more aware of Oben's warm body next to hers. She found herself thinking of how alike they were and more and more wondered how she could turn his strength of purpose to serve her.

After six days of hard riding, Oben climbed off his stallion at dusk and said, "We should arrive at Charity Keep late tomorrow."

One more day until she returned to her uncle's control. Anticipation mixed with fear.

"Are you certain the King and Crown Prince will be holding court when we arrive?"

"As certain as I can be," Oben said.

"Do you know how long they plan to be in attendance?"

"A week. Perhaps two."

Her heart sank. A week was not much time. If she was going to find the courage to act, she would have to do it fast.

"Tell me what you know of the Crown Prince," she said as they prepared for sleep in the small cave Oben had found hidden in the woods. "My father and uncle both told me a great deal about the King. They both fought at his side during the war to reclaim Eden's virtue."

Her father said few wished to depose the old King or the Bastian descendants and disturb the stability of the throne, but the High Lords claimed they had no choice. According to the High Lords, the old King was no longer concerned with the good of the kingdom and continued to raise taxes higher and higher on the districts. People starved and the Xhelozi appeared in larger numbers while the Palace of Winds grew grander and the lights brighter. The High Lords made appeals to the king to ease the taxes and to honor the virtues he was dedicated to serving. Upon their last request, the King sent the body of the messenger back to High Lord Adham with a notice of another tax increase.

Her father had neither been certain war was necessary nor that all the kingdom's ills were the fault of the King, but he felt he had no choice and answered High Lord Adham's call to war. Six months later most of the deposed Bastian royals were killed, and those who survived the battle fled into exile. High Lord Adham was elevated to the Throne of Light. King Adham was said to be cunning, yet fair. Betrice had heard little about either of the King's heirs other than that they were required to train with the King's Guard. Perhaps Oben's desire to strike the King down should offend her, but she had little loyalty or love for anyone who rewarded a man like her uncle with power. To her, that said a great deal about the king's judgment and virtue.

"If you think to speak of your uncle's actions to King Adham or Prince Ulron, it will not go well for you, my lady. Your uncle is a High Lord. He is a trusted friend of the king, and you—"

"I am a woman and of little consequence," she shot back. "I know my position, Oben—better than you may think—and I would like to understand all that I will be faced with when I arrive at my uncle's home."

Oben considered her request for a moment. "I have never met Crown Prince Ulron. He is rumored to be a strong swordsman, but not as sharp of mind when it comes to intricacies of court. Many say his brother is the more natural ruler and that Prince Ulron would prefer to fight his battles with steel instead of wit."

"Which is why he and his father will be happy to have you in their guard. Your strength with steel is a weapon they will believe they can use. Until you turn it on them. Just as the swords pledged to them will surely turn on you." As they'd rode the last few days she'd considered the path he was traveling and what it would mean. No matter how many different scenarios she envisioned, each ended in Oben's death.

"You intend to die?" she asked. "Do you think that's what your family would want for you?"

He spread his blankets then lowered himself onto them with his healing leg stretched in front of him. "I will have fulfilled the oath I made to my grandmother and the memory of my parents. That is all that matters."

She pictured his eyes that stared so intently at the world going blank for eternity and everything inside her went cold. Tomorrow they would ride into Grace City. Oben would return to the barracks where no lady—especially not the ward of the High Lord—could trod. If she was to test how firmly his oaths tied him, now was the time.

Slowly, she knelt next to Oben and placed a hand just above his knee. "Is that truly all that matters to you, Oben?" Her heart jumped into her throat as she moved her hand higher—feeling the flame pulse inside her. His muscles tensed under her touch like a coiled spring. "Can you tell me that there is truly nothing more you care for or want?"

She shifted her hand higher, barely able to breathe as she stared into his eyes, daring him to accept what she was offering. Insisting he admit that there was more than duty in his heart.

His hand clamped around her wrist and squeezed tight. "Stop." He pushed her hand off his leg. "You don't know what you are doing, Lady Betrice."

Yes, she did. Her uncle had taught her. She needed to fan the spark and see whether they could turn into flames.

The last of the sunlight was fading, but she didn't need the light to see Oben's face. She had it memorized—every strong line and imperfection. "I have lived in High Lord Xavier's castle." She leaned toward him, fascinated by the way Oben stared at her. "Do you honestly think I don't know what I am doing, Oben?"

He didn't move an inch, but he wanted her. She knew he did.

Her stomach swooped as she moved fast and shifted her right leg over his body, testing his will and what it would take to make him break his bond. "You gave me an oath, Oben. You promised to truthfully answer whatever question I asked."

His eyes held hers. His breath came fast. As fast and harsh as her own. He was as strong as any in the kingdom, but right now he was in her power.

"Do you want me?" she whispered. She couldn't catch her breath. Need pulsed and warred with good sense as she waited, knowing what she wanted from him.

He found her hand and placed his palm against hers. Her hand looked so small and soft next to his calloused one. Slowly, he wound his fingers through hers, then pulled their joined hands to his mouth.

His lips were warm as one at a time Oben kissed the tops of her fingers, his eyes never leaving hers. He then pressed his mouth to the back of her hand.

"Yes," he said, his breath hot against her skin. "But not like this. Not when I know I have to leave you behind."

He let go of her fingers, shoved himself to his feet, and sent her sliding to the ground as he stalked away. Betrice shivered as the night air cooled her flesh. Then she settled onto her blankets and watched the back of Oben as he stared off into the night. Never did he look in her direction.

And for good or ill, she had the two answers she sought. She clutched the ring dangling around her neck and smiled. The flame had been lit. Now the only question was, could she be the Phoenix her father had talked about. Could she burn hot and bright enough to destroy everything that she once was? And once she did, would she be left in ashes or rise again?

Betrice took her time getting dressed while Oben paced. "Since they do not know when we are arriving, I don't see what difference a few minutes makes," she said after the third time he inquired as to when she would be ready.

Calmly, she looked at her reflection in the small pond. She'd brushed her dark hair until it fanned out in soft, shiny waves framing her face, giving her the appearance of innocence despite the still-healing cut on her cheek.

The innocence ended, however, where her gown began. The blue, beaded bodice of the undamaged lady's frock she wore was so tight she could barely breathe. The swell of her breasts over the neckline was the price of her discomfort.

When she turned toward Oben, she knew by the way he clenched his fists at his side that the time she had taken on her appearance had been worth the effort. Not being able to breathe made it harder to mount Snow, though, and for the first time Oben was not there to help. He pushed the horses hard when they arrived at the wide, packed dirt road that led to Grace City. Had it been the first day of their travels, Betrice would never have been able to hang onto her seat. She had changed since being told she would leave the Village of Night. But as Grace City appeared in the distance, she wasn't sure if she had changed enough.

Anxiety snaked through her with each passing league. Sweat dripped between her breasts and down the back of her gown. Betrice touched her father's signet ring and forced herself to breathe in and out as the walls surrounding the city grew taller and the lake behind the seat of the High Lord of Charity glittered brightly under the heat of the summer sun. And on the walls and atop the castle far in the distance, the blue and yellow banners of the King of Eden fluttered next to her uncle's red and gold ones in the breeze.

"King Adham is in residence," she said as they approached the massive gray stone gates. Shouts of "Lady Betrice!" rang out. Somewhere deeper in the city, bells sounded. Betrice took as deep a breath as she could and looked at Oben. "I fear there is no turning back."

For a moment, she saw regret flicker across his face. "There never was." He reached behind him, unhooked the leather pouch with the bottle of Tears of Midnight, and held it out to her. Slowly she took it. As she clutched the bag, Oben nudged his horse forward, saying, "There is no turning back for either of us."

Betrice barely noticed the city as she rode next to Oben along the cobbled street that led through the most affluent and thus most well-tended parts of the city. Vaguely she was aware of how the people whispered and pointed. Here and there she heard her name—some wondered aloud if it could actually be her. All the while she thought of the bottle Oben had given her—a way to block out dreams or pain. It was clearly the only gift he felt he could give.

The road slanted uphill and Betrice kept her back straight and her eyes forward. Her heart throbbed in her throat as the two windmills that powered the castle and flanked the entrance came into view. The creaking of the gears pulled her nerves tighter. Everything inside her screamed to turn back.

And when her uncle appeared in the center of the archway that led inside the Keep, Betrice flinched and straightened her shoulders as she spotted her quarry standing to the side of him. Prince Ulron's dark blond hair curled around his ears and brushed the tops of broad shoulders. She couldn't see the color of his eyes from where she stood, but the smile that spread across his face when he saw her staring was self-satisfied. Attention from women was clearly what he had come to expect.

Quickly, she looked away from Prince Ulron and focused on her uncle, who had evidently spent more time at the dining table than the training yard in the two years since she'd been gone. His legs looked stubbier than she remembered and his black beard and mop of hair were threaded with gray, but the greedy, narrow eyes that traveled up and down her body were filled with delight and surprise.

"Lady Betrice!" Her uncle waddled forward and took both her hands in his. Her skin crawled at his touch, but she forced a smile as he boomed, "Captain Tarak told us of the ambush. He said he and the three men who helped him kill the attackers searched for you. Your bloody clothes were found shredded in a ravine and there were rock wolf tracks nearby. They believed you to be dead."

"Had it not been for my horse's sense of self-preservation and Oben's aim, I would have been." Betrice looked for Captain Tarak in the crowd.

"You have my thanks, Guardsman Oben." Her uncle moved, blocking her view of Captain Tarak. "You brought my niece back unharmed. I am glad that she and I will have a chance to get reacquainted."

"I am glad of that, too, my friend." King Adham stepped forward and slapped her uncle on the back. Her uncle stumbled forward a bit, but laughed it off as the King turned his gaze to her. There was a long-healed scar on his right cheek that disappeared into a well-trimmed beard of dark blond and silver. His tunic was of the deepest blue that matched shrewd eyes. "Lady Betrice, I am sorry to hear of your troubles on the roads of Eden and am relieved you were able to return safely. I take it personally when thieves are so emboldened as to attack a Lady and an armed escort on one of my roads."

Thieves. She shook the thought away and sank into a deep curtsy. "Your Majesty—"

"Forgive me, my liege," her uncle interrupted. "May I present my niece, Lady Betrice."

As she stood, her uncle turned away from her and strode over to talk with several of his men.

"Ulron," King Adham bellowed. Prince Ulron stepped forward and the king smiled. "Meet Lady Betrice. Her journey here shows that there is much work to be done when it comes to the safety of Eden. It is your duty to do your part to secure that goal. Perhaps you should hear more about Lady Betrice's experience so you are never tempted to take your role lightly."

Prince Ulron's eyes blazed, but his voice and expression were calm as he said, "Of course, Your Majesty."

The king crossed to where her uncle Xavier and the other men were huddled. He said something and the men let out a loud guffaw.

"So . . . ," Prince Ulron said, looking over his shoulder at his father's back. "Would you like to tell me about the attack you suffered through?" The balled fists at Prince Ulron's sides said that despite his polite tone, hearing her story was the last thing he wanted to do.

Carefully, she chose her words and kept them light, as if this conversation was not one of import. "The only story I can tell is one of a girl holding onto her horse for dear life as she fled the fray. It's not exactly heroic, I fear, but you are kind to ask."

Prince Ulron turned to her with a smile. "I am not known for my kindness."

"Perhaps that is something we have in common."

"Really?" Ulron cocked his head to the side. "Most women go out of their way to assure me they are nothing but kindness."

"They must have nothing to lose. Those who have nothing to lose can afford to be kind."

"Well, that explains my lack of kindness," Prince Ulron said quietly. "I have a throne and a kingdom to hang on to. But you, Lady Betrice, what could you possibly be worried about losing?"

"Betrice!"

She flinched at the sound of her uncle's voice and turned to see him waddling toward her and Prince Ulron. "I'm sorry, Your Highness, but after such a long journey, I am sure my niece needs to rest. After all, there is much celebrating to be done." He turned toward the others gathered and bellowed, "I have promised His Majesty, the defender of Virtue and Keeper of the Light, King Adham, a hunt as a way of demonstrating the prowess of the men of my guard. The most talented of which will be returning with him to Garden City to join the Palace Guard. I do hope you'll reconsider coming with us, Prince Ulron. I would like to see the skill your father speaks so highly of."

"My son prefers war to the hunt." The King slapped her uncle on the back again. "But I am happy to see your men in action and show them how hunting Rack Deer is done." The men laughed as they turned and headed into the castle.

"Wait," she called as her uncle's housekeeper and several other woman of the castle appeared and hustled her inside.

What was happening? Her clothes were not found in the river, shredded or not.

Captain Tarak had lied and she couldn't help but wonder why.

6

She pushed open the doors of her old room, stepped inside and sagged against the door in relief. The women said they would be coming soon to help ready her for her first night back in the High Lord's keep. They said her uncle wanted her to look perfect and that he himself had ordered the dress that she would wear. But that was later, she thought, straightening and walking into the room she'd tried to leave behind. For now she would . . .

"Hello, Betrice."

She whirled as her uncle pushed himself out of the high-backed chair near the fire and crossed the cold stone floor toward her.

"It truly is a joy to have you back here at Charity Keep. You have changed a great deal in the time you were gone."

"Yes, Uncle Xavier." Her throat was tight with fear at the look in his eyes. She knew that look. Her stomach churned.

"And your nightmares are gone?" he asked, pulling a jeweled dagger from his belt. Diamonds and sapphires and emeralds glistened in the firelight along with cold, sharp steel.

"Not entirely, Uncle Xavier."

He put his fat, sweaty fingers on the top of her arm and stroked her skin. "That's too bad," he said, putting the tip of the knife at the top of the neckline of her dress in between her breasts. "Perhaps you need better memories to play over and over again in your dreams."

"I don't . . ."

He slashed the knife, slicing the fabric and beads and pricking her flesh. He smiled as she whimpered, but she held still, aware of the knife so close to her heart, while his other fingers slid over an exposed breast.

You are my uncle, she screamed inside her head. But not a word came out as his mouth came toward hers. His breath stank of stale ale. Bile choked her. Her heart pounded harder and harder as anger and tears and fear pulsed and pushed at her. His hand squeezed her breast as his mouth latched onto hers and she knew the only way to live was to go along with what he wanted. Live in horror or die.

His tongue licked her lips and she made her choice.

"No!"

She wrenched away. The knife slashed her upper arm. She screamed and bolted toward the other side of the room, clutching the wound as her uncle spun toward her. Rage and lust twisted his face and she realized this is what he wanted. He wanted her to fight. He wanted to draw her blood.

He stepped toward her, knife extended. Her blood staining the blade and the jewels. He licked a drop of saliva off his lips and smiled. "Feel free to fight me, my dear. I always win."

Something banged on the door.

"Yes?" she yelled, clutching her arm tight to her chest as her uncle snapped at her to be quiet.

"High Lord," a voice called. "The king is ready for the hunt."

Her uncle looked at her and smiled. "Then I guess our hunt will just have to wait until later. The king won't be here for much longer and then we will have all the time in the world."

He sheathed the dagger without wiping it free of blood, then left without a backward glance.

Tears spilled. Her legs trembled and she barely made it to the chamber stall before her stomach emptied again and again, burning her throat and mouth until there was nothing left. Blood dripping down her arm, she ripped at the bodice of her dress, sending shimmering beads flying as she tore the garment from her body and crossed the room to throw it in the fireplace.

For several moments, it just sat there on the fire.

"Burn!" she cried. She needed it to burn. For everything to burn.

The fabric smoked and blackened as the sound of voices echoed from down the hall, and she remembered. Now that the men were going on the hunt, the women would be coming. They couldn't see her crying or in pain. She had to be calm. She had to be who she needed to be to escape this place. If she didn't, she knew that she would die.

Betrice looked for her travel bag. She discovered it in the back corner of the room and fumbled through the contents until she found what she needed. She pulled the cork from the bottle and drank deep of the bitter Tears of Midnight, desperate for the calm it would bring.

And it did. By the time the ladies of the Keep and their maids arrived, her wound had been wrapped in a thin towel and she was seated in a deep red dressing gown brushing her hair. The women clucked and fussed over redressing her cut, assuming she had received it in the attack on the road instead of in the one in her rooms. At least, that is what they claimed, but Betrice was sure at least some might know the truth and yet didn't care as they prepared her for the night ahead.

Deep down, rage simmered, but over the rage was a slick calm from the Tears of Midnight that allowed her to smile at the deep green dress trimmed in gold and nod as the women chatted and giggled and gossiped. None were concerned that Betrice rarely spoke.

Instead, she listened to them as she fixed her plan to escape in her mind. Topics of their chatter ranged from their husbands and sons to the new dresses Captain Tarak's wife had begun to wear. As a woman of Adderton, Captain Tarak's wife was of keen interest and much suspicion. No one thought her new dresses changed that. The conversation then swirled to topics from the king's current mistress, to the prince's seeming disinterest in his possible betrothal and his insult to the women of Grace City in looking for a bride elsewhere.

"Speaking of startling, did you see Lord Vincent's new britches? A man his age . . ."

Finally, claiming exhaustion, Betrice sent even the most persistent of her helpers on their way. At last, she found herself alone in the room where her uncle had just tried to fulfill the promise he'd made years before. She stared at the hearth, at the blackened remains of the dress she had worn, for several long seconds to give herself courage before rummaging through her travel pack again and heading out into the Keep. It was time to light the fire that Kiara had spoken of to her. Time for the flames to burn.

Her first step was finding Captain Tarak's rooms.

She was surprised how well she recalled the layout of the Keep and found her uncle's trusted guardsman's rooms with ease. He was on the hunt with the men, as Betrice knew he would be. His wife was also absent, which Betrice took as a sign. A nearby servant was happy to help find parchment and a quill so that Betrice could compose a message of gratitude and was wise enough not to question what took so long for Betrice to finish the message and place it in a prominent position in the sitting room.

Then, armed only with suspicions about why the Captain had lied, Betrice took a deep breath, straightened her shoulders, and went in search of Prince Ulron who, unlike the other noblemen, had not gone on the hunt.

He was easy to find since it appeared all the maids in the Keep were tracking the prince's every move. He stood in the heat of the sun on a private balcony. It overlooked the guards' practice field and beyond that, Lake Venia.

"Hello, Your Highness." She curtsied and stepped over the threshold of the doorway into the sunshine. "Are you enjoying the view?"

He turned and frowned. "I suppose you expect me to say the view is better now that you are here."

The Prince assumed vanity in others. That could only imply he had a hefty dose of it himself. According to her ladies in waiting, women who threw themselves at the prince had talked of feeling insulted. And no wonder.

"Since you have already informed me that you aren't kind, I assumed nothing of the sort. People don't waste unnecessary words in the Village of Night. I suppose I will have to relearn how to deal with such trivialities."

Prince Ulron's considered her, then shrugged. "The Village of Night sounds . . . restful." He turned and leaned on the ledge, once again staring at the water beyond the city.

"Only if you fancy staring at the night sky for hours on end, looking for meaning that never comes."

He didn't order her to leave, so she took a deep breath and moved to stand next to him. Anxiety churned in her gut. One wrong word could end her plan before it had a chance to begin.

Indecision stilled her tongue. She could feel each precious second slipping away, but she had no idea how to convince the prince to give her what she wanted.

"If you are hoping I will be intrigued by your silent beauty and decide to make you my princess, stop now," Prince Ulron said with his gaze on the horizon. "You might not have heard, but I am betrothed."

Was she so transparent? Her heart beat hard—like the timid rabbit she refused to be. She had to burn bright and without fear.

"Congratulations," she said, willing herself to be calm, like the lake. "Although the ladies who helped me dress sounded far more interested in your upcoming nuptials than you do, my prince. I am sorry if it is not what you wish."

"I wish to secure my family's hold on the Throne of Light and bring stability to Eden."

She nodded and saw the path she must take. "Then, I suppose your father commanded you to go along with the betrothal because Adderton agreed to turn over the Bastian survivors once you united the two kingdoms through marriage. I can see why he believes that to be the case."

"And you don't?"

"Sometimes the obvious thing—the situation in front of you—is only there to serve as a distraction." She sighed. "Seer Zachar liked to say that 'only when you look beyond the obvious, can you open yourself up to other possibilities.'"

"And is that what you think I should do? Look for other possibilities?" he asked.

Betrice continued to look out at the water as if unaware the Prince had turned so he could study her. "It is not for me to tell you anything, Prince Ulron, but when your eyes are firmly in front of you, it can be hard to see what is approaching from behind."

"I thought we were talking about my betrothal."

"We are." This was her chance to strike a spark. "Just because an enemy appears to lay down their weapons doesn't mean they have surrendered." Now she did turn to face him. "I beg you, Prince Ulron, do not trust what is in front of you—not when it could distract from the sword aimed at your back." She bowed a quick curtsy and spun toward the entrance.

"Stop!"

She stilled in the doorway at the Prince's command.

"You dare threaten the life of Eden's crown prince?" Anger crackled like fire. He grabbed her arm and yanked her around to face him, and his fingers bit into her flesh.

"I did no such thing!" Fear slashed through her stomach. "I am trying to give you a warning."

"Then do it." His hand squeezed tighter, and she whimpered at the pain. "No games. No riddles. Or you will face the consequences."

"I do not play games, Your Highness," she panted, desperate to hold onto her composure, but all illusion of control was gone. She was again at a man's mercy. And this man wouldn't keep her alive to toy with her if he was displeased. "My uncle would never forgive me for speaking what I know to you instead of sharing it with him first. No matter what I do, I will pay a high price for my words unless . . ." She took a breath and said, "Unless you promise to take me with you when you leave Grace City."

Pain shot through her arm. Prince Ulron yanked her against him, and hot tears pricked at her eyes. "You're demanding a promise from me? Who are you to do so?"

"No," she begged. She fought hard to keep fear from swallowing her whole. "You are my prince. I can demand nothing. But I am hoping if what I say has value you will remember the bearer of the words as one who would guard your back and see that you become king."

"Speak."

She straightened her spine and reminded herself there were worse things than death. There was life under her uncle's control. "On my journey from the Village of Night, our party was attacked."

"You forget that I know this."

She ignored the barb and said, "Captain Tarak claimed the attack happened on the open road. It didn't. I do not know why he decided to turn us off the more direct road and into the forest. I can only guess. But, it is in the forest that we were ambushed by well-dressed, well-armed men with Adderton blades and insignias. If the King of Adderton has truly pledged an allegiance with Eden, it would be strange to find his men attacking a party wearing the colors and crests of an Eden High Lord. It is also strange that the Captain of the High Lord's guard—the same man who altered our party's course, claimed the attack was carried out by common thieves and that he discovered my dress torn asunder by wolves. Not one of the details in his story is true. Why?"

Prince Ulron's grip eased. The pain lessened, but he didn't let go. "Perhaps you were mistaken about the men who attacked you, Lady Betrice. It is far more likely a seasoned warrior would understand who his foe is than a woman who fled to save her life."

"Of course, Your Highness," she said, swallowing hard. "I could be mistaken about what I saw. But am I mistaken that your father is planning on taking a number of my uncle's most skilled fighters into your guard?" Prince Ulron nodded for her to continue, and she forged ahead, knowing this was the only chance she would have to flee this place. "Including Captain Tarak?"

"I believe he is one of those my father has chosen—for his skill and his dedication to defending those in his charge."

Meaning *her*. Betrice remained silent. Allowed the truth to dawn on the prince.

"Do you doubt Captain Tarak's skill, Lady Betrice?"

"No," she said honestly. "But he volunteered to lead my escort because my uncle promised any who returned me safely back to Derio would be released from their oaths if they wished to join the King's Guard. While many would desire that honor, most are not recently married to a woman from Adderton as Captain Tarak is. Unless you intercede, I am certain he and his wife plan to travel to Garden City with the intent to remove your family from the throne at any cost. If you doubt me, search Captain Tarak and his wife's rooms. You will find proof they are connected to the kingdom that sheltered traitors to Eden. Those who believe your family has no right to the throne. Or simply ask yourself, why would the Captain give up leading his own post to take a lesser position. For the honor of serving you, or because he serves someone else?"

Prince Ulron released her arm and stepped back. Her heart counted the seconds as he stared at her long and hard. "If you are wrong, you will pay with your life."

"Of that I am certain."

The fire was burning. Now had she done enough to rise once the flames burned out?

She dragged a table in front of her door before taking to her bed. The hunting party could return, and her uncle might choose to visit while she slept.

But he didn't come and neither did sleep. No amount of meditation could calm the anxiety churning harder and faster with each passing minute. The cut on her arm throbbed. Her hands ached from where she had scrubbed them with lye soap. Dawn, and the effect of her actions would soon be upon her.

She remembered the Tears of Midnight and raced to the drawer of her dressing table. With shaking hands, Betrice withdrew the tiny flask. She consumed only a thimbleful. A strange licorice flavor spread over her tongue.

And then she remembered no more.

She jolted awake and found the sun streaming through the windows. And her maid was desperately calling her name and pounding on the door.

"Lady Betrice, you have to wake up. The King and the High Lord are holding audience. They expect you right away! Wake up!"

The maid raced to get Betrice tied into a cap-sleeved red and yellow gown. She apologized that there was not time to send for a tray, but Betrice was glad to have an empty stomach when she joined the crowd of nobles streaming into the Great Hall of the Keep.

She walked past Oben, whose expression did not change upon seeing her. It was as if they had never met. Her uncle was already standing on the dais next to his shining high-backed silver chair. She was told each High Lord had a similar seat—a gift from a long-gone

King to show his support of those chosen to guide their part of Eden. Banners representing each of the kingdom's virtues lined the Hall's walls. The banner of red and gold representing the virtue of charity that hung behind the silver chair was much larger than she remembered.

The room went silent as Prince Ulron strode down the center aisle of the Hall, flanked by men wrapped in mail shirts and the blue and yellow tunics of the King's Guard. The guardsman lined the floor in front of the dais as Prince Ulron took his place on the top. The prince scanned the crowd in front of him as her uncle's steward moved to the bottom of the first step of the dais and announced, "His Majesty King Adham, Defender of Virtues, Keeper of Light, ruler of Eden."

More guardsmen accompanied the monarch as Betrice dropped into a deep bow along with those around her. The King ascended the dais, but did not sit as was expected. Instead, he turned and said, "Yesterday, it was brought to my attention that there is one in our midst who seeks to undermine the choices I have made as King. There is one who thinks she can with one stroke destroy the foundation of the peace I want for our land."

Prince Ulron turned his head and looked directly at her. Betrice clenched her hands at her sides and resisted the urge to flee. The guards at the doors would stop her. Oben would not give aid. No one would.

In a way, she was relieved at the way her story would end. She placed her hand on the bodice of her dress and felt the bulk of the ring hanging between her breasts. She would accept the consequences of her choices with her head held high.

She straightened her back, standing at her full height, and met

Prince Ulron's stare as the King announced, "Bring Lady Pardana forward."

"No!" someone shrieked as several members of the King's Guard dragged a woman with tangled auburn hair down the center aisle and threw her on the base of the steps. The King's retainers gasped in horror in front of Betrice and blocked her view. Even on tiptoes she couldn't see the woman who desperately begged, "I have done nothing wrong, Your Majesty. I promise you, I am loyal to Eden. Tarak! Tell them, I am loyal. Tarak!"

"Quiet!" the King bellowed. "There were letters from Adderton found under the rug in your rooms." King Adham nodded and a herald stepped forward with a piece of parchment in his hands.

"My dearest daughter, Pardana," the herald read as everyone else went quiet, and Pardana stopped fighting and went still. "I am glad to know you are well and that you are sowing the seeds that will soon produce fruit. When the Throne of Light is returned to the true and most virtuous rulers, you will be rewarded. Stay strong and walk in the light. The hopes of all in Adderton are with you."

"No!" Pardana shrieked and tried to pull herself free. "This isn't right. It isn't true. Tarak!"

"Let it be known that any plots against the throne will be ferreted out and let your head serve as a message to the Kingdom of Adderton that Eden will no longer tolerate its duplicity. Snakes who lay in wait to strike will be flushed from the bushes and destroyed."

There was the whisper of steel freeing from a scabbard.

"I am innocent, I tell you. Inno—"

Then the sound of the blade connecting with flesh before the two thuds made Betrice's stomach heave—Pardana's body and then her head as they separately hit the ground.

"And let it be known," the king continued. "Since it is now doubtful that Adderton has been negotiating in good faith, my son will not agree to the terms of the betrothal agreement. Instead, his bride will be from a family whose loyalty to the crown of Eden has never been in doubt. I give you Eden's future queen—the niece of High Lord Xavier, Lady Betrice."

Heads turned in her direction. Whispers echoed like the voices in her nightmares.

"Lady Betrice." Prince Ulron stood at the front of the dais with his hand outstretched. Those standing in front of her parted, giving her a clear view of the blood pooling around the headless body of Captain Tarak's wife.

Bile filled her mouth as she lifted her chin. She was careful to pick up her skirts as she walked over rivulets of blood and climbed the steps to take Prince Ulron's hand. From there she could see the woman's head. Next to the steward's feet, Pardana's sightless eyes stared upward as if in shock as the chamber erupted in cheers. Her uncle shouted something about another feast, but she was barely listening as Ulron led her toward the side door of the hall and into the dim hallway beyond.

"You are surprised, Lady Betrice," Prince Ulron said quietly. "I do hope you aren't disappointed at the announcement. You did say you wished to join our party when we rode to Garden City."

Yes. Yes, she had.

"Of course, I'm not disappointed," she said as the Prince watched her with his intense gaze. "I just . . ."

"You didn't expect to become a princess?"

"I didn't think you would believe me."

He smiled, softening his hard, handsome features. "I didn't

know what to believe, but while I might not always see beyond the obvious, I do not ignore any threat. I had my guards search Captain Tarak and his wife's rooms."

Her heart thudded hard.

Prince Ulron turned and paced away from her as he explained, "Lady Pardana had poisons as well as an Adderton-made dagger—a weapon favored by Adderton assassins. The combination sealed her fate and appears to have changed mine."

She felt the fire she had thought dead burning anew. "I am glad you heeded my warning, Your Highness. I would never want you to come to harm."

Prince Ulron closed the space between them and placed a hand on her shoulder. "This court is filled with schemes to acquire influence and power. The Bastians will not disappear just because the heads of Pardana and her husband are delivered to them." Ulron's heavy hand was gentle but firm as it traveled down the bare skin of her arm. "I require someone at my side with the skills to unravel these plots before they have a chance to be spun to fruition."

"I am happy to serve you, Your Highness. You need not make me your princess."

"Perhaps not. But one who spots schemes is just as likely to be able to create them. I find it is easier to trust someone whose fate is tied to my own." He pulled her closer and leaned down so his face was inches from her. "As my queen, you will bear my sons, stand by my side and if I fall, so will you." His lips whispered against hers before he stepped back. "After what has transpired, my father has decided we shall leave your uncle's hospitality today. In case Captain Tarak and his wife's plot extended further than the two of them, we will not be taking additional swords from your uncle's garrison with us when we ride."

Oben's face flashed before her as she thought of what lay ahead.

"I trust you will not object if I select two or three attendants to take the journey with me." She smiled. "I, like you, prefer to surround myself with those whose fates are tied to mine."

Blood pounded in Betrice's ears as Prince Ulron considered her then gave a curt nod. "Of course, my lady. Just make sure you are ready when it is time to leave." He leaned forward, brushed his lips against her cheek and whispered, "Remember, I do not like being disappointed."

"I am not the kind of lady who forgets."

"You sent for me, Lady Betrice."

She turned. Oben stood in the open doorway. The stony resolve she had come to expect had been replaced by an air of defeat.

Good.

She looked at her maid. "Get your own bags and say farewell to your family. I will meet you in the courtyard in an hour. Don't be late."

The girl bobbed a curtsy and scurried around Oben to prepare herself for the journey.

Betrice picked up one of the white gowns she'd worn in the Village of Night and carefully folded it before placing it in one of the four open leather packs on her bed. She would leave nothing of herself behind when she quit this place. Not the person she was now or the girl she had been.

When she finished fastening the straps of the pack, she said, "Come in and shut the door."

She heard the shuffle of feet and the click of the latch before turning. "Do you still wish to go to Garden City with the King?"

Oben's jaw clenched. "The King has decided to forgo taking any of the High Lord's men into his own garrison, my lady."

"Yes. My uncle's men will all be remaining here," she said, slowly crossing the room. "*My* men, however, are more than welcome to make the journey."

His eyes flashed as he limped toward her. "*Your* men."

"My maid is preparing for the journey as we speak, but I have decided I have need of a chamberlain—someone to guard me, manage my personal affairs and help me learn the secrets of the people who reside in the Palace of Winds." She looked up into the face that had compelled her from the first. "Do you know of anyone who might be interested in such a position?"

"I might, my lady," he said.

"Of course," she said, putting a hand on the center of his chest—atop her uncle's crest. "I would require an oath."

Oben tensed beneath her touch. "What kind of oath?"

"An oath that says he is first and foremost loyal to me above all else."

"I have already given an oath—"

"One that I would never ask you to break," she told him. "I will help you fulfill your oath, if you give me your word not to act until the time is right. You want vengeance for a life lost. If you pledge yourself to me, we can both get what we desire."

He cocked his head to the side. "You will be a princess of the realm—away from your uncle's authority. What more could you want, Lady Betrice?"

She reached up and pulled his lips down to hers. "What do you think?" she whispered.

For a second neither of them moved as they breathed mouth against mouth, waiting for one of them to act. When they did, it was at the same time. Oben's mouth pressed against hers, as her lips parted fiercely to match him. His arms pulled her against his chest and she wove her hands into his thick hair as if daring him to try and pull away. Her head spun, and her heart raced faster and faster until she pulled back and stepped away.

"I ride within the hour," she said. Oben stood breathing hard in front of her. He was strong, but she was stronger. Together they would be unbreakable. "And I require an answer. Will you give me your oath and come with me to the Palace of Winds? Will you guard me with your life?"

Oben's dark eyes searched hers. "I will if you answer my question. What is it that you want? And what will you be willing to do in order to get it?"

She wanted what she realized she didn't have the minute her uncle came into this chamber with his knife and his men. "I want control. Jurisdiction over my own life." Holding up her hand, she admired the stain of ink on the inside of her thumb she hadn't been able to remove after she'd finished placing the note she'd written under Captain Tarak's rug. "And I'm willing to do whatever it takes to get it."

"So am I, my lady," Oben said with a low bow.

When he rose, Betrice corrected him. "I am not your lady." She pulled the chain from where it hung between her breasts and unfastened the ring from the links. Holding it out to him, she said, "I am a queen."

HOW FAR ARE THEY WILLING TO GO TO WIN THE CROWN?

Delve deeper into the world of Eden with these novellas!

Forbidden Fruit:
A Dividing Eden Story
also available.